Lady Celina ~ Knight of the Church.

Book 1 of The *Knights of the Church.*
By A. E. Staniforth.

Published by New Generation Publishing in 2013
Copyright © A.E. Staniforth 2013

www.newgeneration-publishing.com

Contents

****

When I started to put pen to paper it was never intended for this manuscript to be published, it was penned solely for my pleasure of writing it. It was only after others had seen parts of the finished work that I found there was a demand to see the complete story; and so, after much deliberation, here it is.
I can only say I hope you the reader will find as much pleasure in reading Lady Celina, Knight of the Church as I did writing it.

Just for Is-obel
My book to enjoy
A. E. Stanford

Lady Celina ~ Knight of the Church.

Book 1 of The *Knights of the Church.*
By A. E. Staniforth.
~ Prologue. ~

Ours is a story of Arthurian tales and stories of witchcraft, sorcery, and magical talent. Its roots lie in the lives of Merlin and Morgana le Fay, and the legends of how they saved the world from a fate worse than death. Our narrative reaches back more than two millennia to reveal how the lives of these Ancients extended their influence to finally emerge in 19th century times and events.

Now read on,
The story will amaze you!

The Eternal Garden

Under a rainbow sky and in the centre of an endless garden stands a white marble pyramid; on the flat top of this pyramid, two figures are seated on stone thrones; figures that are looking over a garden of many intricate and beautiful designs composed of flowers that stretch in every direction to possibly beyond infinity....

Now one pair of eyes was no longer looking out over the garden, but looking at one small but beautiful flower that danced in a gentle breeze that had blown since time began.

These eyes were not admiring the delicate beauty of this blossom with its blue and green petals delicately edged with white, but were looking at a small red spot; a blemish on an otherwise perfect petal.

Lips that had always been a perfect bow now parted for a voice that had never uttered a word to say. "My husband, I fear there is blight within your garden."

Other eyes turned from admiring the endless garden of flowers to study this small delicate bloom with the red spot blighting the one petal. Finally, a voice that had spoken only twice before said.

"This is not of my creation; this blight is from without and must be erased; on this my wife I will contemplate."

Two pairs of eyes now studied the blight; it was Asherah who turned her beautiful face to see for the first time the perfection of her husband, and for a second time spoke.

"If my husband will hear my words; I have a suggestion." Yahweh turned his head to see for the first time the unblemished beauty of his wife as he said, "I will hear your words."

In this beautiful timeless garden, days may have passed or a millennium before the creations of Yahweh, and his wife Asherah were dispatched to banish the blight.

In the Beginning.

~~ 53 B.C.~~

Before the day's first light had stained the mountaintops they had left their home and the last of what they still called their family. Now almost at the top of the rise they had stopped and were looking back into the valley at the huddle of rough stone and turf buildings that had been their whole life for the last eighty years.

Their parents had both been dead these last fifty years, and now even their youngest sister's children looked older than them. People had begun to talk seeing them remaining unchanged as the years passed them by. Turning the man took the hand of his sister and gently asked,

"Any regrets?" Morgana, looking down into the shadowy valley found herself wiping away a mist of tears to see the smoke starting to rise from the hearths in the village below. She shook her head saying,

"No, I suppose it had to be, as people were starting to ask questions, and soon feelings of friendship will turn to fear and then to hate." Then as she turned back to her brother she said. "I'm sad but I know it had to end."

Gathering up their few belongings, they turned their backs on the valley and the surrounding blue-tinged mountains as they faced to a new horizon, and a new beginning.

They set off over the crest of the rise and then down a slope toward the trees, Morgana finding more tears in her eyes as she looked for the last time at the familiar land about them.

Growing along the side of the path was a holly bush with its branches mostly twisted and gnarled. In between these branches grew two almost straight ones. Merlin mentally shaped his defensive *shield into a cutting edge and then pushed it into the bush, cutting the thinner branch before gripping it with his shield and pulling it free.

He then held it out looking at it critically as he turned it this way and that, finding that it was a little less than half the thickness of his wrist.

He held it in both hands studying it and then forming a circle with the finger and thumb of one hand he created a knife-edged shield between them. Running the length of the branch through the circle of his fingers, bark twigs and wood were stripped with ease, leaving the new staff clean, straight and smooth.

Finally, he measured its length against Morgana before he cut it to size, rounding one end with a rub of his hand, and then with a snap of his fingers; he heated the other end to fire-harden it before giving it to his sister.

With a small laugh, Morgana took the staff and looking at the finely finished wood she shook her head as she said.

"You make it look so easy, as if it's the commonest thing in the world."

Merlin then cut the second branch and pulled it out from among the twisted stems of the holly bush, once again cleaning and shaping it as he had Morgana's before cutting it to size. He again worked rapidly and with ease but now also with a bit of panache feeling pleased with the praise he had just received from his sister. Then and with a laugh, he threw the staff into the air and catching it with one hand he said.

*The shield. A mentally projected physical barrier used for protection. The shield may also be shaped to form useful tools.
Merlin and Morgana also believe that there is an internal shield that protects the mind and personality from fading away.

"There you are, and it is easy, but then I've had more practice than you." Examining the heavier staff turning it and testing it for size strength and weight he finally said. "I think that will do."

They weren't in any hurry in their travels, stopping to make their evening camp as and when they felt like it. Evenings were a time to compare and exchange knowledge between themselves.

In this Morgana found great pleasure in teaching Merlin the subtle arts that she knew such as. *Leaning, divining, concealment and especially the art of healing. Merlin in turn taught Morgana the more manly things that he knew.

These included the manipulation and moving of small and large objects, the many uses of the shield. Including how to shape it into usable tools like knives, scraper's spears or even a sword, and most importantly and the most useful of all the **strike.

Merlin showed her the many ways that the versatile strike could be used. Including, punching, heating, and even destroying. Practicing constantly until Merlin began to suspect that his sister was stronger in some things than himself.

Though when all had been said Morgana had to admit she couldn't match Merlin for style and flair, finding he always made everything he did look so easy.

Summer was winding down into autumn when they decided it was time to split up each to go their own way. The decision had not come easily, but each had their own ideas of what they wished to see and do. That evening they had made their camp on the banks of a shallow river where Merlin had caught a nice plump duck for their evening meal. Morgana had plucked it and then stuffed it with a few apples and herbs that she had collected along the riverbank, and now she was cooking it over a small fire

*Leaning Influencing the thoughts and or emotions of another. A very strong telekinetic may even be able to read surface thoughts.

**Strike or cast, telekinetic projection taking many forms and causing intense pain at the point of exit from the body. It was Merlin who in his early years discovered that a strike or cast could be directed through a long bone held in the hand and thereby reducing the pain. Later, this was developed into the walking staff or staff and eventually into the wand.

Merlin who was sitting and looking into the flames thinking about their future turned to her and asked.

"Where are you thinking of going from here?" Morgana who had been looking down the river wondering just what would be downstream replied.

"I think I shall continue east on this side of the river for now, as I have heard stories of the Romans, and I think I would like to see these people, what about you?" Merlin who had been idly poking at the fire with a stick stopped and looked across the river.

"I think I will head south first, and then possibly west. I have heard strange tales from that area, and it could be there are more people like us." Carefully lifting the duck Merlin stirred the embers and then added a little more wood, while Morgana turned the duck before putting it back as Merlin said.

"After all we can't be the only two; there must be others with our abilities." Then they sat side-by-side quietly watching the fire as darkness fell and stars slowly filled the night sky.

It was late by the time they had finished their tasty supper, and Morgana looking at what remained had decided that there was just enough left for a cold breakfast.

The following morning they stood on the riverbank looking at the morning mist hanging over the water.

"Be well Morgana," Merlin said.

"And you Merlin," Morgana replied as she reached up to embrace him before pulling his face down to hers where she gave him a kiss on the cheek, and then with a grimace she said. "I don't like you with a beard, it makes you look old." Merlin laughed saying, "we are old."

"Speak for yourself," she retorted. "I'm three years younger than you." Then with a final kiss on his lips, Morgana turned and walked away along the river's edge, unable to look back as the tears started to fill her eyes. It was too much, she turned and blinking away the tears she called out to the now distant figure.

"I love you Merlin."

"I love you too Morgana," Merlin called back as he stood watching her go. Then he stepped into the river wincing as he *found the water was icy cold, and the bottom stony and treacherous.*

Hurrying across he climbed the opposite bank and looked for Morgana, who was now a small figure far in the distance. There was a brief flash of red from her hair shining in the morning sun, and then she was gone.

It was a lonely man who headed for the distant wood and his uncertain future. However, of one thing he was certain: his could be a long and eventful life.

****

The County of North Yorkshire.
Friday, 8th February 1839.
Lady Mary Carvel.

Snow was falling as Lord Carvel helped his wife climb the two steps up into the carriage. To Lady Mary as she collapsed onto the seat it had felt like climbing a mountain. Groaning as she tried to find a comfortable position, she complained to her husband as he took his place beside her.

"James, you would think that after eight children I would be used to this." Lord Carvel pulled his wife's cloak up around her shoulders closing it tight about her as the morning was cold, cold even for February, and as the hot stones wrapped in flannel that had been provided were doing little to warm them, Lord James pushed a little more heat into them.

"Why do I always choose winter?" Lady Mary asked twisting again on the seat. "It would be nice to celebrate a birthday with good weather."

Lord James laughed at her knowing that the timing was hers and hers alone, although she had admitted that this one had taken her by surprise.

Finding after releasing the block on her monthly cycle, she had fallen pregnant without a single bleed. Now he took her hands in his, surprised to find how cold they were. He felt her tense as a contraction started, as between gritted teeth Lady Mary asked.

"Why is it that as a fully trained doctor, I can place a pain *block on my patients but not on myself?"

Lord James held her hands until the pain passed. Knowing but not understanding his wife and her irrational refusal to allow him to administer the partial pain block for her. Being a surgeon applying such a block was to him a matter of routine, so he consoled himself and his wife by saying.

"It's not that far dear, just another few minutes and we shall be there." The sound of the horse's hooves changed from the muffled sound on the snow-covered road to a ringing clatter on the cobblestones of the swept courtyard as the carriage entered the hospital gates.

A doorman in hospital uniform ran to pull down the carriage step and open the door, and only then as he helped Lord Carvel down from the carriage did he say.

"Careful sir, it may be a little slippery." Lord Carvel slipping slightly himself turned to help his wife down saying. "Careful dear, I can assure you that it is, a little slippery."

As the hospital doors closed behind them, Lady Mary found the reception area to be pleasantly warm. The newly designed coal-fired boilers fitted in the autumn were working well, and for once Lady Mary could not complain about the hospital being cold in winter.

Lord Carvel escorted his wife to the new maternity wing. Lady Mary had missed the opening the previous month, having said at the time. *"I will be seeing it soon enough,"* and now Lady Mary was seeing the new ward for the first time.

Looking around Lady Mary found each of the two wards contained six beds arranged with three beds each side. There was a window at the side of each bed, while between the beds was situated a sink with hot and cold-water taps. Of this feature, Lord

Block or nerve block in this case one that only blocks pain, other nerve functions are left unaffected.

Carvel had specifically instructed the architect, and then had forcibly to tell him.

"As this is my hospital, and as I am paying for the work, I must insist on hot and cold water in abundance in every ward."

Lord Carvel, due to his church training as a surgeon, understood better than many in the conventional medical profession the relationship between dirt microbes and disease, and that cleanliness was essential in keeping infections down.

"Well Mary what do you think?" her husband asked. Lady Mary who had been pleasantly surprised gave her husband that meaningful look. It was a look he knew well and it brought a smile to his face knowing that it meant his wife was now contemplating further improvements to the ancestral Hall.

"It's warmer than our rooms at home," was all she said. It was as Lady Mary was choosing a bed that the midwife arrived closely followed by Dr Roberta, the doctor greeting her colleagues as equals with a cheery. "Good morning James, good morning Mary."

As the doctor pulled the screens around the bed, Lord James settled into a chair to wait for the doctor's report.

Sitting listening, Lord James found the screens did little to hide the conversation going on behind them, and he had to smile as it soon became apparent it was more a social event between three women than a medical one.

Lord James was aware that all three women knew that if anything had been wrong, his wife would have been the first to know and would probably have dealt with it. At last, the screens were pulled back with Dr Roberta saying.

"A few hours yet I think James, so if you wish to stay I can arrange for a more comfortable chair, or we can call you when the time comes." Taking her husband's hand, Lady Mary said.

"You may as well go home James. You know I don't want you here either working or waiting; you only grow nervous and you know that makes me nervous too."

"What and leave you all on your own in an empty ward?" he asked in surprise.

"No I'll be fine, besides the midwife says there is someone else due to arrive shortly." Lady Mary smiled reassuring him and then waving him away as she said. "Now go, be off with you."

Lord Carvel ran his hand annoyingly but lovingly through his wife's hair before giving her a kiss and saying.

"I'll be back as soon as you send for me." Then turning to the midwife he said. "Make sure she calls for me in plenty of time, as I know my wife and I want to be here for the birth."

The midwife a church-trained *Talent herself liked and respected Lord Carvel as a church surgeon, and the Lady Mary as a church doctor.

. Then as she turned away, she smiled to herself as she remembered his words to Lady Mary and the doctor the first time he had been present at his wife's delivery.

"As I have paid for most of this hospital I think I have the right, and I insist that I want to be with you."

It was some hours later that a scullery maid with her heart pounding was seen scurrying down a corridor.

She knew she shouldn't be there, as it wasn't her place to be in the family's private rooms. She stopped at the door to the master's study; standing there and gathering her courage she knocked, a barely audible knock.

"Yes," the reply came from the other side of the door. She opened the door just enough to see in and to be seen by the occupant of the room.

"Yes." Lord Carvel leaned on her prompting her to think of her name, and then catching it as it floated momentarily across the surface of her mind he said. "Sarah."

Blushing with embarrassment, she stammered her reply. "The hospital has sent word sir, they say that it's almost time my Lord."
Lord Carvel rising to his feet said.

"Thank you Sarah." The maid then curtsied closed the door and

Talent. Telekinetic ability that was originally known as 'The gift of God,' but by the end of the sixteenth century, the term 'Talent' had become the normal description of a telekinetically gifted person.

fairly ran back down the corridor, secretly pleased that her Lord had remembered her name.

He stood for a minute or two thinking of the seven other births; so far it had been twin boys and six girls. Could this be a boy or a seventh girl? He didn't know which to hope for, and his wife had always said. "*It's cheating to look.*"

A boy would be nice, but if it were a seventh girl…. well, a girl would make the seventh daughter of a seventh daughter and remembering the old wives' tales, for some reason a shiver ran down his spine.

With a sigh, he looked at the silver stand with its *communication sphere placed prominently on his desk. Knowing that his wife's would still be in her study, he asked. "What was wrong with you taking yours?"
Leaving his study, he made his way down the hall where a smiling footman handed him his hat and gloves before giving him the house servant's best wishes to give to Lady Mary.

Lord James arrived at the stables to find his horse was already prepared and waiting. The groom who had been waiting to assist him now hurried over to ask. "It's time is it my lord?"

Lord Carvel nodded as the groom took his hand and shook it warmly, before bringing him his heavy leather-riding coat saying. "You will need this sir as it's started to snow again sir."

Lord Carvel accepted the coat gratefully, and then it was a case of pulling his hat down over his eyes and riding out into the failing light of a miserable February afternoon.

Once away from the shelter of the hall and out on the open road Lord Carvel pushed a shield around himself and the horse to keep the blown snow and the biting wind at bay, but by the time he reached the hospital, the increasing wind was driving the snow into deep drifts along the side of the road.
Having handed his horse to the porter, the duty doorman on seeing who it was invited him into his little office, and after taking Lord Carvel's hat coat and gloves he said.

Communication sphere used by certain talents for communication over long distances by thought.

"Here my lord, this will warm you up." Pulling out a small flask, he offered it to Lord Carvel saying apologetically. "It may not be quite as good as you serve my lord." Lord Carvel chuckled as he took a drink before replying.

"On an evening like this it's the best brandy in the county. Thank you, although my wife will probably rake me over hot coals for drinking at a time like this." Handing back the flask, he placed his hands over the office's small heater saying. "I think it would be a wise decision to make sure my hands aren't too cold."

Arriving at the maternity wing, Lord Carvel found the local blacksmith stood in the entrance watching the falling snow. Seeing the passing reflection in the window, he turned as Lord Carvel asked him.

"Not the best of weather is it John?"

"No sir and I reckons it'll get worse yet," and then looking towards the ward he asked. "Is Lady Mary here as well?"

"Yes I brought her in this morning." The blacksmith with a chuckle asked.

"Are you going in, they won't let me near my wife, not till it's all over?"

"Don't worry," Lord Carvel laughed. "She's in good hands."

"It's not her that I'm worried about," the blacksmith chuckled again. "It's the hospital folk, my wife Wendy; well she packs a rare punch. Time last she blacked one of the nurse's eyes."

Lord Carvel laughing put his hand on the Smiths shoulder and gave it a squeeze before he walked away.

He knew the hospital and its workers well, as he had staffed it with the best men and women he could obtain, including alongside the conventional medical men, a church trained doctor, two midwives, and four nurses.

What with himself and his wife, he knew that his hospital employed more talent than any other small hospital in the country.

Open to all and catering especially to the poor at little or no charge, the hospital prided its self that no one was ever turned away.

Lord Carvel looking between the drawn curtains found the midwife had already placed a pain block, so Lord Carvel was able to greet his wife with a hug and kiss before saying.

"I wish you would call me yourself rather than sending somebody." His wife smiled as she said.

"James you know I have no intention of letting you into my mind at a time like this." He laughed and thinking of the communication sphere sitting in her study he said.

"Yes I have noticed, but it would have been better than sending someone out in this weather." Taking her husband's hand, Lady Mary said.

"I'm sorry James, is it really that bad, being behind these curtains I can't see out of the windows?" and then more seriously she asked. "You do realise don't you that if this one is a girl it will be the seventh daughter of a seventh daughter?"

Lord James feigned a laugh making light of his earlier thoughts, and giving her hand a squeeze replied.

"Yes I do, and if it is a girl, well I can see that being rather exciting, especially if she takes after her mother."

Just then the midwife, who was trying to concentrate on the baby and at the same time control Lady Mary's unfelt contractions, opened her eyes and looking up at the two of them said.

"No more talking or I shall take the pain block away, and then you my Lady can do this yourself, right now I need to concentrate."

It was about three-quarters of an hour later that Lady Mary was delivered of her baby girl. It was a first cry heard not from one, but from two infants.

The second cry arose from the bed across the ward. It was so close in time and tones that it was as if only one cry had been issued. Lord Carvel looked up startled saying. "I wonder who that could be in the other bed."

It was several minutes later as the midwife placed the now wrapped and sleepy baby in Lady Mary's arms, that a trainee midwife came across from the other bed and put her head around a screen to say.

"This one's a girl, what's yours?" Lord and Lady Carvel looked at each other, as a concerned Lord James asked his wife.

"Who is the mother; it's not the blacksmith's wife is it?" The trainee midwife, who had been clearing away and making Lady Mary comfortable, replied.

"Yes it is Mrs Cooper, and it is her seventh girl." Lady Mary looked at her husband and quietly said.

"Mrs Cooper, I understand was a seventh daughter herself." With a worried frown Lord James looked first at his wife, and then across to the other bed behind the screens. Getting to his feet he crossed over the ward leaving his wife for the nurse to make comfortable while he spoke to the other midwife.

A few quiet words later and he returned to his wife looking even more perplexed as he said.

"Yes it is the blacksmith's wife and it is her seventh daughter," He looked back towards the other bed behind its curtains as he said. "You are right; Mrs Cooper is a seventh daughter herself." Lady Mary took his hand as she asked.

"You know what that means don't you?" Then answering her own question she said. "It's an omen, two seventh daughters of seventh daughters both born together like this."

Lord Carvel whose family was steeped in tradition knew of the ancient practice of bonding in circumstances such as these, and now he asked his wife. "Do you think?"

"You're thinking of a bond?" Lady Mary asked, biting her lip and looking worried.

"Yes Mary, I think it has to be." Hearing this Lady Mary silently nodded. Lord Carvel seeing Mrs Cooper's midwife beckoned her across to ask.

"When you are finished, would you please ask Mrs Cooper if we might see her baby?"

It was about twenty minutes later when the midwife came across carrying the baby. Lord Carvel and his wife looked at the baby girl and then at their own daughter; they could have been twins.

"Do you really think we should?" he asked his wife. Lady Mary nodded as she said.

"I think the Lord must intend it."

16

"Intend it… what makes you say that?"

"Well earlier this afternoon, Mrs Cooper was telling me that this baby was totally unexpected, she says that after Jonathan, her husband had said."

"Eleven is enough, this is the last."

Lord Carvel thinking of his wife's surprise at how fast she conceived this time, and now hearing of the coincidence of the blacksmith's wife's equally unexpected pregnancy, finally accepted the idea.

Looking at his wife, he gently placed his right hand on the head of the Cooper's baby. Then as he took his wife's right hand, she placed her left hand on her baby's head.

The midwife with a look of shock on her face and the sudden understanding of what was being done, and done at such an early age backed away putting her hands to her mouth to suppress her squeal.

Lord Carvel and Lady Mary closed their eyes and with a slight nod from them both, it was done. A life-long bond had been created between the two girls. Lord Carvel turned to the midwife and to complete the bond he formally said.

"When Mrs Cooper is ready we would like you to make an inquiry of her on our behalf. Please ask if she is in agreement that when her daughter is old enough, and due to the unusual timing of her daughter and our daughters' births.

We Lord and Lady Carvel would very much like to bring her daughter into Brimham Hall to complete her schooling, and later to become the personal maid and companion to our daughter."

The midwife who was still shaken at what she had seen looked at the two girls and then across to the other bed before saying.

"I don't think that would be a problem sir. There are eleven mouths to feed in Mrs Cooper's household already." Lady Mary looked at her husband for confirmation as she said.

"In that situation would you let her know that a small stipend will be made available to them when her daughter is able to take up her education." Lady Mary with a smile then said to the midwife.

"I don't think I need your pain block any more, in fact I think I would like to have all the feeling in my legs back."

"I'm sorry my Lady," the midwife said as she placed two fingers on Lady Mary's temples and relaxed the pain block.

As all the feeling in her lower body returned, Lady Mary looked down at her new daughter saying.

"I have a feeling our Celina is going to be something special."

"Celina?" Lord Carvel asked raising an eyebrow. "Why Celina…. I thought it was to be Victoria if it was a girl?" Lady Mary smiled as she said.

"I don't know; it just popped into my head and it…. well, Celina, it just seemed so right; Victoria can wait for the next one."

"I think," Lord Carvel said with mock umbrage. "I shall have to insist that the next one's a boy." Then with a wink at the shocked midwife he kissed his wife.

****

Summer ~ 41 B.C.

Morgana sat watching as the line of soldiers marched down the valley.

"So these are the marvellous Romans," she said to herself thinking aloud. "They look just like ordinary men to me." She shaded her eyes against the mid afternoon sun to see better the man bearing the standard.

"It looks like a bird of some sort," she murmured. Then turning and looking along the valley she said. "I suppose they will be going to make camp at the ford on the river just as the headman in the village said."

Morgana sat watching and waiting until they had marched out of her sight before getting up to follow them.

It was almost dark when she finally caught up with the soldiers. Morgana, who had kept to the high ground, now stood looking upstream of the ford where she could just make out a fair-sized town that was spread out on the far side of the river. With the light failing Morgana struggled as she tried to count the houses and eventually decided there must be at least thirty.

Morgana turning her attention to the Roman camp where the Romans she had been following, having crossed the ford had now been lost in the large number of soldiers who were encamped there.

Morgana standing looking at the camp had tried to gain an idea of just how many men there were by counting the camp fires, and found she could easily count a hundred, the great number prompting her to ask.

"Do you know what I think? I think that's a very large camp.... what do you say?" There was a short silence and then a voice answered her saying.

"Do you normally talk to yourself?" Morgana who was a little surprised at the question had to admit that it had become a habit of hers, so she replied.

"Quite often as I find that I usually get sensible answers that way, but just now I was talking to you." It was a small boy who Morgana guessed to be around seven years old who rose from concealment a mere ten feet from her.

"You didn't know I was here," was his indignant reply.

"Oh but I did."

"You didn't," he retorted. Morgana looked around and finding a suitable-sized grassy hummock she sat down bringing herself more to his height. Then looking the child in the eyes she said. "I did; you came from over there down by that bush, and then you crawled up here." The boy went quiet for a moment and then said.

"You're good." Morgana who had been studying the boy could feel there was something wrong about him as she replied.

"I'm better than good. Now, what did you do to your hand?" The boy who had his hand tucked loosely inside his scraggy cover reluctantly replied.

"I burnt it."

"Let me see it." Morgana held out her hand while leaning on him just enough to calm his fears. Hesitantly, the boy took out his hand; though his face remained expressionless Morgana could see the pain that showed in his eyes.

Morgana was shocked to see that it was a fresh burn and a bad one, and just how the boy was managing with the pain she had to probe to find out.

Leaning she found that he was a chief's son, and that pain was to be endured and ignored. How he could endure that pain Morgana didn't know, but she knew she couldn't tolerate it as even sensed second-hand it had brought tears to her eyes. She hurriedly ceased her probing. Holding her hand out to him, she said.

"Give me your hand," but the boy shaking his head had started to back away. "It's all right," she said reassuringly. "I heal people and I can help you." She leaned again now putting trust into his mind. At last he came forward hesitantly while not taking his eyes off Morgana's face, and as he drew close he slowly held out his hand.

He was now close enough that even in the gathering darkness Morgana could see how bright his eyes were. 'He must have been crying,' she decided, 'or he has the start of a fever.'

Morgana did not touch his hand not wishing to cause him more pain. Instead, she took hold of his arm and even then she felt the boy wince as she asked.

"How did this happen and when?" The boy sniffled as he said.

"Yesterday, I fell into the fire." Morgana immediately felt the untruth of his answer; he had been pushed, or even held in the fire.

"It hurts," the boy sniffed as he said. "My mother says I'm going to die." He sniffed again and with tears starting to run down his cheeks said. "So I ran away, I don't want to die." He was now silently crying as Morgana sat him down and then probed for the pain, finding it she deftly applied a pain block cutting it off.

The boy jumped back with a gasp almost pulling free from Morgana's grasp and asking.

"How did you do that?"

"I told you I heal people, and now we have to make your hand better, so come with me."

Morgana led him back to a sheltered water worn gully where she quickly kindled a fire, holding her staff close to the sticks to hide the heat strike she sent from it into the heart of the kindling.

20

Then pulling a pot from her pack and filling it from the stream, she set it to boil while she again examined the hand.

It was bad and starting to fester; Morgana found the skin was dirty and the flesh badly burnt. Without the use of her abilities, the boy would most certainly lose the use of his hand; though it was far more likely he would sicken and die.

Once the water was boiling, she combined her usual mixture of herbs and powders to make a smelly poultice, the one she used as a cover for what she really did. Only then did she begin using her other abilities to defeat the infection and encourage a fresh growth of skin.

It still took ten days before Bard, as he was called was ready to return to his family where he proudly took Morgana to start her new life as a healer and wise woman among his people. Morgana was also ready to have words with the father who had held his son's hand in the fire.

JANE

The early years that Jane spent at home were filled with long days playing with her brother Jonathan. Jonathan was two years older than Jane almost to the day, and it seemed that he knew everything, especially how to get into trouble.

He knew where the deepest mud was at the sides of the little beck, and how to find the stepping-stones to cross it where it ran at the back of the house.

He knew the best places to pick blackberries, and how to sneak into the church orchard without being seen. Summers seemed to last forever and sharing them with Jonathan had only made them better.

Wintertime also held special memories for her; she recalled being pulled on Jonathan's sledge, or more likely than not pulling his sledge.

At other times she would watch her mother in the warm kitchen savouring the smells, as large and delicious meals were prepared. Christmas memories were of sitting around the fire and eating chestnuts or her mother's Christmas pie.

The spring weather had turned cold and wet as the ringing blows of a hammer on steel drew Jane like a magnet towards the forge, a place she was always being told was no place for a girl.

Standing peering around the door she stared in wonder, seeing the hot coals and the glowing iron taken out of the fire. Jane watched fascinated seeing the metal take shape in a shower of fiery sparks.

Her father, who was busy shaping the end of a bar of iron for the Cathedral's organ loft became aware of a feeling of being watched. Missing a beat of the hammer he looked towards the door and seeing the blond-haired head of his youngest daughter peering around the doorpost he asked.

"Well little miss, what are you doing here?" Jane coming further into the Smithy, and watching the rapidly cooling bar of iron her father had been working on asked.

"What's tha doing Da?" Her father having pushed the iron back into the fire turned to his daughter and with a disapproving look said.

"If you speak properly I will tell you, now what did you say?"

"I'm sorry Father but my friends all make fun of me, and it's just that I forget sometimes."

"Well you're five now and long past that common talk, and some day you will find being well spoken will be of a great advantage, so just you remember that. Now what did you ask me?"

"I just wanted to know what you were making, and if I can watch." Her father studied the long skinny frame of his youngest child, and then turning back to the forge and starting to pump the bellows he said.

"It's a part for the staircase to the organ loft at the Cathedral, and if you don't get in the way, yes you may."

Jane watched studying every move as her father pumped the bellows and turned the iron in the fire.

"Why do you do that Father?" Jane asked pointing to the bellows.

"To make the fire hotter, fire is like a horse. It needs to breathe if it is to work hard and the bellows push air into the fire making it burn hotter and stronger."

22

Jane watched as the glowing iron was laid on the anvil and with blows of her father's hammer drawn out to a point, reheated and twisted into a spiral before being put among the other finished work.

That night Jane lying awake in the bed she shared with three of her older sisters ran through in her mind what she had seen and been told, and to work iron like her father seemed to be the most magical thing in the world. Lying there in the dark Jane decided that she would be a blacksmith.

The following morning Jane was back sitting in the smithy, watching as her father and his striker Simon loaded the wagon with the finished ironwork ready for Simon to take to Ripon.

Without his striker Jane's father started on the numerous small tasks that had been put aside while he finished the heavy iron work for the Cathedral staircase, the little things like hinges for the oak doors, brackets for the torch and candle holders, and many other items.

Jane watched and took it all in, seeing her father struggling to work the bellows and hold the iron in the fire. The way he used his hammer, Jane felt it was like a fist beating the iron into submission, and then gently teasing it into shape. It fascinated her, and she found her fingers itching to help.

As the days lengthened passing from spring into summer, Jane became a definite help in the smithy, fetching, carrying and generally helping with the small things that needed doing. It was towards the end of harvest time when Simon his striker was out, and her father was putting the finishing touches to a large hook before finishing for the night.

Jane seeing her father struggling with the big bellows; and at the same time trying to keep the iron turning in the fire decided it would be far easier if she worked the bellows and her father worked the iron.

Once the decision had been made there was no stopping her. Jane was off the bag of coke she had been sitting on and saying.

"Father I could do that for you." Her father stopped pumping the bellows and wiped his brow with the back of his hand as he said.

"No Jane I don't think so, its hard work even for a grown man." Jane's face immediately assumed that stubborn look that both he and his wife knew her intention was to do something no matter what, and so with a condescending smile her father stepped aside.

Jane as she had seen both her father and Simon do spat on her hands, and then with both hands she took hold of the arm of the bellows. With a look at her father that said.

'I told you so,' Jane pushed down on the arm. Jane's father wanted to laugh knowing that Jane probably hadn't the weight, never mind the strength to push down the arm of the big bellows, but he stood watching as Jane came up onto her toes as she pressed down, and then settled back onto the flat of her feet.

To his amazement, the arm went down and then up as Jane worked the bellows. Watching her he could see it was hard work but she was working them steady and sure.

After possibly six or seven operations of the bellows Jane stopped and wiped her brow just as she had seen her father do before turning, and with another. 'I told you so' look she waited for him to take up the part-finished hook.

It was later that night after the children were in bed, and John and Wendy were settled in their own bed that Wendy, who had been worrying about Jane's spending so much time with her father asked.

"Do you think its right for our Jane to spend so much time in the smithy? After all it's not the kind of thing a girl should be doing."

John lay silent turning over in his mind what he had seen that afternoon, until just as Wendy was about to ask if he had heard her, he said.

"How much would you say our Jane weighs?" Wendy puzzled considered the question before replying.

"Well she's tall for a girl her age but skinny with it, so possibly a little underweight why?"

"Would you say our Jane was particularly strong for a girl of her age?"

Wendy turned on her side looking at John as he lay frowning up at the ceiling, and now curious with the question she asked. "No, why do you ask that?" John turned to face his wife.

"I think I've seen the impossible today." Wendy heard his reply and becoming even more puzzled she asked.

"What do you mean you've seen the impossible?"

"Our Jane worked the large bellows for me this afternoon, and if I hadn't seen it with my own eyes I would never have believed it." Now it was Wendy's turn to think; could Jane be that heavy? Wendy couldn't believe it.

"You mean she pushed them down?"

"No, I mean she worked the bellows for me to finish what I was doing. Do you know what I think? I think she could be talented." Wendy with a shake of her head confidently replied.

"No, Lady Mary would have known, after all she's seen our Jane often enough when you have spoken to Lord James at church."

Over the next few weeks John kept an eye on Jane and finally decided that she was strong for her age but nothing more.

As the weeks passed and the time approached for Jane to start school, she finally managed to get her father to let her work with some hot iron, and in doing so surprised both Simon and her father, how quickly she learned from them.

As the days turned into weeks they both found themselves having to admit that she had a natural ability in the craft. Then with the months passing and as Jane became more skilled her father found that word of his girl apprentice had spread, bringing in extra work from far and wide just to see Jane at work.

It was cold and wet, Jane who having just celebrated her twelfth birthday, and having received as her present her very own leather apron from her mother and father, now wanted to wear it, but it was a Sunday. .

Her father may not have been a particularly religious man but he had a rule; no work on a Sunday. Now feeling bored, she was walking along the beck away from the smithy so as not to be tempted.

Ahead of her where a group of willows overhung the beck, she could hear voices raised in excitement, and as she drew nearer she recognised them as belonging to two of her elder brothers, Albert who was five years older than her, and Ernest who was a year younger than his brother.

As she came around the willows, Jane found Andrew a boy of seven from the shop in the village knee-deep in the water, being kept there by her two brothers who were refusing to let him out.

Jane didn't know how Andrew had come to be in the beck, but seeing her two brothers keeping him there set Jane's temper to boiling.

Jane walking up unnoticed behind Albert pushed him in the back, almost sending him to join Andrew in the beck as she said.

"Don't you think you're a little old for bullying a seven-year old?"

Taken by surprise both Albert and Ernest spun around. It was Ernest who recovered first and pushed his face close to Jane's while copying her speech as he said.

"Well if it isn't our little miss high and mighty all hoity-toity with her posh voice," and then with a shove. "tak yer sen off afore I push yu in wi' im." Jane caught off guard almost slipped on the muddy bank, catching Albert a dig in the stomach with her elbow as she recovered her balance.

"Watch what yu do yu silly lass!" Albert gasped pushing her back into Ernest, who had just turned to stop Andrew climbing the bank, and with Jane bumping into him he now found himself stumbling down the bank to join Andrew in the water.

Seeing his brother in the water Albert grabbed Jane by the collar of her coat saying.

"Look what yu dun yu silly lass, now thee can go in wi 'im," pushing Jane towards the bank's edge.

That was it; Jane bunched her fist and struck with all the strength in her young body. Albert lurched backwards clutching his eye and screaming.

"Yon's put me eye out yu blinded me." Struggling up the bank and seeing this Ernest made a grab for Jane, and getting a hold of her shoulder he pulled her around. Only to receive a right hook under his chin that took his head back with a snap. His knees buckled, and down he went not moving.

Beckoning to Andrew, Jane grabbed his hand and dragging him out of the beck she hurried him away, risking a quick look back at her brothers, to see one still laid on the bank and the other on his knees covering his face with his hands. Arriving back in the village she told his mother that she thought he had slipped into the beck.

Jane was looking forward to her thirteenth birthday as it meant she could leave school, and that she would be able to work with her father every day.

After the marriage of three of her sisters, Jane now had her own bedroom and had just climbed into bed when her mother came in, and sitting on the bed said.

"Jane I know how much working with your father means to you, but it will have to stop."

Jane felt her heart freeze; she could see her mother was serious though she knew of no reason why her mother should say this. With a throat that had closed she asked.

"Why Mother, Father never said anything today?" Her mother sat looking at her hands as she fiddled with the thin eiderdown, and then looking at her daughter she said.

"It has to do with the day you were born." Jane now sitting up in bed shook her head; it didn't make sense. Why would something that happened thirteen years ago mean she couldn't work with her father?

"You were born on the same day as Miss Celina, did you know that?" her mother asked. Jane hadn't, and it still didn't make any sense to her as her mother said. "It wasn't just the same day Jane; it was at the same time; and I mean exactly. You and Miss Celina both took your first breaths and cried together just as if it was only one cry."

Jane who could still see no reason why this should stop her working in the smithy listened with a sick feeling as her mother said.

"Not long after you were born Lord Carvel asked if he and Lady Mary could see you. Well, a Lord and Lady.... I couldn't say no, and then after seeing you they were so taken with you that they asked that when your schooling was finished for you to become the companion of their daughter and live at the hall." This left Jane sick and desperate as she said.

"I can't mother; I can't live in the hall. I want to be a blacksmith just like daa." Jane fell silent even as she said it she knew she had no choice, and now she said.

"Mother I so wanted to be a blacksmith," and then knowing in her heart that there was no hope she asked. "Does it have to be Mother?" Her mother with a nod took a quietly sobbing Jane into her arms.

It was on her last morning at home while working in the forge with her father, that she came to ask about a sword that had hung on the wall at the back of the smithy for as long as she could remember.

"Father," she said pointing at the sword. "Who did that belong to?" Her father looking over his shoulder replied.

"No-one lass," he then reached up and took down the sword. It was in a plain leather scabbard with the upper scabbard locket, and the chape at the scabbard tip both fashioned in brass.

The sword's pommel capping the hilt and its cross guard were also made in brass inset with polished black jet, while the grip was bound with black leather. A leather belt with two bolts to hold the scabbard in place was taken down too.

Jane had never seen it taken down before, and as she ran her hands over the leather belt, she found there was no dust or dirt on it. Indeed despite its great age the metal and leather were all as shiny as new.

"Has it belonged to no-one father?" she asked again. Her father held the sheathed sword turning it as he said.

"It was made many years ago by one of my great-great-grandfathers. He made this sword as a test at the end of his time as an apprentice." Then seeing Jane's puzzled look he explained.

"It was expected of a journeyman in those far-off days to show he was a capable sword Smith. When it was finished the man who had commissioned it never came back to collect it so it was offered to one of Lord Carvel's great-great-grandfathers.

It was strange; you see when that Lord Carvel tried to draw the sword he found he couldn't; yet my great-grandfather could draw the sword with ease.

Lord Carvel said the sword was waiting for its rightful master and should remain with its creator until that man arrived."

Her father snapped the scabbard back onto a beautifully worked leather belt as he said. "It has resisted all attempts to draw it by any other but the head of our family right up to myself." Taking the sword by the grip, he withdrew it. Jane watched wide-eyed as the blade sparkling and shining in the light from the forge slid from its scabbard.

"So," her father said. "It hangs there waiting for its true master," and with that he re-sheathed the blade and replaced the sword and belt back high on the wall, while Jane's eyes large and round followed his every move.

"Now little miss we had better to be started as we have work to do that is if you want me to be at your birthday celebration."

The following day Jane and her mother walked to Brimham Hall with Jane nervous to the point of almost being sick. It was as they approached the Hall itself that Jane began to feel herself to be about two feet tall, finding herself looking up at its walls as it towered over her like a beast about to devour all before it.

As they approached the side of the house, a young man dressed in the livery of the house met them with.

"Good morning Mrs Cooper," and turning to Jane with a small bow, "and to you Miss Jane. Lady Mary is expecting you." Jane found herself tongue-tied and blushing having been greeted this way by so handsome a young man.

The young man took Jane and her mother through a splendid hall and then into what to Jane was a very large and elegant room, where they found Lady Carvel sitting by a window.

Jane found herself so frightened she was unable to move, until Lady Carvel coming to greet her, smiled in a way that suddenly made her feel better and even welcome.

Getting to her feet, Lady Carvel who was as tall, slim and elegant as Jane's mother was small and plump approached Jane and her mother, and seeing that Jane had started to look tearful and frightened leaned slightly to ease Jane's fears.

Lady Carvel taking hold of both Jane's hands while still lightly leaning said.

"Don't be frightened Jane. You must look on this house as your own to come and go just as my daughter Celina does," and then without even looking up Lady Carvel said. "Look she's coming to join us now."

Jane heard the door behind her open and turning; she found a girl with the most beautiful dark-red hair and the greenest eyes she had ever seen coming into the room.

The two girls looked at each other for a moment; both were tall and slim, one with dark-red hair and the other a golden blond. Apart from their hair and eyes, they looked so alike that they could have been twins.

At that moment feelings of loss separation and longing welled up inside Jane and drove her towards Celina. They reached out tentatively, touched and then fell into each other's arms crying. It was as if they had been long-separated sisters. Indeed from that moment on they were inseparable.

Jane found Lady Mary to be a second mother, although sometimes a little more distant and reserved, and demanding a higher standard of behaviour than her own, while Celina found Mrs Cooper to be a more relaxed and playful mother.

It wasn't long before Jane Celina and Jonathan were known throughout the village as the 'terrible trio.' With Celina sharing Jane's fascination with the smithy and happily spending many an hour helping Jane, and with both suffering many a scolding or even worse from Celina's mother about the state of their clothes.

Celina and Jane were inseparable in all things but one. All in all, Jane took the same lessons as Celina and soon made up for subjects not taken in the village school. However, to Celina's education had been added special lessons given by the Reverend Dr Richard Bird.

After only the second week of lessons Jane ran crying from the classroom and refused to go back. When asked why by Celina,

Lady Mary or her mother none could get her to give a reason other than that the lessons simply weren't for her.

Celina

The smell of beeswax polish on brown wood, for Celina this would always bring back memories of a childhood full of sunlight and shadow playing across the nursery floor.

A place where there were always soft pillows for her to sleep on when she was tired, her older brothers and sisters. Then later when she was three, her baby brother came along, all helpless and very noisy.

Celina knew she was special in her mother's eyes because when her baby brother Robert was out of sorts and crying, her mother or the nurse would place him on her knee to nurse.

This always had a magical effect soothing Robert and soon sending him to sleep. Nurse also found that if Robert were to sleep in Celina's room on a night, it ensured a peaceful night for her. By the time Celina was six it was usual to see Celina and Robert playing together either in the nursery or in the house grounds.

As the years passed, Celina joined her older brothers and sisters in school. Robert was still too young for school, but he listened attentively to Celina repeating her lessons each evening.

To their mother's surprise, Robert was soon able to understand most of Celina's lessons and learned readily from his sister. While Celina found going over her lessons with Robert helped her better to understand them.

Celina was eleven when her life changed forever. She was playing in the nursery, when the ball thrown by Robert found the open window, and ended on the lawn one floor below.

Celina, who was now tall enough to look out of the window, could see where the ball had come to rest close to a flowerbed.

Before the nurse could take Celina away from the window, she had lifted her arm and plucked the ball out of the air as it flew back into the nursery.

That night Celina's mother and father had a talk with Celina about what she could do. Her mother found that with a little coaching, Celina could move quite heavy objects from a distance of several yards.

Her mother also found Celina could manipulate small objects with a precision and dexterity that startled her.

More astonishing still was the fact that without knowing it, Celina had been leaning on Robert since he was a baby, comforting and soothing him as and when needed.

From that day on, Celina's life was never to be the same again. As her father took great pains explaining to her, that the use of what she now knew as her 'talent' in public, was not allowed, not even in front of her brothers and sisters.

Celina having heard all this from her father, rightly or wrongly decided Robert was not included in this ban.

Her school lessons now differed from those of her brothers and sisters as she began her studies with the Reverend Dr Bird. He was a man of about thirty-five years of age, which to Celina seemed quite old, although she found him to be very nice.

He not only taught her all the normal school subjects, but he also tutored her in what he called her 'special subjects, and it wasn't long before they became firm friends.

Each evening Celina and Robert would compare notes on school. Celina was proving to be an excellent teacher herself with Robert doing consistently well in all subjects.

It was as she approached her thirteenth birthday that her mother told her of the special circumstances of her birth, and that another girl her age would soon be coming to live at the Hall to be her friend and companion.

Celina wasn't too comfortable with this. After all she already had Robert, and she didn't feel that she needed anyone else. Indeed as her thirteenth birthday approached, Celina started to worry about this new companion. What if they didn't like each other…. What would happen then?

The day of her new friends coming eventually arrived, finding Celina watching from behind the curtains of an upstairs window as a small and rather dumpy-woman accompanied by a slim blond girl came up the drive to be met by a footman.

Celina who had crept down the stairs and stood listening at the door heard her mother introduced herself to the girl. Celina now felt a strong pull from her mother who had obviously known she was there listening.

With this urging, Celina knew it was now time for her to make her entrance. Putting on her most regal and intimidating air Celina opened the door and entered.

The blonde girl who Celina found to be of her own height and build was standing with her back to the door. Once through the door Celina found a strange feeling of need was pulling her forwards.

It was as the girl turned and they looked at each other that this need welled up inside her. Something beyond words grew in her. It was with a feeling of need, love, and long separation so mutual and strong that they fell crying into each other's arms.

At that moment, both knew they were part of one whole, as between them a bond was created that went beyond words.

Celina finding all her previous worries driven from her mind knowing that in this girl, she had met a trusted and life-long companion. Celina found that this girl was the twin sister who should have been but never had been.

Jane

From the day Jane arrived Robert found he was no longer the centre of Celina's attention. Feeling hurt and lost he took his frustration out on Jane being as nasty as a younger boy could be to an older girl.

To her credit, Jane made it clear to Celina that she fully understood why Robert so obviously disliked her, while doing her best not to retaliate.

It was several months later when Jane witnessed the animosity that happens from time to time between brothers. The twins had never been particularly close to Robert with Celina being between them in age, and now when Celina was at her lessons and leaving Robert alone they had started to torment him, sometimes to the point where physical violence occurred.

33

Jane was bored; it had been a wet morning and now the afternoon was promising more of the same. Celina was having her special lesson with Dr Bird, and Jane had been wandering around the stables making friends with the horses and talking to the stable boys. Eventually, curiosity found her exploring the empty stable blocks furthest from the Hall.

Jane was approaching one of the stables when she heard a voice she recognised as belonging to Henry saying.

"What do we have here, and has our baby brother been trying to hide from us?" Jane crept silently towards the open door as she heard James say.

"You know it's no good trying to hide from us, as you know we always find you, and when we do you know what happens don't you?"

Jane who had reached the open door stood quietly to one side hidden from view as Celina's two elder brothers pushed a wet muddy and now crying Robert around.

Jane silently waited and watched unobserved until the twins had their backs to the door before she stepped into the doorway. James having taken hold of Robert's hair had pulled his head back as he sneered with obvious relish into Robert's face.

"Your big sister doesn't want you any more does she? She's left you for a peasant hasn't she."

Jane who had quietly walked up behind him now prodded him firmly in the back, and though James was heavier and inches taller than her Jane said.

"If you want to bully someone try someone your own size." Both James and Henry spun around. It was James who recovered first saying.

"Well if it isn't our little peasant girl, have you come to join in?" Then the two boys started laughing.

James obviously the main instigator started to walk around her making comments about 'village trash,' before he began pulling prodding and tugging at her clothing.

Jane stood silently waiting with her arms folded until eventually; tiring of this he stopped and turned to Henry to ask.

"What should we do with this one then?" Henry looked her up and down as if she was something dirty, and then turning towards the horse trough he said.

"We could give her a bath; the trough is a big enough one, and she might even drown in it." Then he laughed as James with a snigger said.

"With a bit of help, come on let's get her undressed and give her a good scrub."

James who had now turned his back on what had become a very annoyed Jane stood watching as Henry walked to the back of the stable, finding there an old hard bristled brush which he began rubbing across his hand while saying.

"This should get the dirt off." By now, a very annoyed Jane decided enough was enough, and reaching out she took hold of James's collar and the seat of his trousers.

James who was a boy two or three inches taller and much heavier than Jane, found himself lifted completely off his feet, and then ignoring the thrashing of his arms and legs Jane marched across to the large and deep horse trough where she dropped him in.

Then despite Jane's lack of weight and his best efforts to resist her, he found himself pushed down under the water and held there until he was thoroughly soaked. Henry who had stood for a moment speechless dropped the brush and ran across to help his brother shouting.

"You…. you stop that." Jane was ready for him catching hold of one of the arms reaching for her; she spun him around tripped him and dumped him unceremoniously on top of his brother in the trough. Then with two hands full of hair Jane pushed the two of them down faces-first under the water.

After a moment, she pulled their heads up out of the water holding them by their hair while they coughed and spluttered as she demanded.

"Now say you're sorry, and I do mean truly sorry to both of us." When she didn't get an answer from the spluttering boys, she dunked the both of them again, after which she repeated her demand.

35

This time she received a stream of words that boys their age shouldn't know, so once again she dunked them. The two boys came up gasping, spluttering and splashing water all around soaking Jane as she asked.

"Now do I have to ask again?" There was still no answer from the boys, whether they were unwilling or unable too Jane wasn't sure so once more under the water they went. This time Jane held them down even longer having to use one foot to hold a struggling Henry's rear end under the water.

All this time Robert had been standing with his mouth open, trembling, watching and wondering.

The two boys came up gasping spluttering and with arms and legs flailing spilling more water all around and soaking the few parts of Jane that had remained dry.

"Now I don't want to have to ask again," Jane said still holding them by their hair.

The two boys looking like drowning rats and gasping for air finally managed something that sounded like an apology, so Jane pulled them out one at a time and threw them towards the door saying.

"Don't ever try anything like this again because I'm here, and Robert's my friend now, do you understand that?"

It was a very wet Jane, who watched as the two older boys ran dripping water back towards the house. That left her with a shivering wet cold and muddy Robert.

Jane looked him up and down with a thought running through her head. *This has happened before,* remembering Andrew, after which the words. *I wonder if I'll go through my life rescuing little boys?* almost came from her lips.

Instead, Jane took his hand and said. "Come on we'd better get you cleaned up before your mother or nurse gets to see you."

Taking him through the servant's entrance, she managed to get him into a bathroom without being seen. Then leaving him to clean himself up as best a ten-year-old boy could she went in search of clean clothes for the two of them.

Celina was rather surprised and pleased when a bond suddenly developed between Jane and Robert, as it meant the three of them could be friends at last.

Celina also noticed that whenever her two older brothers were in the room, a certain look and smile would pass between Jane and Robert that would send them scurrying out. It was several years later before she finally heard the whole story from Robert.

Celina

Celina's lessons just lately with Dr Bird had been rather boring lectures on what was permissible under talent protocol and what was not. His words on what Talents were allowed and not allowed to do; well most of them had gone in one ear and out of the other.

Even the mystery of why Talents normally touched hands briefly had aroused only mild interest, answering her curiosity on this practise as she heard that it was so as not to be accused of leaning.

Celina's lessons today had been two of the more interesting ones; to be precise the shield, and basic instruction on the broom. Now the lessons were over and Celina was wandering around the stables practicing her shield.

The bubble shield was easy; you just created your shield around you so you were enclosed in a bubble, but that was it as you were trapped unable to move.

A proper shield to enclose oneself was much harder, and at the moment it was taking all Celina's concentration. It had to be created away from your body and outside your clothes, because as Dr Bird had said.

"If you just create a shield and then push it away from you, you will end up naked as it will rip your clothes off your body as you expand it. All right using a skin shield or partial shield will protect you, but it will not protect your clothing and again that could become embarrassing."

Now Celina had created a proper shield, and she was struggling to control it as she moved around. It had to follow not just the movement of her body, but also the movements of her clothing, and it had to be kept unnoticed where it passed under the soles of her shoes, while at the same time allow her to walk.

It was difficult but Celina was mastering it, and at the same time finding herself intrigued by how it had changed the world.

The breeze that was no longer blowing against her skin had become a pressure against her shield, while sounds from outside had deepened slightly, and the shield under her feet felt different to how the ground had, some how flatter or smoother. As she looked around she found it was only the sunlight and colours that seemed unchanged.

By the third time around the stables, the shield had become almost a natural extension of her body, so Celina's thoughts turned to this afternoons other lesson, basic instruction on the broom.

Her wanderings had now brought her to the tack room where her parents stored their brooms. Pulling the door open Celina looked in. By the wall, she saw three brooms resting in place on their *racks, while the fourth ones place was empty.

Celina wandered in trailing her hand across the wicker rear seat of her mother's two-seat broom. It rocked under her touch surprising her by rising from its rack like an eager pony ready for a gallop. Celina hesitated; her mother was out for the rest of the afternoon, and her father would probably be late back, so she decided, "why not?" With only a slight push the broom moved forward.

Celina kicked the rack so it swung up and out of the way before she floated the broom toward the door.

Once outside Celina slid into the rear seat just as her mother always did. Then with a quick look around and finding no-one in sight, she gave a gentle push down and the broom lifted up.

Celina was so surprised that she was a good hundred and fifty feet in the air before she stopped pushing. The broom then hovered there drifting slowly with the breeze as Celina sat waiting for her heart to stop thumping.

That was easy,' she thought to herself. *'Now just a slight push,'*

*Rack. A stand attached to the broom that is swung up out of the way when the broom is in use.

and the broom drifted forwards.

'A little harder…. there now that's better.' The broom was now moving as fast as a horse could run.

'Just a little harder…. maybe a bit more,' she thought again. *'Well, this is easy,'* Celina thought as she eagerly looked around. *'This is far better than being a passenger, and I can go wherever I like on the estate.'* Celina may have been headstrong and reckless at times, but even she knew better than to be seen off the estate on a broom.

Pushing hard and full of excitement Celina flew towards the druid's rocks with the broom crossing the fields so fast that they had started to blur under her.

It was as she was twisting weaving and diving around though and between the druid's rocks flying far faster than a horse could run that she found herself laughing and screaming with the thrill of it all. *'This is great!'* She thought as her heart raced with excitement. *'The sooner I can have a broom of my own the better.'*

At first it was great fun just to fly from one end of the estate to the other, but after about an hour or so of being on her own the novelty started to wear off. *'I wonder,'* she thought. *'If I go over to Jane's, I can bring her back with me.* Celina mentally hugged herself unable to find any adequate words to describe her feelings. *This is fantastic and so easy.'*

Taking the broom even higher into the air, she found the miles flew by as she headed back towards the village intending to stop first at the smithy.

It was as she crossed the meadow towards the beck that she saw Jane with some friends of their age from the village. Celina dived swooping down low over their heads and waving to Jane only to find that possibly with the noise they were making none of them thought to look up to see her.

In doing this Celina had become so engrossed in the group below her that she completely missed seeing the old tree in the middle of the meadow.

The next thing she knew it seemed like something had plucked her from the broom; spun her round and smacked her hard. Then she was falling, bouncing from branch to branch until she reached the thicker bottom branches.

In a shower of broken branches and leaves she reached a spot where the branches could support her weight. There was a tearing of fabric as her skirts caught and pulled up over her head, leaving her hanging with her legs dangling through the lower foliage held there suspended by her skirts.

Try as she would all her efforts to free herself proved fruitless; she was stuck. A boy's voice came drifting up from below saying.

"I've never seen a bird with feathers quite that colour before." After which a lot of giggling and laughter drifted up. Celina could feel herself blushing as she called.

"Get me down." It was Jane's voice that came up from below asking.

"Celina is that you?" Celina's scream of, "Yes," was followed by a pleading. "Please Jane, get me down!"

"I can't," Jane called back. "You're too high up and too far out, I'll have to go and get help just stay there until I get back." Celina fumed as she shouted back.
"Where am I likely to go?" Celina hung there as more and different voices drifted up discussing the view from below.

"Don't you dare to look," Celina shouted now near to tears. Only to be greeted by more laughing, cheers and some very personal observations about the view from below.

By the time Jane arrived back with her mother and father, with her father carrying a ladder Celina was beyond blushing and in tears.

Jane looking at the crowd standing under the tree decided just about every one between six and thirteen in the village was there, probably about twenty in all.

A few sharp words from Jane's mother Wendy quickly sent them all scurrying back home, especially those of her brood.

Once Jane's father had the ladder safely in place; it took him about twenty minutes carefully to cut away most of the branches holding Celina in the tree. Then with Celina standing on his shoulders having extracted a belated promise from him not to look up, they waited for Lady Mary.

Lady Mary, who arrived on a borrowed horse at first found herself feeling angry, but then after seeing Celina's predicament she found she didn't know whether to laugh or cry, but eventually she managed to ask.

"Celina are you all right?"

"Mother," Celina sobbed. "Please get me down and take me home; I want to go home."

Lady Mary taking out her wand and lifting Celina's weight off the branches said.

"All right Mr Cooper I've got her now." Hearing this, Jane's father started back down the ladder accompanied by a loud wail of. "Motherrr!" from Celina.

"Take the ladder away please Mr Cooper," and then with a further lift using her wand, Lady Mary lifted Celina up and unhooked the rest of her skirts from the few remaining branches before lowering her to the ground. Where her daughter sat with both hands covering her face, sobbing in distress and embarrassment as her mother sternly informed her.

"You young lady, when your father gets home tonight we shall both have something to say to you." Then turning to Jane's father she asked. "Mr Cooper, would you please put my daughter on my horse?" Jane's father picked Celina up and deposited her on the horse as her mother said.

"Now young Lady, you stay on that horse and go straight home," and then turning to Jane. "Jane you go with her and make sure she stays out of further trouble."

Lady Mary found she had to laugh as they watched Jane with Celina sitting behind her ride away. Finally turning to Wendy, she said.

"If it wasn't so funny I'd be really angry; I just hope that this teaches her a lesson." Then looking at the broom lying on its side in the grass she mused. "And with no wand, I wonder how she managed that. Still I doubt if it will put her off."

"Well," Wendy said with a small chuckle. "I doubt if she'll be in a hurry getting back to the village again."

"Oh, why not?" Lady Mary asked. Wendy now laughed as she replied.

"Most of the lads from the village were here and saw her hanging in the tree." Lady Mary who was still stood under the tree looked up frowned and said.

"Oh my, that does make a difference." Then they both laughed.

On the day after her sixteenth birthday, Lord and Lady Carvel took Celina to Fountain's Abbey. Jane again refused to go stating it wasn't something she should do, saying that she would go back to her mothers for the day.

On their arrival at the Abbey, the High Abbot himself greeted the party and ushered them into his private rooms. There he had a long talk with Celina on the responsibilities of being a Church Knight.

Regretfully and as usual with Celina, most of what he said went in one ear and out of the other, although he took pains to have her repeat the more important points back to him.

He then took them all into his study where a selection of wands awaited. To the surprise of all and not even waiting for the wands to be taken from their sheaths, Celina ran her hand over the line of wands that had been set out.

She shook her head and then looked around the room to where an open cabinet with fifty small square pigeonholes caught her attention. It was as if something in the cabinet was calling her name. Walking over to it Celina reached out and without hesitation, she withdrew a wand from one of the upper levels of pigeonholes.

"This is the one," she said confidently slipping the wand out of its sheath. It was black and almost thirteen inches in length, with a thin line of silver running along its full length.

As she held it and turned it in her hands they all watched as the following words appeared along the length of the wand in silver.

"I WILL PROTECT."

"Oh my!" the Abbot exclaimed. "I didn't expect that." Lady Mary looked at him with her question dying on her lips as she heard him say. "That wand is over a thousand years old, and it is believed that it was Morgana-le-Fay's wand."

He looked at Celina, who apparently hadn't heard a word as he said. "There are three wands that have *refused all candidates up to the present. There is that black wand," the Abbot said pointing to the wand in Celina's hand. "Then there is a red wand that is held at the Abbey at Glastonbury, and there is said to be a small white wand that hasn't been seen for centuries."

He stopped and looked carefully at Celina, who was standing and turning the wand in her fingers seemingly mesmerised by it, and oblivious to the Abbot's comments and everything around her while she accepted the wand as a living part of her.

"Celina," the Abbot finally said attempting to get her attention. Celina continued to stand as if in a trance.

"Celina," her mother said as she put a hand on her shoulder, making her jump.

"Yes Mother."

"The Abbot wants to speak with you," her mother turned Celina in his direction. Celina looked at the Abbot as if seeing him for the first time and said.

"I'm sorry my Lord Abbot."

"Celina, we need to go to the chapel." The Abbot hesitated and looked at the wand once more before he said. "You have to take the oath."

Celina again looked blank for a moment or two and then with a visible effort she pulled herself together. With a feeling of great reluctance, Celina with her mother's help replaced the wand back in its sheath, after which she let the Abbot fasten the sheath to her belt. On the way to the chapel Lady Mary whispered to her husband.

Look at Celina; she's lost to the wand." Celina was indeed; she had taken the wand out of its sheath again and was carrying it, turning it and stroking it.

Once in the family's private chapel Celina knelt before the altar as her parents took a kneeling position behind her.

Celina took her wand holding it between both her hands as if in

*It is said that a wand is almost alive and chooses its talent, not the talent who chooses the wand.

prayer as she repeated the oath as dictated to her by the Abbot.

It was the same simple oath as taken by the Knights of the Church since the time of King Arthur, with the Abbot finding it unnecessary to insert any words at the appropriate points in the last lines of the oath.

"My life I will give to the Church I serve. All people 'I will protect'. No wrong or harm to man will I do; by the name of the God I serve, all evils I will fight."

With the oath taken the Abbot taking a small bowl of oil made the sign of the cross on Celina's forehead. Then taking one of Celina's hands in his he raised her to her feet. It was only then that her mother and father stood and embraced her.

Following the taking of the oath, they all returned to the Abbot's private study. With Celina seated in front of his desk the Abbot produced a large and ancient black leather-bound book.

It was the Abbey's book of names of the Knights of the Church since the day King Arthur had founded the order of the Round Table in the year 530 A.D. In all those centuries only seventy pages had been used; and now Celina's name was to be added to the list.

As the Abbot started to write Celina's name in the book, Celina who was looking over the desk asked.

"How many names are recorded in that book?"

"Nine hundred and forty-six," the Abbot replied, "and you will make it nine hundred and forty-seven." Celina who was still looking at the book now asked.

"How many are alive now?"

"About sixty Knights of one calling or another are working permanently in the Abbeys. Then there are probably as many that are working for but outside the Abbeys so about one hundred and forty." The Abbot now took out a sheet of paper saying.

"This is the official application for your warrant, and once we have filled it in it will be sent first to the Archbishop and then for royal approval before being delivered, signed and sealed to you."

Celina suddenly found herself thankful to be seated as she realised for the first time just what becoming a Knight of the

Church really meant, and the enormous obligation it had put upon her, an obligation that would last for the rest of her life.

Later that evening the family attended a service in the Abbey's small private chapel, and afterwards Celina was introduced to the talents on the Abbey's staff. *'Only twenty'* she thought. *'Sixteen women and four men.'* Not only that she found only one a woman was actually a Knight while the rest were talents of one calling or another.

"Of course," the Abbot explained. "A number are away from the Abbey at the moment."

That night as they prepared to retire to the Abbey's guest apartment, Lord and Lady Carvel presented Celina with their own small gift, a gold ring with the family seal embossed on it, and a gold wand safe that fitted her wrist like a bracelet.

"There," her mother said as she closed the band around Celina's right wrist. "If ever you use your wand in difficult circumstances, always make sure it's attached itself to your wand safe and that way you won't lose it."

Jane

Jane had watched Celina with her mother and father depart for Fountain's Abbey with mixed feelings. She had been invited to join them but the thought of what was to occur there made her feel sick. She was even worried about what it would be like when Celina returned. Other people's wands were bad enough; but one belonging to Celina.... the very thought of it made her shudder.

It was still early and in the east the first glow of dawn was spreading across the clouds as Jane set off toward her mother's home. Jane knew the road well so setting a brisk pace and wrapped in her cloak, she found she wasn't too cold.

Her first stop was to see her father at the forge where she found him coaxing the fire back to life and not hearing her approach.

"Good morning Father," she said. Her father turned smiling to see her standing at the door.

"Jane," he exclaimed as he pulled her close to him. "Happy birthday for yesterday, did you get your presents?" Jane with her arms clasped tightly around her father said.

"Yes Father, they were lovely." Her father leaving the forge and linking his arm with her said.

"Come on into the house; your mother missed you not having seen you yesterday." Arm in arm they walked down the road to the house.

"Mother," her father called out, "come and see who's here."

Her mother appearing at the door squealed.

"Jane oh Jane," as she hugged her and called for the rest of the family, and from then on pandemonium ensued as Jane unpacked her basket of bits and pieces to show everyone.

Finally, things calmed somewhat and then it was on with some of her old working clothes before she headed out to the forge. Her father seeing her carrying her leather apron smiled as he said.

"It's a pity you're a lass; you would have made a first-class blacksmith." Jane laughed saying as she put her leather apron on.

"I'll remember that Dad, if Celina ever throws me out, well then you will be able to give me a job."

Later, she took the hinge she was working on and plunged it into the water barrel before passing it to her father asking.

"How does that look, or have I lost my touch?" Her father gave the hinge a thorough looking over, considered the weight of the barn door it was to be fitted on and then pronounced that it was perfect. Indeed as good as any man could do. Jane looked into the back of the smithy saying.

"I would be truly good if I could make a sword like that one. I see it's still there and no-one has claimed it yet?" Her father looked up at the sword and replied.

"No and I don't expect to see yon claimed in my lifetime now."

"You never know Father; it must be intended for someone somewhere." Jane then pulled some more iron out of the fire and started on a second hinge, taking great pleasure out of striking the iron and seeing the sparks fly as the metal was shaped.

That evening sitting by the fire Jane wasn't too sure just how much she still enjoyed the work. She found her arms back and shoulders ached, and she certainly knew she had worked a full day in the forge. Even so she felt that she was happy and contented with her day's work.

As her mother applied soothing liniment to aching muscles before bed, she asked Jane about herself and Celina. In particular, what Celina was and being what she was, was Jane happy.

Jane sat quietly looking into the fire for a moment and then said.

"Yes Mother I am happy; Celina truly treats me like a sister." Then as Jane thought about Celina's other sisters and how she treated them, she said. "She treats me better."

"What about what she is?" her mother pressed further. Jane looked up and said.

"Mother if I tell you this you must never tell anyone what I've told you." Her mother looked at her daughter and considered for a moment before saying.

"All right; if you feel's you want to tell us I promise." For a moment Jane looked into her mother's eyes and then quietly she said.

"Mother, I know that I have some talent too." Her mother stopped rubbing and exclaimed.

"You can't have."

"I have Mother but I don't mean talent like Celina is talented. I think Celina suspects that I have some form of talent…. She thinks it is just a small amount but she's wrong. I don't know exactly how much I have but I know it's there. I may not be gifted in the same way Celina is, but I do know I have a power."

"How'd you know?" her mother asked as she continued to rub the liniment into Jane's shoulders.

"I just do Mother." Jane fell quiet for a moment before she asked her mother. "How many girls my age could strike for their father with a seven-pound hammer for two hours at a time and keep up with him. Or pick up a full bag of coal in each hand?

Mother it's not just that I'm strong; I can feel something inside…. something is helping me. I tried making a horseshoe once out of cold metal. I found I could do it easily with my bare hands."

Jane held out her hands and looked at them. They seemed the same as any sixteen-year-old lady's hands as Jane turned them so her mother could see the un-marked backs and palms, and as she did so she said, "It wasn't a perfectly shaped horseshoe but it was a good shape." Her mother sat thinking and then said.

"You could have a talent for strength I suppose." Jane looked at her mother before she said.

"Mother look at me, I've worked all today in the smithy; oh I know I ache a bit but look Mother." Jane held out her hands again. "Not a blister, my hands are as smooth and clean as Celina's and she's never done a day's work in her life." Jane looked at her mother as she asked.

"Have you ever seen me with a burn or a blister or a cut? Not only that, I don't bleed. I'm sixteen, and I've only bled once and that was at the same time as Celina. I was there when Lady Mary told Celina how to stop it until she wanted children, and I found that I could do the same."

Her mother started to protest, but Jane was saying. "Then when I was with Celina while she was taking her special lessons, I felt that the more I learned the more it was wrong for me, so I had to leave. Something kept telling me to go, it was not that I felt what Celina was learning was bad; it was just; well, I felt that it wasn't yet time for me.

The feeling was strongest when Dr Bird started to explain about wands; and then when he took his out." Her mother tried to speak, but Jane wouldn't let her as she said.

"Oh I know about not being able to touch other people's wands; and that once a wand has bonded only the person bonded to it can touch it. This was different; Dr Bird's wand actually wanted me out of the room. It was like it was telling me that it was too early and to go."

Jane fell silent as her mother continued to rub the liniment in thinking. Then her mother quietly said.

"You should be telling this to your Dr Bird or Celina."

"No, not yet," Jane said. "That just doesn't feel right; this is something that will have to work itself out, but it will be Celina that I tell first." Her mother sighed and then said.

"Well then lass go to bed. The morrow's another day and you've to be back early to the big house, so we'll keep this just between the two of us." Her mother gave her a gentle push in the direction of the bed saying. "Go on now." Jane paused for a moment before she said.

"Thank you Mother, I feel better just having told you."

"Well then think about telling your Dr Bird," her mother said as she closed the door.

Later that night, Wendy having first sworn him to secrecy told John all that Jane had told her. John lay quietly for a while just thinking, and then he said.

"Some years ago Simon told me about something that happened with our Jane." Wendy turned on her side to face him.

"Let's see," he said. "It was early spring so our Jane would have been just about twelve."

Simon's story.

Jane watched her father as he drove their wagon down the road until he disappeared into the early-morning mist. She had to light the fire in the forge before Simon arrived so she started cleaning out the cold ashes. By the time Simon arrived Jane had the forge hot and ready. Accompanying Simon was Farmer Brown leading old Ted, the largest and nastiest Shire horse in the county.

"Where's John?" Farmer Brown asked.

"He's taken some parts for a plough over old man Todd's way," Jane replied. Farmer Brown scowling turned to Simon as he said.

"I need old Ted here seeing to; he threw a shoe on the first pull this morning so can you see to him?" Simon looked at old Ted and to Simon it seemed the horse glared back; he shook his head saying.

"The best one to see to him would be Jane here, as I'm only the striker and I've never done a horse afore."

Farmer Brown looked down at Jane and then said pointing at old Ted.

"I need that horse this morning as I've a field to finish, and now you tell me there's no blacksmith." He then swore angrily.

49

"I'll see to him Mr Brown," Jane said. "I've seen to Shire horses afore."

"You, a slip of a lass the likes of you? You wouldn't have the strength to get him in here." Simon laughed as he sprang to Jane's defence saying.

"Don't underestimate our Jane; she's nearly as good as her dad she is." Farmer Brown only snorted.

Jane looked at him as he stood there glaring at her, and then she turned and with her back straight and her head held high, she walked over to old Ted. Beside the massive Shire horse Jane looked tiny, with her head just reaching the tops of his legs as she walked him up to the rail. Once there she carefully wrapped the halter around the rail tying it securely. The one thing she didn't want was the first horse she shod unsupervised running away.

Then taking hold of Old Ted's front knee she gave it a tap at the back and old Ted politely allowed Jane to lift his hoof. It took just a quick look for her to estimate the hoof size, after which Jane took three of the part-finished shoes from the rack. With another tap, old Ted again lifted his massive hoof.

After cleaning and trimming the hoof Jane checked for the shoe that would give the best fit with the least alteration. Selecting one she made a final check running her fingers under and then around the hoof to see if she could find any other hoof damage roughness or bruising.

This was what old Ted had been waiting for; tipping his hoof forward to catch her fingers he stamped down hard. Most of the blacksmiths and farriers in the area knew of old Ted's habit and quite a number who had been careless or had forgotten had ended up with crushed or broken fingers.

Both Farmer Brown and Simon swore to John afterwards that the hoof had never moved. Instead old Ted had just rocked as if he had trodden on a step.

Knowing what the horse had tried to do Jane lowered the hoof to the ground. The horse stood frozen unmoving as Jane looked up to where its long head towered high above her. She could see a white ringed eye, and Jane knew that when the white around a horse's eye was showing that it was either angry or frightened.

Instead of moving away in fear Jane just reached up and put two fingers up a pair of extra-wide nostrils, and then she proceeded to pull the startled horse's head down to a point where her left hand could take hold of an ear.

Despite old Ted's resistance, Jane's feet stayed firmly on the ground as she pulled until finally taking hold of and twisting an ear; the horse's enormous head came down to her height. Then putting her mouth next to the ear she said.

"You do that again and you'll be horse meat; I'll have you down to the knacker's yard so fast you'll...." She then gave the ear a good twist that brought a squeal of pain and surprise from the horse. Letting go she gave the horse a friendly pat on the leg and took the shoe to the fire. The horse, Simon and Farmer Brown just stood there frozen in shock and surprise.

After Jane had finished Farmer Brown came over and shook Jane's hand while shaking his head as he said.

"I think I'd better say now't about this lass they'd say I was barmy, but well done lass."

From that day on whenever Jane was working in the smithy Jane always dealt with old Ted, and she never had any trouble with him. Jane said it was the carrot or the apple she gave him when she had finished. However, Farmer Brown and Simon both knew better.

John lay beside Wendy in silence for a moment before he said.

"I think our Jane is different from other girls." He paused again and then said. "I think she has a task to do, our Jane and Celina both." They lay there in silence for a minute or two longer before John said. "I hope they're up to it." Wendy looked at him as she replied

"I reckon they are John; I reckon they are."

****

Celina was waiting for Jane in the morning room bursting to tell her everything that had happened; the first thing though was to show Jane her wand.

Jane had never moved so fast in all her life as without conscious thought her hand reached out and pulled Celina's hand away from the wand's sheath.

"Don't Celina, please don't," Jane found herself begging. Celina startled stopped with her hand pulled away from the sheath.

"Please Celina, I couldn't stand it," Jane sobbed as she stood there with tears starting to run down her face. It was just that Celina seemed so happy; yet being so close to the wand was too much for Jane, it actually hurt.

Even with the wand in its sheath the feeling pushing her away was too much to bear. It rang in Jane's head not with words but with feelings…. feelings of, *'not yet, too early, not right.'* At last between sobs she managed to speak saying to Celina.

"I can feel the wand even in its sheath; it's telling me to go; it doesn't want me near it." Celina stared at her at first not believing and then said.

"How do you mean you can 'feel' the wand? You can't; it's not possible."

"Yes it is that's why I always had to leave your lessons, I just couldn't stand it. Something, a wand, Dr Bird's wand was pushing me away." Celina stood, hesitated for a moment and then turned pulling Jane after her saying.

"Come on we have to see Dr Bird right now."

Dr Bird opened the door to his room in his dressing gown to find Celina standing there holding a tearful Jane.

"Celina, Jane whatever is the matter?" Dr Bird asked as Celina pushed her way into the room dragging Jane behind her.

"It's Jane," she began and then turning to Jane she said. "Go on Jane tell him, tell him what you told me."

"It's everything about the wands," Jane sobbed. "They don't want me near them; they push me away and tell me to go and now Celina's got hers, and it's…. just terrible." Dr Bird was visibly shocked knowing that Jane had no noticeable talent.

"How…. what do you mean?" he stammered.

"They push me away," Jane said. "It's as if they don't want me near, it's not hate, it's just a feeling that I shouldn't be there with them." Dr Bird stood thinking and then asked.

"Can you sense my wand and Celina's right now?" Jane nodded and said.

"Celina's is more forceful than yours, Celina's is saying. No, not yet, go away', and then it's pushing at me pushing me away. Yours.... well, I just get the feeling it wants me away and out of the room."

Dr Bird got up and paced across the room thinking. Then turning to Jane he said.

"It's obvious even if it is very slight that you must have some level of talent, or you wouldn't feel like this, and if that's the case you should be able to block." Jane looked confused not understanding. "Block?" she asked.

"Yes, you should be able to hide yourself, your inner self from other people and wands." Then he turned to Celina saying.

"After breakfast I want Jane and yourself in the classroom as I might as well show the two of you at the same time," and taking hold of Celina, he said. "You My Lady will leave your wand in your room; as it's too strong for Jane at the moment."

By day three Dr Bird was convinced that Jane could block with ease but was hiding that fact. Celina most certainly could block but Jane.... To Dr Bird, Jane remained a conundrum.

Jane, on the other hand was rather pleased with herself. She had managed to conceal the fact she had a talent of some kind, and blocking had proven much easier than she had expected. Wands no longer bothered her sheathed or unsheathed. Even Celina's wand was now only a distant feeling that said. "I am here but you are not ready yet."

****

Spring ~ 20 B.C.

Morgana looked back as she reached the first turning in the path. It had been twenty-one years; and now it was time to move on and find a place away from people to give them a year or two to forget. She could move north, south or in some other direction and as to which, well to her it didn't make much difference.

Morgana had heard of a Roman city in the north called Eboracum; she had never been north and the name Eboracum sounded interesting, something to do with yew trees.

The soldier's trading with the people of Bard had interested her with their tales of strange lands and customs to the north, so with that in her mind she slowly made her way up country. She had the time; after all what were years to someone like her?

Eboracum.

Morgana sat on the banks of the River with her staff across her knees as she watched the comings and goings of the soldiers and others. She had never seen so many people all together. Eboracum was so large and had so many buildings that it was almost frightening.

She spent several days moving around the outskirts of the city absorbing the wonders, speaking to the soldiers and listening to gossip. Eventually, she made her way into the city and finding herself lodgings she gradually settled in as a healer.

Once recognised as such by the soldiers, she was able to make a fair living, and over the years she moved in and out of the city several times. Each time she returned she took a new identity but always returned to her chosen role.

****

Sunday 16th October 1859.

Excerpts from the journal of
Lady Celina Carvel.

At last, my father has given permission for my project, though I think having the backing of the high Abbot helped. After the Abbot explained to father about the artisans living on church lands who were unable to find a market for their wares, and after he had explained the drain this imposed on the Abbey's finances my father had little choice but to assist me. Now I am to move into part of my father's apartments in London. Some of the household servants are to travel down on Wednesday next by the railway to open the rooms and ready them. My mother and my father along with his man Mr Ross who is to fly with Father are to travel down on the following Friday. I am to fly with them, and this is going to be the longest flight I have ever made.

~~~

Lady Celina Carvel had started packing, or at least Jane her maid and childhood companion had. Jane had started as soon as word reached her of Lord Carvel's orders for the household servants to travel to Belgrave House, the family's London residence.

Privately, Jane regarded Celina's assistance as more of a hindrance than a help. With Celina wanting to select dresses and other clothing that Jane felt were mostly unsuitable, requiring Jane to constantly unpack and repack portions of the luggage.

Finally, Jane had to enlist the help of Lady Mary to persuade Celina that the busy streets and shops of London were best suited to straight slim dresses, contrary to her more elaborate skirts that extended to many feet in diameter.

It was hard work for Jane as all the packing had to be completed before Tuesday, with Lord Carvel having arranged for all packed items to be transported to London on the railway that night.

When Celina had broken the news to Jane that she was to follow with the rest of the servants on Wednesday by the railway, Jane found she wasn't at all happy about this arrangement.

Jane had only heard of the railway and the thought of travelling at forty miles an hour, well. It brought visions of monstrous fire-breathing machines pulling carts passing before her eyes.

To Jane the alternative of not going by the railway was far worse. The thought of the railway only frightened her, while the alternative of flying with Celina Jane knew to be totally impossible for her.

Jane found as the day for departure approached, her tattered nerves reduced her normally brave and sensible nature to one of almost panic.

Though Celina's father was a major shareholder of the railway, and sat on the railway board. Celina knew very little about the railways.

Still she did her best to explain about Mr Anderson's wonderful railway in an effort to set Jane's mind at ease.

Wednesday finally arrived, and it was time to set off with coaches for the servants and a wagon containing their personal luggage.

Arriving at the railway station, Celina was surprised to discover just how intimidating the railway engines were. Jane herself saw the engine pulling into the railway station as a massive clanking black monster belching smoke and steam, drawing behind it a line of coaches.

Jane looking along the line of coaches saw some had glass in the windows while many at the back of the train did not, causing some concern to Jane and the servants.

"Don't worry Jane," Celina said taking her hand reassuringly. "Father has had one of the Director's coaches put on for all of you to ride in."

Jane gave Celina a weak smile as Samuel the Butler, with much shouting and waving started to organise the boarding of the servants.

After a tearful farewell, the two-hour journey from Ripon to York began. There was a shriek from the engines whistle followed by a jerk and a loud clattering and banging from the train of coaches.

Having travelled a few miles and with nothing disastrous having occurred, Jane started to relax and take note of the countryside they were passing through.

Cook was a great help keeping them all entertained with stories of earlier days on the railway. She told about the days when her father had worked the 'tokens' on the pit line, and how as a little girl she had taken his meals to his small wooden shelter, and then sat watching the old-fashioned engines pulling wagons laden with coal go by as he ate.

The York railway station proved to be a revelation for most of them as it was enormous. Samuel had visited York many times with Lord Carvel, so he knew the area around the station well, and as on his previous visits, immediate use was made of 'The Railway Hotel,' situated just across the road from the station.

Jane found this small hotel, and the refreshment area run by a rather fat jovial man, a pleasant way to pass the hour waiting for the London express to arrive.

If Jane had thought the elderly engine on the Ripon branch line was large, the one pulling the London Express soon changed her mind. As it thundered into the station, the noise heat and steam that immediately surrounded them drove everyone as far away from the platform's edge as they could get.

The iron monstrosity was enormous, over three times the size and four times as fast as the Ripon branch line engine, and taking them in luxury to London in just three and a quarter hour stopping only once.

London was large and noisy, although Jane and the rest of the servants now considered their selves seasoned railway travellers. The sprawling streets of London provided yet another travel experience, as they made their way to Lord Carvel's apartment in a perpetual state of wonder. Cobbled streets nine or more yards across with raised paved walkways at the sides. Open spaces with parks full of trees all evoking admiration and surprise.

Jane watched as steam coaches and wagons trundled almost silently along belching the odd burst of steam as they went. Everywhere she looked there were people whom she assumed to be ladies and gentlemen in marvellous clothes.

The London apartments, 'Belgrave House' as kept by Lord Carvel, Jane found to be a four-storey town house taking up the East side of Belgrave Square.

Ten years previously, when 'Belgrave House' was being built, the facilities it boasted had been the most modern and luxurious in London.

A coal-fired boiler in the cellar produced ample hot water at the taps, and heating in the rooms for winter, allowing all the family and guest rooms to have their own bathroom and water closet, supplied with hot and cold running water in abundance.

There was even a bathroom and water closet for the servants in their quarters.

Samuel made sure that the entire load of luggage had been delivered and checked before setting Cook and her helper to work in the small servant's kitchen that was to be used for their stay.

Jane who was in charge of unpacking her mistress's things and preparing her rooms for her arrival, found the Rooms for Celina and her parents to be situated on the first floor.

Celina's rooms were comprised of a sitting room with two large windows that overlooked Belgrave Square, giving a view of the park and a small lake through the trees. Celina's bedroom had attached a reasonable size dressing room, and by a short corridor, a bathroom.

Jane found she had the luxury of adjoining rooms. Her rooms included a sitting room with a window overlooking the square, a reasonably large bedroom whose window looked out onto a side street, and by the same short corridor, the bathroom she would share with Celina.

All told, Jane was very happy and looking forward to the arrival of Celina.

Opening the few rooms that were to be for Celina's use, the servants found that in spite of the dust covers, there was still a large amount of cleaning to do. Prompting Kate the young maid to complain about how dirty the house had become in the six months since her last visit.

Jane was already hard at work black-leading the fireplace when Kate asked for her assistance in moving a heavy desk.

As Jane turned to Kate, the brush she was using caught the fire irons knocking them over and the open tin of black lead into the pan of ashes.

Picking up the poker Jane turned to Kate and jokingly said. "I think it's about time this house learned how to keep itself clean don't you?"

Then imitating Celina, she waved the poker as though it was a wand and said. "House after today be clean. Oh my God!" Jane exclaimed, dropping the poker with a shudder.

"Are you all right?" Kate asked.

"Yes it's just that I think someone walked over my grave that's all." Then with a laugh Jane picked up the fire irons and wiping her hands clean she went to help Kate with the desk.

By Friday lunch, all arrangements for the arrival of the family were complete, and as a reward for their hard work, Samuel had arranged for the steam carriage to be readied in the afternoon for a tour of London, or at least a visit to some of the best shops and one or two other sights.

He said it would be a treat for those on their first visit to London. Jane, Cook, Thomas the young footman, and Kate were four of those included.

Then upon their return, it was a final rush and by late evening all was ready. Jane could hardly wait; she had missed Celina as she always did, just as she knew Celina would have missed her too.

It was shortly after two in the morning when the sound of voices in the stable yard alerted the house servants to the arrival of Lord Carvel and party.

Jane was on tenterhooks as she could feel Celina's excitement even before she reached the door.

Lady Mary's maid and Jane were ready to help their mistresses out of their heavy travelling coats, while Thomas took the brooms and put them in the stables as Cook bustled about with the hot drinks and savoury pies that she had made for their arrival.

Saturday 29th October 1859.

We arrived just after two of the clock in the morning. I must admit I was very relieved to arrive as I found it quite tiring flying that distance. The servants had waited up with hot refreshments, as it was a cold night. This is my first visit to London, and I find my rooms are most pleasant. Jane has worked her magic as usual, and I am most thankful.

Lord and Lady Carvel together with Celina and Lord Carvel's manservant Mr Ross arrived cold and tired just before two in the morning. Lady Mary like Celina was pleased to be reunited with her personal maid, who like Jane had travelled down with the rest of the servants on the railway.

All the new arrivals were grateful to find Cook ready with hot soup and warm food, and then after a quick inspection of the house by Lady Mary it was bedtime for all.

Celina woke early that morning and was taking a bath as Jane laid out her town dress and other essentials.

"Jane, I'm so excited," Celina called out from the bathroom. "Just think we're in London the greatest city in the world, and on Monday I start looking for a suitable shop. Father has decided to leave Cook, Thomas and Kate as servants. He says we only need a few rooms for now, and if we need additional servants they can come down later, isn't it marvellous?" This was followed by a pause before Celina's voice came again from the bathroom. "You're laughing at me."

"Yes my mistress," Jane admitted with a smile.

"Don't start; we've been together too long for that," Celina called back from the bathroom, "though I suppose I do sound like a schoolgirl on her first outing."

"Yes my Lady," Jane said still smiling. Celina appeared from the bathroom in her dressing gown to say.

"Stop it, I need my hair seeing to, you know I can't do it myself, and if I dry it, it goes all horrible." Jane turned laughing having seen the results of Celina using talent to dry and arrange her hair. Taking up a towel, she began to dry Celina's hair as she said.

"It's so nice to have you here; I missed you."

"I missed you too Jane, nobody can do my hair quite like you."

"Thank you mistress," was the sarcastic reply from Jane at which they both dissolved in laughter.

With breakfast over Celina went looking for her mother, finding her sitting in the window seat of the day-room reading. With a smile Lady Mary made room on the seat for Celina.

"Is it interesting?" Celina asked pointing toward the pamphlet her mother had been reading.

"Not really," her mother replied. "It's a medical publication, and it's not that up to date." Putting the pamphlet down on the seat Lady Mary looked at her youngest daughter and was lost for a moment in thought. *'How like I was at her age, but so....'* Lady Mary couldn't put words to her feelings.

"You wanted a word with me?" Celina asked. Her mother nodded with a slight frown creasing her forehead as she said. "You know I'm not happy about all this don't you?" Celina put her arm around her mother snuggling up to her.

"I know Mother but it's something I have to do to prove myself.... even if it's only to myself." Her mother gave her a squeeze as she asked.

"But Celina why? There's no need it's not as if you need the money or anything like that."

"Mother I'm your youngest daughter, and as your only child that is a Knight, I feel I have to make something of myself. Besides I like the High Abbot."

"We all like the Abbot," her mother replied.

"It's not just that Mother; it's the people on the Abbey lands too; he worries about them. Some of the small tradesmen wouldn't have been able to pay their rent last year, and by rights he would have had to evict them."

"I know that, your father told me how he loaned the rent to those unable to pay their rent until they started the new market, but what has that got to do with you?"

"Well I talked to the Abbot about them, and he said he didn't want to evict them, so I suggested getting them all together so they could sell their products under a more recognisable brand, and as you know they started a market in Ripon, and it worked. Now the Abbot wants them to expand. You know that they've started selling on the market at Selby?"

"I know about that but why in London, and why you?"

"Mother I just have to; I started it all and I want to make it work. The Abbot thinks I can and I think I can too, and as for London that is where we feel we can really sell Fountain's products.

As you know the Abbot has entrusted me with five thousand pounds of Church funds, so I can't let him down. I have to make a success of this venture not just for him and the North, but for myself as well. I have to prove myself to myself; I can't be just a Lady 'swanning' around looking glamorous and being a complete waste of time. Mother I need to do something with my life."

Lady Mary looked at her daughter closely. Ambition, sincerity and loyalty; any one of these could have been the word she was looking for, and yet she still couldn't find the right words to describe her daughter.

"Very well Celina, I can't stand in your way as your father has approved of this venture of yours, but a shop selling, what? Bric-a-brac?" Celina laughed saying.

"I hope to sell very expensive bric-a-brac once I find a shop. Not only that, but the Abbot is also arranging for me to sell

Fountain's products to Talents; after all there must be at least as many if not more here in the south."

"I'm still going to worry about you in London; it's not like the cities in the North, and here you'll be entirely on your own."

"Mother I have Jane with me, and if between the two of us we can't look after each other, then we are a sorry pair."

"Neither you nor Jane has any experience of London," her mother rejoined. "Yes I know you do have talent that you can use if you meet trouble, but what about Jane?"

"Mother, Jane is more resourceful than you think, and I do know she has some latent talent." Celina's mother straightened up with sudden interest.

"That can't be," she said. "I would have felt it."

"Well, that's part of her talent," Celina said smiling. "Jane is really good at blocking."

"Jane can block?" her mother asked with surprise.

"Have you ever tried to lean on her?"

"I wouldn't dream of doing such a thing," was the indignant reply from her mother.

"Well you can't, it all started when I was chosen, it turned out that Jane could feel my wand. Not just feel it, she couldn't be in the same room with it even when it was sheathed. As it turned out all wands affected her to a certain extent, so Dickie taught her how to block and shield from wands. Not only can she block; I know she uses her talent to suppress her body just as I do."

"Why didn't Dickie tell me?"

"Jane asked us not to tell anyone, but now that we are here in London I think you ought to know that there is much more to Jane than meets the eye. You know Mother, I think when you and my father bonded us; you did more than you realised."

"How do you mean?"

"I don't know exactly; it's just a feeling, intuition if you like." Celina's mother gave her a questioning look and then shook her head as she said.

"We will just have to wait and see." Then looking at the clock she said. "We need to be going as your father wants to introduce you to his London solicitor this morning."

Monday 7th November 1859.

My mother and my father accompanied by his manservant left late last night. The other servants are catching the nine o'clock railway and have just left.

Jane has helped me with my hair, and now I am looking forward to exploring London and looking for a small shop suitable for my needs.

The Abbot has been very generous with finances, having made available from Church funds five thousand pounds for the purchase of property and stock. I must be careful.

Lady Celina's feet hurt; she had walked the streets of London for four hours and looked at four shops, not one of which was a suitable candidate for her requirements. As she now made her way towards the top end of Holborn Hill feeling weary and hungry, she found a small tearoom that looked very inviting.

Opening the door and looking around, she found it larger and even more inviting than it had looked from outside. Her attention was drawn to a corner table where a small rosy-faced man with greying hair, and sporting a goatee beard sat teacup in hand reading. As she hurried toward him, a smile broke over her face as she said.

"Mr Jones," the man looked up and seeing Celina he rose to his feet and with a smile of pleasure and a small bow, he greeted her by pulling out the chair opposite and holding it for her as he said.

"Lady Celina, please do join me," and then as she seated herself. "What if I may ask are you doing out and about in London?"

"Please just Celina, I'm incognito," she said in hushed tones as she placed her purse on the side table provided. "I didn't expect to see my father's London solicitor in a small tea shop like this." He laughed as he said.

"I didn't expect to see Lady Celina Carvel in a small tea shop like this either. As for me being here, well the food is very good and the price is fair, so here I am. Now what keeps you in London?"

"Oh, this and that," Celina replied. "Just now I'm looking to open a small shop selling rare old books and other things like antiques, along with some very exclusive jewellery and unusual collectables, all expensive and one-of-a-kind in nature…. that is, when I find somewhere suitable."

"Well," Mr Jones said. "I will certainly keep an eye open as I sometimes come across vacant premises in my line of work." As he spoke a young man arrived at their table with an order book in his hand.

Celina looked through the menu and asked. "What would you recommend Mr Jones?"

"The duck is very nice," he replied.

"Thank you," and turning to the waiter. "The duck it is then." Talking to Mr Jones and discussing property, Celina gained an impression of the rent she would have to pay. Privately, she decided that ten to fifteen pounds a month would be her limit. Just how much would depend on where the shop was situated, how large it was, and its condition. Celina certainly didn't want to have to do a lot of work to make it presentable.

After a very enjoyable meal, Celina said good-bye to Mr Jones. Leaving the tearoom and feeling much refreshed, Celina crossed the road to continue her quest. As she once again crossed Holborn Hill her eye caught a view of Church Street. It was a short side street that ended in a square of several large houses, while at the end of the square was a small church. What particularly caught her attention was the presence of six shops on each side, with the second one on the far side being a milliner's.

Looking in the window she found not only some of the best and prettiest hats on display, but Celina could see in the shop there were gowns and dresses that almost took her breath away. "When I have time," she told herself. "I must call back here and have a good look."

Once more surveying the street and looking at the shops along both sides, she decided. *'This street has some very nice-looking shops; It's a pity none are vacant.'* By the time Celina reached the end of New Oxford Street, it was sore feet that decided her that it was time to call a cab.

Arriving back at Belgrave House, it was Jane who greeted Celina at the door and as Celina limped in Jane seeing her limping decided that a good soak was what Celina needed, so taking her outdoor things she said.

"Celina you look terrible, go upstairs and I'll run you a bath, and then while you have a soak and a drink I will have Cook fix you something special."

"Thank you Jane that will be very nice. I'm not used to paved streets and they hurt your feet." As she said this Celina dropped into a chair and pulled off her shoes; and then wrinkling her nose she threw them toward the door, calling after Jane. "Tell Cook just to make it something light and not too much of it please." Later after her bath and telling Jane all about her day, Celina mentioned the milliner's shop and the hats in the window saying.

"I shall have to go back there some day for a better look."

Thursday 22nd December 1859.

I think I have found a suitable shop in a side street off Holborn Hill. I have arranged to view it tomorrow morning at nine of the clock.

~~~

Breakfast over, Jane was sitting and looking idly out at the park as Celina came into the day room. Celina seeing Jane at the window said.

"Jane, I have had enough of traipsing around London looking for a shop, so today we are going shopping." Seating herself on a couch across the room she asked.

"Do you remember that small shop I told you about? The one selling hats in a road just off Holborn Hill." Jane, who had been watching a lone gardener in the park, nodded her reply.

"Well, as its Christmas, please Jane come and sit over here." Celina patted the seat beside her and waited as Jane crossed the room to sit with her before saying. "We are going to treat ourselves, first though I need to know something about the servants." She paused to look at Jane before asking.

"Do you know what the servants would like to do over Christmas; would they like to go back up north, stay in London, or have they planned something else?" Jane considered for a moment before she asked.

"Are you planning to stay in London?"

"Yes, but if they would like to go home I can manage for a day or two; after all I'm not completely helpless you know." Suddenly Jane had visions of Celina looking after herself floating before her eyes. With a shudder, Jane decided that she didn't dare even to think about it, as Celina's idea of managing almost certainly included her being there to keep Celina out of trouble.

"Well if you are stopping in London I think the servants will want to stop with you. In fact I know they would prefer to be in London as the work here is easier."

"Good, I was hoping that would be the answer. Now we need to do some Christmas shopping, so let's get our hats and cloaks, and then we can make a start."

By one of the clock two large emporiums had provided numerous sugar delicacies for the festivities, and a variety of small presents for the servants. Celina had even managed to secure two presents for Jane without her knowing it. Presents which now resided discreetly in her purse.

Having arranged for everything else to be delivered into Jane's care the following afternoon, food was the order of the day. They found this need met most satisfactorily by the small tearoom on Holborn Hill, the one that Celina had previously visited.

Once rested and fortified Celina and Jane made their way across the road; but reaching the corner Celina stopped in surprise. The milliner's shop was now standing empty.

Running across the road to look in the window, they found a notice on the door stating that this shop was available for lease, and a second notice providing the shop's new address. Seeing this all thoughts of hats and gowns instantly went out of Celina's head.

"Jane I don't believe it," she said excitedly. "Look, there's even a Telson number to call." Jane ever practical and prepared took out a small notebook and copied down the name and number as Celina said.

"There's a postal office just up the road and I do believe it has a Telson office, come on."

Celina almost dragged Jane across the road and then back along High Holborn Street to the postal office. In one corner of the postal office two Telson units hung on the wall.

Celina approached the counter where a man in a Telson uniform sat in a small alcove. The man who was wearing a set of ear speakers and a sound collector watched in a mirror as Celina approached before turning his swivel chair away from a panel festooned with wires to say.

"Good afternoon ladies, may I be of assistance?"

"I wish to make a Telson call," Celina announced.

"Certainly Miss, do you have the Telson number or the name of the person you wish to speak to?" Jane gave him the number.

"Thank you," he said looking at the number. "If you would be as kind as to wait I will contact this number for you and put it on number one Telson." He indicated the first unit with a large number one above it.

Celina waited and only a few moments had passed before the Telson unit buzzed. Picking up the ear speaker Celina heard a tinny voice saying.

"Good afternoon, Pickering and Simms at your service, Mr Simms speaking."

"Good afternoon," Celina replied. "My name is Celina Carvel, and I am interested in the shop that is to lease in Church Street, the street off Holborn Hill."

"Miss…. is it Miss?" the man asked.

"Yes it is Miss," Celina answered and then listened with growing excitement as the man said.

"The shop has only become available in the last few days, and as you can see it is a very desirable property in a very good location and," the man stressed. "I can assure you that it has been very well maintained." Celina thinking for an excuse for an early viewing of the shop quickly improvised saying.

"Would it be possible to view the property tomorrow as I cannot say how long I will be in London?"

The man paused. "I think that is possible." He paused again before saying. "Early tomorrow at nine of the clock is available; would that be suitable for you?" Celina smiling to herself said.

"That would be just perfect, and it will not affect my other arrangements." Celina turned and smiled at Jane, who could only hear one side of the conversation and was looking puzzled.

After a few pleasantries, Celina ended the connection and then turned to Jane saying.

"Well I have arranged for a viewing first thing in the morning. The shop is still to let and it looks hopeful, so now I need to call my father's solicitor." Celina went back to the desk and asked the Telson man.

"Can you contact King, Jones and Smith; the solicitors on Regent's Street for me please?"

"Certainly Miss," he replied. "I will put it on to number one Telson again." Celina returned to the Telson and after a few moments it buzzed. Picking up the ear speaker Celina heard what seemed to be the same tinny voice saying.

"Good afternoon King Jones and Smith solicitors."

"Good afternoon could I speak to Mr Jones please?"

"May I ask who is calling?" the voice inquired.

"Miss Carvel," Celina replied.

"One moment please," Celina heard the voice say. There was a short wait, and then she heard a more familiar voice.

"Celina once again," she heard a rather amused sounding Mr Jones say. "I take it that you are still incognito and I assume you are still in London; now how may I be of service?"

Celina explained about the shop and how the arrangements had been made to view it. Mr Jones had a little chuckle at her small deception feigning her imminent departure from London, but he had to agree it was a good ploy to get an early appointment.

"Now Lady Celina, I know of the property and they will want as a starting point a rent of about thirty guineas a month. They will ask for more but don't accept their first asking." Celina's eyes widened and she explained that she hadn't expected that amount. Mr Jones chuckled as he said.

"I know these people so don't be put off by that amount, and that is all I am going to say about them."

Hearing Mr Jones tone of voice Celina had a definite feeling that he didn't exactly approve of Pickering and Simms, but Mr Jones was saying.

"I believe the last tenant was paying oh in the region of fifteen guineas or so, so you should pay twenty at the very most."

Celina smiled, thinking that fifteen was more like it. Having thanked Mr Jones profusely she returned to the Telson man at the counter and paid him two pence halfpenny for her calls. Then she explained the unheard half of her calls to Jane as they walked back to the shop for another look. Cupping her hands to one of the windowpanes, Jane peered in saying.

"It's bigger than it looks; it goes back quite a long way." Celina who was looking through the glass window of the door asked.

"Should we go in?" Jane thought for a moment and then answered.

"I don't think it would be right do you."

"No you're right," Celina agreed. "I suppose it could be called an abuse of power. Let's go home."

****

Morgana

He was handsome; in his early twenties and hurt. His comrades had brought him to see her tied to a simple carrying board saying that he had taken a bad sword wound in his side from a practice bout two days ago, and now the camp surgeon had determined that he had lost too much blood and as infection had set in he would die.

A man elaborately dressed as a high-ranking Roman was walking with them. He introduced himself not by his rank as most Romans did, but he simply said.

"I am his father, please can you help him? The camp surgeons say he will die, but his comrades say you will be able to save him." Morgana didn't need to lean to feel his sincerity and obvious love and fear for his son, she found this impressed her more than his splendour.

Pushing the others outside, Morgana enlisted the father's help in moving the young man to a table. It was a table that she kept well scrubbed and clean solely for her examinations and surgery. Removing the bloody and dirty cloth she found that the wound was deep, too deep.

The camp surgeon was right. The wound was red, inflamed, smelling, oozing puss, and having removed the cloth, she found it was still bleeding profusely. Without her help he would be dead within days. Morgana explained to his father that before she could do anything for him, that the wound would have to be cleaned first with boiled water to remove the caked blood and dirt.

It was at this early point in his treatment that she and the father nearly came to blows, as his father became extremely angry when he found she intended to treat the dead and festering flesh with a poultice of maggots. Morgana explained with some frustration.

"If the wound isn't cleaned inside as well as outside he will die. If he dies there will be nothing I can do for him and my reputation will suffer, but if the wound is clean I might be able to save him." She stood glaring at his father. Then taking the hand of the father and leaning slightly pushing trust she quietly asked him. "Do you want him to live or die?"

Up to that point the father had stood stiff and proud with his back straight and head held high. Now he slumped defeated and looking down at his son, he nodded and said.

"Do as you believe best. The surgeons in the camp have given him up as dead already, and they say they can do nothing." He looked up at Morgana.

"At least you say that maybe you can help." He looked at her a broken man as he said. "Please help him."

****

Friday 23rd December 1859.

The shop is perfect. It has a pleasant front area with a small office toward the rear. The office has a window looking into the shop. At the back is a storeroom, and to one side is a smaller room with only a small window located quite high up in the wall. This will be just the thing for my other private sales. It also has a small enclosed yard with a stout door.

In addition, there is a small building outside for storage, and a room containing a water closet. The door of this is in need of repair, but the rest seems clean and in good working order.

A big advantage is the fact that all the rooms have gaslights using the new limelights, so I had the man demonstrate them to us. I think I will try to persuade father to have them put in at Belgrave House.

At nine of the clock, Lady Celina and Jane arrived by cab at Church Street where a rather portly smartly dressed man wearing a top hat, black trousers a tailed coat with a velvet collar, and shoes that were so shiny you could see your face in them stood waiting.

"Good morning…. Miss Carvel I believe," he asked. Then taking Celina's hand in his, he bestowed a kiss to it. "Let me introduce myself; I am Mr Simms of Simms and Pickering at your service." Turning he opened the shop door as Celina and Jane exchanged amused looks.

Once inside the shop Celina was pleasantly surprised as she found it was longer than she had thought. To light the shop itself were two gaslights suspended from the ceiling with each having a long bar supporting four glass shades, and most intriguing the new limelight gas mantles.

"Very impressive," Celina said giving Jane a nod of approval after having had Mr Simms demonstrate them.

Inside the shop there was plenty of room for books on both walls, while some attractive display units had been left pushed together down the centre of the shop. At the end of the shop there was a small office with a glass window that Jane decided was so the manager could keep an eye on the shop staff.

Beyond the office was a room about three yards by two and a half with a small window at a high level, once again with gas lighting, a single limelight this time. Finally, the passage ended in a larger storeroom again with a single limelight. It had a window over a sink that was supplied with cold water by a tap, and in a corner was a gas ring.

Jane who had been looking at the shop with a servant's eye was not as impressed as Celina. The shop was dirty and Jane could see there would be a lot of cleaning to do. Looking at the area around the sink she found it to be grease-encrusted, while the cast iron gas ring she found to be in a terrible state with many of the gas holes blocked. Muttering to herself about filthy and lazy staff she idly picked at the grease saying.

"When we move in the shop will be much cleaner than this and it will stay clean." Jane jumped dropping the gas ring; something had caused a shiver to run up her spine.

There was a door that when opened revealed an enclosed yard of quite a reasonable size. To one side of the yard was a lean-to building containing a small store, and forcing open a second door Celina was surprised to find a water closet, which as Mr Simms proudly said.

"It is of the latest type and in full working order, and was connected to the main drains' only last year."

"The door will need putting right," Celina observed seeing that it had only one working hinge, Mr Simms made a note. At the end of the yard there was a stout locked door, quite a large one as Celina noted.

"There is a back way for goods through this door," Mr Simms said as he opened the door to reveal a wide paved alley. Back in the shop Celina posed the important question asking Mr Simms just how much the lease would cost, and over how many years.

"Forty-five pounds a month on a five-year lease," he replied. Celina shook her head as she said.

"That is far too much, ten is more like it." Mr Simms assumed a look of horror and dropped his price by five pounds.

Celina pointed out that at this time of the year just before Christmas and right after that few businesses would be looking for premises, as trading would be slow for some time to come. A little more bargaining followed and the price came down to thirty-five pounds.

At this point Celina decided that all was fair in bargaining and war and started to lean on him. Feeling this Jane's mouth almost dropped open in shock and surprise.

A thought ran through Mr Simms head. *'She's a lovely-looking lady, if only I were single and twenty years younger.'* He then said. "I can come down another five pounds." Celina leaned a little harder and countered again with her ten pounds.

It was at this point Jane left the shop totally disgusted and horrified. She knew Celina wanted that shop but to lean on a non-talented person as heavily as Celina was doing…. well it just wasn't done.

Mr Simms shook his head and said. "I'm sorry but I can't drop below twenty five…. well for you twenty." *'What lovely hair she has and I do like red hair,'* was the thought now running around in his head. Celina decided she had won and offered him fifteen pounds.

"Very well," Mr Simms finally conceded, "but only if it is fifteen guineas a month and only for three years." At last after ten hard-fought minutes at least for Mr Simms an agreement was reached. A price of fifteen guineas a month for three years was set and a rather confused and slightly dismayed Mr Simms had agreed to it.

"It must be because you are such a charming young lady." He said as he thought to himself, *'and I do so like red hair.'*

Mr Simms then arranged for the papers to be sent around by hand that afternoon to Belgrave House. As Celina left the shop and thanked Mr Simms she found Jane waiting for her in the cab with a look as black as thunder on her face. Once the cab was moving Jane started to admonish her wanting to know.

"How could you, if your father finds out?"

"Well he's not going to is he?" Celina interrupted her smiling cheerfully. "No-one is going to tell him are they? After all how would anyone know as it takes talent to tell if someone is leaning, and I was the only one there with that level of talent wasn't I?"

Jane was stopped in the middle of her admonishment. She had no argument without admitting how strong her abilities were.

"But we shall have to have words about this later." Jane sank back into the cab's seat feeling mortified. Celina knew she had talent but she had not been aware until now just how strong it was. Celina had caught her out well and truly.

That evening Celina broached a subject that had been opened and closed a number of times. Celina had been certain that Jane had more talent than she admitted, and had been sure that for a number of years she had been suppressing it. However Jane had always adamantly denied this. This time someone with talent enough to sense its use had caught Celina in the act of leaning, and Jane wasn't supposed to be that talented. Jane sat with her head down not looking at Celina as she said.

"It's very little and not always there."

"Jane if there is the slightest hint of talent it needs training." Jane sat with her hands clasped on her lap as Celina reached out and lifted her chin, and then looking her directly in the eyes she said. "Jane I want you to accept help, someday you will need to use your ability to its fullest extent, and as things are you won't be able to. Please think about it. If your talent is as slight and unreliable as you say it is it won't change you."

Jane looked down again and then nodded saying. "I'll think about it."

Celina and Jane took the papers to Mr Jones for his approval the following morning. Mr Jones was to say the least surprised at a rent of fifteen guineas a month but he most certainly recommended

that Celina sign them, and he would arrange to have them
delivered later that day.

Monday 2nd January 1860.

*I have taken the lease on the shop. His original rent request
was a little exorbitant; the man wanted forty-five pounds a
month. However, with a little leaning he settled for a more
realistic fifteen guineas. Very naughty of me as: Jane has
informed and admonished me.*

*I open on Monday next. Now I have to prove to mother and
father that I am capable of making my own way in the world
rather than being a drain upon the family.*

~~~

The first days in the shop weren't very promising. Celina and
Jane spent most of these days rearranging the displays to make
their meagre stock look more substantial. The few customers who
came in did so in order to browse, while others just looked in the
window.

Celina had arranged that afternoon to contact her father and the
Abbot by Telson. Talking with her father and the Abbot she
arranged for the Abbot to supply more of the locally produced
items, including clothing, decorative items and jewellery that she
wished to sell.

The following morning Jane posted several letters, and then with
a list of warehouses and importers in her bag Celina sent her
shopping. Jane started by looking around the local markets and any
other places where she might find ideas to interest her. While back
in the shop Celina sat and waited for any customers.

It took three or four days before the posted letters bore fruit, and
then for the next few days Celina found she had a steady stream of
salesmen offering various saleable objects. Few were of interest to

her but one or two of the salesmen while not having quite what she wanted with them could obtain and supply some of the items she was seeking.

Jane was having far more success on the south side of the Thames. There among the immigrant communities she found handcrafted articles from India and the Far East. She came back with samples of artwork silks and other saleable items that perfectly met their needs, and so it was by the end of January that quality stock was starting to fill their shelves.

Jane however complained she had changed her occupation from maid, to jack of all trades, to travelling buyer. Celina with a laugh had said that Jane had started out as a blacksmith.

Things for Jane had indeed changed, nevertheless Jane found herself enjoying the work, and she was developing an increased self-confidence that allowed her to enter places not usually open to a woman.

Friday 27th January 1860.

My father has inventoried and cleaned out his library. He sent over 150 books some quite old and rare. His instructions are to get the best price I can, and I may have 10 per cent of what they bring. Jane has made a suggestion for the name of the shop. I think it is very interesting.

With her father's books and the new Northern stock, stock all of good quality and sold at a reasonable price sales at last started to increase. This is not to say that Celina was ever rushed. The special stock in the back room for Talents was still there and untouched. What she needed was a means of advertising them, and it was Jane who came up with the idea over a cup of tea one afternoon.

Jane had just put down her cup and was looking at the day's meagre takings when she said.

"What you need is a proper sign outside the shop, after all no-one really knows what you are selling, it should be something to get people interested from clear across the street."

Celina considered her suggestion carefully, and it took her a few moments before she replied, saying.

"I could have something like books on a sign, but how do I show the other things?" They both sat and thought in silence for a time. Finally, it was Jane who looked up and said.

"What you need is a name for the shop, a name that helps to explain what you have. It should be something to describe your goods and tantalise passers-by. It could be something like 'RARITIES,' and then in smaller letters, 'Rare, Old, Beautiful and Curious'." Celina thought it over before saying.

"I could always include the old Fountain's Abbey symbol to refer to my Fountain's products." Jane considered this and then said.

"What about a picture of Fountain's Abbey? It would show people where they come from." Celina sat forward with growing interest and asked.

"Do you think I could get away with putting a communication sphere and fake wand in the window below the picture of the Abbey?" Jane thought for a moment before saying.

"No, but you could put up a poster with something about the Abbey, a bit of history or something that will be of interest to normal customers then…." Jane paused again before she said. "Maybe a sphere and an imitation wand might be all right tucked away in a corner. You could also contact the High Abbot and see if he will arrange a delivery so you can sell some more and different Abbey products; after all he has a vested interest in our sales."

By the time the shop closed that evening Celina had spoken to the High Abbot at great expense by Telson, and an order had been placed for more things than Celina or Jane on their own could ever have thought of. These included some very special pieces of jewellery described by the Abbot as.

"Very beautiful hand crafted enamelled jewellery created with semi-precious stones found locally in and around the Abbey area."

Then as an afterthought he said. "Later there could be some pieces crafted in silver and Whitby jet that are truly exceptional."

With some professional help, an unusual sign was developed. At the artist's suggestion, it was to cover the whole length above the shop windows and door rather than being limited to a small sign protruding over the door. However, the special items took some work to integrate into the overall design without the artist knowing their meaning. Once these difficulties were overcome; the finished product left Celina feeling rather pleased.

With the windows redecorated and restocked sales improved still more. It was only a few days later that a woman broached the subject of the symbol on the sign and in the window display. It turned out that she had a daughter of thirteen who had already started church training in her talent and needed some of Celina's products. After quickly showing her the range of books and learning aids available arrangements were made for the family to visit at closing time the following day.

The whole family arrived at five of the clock, prompting Celina to close the shop and retire to the private store. Once inside Celina displayed her educational books, various implements for training and strengthening talent, all of which could be supplied by the Abbey.

Even though it was only the girl's mother who was a Talent, both the girl's parents took a keen interest obviously wanting the best for their daughter. Celina hearing about the training that their daughter had started felt hopeful that the young girl would be more than acceptable as a nurse.

As the days passed Celina noticed that Jane was having a greater success with sales than she was. In fact, customers would sometimes wait for Jane to become available so Celina took to discreetly watching her. It was late one afternoon when Celina finally picked up enough courage to call Jane into the office and ask her why. Celina hesitantly began.

"Jane would you please tell me just what I am doing wrong?" Jane shook her head in confusion as she asked.
"I'm sorry; I don't know doing what wrong?" Celina burying her pride asked.

"Why is it that customers would rather be served by you?" Jane sat thinking before she replied saying.

"It's going to be difficult to explain this, but I'll try.... it's like when I'm serving I'm 'Jane the shop girl'." Jane could see that Celina still didn't understand so she changed direction saying.

"When you're serving people you are still Lady Celina, and it makes a difference." Celina with a frown asked.

"How do you mean?"

"Well when you are serving a customer that customer is, how can I put it best? When you are serving others, you must not appear better than them. When you are in service you are not even their equal.

You have to remember the customer is your better; after all he is the one who is paying you. You have to remember that the customer is always right, do you see what I mean?" Celina considered this carefully before she said.

"I think so. What you are saying is that as I have been brought up as a person of some high standing and importance, I may give others the impression I'm looking down on them, and possibly I feel I am above them."

"Nearly, yes," Jane said. "It is something like that, but it's not as bad as you make it sound." Jane paused again to think and then said. "When a customer comes into the shop you have to try to make that customer feel that they are the most important person in your life, and to do it without seeming patronising, and that's actually the hardest part."

Celina sat silent thinking over what Jane had said until the shop door opened and interrupted them. It was Jane who rose and went into the shop while Celina discreetly followed watching and listening from a distance.

Over the next few weeks Celina watched and learned a lot, and as she did so, she put it into practice. Her sales technique improved to the point that Jane simply had to compliment her. Celina had changed her mode of speech, her approach and whole attitude until one day it became apparent to Jane that at times Celina was actually flirting with the customers. To make matters worse it looked to Jane as if both parties were enjoying it.

Even more upsetting for Jane was the fact that Celina was taking on menial tasks in and around the shop, tasks that Jane had considered in her domain. Jane found to her annoyance that Celina had taken to sweeping the front pavement and cleaning the windows. Not only that, but Celina was doing it the hard way, saying it gave her a chance to get to know people. One day finding Celina sweeping the pavement Jane complained.

"Even the man who sweeps the road is on first-name terms with you." Cook Thomas and Kate also noticed the change in her attitude to them. Celina became less distant and more likely to pass the time of the day in idle chatter. She actually shocked Cook and Kate one morning by taking hold of the coal bucket and helping Kate up the servants back stairs while Thomas was out. It seemed to all that Celina was becoming a very changed person.

Wednesday 21st March 1860.

The takings from the shop now easily pay the lease and give me a working profit. My father's books were in great demand, and they have created a regular customer base for me that is expanding daily. Some of my imports are in danger of selling out, especially the imported artwork.

81

Marcus

The letter was addressed simply.

Marcus Thomson.
East India Oriental Line.
Nan tong,
Shanghai,
China.

Marcus didn't get much in the way of personal mail from England; the odd letter from his mother and that was it. This letter most certainly wasn't his mother's hand. Slipping the blade of the letter opener into the top of the envelope Marcus deftly opened it, pulling out a single sheet of paper he read.

My dear Marcus.

Much as it pains me to write this letter, I feel that I have to. When I broached the subject with your mother and said I was going to write to you, your mother absolutely forbade it. She said there was nothing you could do and what you didn't know wouldn't hurt. She also worried that if you did know you would leave your position to come home. However, I say that decision should be yours.

I regret having to inform you that your mother has been visiting the hospital for the last three months. They say due to her age there isn't much more they can do; they now just try to keep her comfortable. At the moment I am staying with her at her house, though for how long I don't know. Regardless I will stay until the end. According to the doctors, this could be at any time between three and six months. At the tine I am writing this she is not in any great pain, as the medication along with a visiting church nurse is helping to ease what pain she has.

As I said I am so sorry to write with bad news. Please write to me at your mother's home.

Sincerely,
Your loving Aunt Edith.

Marcus put the letter down and closed his eyes realising that it was happening again; here he was half way around the world when the word had come. His hand went to his face as memories of how five years ago in Cairo he had received word of the death of his father, and now it was his mother. Well, this time he would do his best to be there.

Slipping the letter into his coat pocket he rang for one of the numerous Chinese clerks. It was Win his translator and assistant who entered his office to be asked.

"Win, will you arrange transport for me for early tomorrow morning to Shanghai, I have to see the shipping manager urgently." Win as was his way silently nodded and with a bow quietly backed out of the office.

It was late in the day when Marcus arrived at the main shipping office. John the manager and shipping director was an old friend and ushered him into his office as he called to his secretary for tea before saying.

"Well Marcus I didn't expect to see you until next month, no trouble upriver I hope." Marcus only shook his head as he took the letter out of his pocket and handed it over. John read it in silence and then giving the letter back he said.

"Marcus what can I say? I know how you felt about your father and now this, all I can say is I am truly sorry and how can I be of assistance?"

"Thank you John, what I need is a fast passage back home. When my father died I didn't get back home in time to see him so this time I have to be there and be with my mother."

John sat back and then pushing his chair away from his desk pulled open a drawer and from it he took out a bottle and two glasses.

"Purely medicinal," he said filling both of them before pushing one across the desk to Marcus. Then from another drawer he took out a large ledger and looking into it, he said. "There is a fast mail steamer that's due out of here in a week as of yesterday. Can you be on it? It makes just four stops to London and only takes seven weeks."

"How much?" Marcus asked. John pulled his chair back up to the desk saying.

"Marcus we've been friends since….well since I can't remember, long before you started working for the company, so we'll put it down to company business. I have a special delivery for the head office that I was going to send with my secretary, but as I haven't told him yet there's no problem." Marcus got to his feet and reaching over the desk, he took John's hand and shook it saying.

"I don't know how to thank you, but if there's anything I can ever do for you just let me know." John getting to his feet and putting his free hand on Marcus's shoulder said.

"Someday Marcus maybe, but right now you'd better make arrangements for travelling, and I'll get someone to take over your office. Oh and send your things down as soon as you can and I'll see that they're loaded for you." A knock on the door heralded the arrival of their tea.

As the day for his departure drew near several members on his staff approached him with condolences and with notes containing the personal addresses of family and friends written in both English and their local script, and as they said.

"You never know what you may need back in England." These were the people he knew who if he needed it, could lay their hands on it. Their thoughtful efforts left him feeling touched and grateful as tears threatened his good-byes.

Though the mail steamer made good time, to Marcus the journey seemed to take forever. Little on the journey raised any interest for him as he spent his days in his cabin with his requirements provided by a sympathetic steward, and when walking on the deck the crew allowed him his solitude.

He didn't even leave the ship when they stopped to pick up coal or mail. It was only as the channel coast came into view that Marcus became more alive and more impatient. The crew now found Marcus out of his cabin and standing at the rail watching the coast as it slowly passed by.

At last and in just under seven weeks he disembarked on the company wharf in London's rebuilt Docklands. There with the shipping manager's package safely handed over to the senior manager at the head office, he took one of the new steam cabs directly to his mother's home. Martha his mother's elderly maid who opened the door looked shocked.

"Oh Master Marcus," she exclaimed. "We weren't expecting you. Miss Edith!" she called out before saying to Marcus. "Miss Edith is in the front sitting room; and she will want to see you before you see your mother." Over Martha's head, Marcus saw his aunt Edith come into the hall. To Marcus though she was only fifteen years his senior, Edith now looked old and worn.

"Marcus," she said hurrying forward, and putting her arms around him she gave him a hug.

"I'm so glad you got here," and then as she took him into the front room she called. "Tea please Martha, now Marcus sit down and tell me when did you arrive back in England; I presume you did get my letter?"

"Yes I got your letter and thank you, but tell me how is mother?" His aunt Edith looked distraught as she said.

"Not very good I'm afraid, the doctor has said it's only a matter of weeks. I'm so glad you managed to get here; I know how you felt about your father so I wrote to you without your mother knowing." Edith sat looking down and twisted her hands on her lap as she said.

"Your mother absolutely refused to let me tell you, so please don't mention the letter." Marcus nodded and putting an arm around his aunt he said.

"I'm so glad you did write." He looked at Edith for a moment; she had always been small but now to Marcus she seemed not only to have aged but also to have shrunk.

There was a tap on the door and Martha came in with the tea, while Cook stood waiting in the doorway as Martha arranged the tea things before saying.

"Master Marcus, we are so glad you came home before." Martha stopped with tears in her eyes unable to go on before turning and hurrying from the room, leaving Cook standing just outside the door wringing her hands and saying. "Master Marcus I'm so sorry," before hurrying after Martha.

Edith poured the tea and said. "Your mother's not been well for nearly a year now, but you know your mother and seeing a doctor. When I finally persuaded her it was too late, what with her age and having let it go so long there was nothing the doctors could do. I am sorry Marcus I did all I could, but I think she's decided she just wants to join your father. She says there's nothing left for her now, not without him." Marcus taking his aunt's hand said.

"I know my mother and she was always stubborn; you couldn't have done more." Marcus hesitated before asking. "Tell me is she in any pain?" Edith shook her head and said.

"No; between the church nurse and the doctor, they are keeping the pain away. She just sleeps a lot."

"Is Mother awake now?"

"I think so; come we'll go up together." Back in the hall Edith said. "I'll get Martha to put your bags in your old room later."

"No I'll do it; Martha is getting a bit too old to be carrying heavy bags like these." Marcus picked up his bags as they made their way to the stairs.

Marcus's mother lay in her bed propped up on cushions with her eyes closed. He was shocked at how small and frail she had become, but pleased as when he took her hand she opened her eyes exclaiming.

"Marcus, oh Marcus it's so good to see you." Then pulling herself more upright and into a sitting position she asked. "Why are you here?"

It had been nine weeks now since his mother's funeral, and Marcus was sitting in his father's old office. On the desk rested two of the four sealed burial urns his father had left to him in his will, still sealed only because as his father used to say.

"It is more exciting not knowing what is in them than knowing." To Marcus however, they were ugly things. He had only kept them because of his mother, and the fact that they reminded him of his father and of their time together in the Egyptian desert, but now he felt he wasn't sure about keeping them any longer.

Picking one up, he felt the weight; burial urns could contain important documents, unusable oil, undrinkable wine or inedible food. Only one of these was worth anything, and he was sure these didn't hold that. He looked around the room. Another one of the urns stood by the door ready to prop the door open, and yet another one stood by the fireplace.

He had constantly to remind himself it was his door now, his room and his desk. His parents were dead and as their only child it had all passed to him along with Cook, Martha the maid, and the debts. After his father had died his mother had let the other servants go, or rather she had not replaced them as they left until only the two oldest remained. These two had insisted that as they had been the first servants in the family that they would stay to the end.

Martha hadn't stopped long after his mother's funeral, deciding to take the pension his mother had arranged for her and Cook when they were the only two left. Cook had finally left last week taking her pension with great sorrow, so she could look after her ailing sister.

Now the house seemed empty and cold. In front of Marcus on the desk were some bills that needed paying; he sighed thinking it was a pity that he wasn't left a smaller house and more money as the finances were definitely getting low.

His mind drifted back to the days after his mother's funeral. At first, he had spent his time visiting the museums in London. In them, he had looked at what he had catalogued when he had been working in Egypt, and remembered how in China, he had initially missed the interesting work he had done there with his father sorting and identifying the new finds and exhibits coming in from the desert.

Now looking at his father's books, they no longer seemed to hold the same attraction for him, not after reading the ones in the museum of Cairo.

Marcus was bored, primarily because most of the people he had known were no longer living in London. Marcus could not remember ever being so bored in his life. He was missing his old job with his ex-employers, The East India Company.... a letter, an application for work lay on the desk. He was certain that his application would be received favourably, after all few Westerners were prepared to work in China.

He'd made friends there among the Chinese, and the trade through his office had increased four fold in the two years since it had been made his responsibility. Picking the letter up he looked at it still undecided, and then put the unfinished letter in the top drawer.

Now Marcus found he was spending his days sitting and looking out of the window, or if the weather were clement, he would be found sitting on the low wall outside his mother's house.

Today being cold and bright he was walking around the streets of central London. A nearby church clock was striking the hour of one as he approached a small teashop near the top of Holborn Hill. Marcus stopped and looked in the window.

'It's getting late' he thought, 'and *it's rather cold.'* Looking at the menu chalked on the slate outside, and then at the money in his pocket, he decided he could just manage a pot of tea and a buttered scone.

Marcus chose a table in the window reasoning it would be more interesting to watch the street than just sitting. Taking his time Marcus managed to make his stay in the tearoom last the better part of an hour.

The street almost opposite had now gained his attention. It contained about a dozen small shops and watching he found that the second shop on the far side of the street seemed to be attracting quite a lot of attention from passers-by. Paying for the tea and scone and leaving a small gratuity he made his way across the street and approached the shop.

Marcus had little idea of what the other shops on the street were selling, but he found this shop was selling books, or at least that's what some of the items in the window were. As he stood looking in the window, he found an interesting mix of old books along with carved objects of Jade and other stone.

Some of these he recognised from the markets of China as the shop had both Chinese and Indian jewellery on display, along with some other exquisite and unusual pieces of jewellery from the north of England. Looking closely he found mixed in among them were some very nice pieces of jet mounted in silver from the coastal area around Whitby.

'Well it will pass some of the afternoon;' he thought as he opened the door, *'and it will be warmer inside than standing out here.'* Inside it certainly was as two gaslights with four shades on each kept the shop quite warm. Looking around the shop a chair just inside the door caught his eye. Taking off his overcoat and gloves, he put them over the chair.

Looking around the shop, Marcus found it unusual in the way it was arranged; instead of the usual shop counter the shop had alternating bookcases and glass fronted display cabinets down both walls. While down the centre of the floor were five display units with glass doors giving the sales area of the shop an open and even spacious look.

A young woman with striking dark-red hair seemed to be the only one serving customers. Marcus took special note of her. *'Definitely a very striking young woman,'* he thought to himself.

Marcus moved to the first section containing books. Looking over them, he selected one at random. It was a large book on flowers found in the coastal areas of Dorset, and as Marcus found beautifully illustrated. A ticket in the book with details of the book gave the price at five shillings. *'Not that bad a price.... I've seen newer books in poorer condition that were a lot more expensive,'* he decided as he put the book back.

In the display cabinet across from it was a selection of silver jewellery apparently from the north of England, and with much of it inset with either Whitby jet or local polished stone. Between the bookcases, Marcus found a display of Indian carvings. Then, there was a collection of books referring to the Far East. Picking out one at random Marcus found it to be a travel journal written by; he didn't recognise the name, so he put it back. Then a section on Egypt caught his eye.

It was as Marcus turned to cross the shop that he saw a small elderly man with rather thick glasses perched on the end of his nose had entered the shop. Intrigued, Marcus watched him as limping and leaning heavily on a walking cane he made his way towards the Egyptian section. Standing a little way back, Marcus watched as with his nose only inches away from the shelves the man searched the titles before finally taking one. It was a book summarising the research done on the mummification of the Pharaohs.

Marcus reached over the gentleman's shoulder and taking a book from the upper shelf passed it to the man saying.

"I think you will find this is far more detailed and up to date." Taking the book and turning to see Marcus the man asked.

"Do you know about these things?" waving the two books in Marcus's direction.

"I worked in the Museum of Cairo for four years doing research, and I met the author of this book several times, in fact, I worked with him on the first draft of this book." The elderly man now looked at Marcus with interest as he asked.

"You worked at the museum, and you know Professor Deville?"

"I most certainly did; I also worked with my father and Professor Deville for several months on excavations, would you know him?"

"Professor Deville is my younger brother," the man exclaimed. "We worked together about ten years ago, but after my accident," he tapped his leg with his stick. "I can't get about anymore."

He then went on to tell Marcus about his accident, and leaving with Marcus's name for the next time he wrote to his brother, along with the book by his brother and several others. Leaving Marcus with a problem, what to do with the money. He managed to solve this problem by removing the price tags and putting both the money and the price tags on the office desk.

Friday March 23rd 1860.

Today I took on my first member of staff; or rather a man set himself on and sold more in three hours than I normally sell in a day.

~~~

The day had started off with a customer waiting at the door, and then for Celina the day went from bad to worse. That was not to say that there were no customers or sales but just the opposite. At times Celina found she was serving two or three customers at once.

Closing time for lunch was long past with the shop still busy, so busy in fact that Celina almost missed noticing a man in a rather old and well used jacket standing at the Egyptian section of books talking to an elderly gentleman who was leaning on a rather elaborate walking stick. Later, the man approached her with a decorated Chinese box in his hand asking.

"Could you price this for me please?"

"Three shillings and six pence," was her quick reply. Five minutes later he appeared with a book of watercolours depicting flowers in the Southern Alps. It was at this point Celina started to take a little more notice of him. She watched him as he moved over to a tall man standing in front of the Egyptian book section.

The next time she looked, they seemed to be involved in an animated conversation. Moving a little closer she found the two deep in conversation over the difference in the findings of two books on the early Kings of Egypt. Then Celina was swept away and lost track of him again, and it was all she could do to try to keep an eye on his behaviour.

By five of the clock, it became easier, and it was as the last customers left the shop that the man made his way over to her again saying.

"You looked as if you could do with some help, and as I'm quite interested in old books I seem to have ended up assisting you. I hope that was all right; I found your pricing system on the tickets, so the money and the tickets are on the desk in a box I found. About nine pounds I think."

Celina was surprised; nine pounds was as much as she usually took in a day.

"I'm sorry; I should have introduced myself; I'm Marcus Thompson, and I saw your shop from the tearoom across the road and I thought I'd have a look at what you were dealing in."

"Well I'm glad you did," Celina said. "I heard you talking about some books on Egypt earlier, and it sounded as if you knew what you were talking about."

He laughed as he said. "I should, I spent four years cataloguing and identifying artefacts brought in from the Egyptian desert for the museum in Cairo. On any given night and on my days off about the only thing to do was drink, play polo or read, and as I'm not a great drinker, and as I don't ride well that only left reading, and with the entire Cairo museum library at my disposal…. and, well like I say, I read quite a lot."

Celina nodded and then without really knowing why or even considering what she was saying she asked.

"You wouldn't be in need of employment would you by any chance?" His eyes lit up with interest as he said.

"Well as it just happens I would. I haven't been back in the old country for very long, but my finances are getting a little thin."

Celina found herself liking Marcus, finding he had an easygoing and cheerful manner, and she began to feel that he could be a definite help as at times over the last week things had been rather hectic.

"When I was working abroad I had contacts with various people working or dealing quite legitimately in items like you sell." Looking around he said. "Take for instance those Chinese trinket boxes. I know where you can buy them direct from the people who make them." He picked the one up off Celina's desk that he had used as a cash box and turning it over, he said.

"Not only that but of much better quality." Celina looked and then she leaned just enough to see that he believed what he was saying. She considered him again before saying.

"Look, I can pay you thirty one shillings and six pence a week; we open six days from half past eight in the morning to six in the evening. I can give you a month's trial, and then we will see how it's worked out."

He looked doubtful so Celina quickly said, "also two pence in the pound on all your sales." Marcus did a quick calculation; what he had sold today would have brought him an extra one shilling and six pence. Marcus considered it; a possible one and six a day on top of his salary….

"When do I start?" he asked with his face lighting up again. Celina could feel his excitement without any help from her talent as he fairly radiated it.

"Will Monday at nine suit you, as that will give me time to open the shop before you arrive?" A smile split his face as he replied.

"That will do just fine." Celina stood up and took the loose money off the desk; placing it first into a linen bag before putting it into her purse along with the price tags, and then turning to Marcus she said.

"Right now I'll just show you the shop, and then it will be time for me to close." Marcus held the office door open as Celina led the way to the storerooms. Reaching the first storeroom she improvised saying.

"This first storeroom is where I keep various items that are reserved so it's always locked. The larger one at the back is for general stock." She opened the door for Marcus to look in.

By the small amount of light from the door, he could see in one corner a sink and a gas ring. Two cups stood on the side and a few tins, but it was too dark to see whether they were tea or coffee.

"There is a yard out at the back with a water closet and a store."

Celina looked at him for agreement, and he nodded his acceptance. They returned to the office where Celina gathered up her things before Marcus blew out the oil lamp and closed the office door. Then with Celina pulling her coat around her shoulders, they walked to the door.

It was just as Celina opened the door that Marcus picking up his things from the chair asked.

"What about the gas lights?" A flustered Celina who would normally have turned off the gas with a simple thought now found herself lost for words, and finally settled for simplicity saying.

"I forgot all about them, would you mind putting them out for me?" Marcus walked back into the shop smiling as he pulled the cords to turn off the gas.

Celina rummaged through her bag thankful that she had kept the shop key. Handing him the key for the door she said.

"Would you? I always have trouble with it." Marcus struggling to turn the lock said as it finally turned.

"I don't know how you manage this lock, it needs some oil."

Celina watched with curiosity as Marcus walked away. *'Oil?'* She wondered. *'It needs oil?' What do you do with oil?'* Celina stood looking at the key as thoughts spun around in her head. Looking up she saw the cabdriver who was sitting looking at her and smiling give her a knowing wink. Celina put her nose in the air, and ignoring his laugh she climbed inside the cab.

It was not until then that it finally hit her; her heart dropped into her shoes only to find them occupied by her stomach. Suddenly, she felt sick as the realisation of what she had done became clear to her.

'Oil, it needs oil.... Oh my goodness!' she thought. *'I've taken on a normal ordinary human being and there's not a trace of talent in him. I don't know anything about being normal; I've never had to act normal, and I am going to have to work with him all day and every day. What have I gone and done?*

What if I have to make tea? How do you make tea? I'm going to need all sorts of things.... I need things to light things, not to mention a kettle. I've never used anything but talent to light things in my life. I know; I shall have to see Cook and get her to show me how to make tea and, and coffee, yes that's what I'll do.'

Tea and coffee had always come to Celina made in a pot and ready to be poured out with the possibility of having milk and sugar added. *'How do I light the gas? What do I do if I make a mistake and do something my way.... oh what have I let myself in for??'* Thoughts swirled within her head as the cab took her home.

Celina was quite subdued over dinner to the point that Jane started to worry. It was later that evening that Celina worked up enough courage to ask Jane to call Cook in to see her. Then she found herself looking from one to the other not knowing where to start. It was Jane who knowing Celina better than anyone and knowing trouble when it was staring her in the face finally asked.

"All right what have you gone and done?" Celina started her explanation by saying.

"It was rather busy today, in fact.... In fact; it was so busy that I couldn't manage." She looked from one to the other and then said. "A man came into the shop."

Jane's eyes narrowed as a thought ran through her mind. *'I hope she doesn't say she's fallen for some man, or worse still she's had to do something about him that she shouldn't.'* Jane had just started to worry when she heard Celina saying.

"When it had quietened down, and I could see what was happening and, well I found he had sold over nine pounds worth of goods." Desperately, she looked from Jane to Cook looking for some understanding as she finally blurted out. "So I've employed him," and then quickly she said. "He knows all about Egypt and the Chinese and…." suddenly she stopped. Jane and Cook were laughing so hard they were barely able to say a word.

"So it's finally come home to you has it that you need help in the shop?" Jane asked wiping away her tears.

"It's not that," Celina looked helplessly from one to the other. "It's just; well he's so normal; he has no talent at all."

"Oh my," Cook exclaimed in sudden understanding as she turned to look at Jane, who had that look on her face that said she had completely missed the point.

"I see," Cook said starting to look serious. "You have gotten yourself into quite the mess now haven't you?" Celina looked down, and in a little-girl voice asked.

"Do you think you can show me how to act like a normal ordinary non-talented person before Monday?" It was at this point that enlightenment finally came to Jane. Cook taking charge sat back and began by saying.

"Well I think first Jane and myself will need to see what you need, and then Jane can have." A concerned Celina interrupted her saying.

"Marcus is starting on Monday."

"A look at this man on Monday," then turning to Jane, she said. "Tomorrow we can at least see what Celina needs in the shop to make her look like an ordinary shop keeper."

"Does he know who you are?" Jane asked. Celina shook her head in response.

"That's one good thing at least," Jane said.

"Come on," Cook said getting to her feet. "I think you two are needed in the kitchen." In the kitchen Cook lined up some of what they thought Celina would need as Jane began.

"This is called a kettle," waving it in Celina's general direction. "You fill it with water and put it on the gas to boil the water in."

"I know that," an annoyed Celina growled.

"That's a start anyway," Jane muttered giving Celina a dig with her elbow. Celina glared, and Jane smiled.

Cook started with the making of tea and two hours later Celina could make a passable pot of tea or coffee, actually heating the water with the gas, and had also added several tips from Cook to her idea of how not to give orders as a lady of high station.

Monday morning and arriving at the shop, she had used a key to open the shop door as Thomas had oiled the lock on Sunday at her request.

Then she used a Lucifer and taper to light the gaslights, actually managing to do this without damaging a single one of the limelight mantles. In the storeroom, a very nervous Celina surveyed a kettle and teapot, sugar, tea, coffee, and the other thing's Cook had supplied.

Last of all with a Lucifer, she lit the oil lamp in the office.

Sitting down in the office at last, and feeling rather proud of herself but nervous she waited for Marcus to arrive.

The first few days could have been a disaster for Celina, but Marcus had an easygoing way and was willing to do most things in the shop from making drinks to dusting. However he did mention as he shook a dust-free duster, that dust seemed to avoid the shop.

It was late on Friday afternoon; Celina was sitting in the office with a list of requirements from Lord Hamilton on the desk in front of her as Marcus brought in the tea.

"Look at this," Celina said passing him the list. "I don't know why but if it comes out of Egypt everyone wants one. Where can I find things like these?" Marcus looked over the list.

"Well the first one you can't get as it's kept in the museum of Cairo. The next two shouldn't be too hard to obtain, but the fourth one is a myth; it doesn't exist. The last two are easy, in fact he can have four, and he can buy them from me."

Celina stared at Marcus only half-believing her ears as she asked.

"You know where these can be obtained?"

"All but two," he replied.

"Marcus you're a gem," she declared. "That's brilliant, and you say you have four burial urns?" Marcus nodded.

"Two small ones and two," Marcus held his hand a little higher than waist-high, "large."

"Do you know how much Lord Hamilton will pay for those urns of yours?" Celina asked incredulously. Marcus shrugged.

"As far as I'm concerned he can have them; I think they're horrible and should have been smashed thousands of years ago."

"He…." Celina stopped to take a breath before starting again. "He is willing to pay at least fifty guineas each and more if they are in good unopened condition." Marcus sat down in surprise.

"I use them as doorstops," he said weakly. "They belonged to my father." Celina was smiling as she said. "Now where can we find the others?"

"With your leave I will contact some merchants I know in Cairo, merchants who I know can legally export these types of artefacts. I shall ask for price and delivery as they will be heavy, and can I say there may be more sales to come as if I do I think they will give me a better price?"

"In that case do so," Celina said and then thinking over what Marcus had been saying she said. "I think we can come to an arrangement on your commission for these special orders."

Oct 1860.

<u>Claire</u>

Africa, why did it have to be Africa? Africa was dry, dusty and hot. She had spent four months there six years ago when at the age of twelve; she had travelled with her mother and father en route to his posting in India. It had dried her out, made her ill, and the dust had affected her breathing. Indeed, she had been a month at sea en route to India before she felt well again; and now her father was being posted to Africa for up to two years. Claire felt she just couldn't go. Somehow she had to persuade her mother and father to let her stay in England.

Major Ferguson sat at his desk studying a large-scale map showing in detail the supply route that he would be responsible for the protection of over the next year and a half; he looked up as Claire put her head around the door.

"Father might I come in?" she asked. Major Ferguson smiled and pulled a chair across for Claire beckoning her in.

"I expected you," he said as she seated herself. "All right I know you don't like Africa, but I'm not sure about you staying in England. After all, where would you live? You can't remain here as we only rent this house."

Claire was now thankful that she had made some preparations before broaching this issue with her father and so was able to reply.

"I have written to Aunt Mary and Uncle Philip, and they both say they would love to have me stay with them." Her father took her hands in his as he said.

"Claire I have to tell you that London isn't the best place for a young girl," only to find Claire was ready with an answer as she said.

"Aunt Mary says I could actually be of help to her, and in turn she would show me the sights of London. Please Father it can't be any worse than Bihar or Calcutta, after all everyone here at least speaks English." Major Ferguson laughed.

"Well almost," he said. "Some of those Londoners could do with a few elocution lessons." He looked at his daughter for a moment as he considered the effect that Africa could possibly have on her, and then he said. "I will speak with your mother about this tonight. Now let me finish this, and then I have some letters to write."

Leaving her father's study, Claire ran down the stairs to find her mother sitting in the day room reading. Her mother looked up as Claire entered and seated herself on the arm of her chair. Putting an arm around her mother's shoulders Claire said.

"Mother," as she passed a small sealed envelope to her mother. "It's from Aunt Mary."

Her mother looked down at the envelope and said. "I thought you had received a reply this morning." Claire blushed as she said. "You knew I had written to Aunt Mary?" Her mother nodded and then opened the envelope to read the letter.

My dearest Emily,

It was so nice to hear from your daughter, she writes a very elegant letter.

Claire's mother looked up at her daughter and then continued to read frowning as she considered the letter's contents. When she had finished she looked again at her daughter and said.

"Well there's not much I can say after this is there? I suppose you know what is in this?" Claire with a shake of her head replied.

"No mother, I only know what was in my letter." Looking at Claire her mother passed the letter to her and waited quietly while her daughter read the contents. When Claire had finished reading and looked up her mother asked.

"It doesn't leave me much of a reason to say no does it, so I'll talk to your father after supper. Now off with you as I need to think about this."

It was a jubilant Claire who ran up to her room and flung herself on the bed hugging herself. She knew she had won. Aunt Mary's letter had been the last bullet of the battle; of that she was sure.

Later that evening her mother and father retired to his study to talk, and to Claire waiting impatiently in her room it seemed that the discussion lasted forever as she tried without success to read.

After what seemed to be hours, Claire heard her mother leaving the study and coming up the stairs. Coming into the room, Claire's mother found Claire not just waiting but ready for her saying almost before she had closed the door.

"Please, please Mother!" Claire dropped to her knees throwing her arms dramatically around her mother's legs. "It's only for a year or two and Aunt Mary says she would love to have me stay, and you know I don't like Africa, please mother."

Claire's mother felt tightness in her throat as she took her daughter's hands and lifting her from her knees she said.

"All right Claire, I've spoken with your father; and as Mary agrees you can stay, your father says he will let me have the final say."

"Can I stay then Mother?" Claire asked again pleadingly.

"As long as you do as your aunt tells you, then you have my permission. As you know I'm not keen on Africa myself, but I have no choice as I have to be there with your father, and as you say we shall only be away for at the most two years." Claire threw her arms around her mother hugging her.

"Thank you mother, thank you. I'll do just as Aunt Mary tells me I promise."

"You'd better go and thank your father." Her mother then had to call after her as Claire ran excitedly from the room, "and then you should pack your things." Watching Claire; her mother found she was blinking tears from her eyes.

Major Ferguson was seated at his desk as Claire burst in, Claire just giving him time to put down his pen before she threw her arms around his neck. He swung his chair around as Claire dropped onto his knees sitting with her arms around him saying.

"Thank you so much Father." Major Ferguson smiled at Claire affectionately; she was an only child and the apple of his eye, and he knew it was going to hurt leaving her in England, but as his wife had said.

"At eighteen she should be allowed to stay, especially as Africa doesn't suit her." He remembered how the last time they had stopped over for just four months when en route for India, Claire had not been well at all, as the heat and dust had been too much for her.

"Well just make sure you do as your aunt says," he said with mock gruffness. "You know we shall miss you so please do make an effort to write at least once a week or your mother will fret."

"I will Father and you can tell Aunt Mary to make sure that I do. Mother says I've to pack but can't I stop to see you off?" Taking Claire's hand he said.

"No you're to take the railway to London the day-after tomorrow; we will see you on to the railway and Aunt Mary will meet you at the station in London."

Two days later it was a very nervous young lady who stepped down onto the platform to be greeted by her aunt. A ride in a cab followed to what was called a small townhouse in north London. Once inside a very fussy maid showed Claire to her room, while her aunt bustled around arranging the refreshments that had been especially prepared for her arrival by Cook.

The house a new one was really quite large and very modern, with Claire's Uncle Philip who was a banker in London saying, the house was his castle as well as his home. Uncle Philip whom Claire had only met once before was a small round-faced jolly man. He was totally different from her father, and Claire found herself taking an instant liking to him. He also claimed that Claire's presence in the house added a new and pleasant 'family' feeling to their home.

Claire found life in London very different from the life she had lived over the last four years in India. Here, there was only a maid and Cook instead of the many servants she was accustomed to having available. Claire found herself doing things she had never dreamt of, like dressing herself, seeing to her own hair, and even helping around the house. Strangely, she found that she actually enjoyed such things.

Claire's aunt would often return home to find Claire in the kitchen assisting Cook with the preparation of the evening's meal. Cook soon found Claire had a natural aptitude for cooking and quickly started encouraging her in her culinary pursuits.

As the months passed Claire was able to explore the north of London both in company with her aunt, and at other times alone. She found London to be a city of wide avenues, beautiful buildings and spacious green parks.

The roads may not have been paved with gold, but they were fully paved or cobbled. Claire finding that every road had on each side a paved walkway that was raised above the level of the road making walking around the city easy and pleasant, and as Claire found there was no need to contend with either the dust or mud as she had in other cities.

The rebuilding of London after the great fire of 1762 had seen for the first time a city planned from the very start. Lessons learned from the spread of the fire were also put into practice. Claire found that all the buildings were built in either stone or brick, with roofs of either slate or tile.

The roads were wide, and even the alleyways were at least ten feet across with no overhanging roofs or other structures. It was all designed to help inhibit the spread of fires. The streets were clean with pipes underground for the drains, water and the gas for the gas Street lighting.

Claire loved London in part because it was clean and didn't have an unpleasant smell, at least not in the rebuilt areas north of the Thames that had now become a very large area of London.

Claire loved the parks in particular, and on sunny days she would take a packed lunch and explore them, often spending a full day wandering from park to park and then visiting the shops in between.

Attending the theatre with her aunt and uncle became an adventure into a new world of make-believe. The autumn and Christmas were just as she remembered them from her childhood.

Christmas was a magical time of snow, carols and presents. Nights when she sat in front of a coal fire roasting chestnuts, it was all well…. Magic to Claire, and when the weather improved, and the spring flowers were starting to appear; Claire hoped to resume her exploration of London.

It was on one of these winter outings not long after Christmas that Claire came across a shop selling not only outdoor clothing and Jewellery, but also some fascinating objects from around the world. To her amazement, there were even some items from the very region that had been her home for the previous four years.

It was as she was admiring a Jade statuette that a tall handsome man approached her and offered to show her more. As they talked, India became a major part of their conversation with the man showing a keen interest in her knowledge of the region, and even mentioning that the owner of the shop was looking for an assistant with some familiarity of India.

Claire was intrigued, and as he told her more about the shop and its owner, Claire began to consider how a position working at the shop would get her out of the house and earn her some money of her own; not that her allowance was small, but a bit of independence would be nice.

The man who told her his name was Marcus had said he would introduce her to the owner, following him to the back office Claire discovered the owner to be a woman not much older than herself, and very nice. It only took twenty minutes with Celina before Claire was convinced she wished to work there. Claire was then given a look around the shop, before with her head in a whirl she was given instructions to start on the following Monday.

Monday 21st January 1861.

Sales on Egyptian and Chinese work have more than doubled since Marcus took over that area. Now I need another 'Marcus' for Britain, India and Europe. To this end, I am looking for a second member of staff to fill this gap.

~~~

Celina felt despondent; she had seen six applicants over the last few days, and she felt none were satisfactory. No…. Celina was a Knight of the Church. A Talent, and she knew none were what she wanted. The last man had just left the shop when Marcus who had been serving customers came into the office saying.

"Celina, do you see the young lady over there?" Celina looked to see a fashionably dressed woman of about eighteen or nineteen years of age. "I think you should have a word with her," he said with a slight nod with his head in the young woman's direction. "She may just be what you want." Celina looked again and then asked.

"Do you think someone of her standing would want to work as a shop assistant, and I didn't exactly have a woman in mind?"

"I'll bring her across as I think you may find she is just what you need." Twenty minutes later Claire as she gave her name left the shop as their new employee. Celina now pushed back her chair and sat looking at Marcus who was attending to an elderly lady and had his back to her.

Celina continued looking as she thought. '*If I didn't know better I'd say he was talented, some way or another.*' She shook her head and watched him until he returned to the office to complete the sale.

"Well?" he asked as he dropped the money from the sale into the cash box. Celina just looked at him for a moment and then said.

"She starts on Monday; and she says that she has travelled all over Europe and India with her family. Her father's in the Army, and she says she's met and knows a lot of people, important people both in Europe and India, and frankly it would seem she's perfect."

Monday 28th January 1861.

Claire arrived early today; she was waiting on the doorstep when I arrived. She seems to be a good choice but time will tell.

~~~

Claire's first month proved to be a complete success; and now Celina with Claire by her side stood outside the shop looking at the new display in the window.

"I think that's a definite improvement don't you?" Celina asked. Claire nodded and then asked.

"That picture of the Abbey with…. what is it, a crystal ball and a pen?" Celina turned watching Claire as she replied. "Yes."

Claire cocked her head to one side still frowning and said. "I think I could do something else with that, the pen doesn't go with it; it should be a magic wand not a pen; a pen goes with a book."

It took all of Celina's self-control not to burst out laughing; so much so that Celina only just managed to keep a straight face as

104

she said. "Claire if you think you can make anything look better, please try, after all I can only say no."

In just an hour a beautiful pencil sketch arrived on Celina's desk, it was a sketch of a crystal ball, and what Celina took to be Claire's idea of a wand. Claire had also incorporated a book with a quill pen overlaid against a background of the Abbey, along with a brief history of Fountain's Abbey. Celina called Claire back into the office to say.

"There is a printer's shop further along New Oxford Street; it's only a small one so watch for it carefully. Go and have this framed as it is much too good to just lie in the window, to be at its best it should be displayed properly."

Claire was pleased at Celina's praise; she had always thought of her drawings as being reasonably good, but to have Celina say it needed framing, and that she wanted to display it in the window.... well it left her feeling proud, embarrassed and lost for words. Celina took two shillings from the cash box and sent her on her way.

Over the next few months' things at the shop settled down to a routine; Celina arranged for them all to have a half-day off in turn, and eventually had a Telson installed, not only in the shop but also in Lord Carvel's apartments. This made it possible for Celina to keep in touch with her family, and to be easily contacted by Marcus or Claire if needed whenever she was away from the shop and at home.

Ixcte ~ 1.

The black had returned, and Ixcte could feel its presence now. It had started off as just an occasional touch against Ixcte's nervous system, but now it was there all the time, flaunting and taunting as was its way and making no attempt to hide. If the black had returned from the dead so could others, a prickle of apprehension ran along Ixcte's length.

Memories of pain and near death came back. It had been a long time ago when Ixcte had been reduced to a pod having to exist on small crawling things. Now Ixcte was powerful again, more powerful than before, but Ixcte was still fearful. The black must be destroyed.

Ixcte had called for a Cesdrik, food/slave/pet, and now Ixcte raised a head from its hood and looked down on the food/slave/pet which lay prostrate before it. The Cesdrik had large yellow eyes and a red skin that blended with the red sand upon which it lay as it looked up.

Ixcte's presence filled its mind. "The black has returned and must be destroyed." Ixcte declared projecting the thought forcibly. "Take what you need and do as you must to find and destroy the black, it must be done in one rising."

The food/slave/pet raised its head with its yellow eyes blinking; Ixcte could feel the fear and dread within it.

Ixcte looked hungrily at the Cesdrik savouring the anticipated flavours as the food/slave/pet backed away. Ixcte now called for more food/slave/pets to satisfy its hunger.

****

125 AD

The old man sat with tears filling his eyes, held tightly in his hand was a silver brooch. Memories flashed before him of a woman with sparkling blue eyes and dark-brown hair, memories of a woman with a flashing silver brooch holding her long single braid. At first when her hair had been dark, she had worn the brooch securely fastened in it. Later as her hair gradually gathered a few silver strands she had started wearing it at her throat. They had shared seventy years together.

At first, he thought he could hold back the years, with his help at fifty she was still young and dark of hair. He closed his eyes remembering.... At seventy-five there was still just a little grey in her hair as she ran and played with her great grand children. For seventy years, he had held back the march of time, but he was never quite able to stop it. Then in her eighty-seventh year it had started. No matter what he tried the years had caught up in a cascading rush.

Her body failed, and her health faded away. Finally lying in his arms she had begged him to let her go. It was with a last kiss, and with his lips still on hers that she died. He could still feel the last breath and her sigh, and now she was gone and only memories remained.

Looking down again at the brooch, he lovingly wrapped it in soft deer hide before putting it safely in his belt pouch. Finally, he looked around the room, at his things, her things; now they had lost all their meaning, and so he was leaving it all behind.

Getting to his feet he reached for his staff, it was old now and the wood was polished with use and red with age. Its end had been tipped for many years with iron; strong and sturdy it had served him well.

Holding the staff, he was now ready to depart; even so he still felt he was leaving the only woman he had ever wanted; the only woman he would ever love. Tears still misted his eyes as he dismissed the small spark of light hanging over his head and made his way into the dim light of a false dawn.

He walked briskly strong and upright for an old man covering the miles with ease. By midday, some twenty miles separated him from the village, and now he sat at the side of a stream musing over the past until finally deciding.

Many years ago, he had said he would first go south and then later he would go west. He had been to neither, and now he decided it was time to go south.

He followed the stream until he found a still pool where he stood and looked at his reflection. An old man with long grey hair and straggly beard stared back at him.

He shook his head; the grey would have to grow out but with a little trim here and there....

Setting to the task he didn't bother with his knife, instead he used his shield, shaping it into a razor he knelt and looked at his reflection in the still water as he trimmed his hair and beard. Finally, it was a much younger clean-shaven man with close-cropped grey hair that looked back at him from the pool.

Over the next few weeks, the sun and rain returned his hair to a more natural shade of brown, and by the time he reached a fair-sized town of some twenty dwellings grouped together inside a wooden stockade; he looked his usual youthful self. Presenting *himself at the gate, he announced himself as Merlin, the great entertainer.*

****

Friday 6th December 1861.

Jane woke me in the early hours this morning. Apparently, I was shouting in my sleep. I remember something about a red sky and a desert of red sand along with a feeling of hate and fear. Jane stayed with me for the rest of the night. I am very grateful to her.

I arrived at the shop this morning to find a notice of unusual interest to me affixed to the door of the offices above the shop. It was so unusual I had to make urgent enquiries.

~~~

December found Celina considering the fact that the shop had become too small. The sales from the north of England had picked up nicely, and the book sales now took second place to sales of goods from the Abbey, while the various imports from China and India were also doing well.

The larger Egyptian sales by now had become too expensive, and apart from the very rich totally unaffordable. In reviewing her situation Celina felt quite pleased with the shop as a whole. She had taken Thursday afternoon off so it came as a surprise on Friday morning to find a notice on the door to the offices above the shop saying.

Property to let.

Celina's heart skipped a beat as Marcus crossed the road and joined her saying.

"That wasn't there last night when I locked up." Marcus looked at the empty shop and then up at the rooms above Rarities and said. "Do you know the extra room could be just what you need?"

"Come on," Celina said, and in her hurry she almost unlocked the door without using the key. Once inside she hurried into the office. Marcus was lighting the gaslights and not looking, and so with a quick strike the oil lamp in the office flared into flame. Celina picked up the Telson and was soon talking to Mr Simms. Marcus walked into the office to hear Celina say.

"Mr Simms says they want sixty five guineas a month; so I've arranged to see him this afternoon, and I am going to have that lease as it's too good to miss, but I'm most certainly not paying that amount."

At two of the clock, Celina was shown into Mr Simms office where he greeted Celina with a small bow before escorting her to a chair. Celina smiled to herself thinking, *'a little small talk to make me feel at home and then to business.'* However, the pleasant small talk also gave her time to do a little leaning, only to find the sum of twenty five-pounds in his mind, prompting Celina to decide she would be happy at twenty pounds; and if she was happy at twenty pounds then Mr Simms would have to be happy at that sum too.

It was as Mr Simms excused himself and went over to a cabinet for the ledgers on the shop that Celina felt she was missing something, something to do with; she struggled to feel the thoughts flickering across the surface of his mind…. *'Money, and an old lady?'*

As his back was turned, she eased her wand from the sheath hidden in the folds of her skirt and let it attach its self to the wand safe where she could let her fingers touch it. Mr Simms returned with an envelope from which he drew out a plan of the upper floors.

"As you can see," he said turning them to face her. "It is a much larger property than the one you already lease, as there are three good-sized rooms on the floor above you and two smaller ones in the attic…. oh and there is a small kitchen and water closet in these two small rooms at the back." Celina pointed at an area at the top of the stairs and asked.

"Is that a storage area?" Mr Simms swung the drawing around to study it. Celina rested two fingers on her wand and leaned heavily, pushing Mr Simms to think about the offices and the accounts. Mr Simms frowned and then said.

"I need to have a look in the ledger, if you will excuse me." Rising and going back to the cabinet a slightly befuddled Mr Simms started leafing through the ledger for the page he wanted. He stopped and looked at it; Celina leaned again pushing him to look closely at the account. Running his eyes down the page, he came to the expenses and income on the account.

Holding her wand Celina leaned heavily aware of his feeling of satisfaction as he looked at the final figures. Once more, Celina leaned struggling to absorb the more complex thoughts now shouting at her from the surface of his mind. Then she half-stood in excitement before sitting down heavily in disgust at what she had found.

Her shop, the property above the shop, and the properties either side were bringing in eighty pounds a month. Of this the owner a widow was receiving only twenty with the rest going in charges, expenses and repairs. It was with great difficulty Celina managed the next thirty minutes finally arranging to give Mr Simms an answer in a week's time.

Marcus knew something was wrong the moment Celina walked through the door. For one thing, she threw her coat over the chair in the office instead of hanging it; this was something Marcus knew she had never done before. Then leaving her coat where it lay she stormed on into the back room. Marcus picked up her coat and hung it in the office; he then checked the shop for customers before following Celina into the back.

"Do you think your uncle could help?" he heard Celina asking Claire. "I need to know today if possible, or by tomorrow at the latest." Claire with a look towards the office said.

"He should be in his office, and if I use the Telson I'm sure he will speak to you."

Celina waved her towards the door and then seeing Marcus; she turned and picked up the kettle and then as she filled it under the tap she asked. "Tea?" Marcus with a nod of agreement took the kettle from her hand and put it on the gas ring to boil.

"That man." Celina said surprising Marcus with the anger in her voice. "Is collecting eighty pounds a month from the five tenants in this building." Celina indicated the property's either side. "Yet he only gives the widow who owns them twenty pounds a month, and out of that she is still expected to pay for repairs and maintenance. I estimate that last year she received less than one hundred and thirty pounds, and he's been doing that for the last ten years."

"How do you know this?" Marcus asked.

"I managed a look at the building accounts while he was occupied." Celina said stretching the truth with a completely straight face.

"Celina." Claire called from the office. "It's my uncle Philip." Back in the office Celina took the Telson from Claire saying.

"Hello Mr...." she gave a quick glance at Claire for his name. "Ellis; this is Celina Carvel, and I need a little help. I don't know how much Claire has told you about me, but I've decided that I need more space, and I think I may be able to buy the shop out right and possibly the two shops on either side as well."

Celina hesitated waiting for Claire's uncle, she could almost see him thinking, and then the voice over the Telson asked.

"I take it that you would need a loan; and if so would you have any security?"

"Well...." Celina began, and then hesitated herself. Should she tell him her title and family? No she decided against it as Marcus and Claire would also hear. "I would have the property as security," she reminded him. "Also it would only be a short-term loan of four to six weeks at the most." Again, there was a short pause followed by.

"From that I assume you have the capital available on reasonable notice?" There was hesitation again before he asked. "How much do you expect you will need?"

Celina considered before saying. "It is a property comprised of three shops and two offices in central London, so what would you suggest?"

There was a silence as Mr Ellis considered what he knew about the location and property from Claire before he replied.

"I would consider having available possibly two thousand or two thousand two hundred pounds."

Celina thought this over for a moment as it would eat into her reserves, but it would be worth it, so she said. "That sounds reasonable so when can I arrange to see you?"

Again, there was silence for a moment or two before Mr Ellis replied. "I assume you are in a hurry?" Celina explained.

"The contract for the people managing the lease runs out at the end of January, and I would like to have everything settled before then." Celina found herself holding her breath as she awaited Mr Ellis's reply.

"Well let me see…. yes, Friday at three will that be suitable?" Celina breathed again as she said. "

Yes that will be just fine as it will give me time to consult my solicitor as well."

"Very well," the reply came, "and I must admit I do so look forward to meeting my niece's employer in person after having heard so much about you." Celina put the Telson down and turned to her two assistants saying.

"Things are looking promising; so now let's get back to work." Celina then turned back to the Telson thinking. *"Now I need to call my father's solicitor."* A few minutes later Celina was speaking to Mr Jones and telling him about Mr Simms.

"So I see you aren't satisfied with just running a shop," Mr Jones said with some amusement. "You're looking to branch out into owning property now are you?"

"It's not that," Celina replied feeling a little flustered. "I just don't like anyone to be treated and robbed like that widow; it makes my blood boil."

"No it's not a very nice thing to come across," Mr Jones acknowledged. "However, it's surprising the number of unscrupulous so-called 'reputable' firms you can find in London.

Not ours I must hasten to state, as we do our best to treat everyone fairly."

"I'm glad to hear that, so can you find out about the lady in question for me, all I have is her name and address?" Mr Jones considered this and then said.

"I will certainly try and I will let you know by Friday morning at the latest." Celina now feeling much happier gave him her thanks and put the Telson down.

That night Celina told Jane the whole story despite knowing the reaction she would get for her immoral leaning on Mr Simms. To her surprise, Jane said nothing about it, and Celina even began to feel she might secretly have agreed. As for Celina's plans to buy the property, Jane just said. "If you can get it at the right price, and you do not cheat the old dear I think it would be the best thing to do."

****

159 AD

Morgana remembered how her mind had been in turmoil on the day Julius and she were to be married. Marriage was something she had never believed could happen for her. Yet after his recovery from the sword wound his father had showered her with gifts, but Julius had given her more. Truly, even after she had told him about herself, he had loved her.

Memories of how they had moved into a villa with twenty-six rooms and over one hundred and fifty slaves. She closed her eyes as tears formed and a host of memories ran through her mind. There were memories of their three girls, she could still see them playing as children. See them growing up and then marrying. Memories of her first grandchild.... those had been happy times.

The sound of her slave making up the bleach she used to grey her hair brought her back to the present. It had been seventy glorious years filled with more happiness than she could ever have believed possible. Their three children had given them eight grandchildren, and she had loved them all. Now Julius was dead and her life here was over, and she knew it was time to leave. Turning to the slave she said.

"Don't bother with that, I won't be needing it again." The young woman looked up and said. "Mistress."

Morgana looked at her feeling as if she was seeing her for the first time as she asked,

"How old are you?"

"Twenty–five I think mistress," the girl replied.

'Only twenty-five' Morgana thought to herself. 'She must have been just ten when Julius first gave her to me, and I don't even know her name.'

"What are you called?" Morgana asked.

"Manora mistress,"

Morgana then asked. "Have you been happy in service to me?"

"Yes mistress," the slave said as she stood with eyes downcast looking at the floor. Morgana hesitated before asking the next question not really wanting to hear the answer.

"You know I'm not like other women don't you?"

"Yes mistress," the slave answered. Now the slave was looking uncomfortable about being asked so many questions from a mistress who rarely spoke to her. Now it was time for Morgana to ask the question she had never dared to ask; having always been fearful of the answer she would get.

"What do you think I am?" The slave was now looking frightened as Morgana rose and took her by the hand; sitting her down in her place she gently leaned to comfort the slave as she said,

"Don't be frightened, I would never harm you; I just want to hear what you and the other slaves say about me." The slave fixed her eyes on her hands that she had nervously clasped on her lap. She had heard of slaves that had been whipped for sitting in the presence of a master or mistress, and her voice trembled as she replied.

"At first I was frightened of you; I had heard stories and I thought you were a monster of some kind. Then the others told me you were a goddess living as a woman because you had fallen in love with a mortal man."

114

"Is that what you all think?" Morgana asked knowing her slave spoke the truth but not wanting to believe it.

"We all think you are a goddess mistress, and we pray to you." Morgana felt she should have been shocked speechless, but instead she found herself saying.

"Don't ever pray to me. I am no goddess, indeed I am far from it." The slave looked up a question in her voice as she said.

"Mistress? Morgana had turned away as she said.

"I am only a woman; I was born just as you and I grew up just as you, but I feel I must have been cursed, cursed never to grow old." Tears started to fill her eyes again. "Always to lose the one I love."

Memories of Julius swept over her as the tears started to run down her face as she admitted to herself. 'I can never have a home; I must always keep moving on.' Morgana sat on the bed crying silent tears having finally faced the truth. Knowing now that she would always have to be alone and unable to love or be loved.

The slave rose and slowly came across to where Morgana was sitting. Hesitantly taking hold of Morgana, she held Morgana's head against her breast, holding her close until Morgana had cried herself out. Waiting until Morgana's sobs had eased before she wiped her mistress's eyes; smearing the paint that Morgana used to make herself look older. Morgana looked up to find another tear-stained face looking down on her.

"You have been a true and faithful servant," Morgana finally said. Now she hesitated wondering why she needed to unburden herself like this to a slave. Morgana again found herself looking into a pair of moist blue eyes only to find reflected in them the long road that they must travel together. Now she knew what she must do.

"Tonight I must leave this house and this city, but before I go I will give you something." Morgana went to her press and took out a small square of deer hide, and then running her fingernail across it; she burnt words into it. Morgana gave the deer hide to the slave saying.

"This is my word from me to you, giving you your freedom. Take this and now you are no longer a slave." Then reaching into *the same press she brought out some coins, gold coins. Morgana then counted out fifteen into the woman's hand.*

"There," she said. "One for every year of service to me, my husband gave you to me to do with as I wish; and you have served me well. The house and house slaves are my nephew's now; I am sorry but I cannot help them."

The slave looked at the fifteen gold coins in her hand and the writing giving her freedom. Then she fell to her knees clasping her arms around Morgana's legs sobbing and looking up into Morgana's face as she asked.

"You are going away?" Morgana nodded. "Please take me with you," the woman pleaded with her. Morgana knew the rightness of the request feeling it pulling at her as she said.

"I have a long road to travel, and you are free and wealthy now so why travel with me?" Manora looked up and answered.

"Because I want to; because I have to." Reaching down and lifting her to her feet Morgana said.

"Very well but you will need stout footwear and travelling clothes, also any other things a woman needs. You will need to bring enough for several months if you wish to come with me, so go now and get them."

Morgana watched her as she hurried out, and then she turned and washed her face. A polished silver mirror showed her to be a grey-haired woman, yet it was a woman whose face didn't match her hair. In a large wooden chest, Morgana found her staff and travelling clothes still serviceable after all the years except for her footwear, Morgana held them up saying to them.

"I'm sorry my old friends, but I think you will have to stay." Putting them aside, she pulled out a pair of stout new boots made to her own instructions. She then proceeded to do something she had not done for over seventy years; she dressed herself. She dressed herself in her old travelling clothes, and then she sat and waited for Manora.

As they looked back at the flickering lights of the city, Morgana turned to her companion and said.

"You still have time to turn back." Manora with a shake of her head turned to face the dawn as she said.

"With you I will see some of the world, and then I shall be able to die happy.

<u>Claire</u>

Claire and her uncle had a long talk that night. He couldn't tell her a great deal about what Celina had said to him other than what she had already heard, but Claire was able to tell him most of what he needed to know about the shop.

The one thing that still puzzled him was how a twenty-two-year-old woman running a medium-sized shop could say two thousand pounds was reasonable, and sound so comfortable and calm about it. Yes that really did puzzle him. Patting Claire's hand he said.

"Your employer sounds very interesting to me, and I'm really looking forward to Friday and meeting her." He found the look Claire gave him strange as she said.

"Be prepared to be impressed, be prepared."

Friday 13th December 1861.

Today I received a letter from my father's solicitor, and it made interesting reading. It also makes me more determined than ever to purchase the properties.

~~~

Friday morning Celina received a letter from Mr Jones about her little old lady, and reading it at the breakfast table her worst fears were confirmed.

"Jane listen to this," Jane picked up the envelope and looked at the handwriting.

"From Mr Jones about the old lady?" she asked.

"Yes Mr Jones says she lives alone with just her maid. He says her maid works for board only, as Mrs Allen cannot afford to pay her a salary. In fact, it looks as if Mrs Allen can barely afford to live in her house. It's a very large one on Chancery Lane bought by her husband some years ago, and he bought the property on Church Street as an investment only six months before he died.

Oh and Mr Jones says as far as he has been able to discern the property on Church Street is Mrs Allen's sole source of income." She looked up at Jane over the top of the letter and angrily said. "That man wants flaying alive cheating an elderly lady like that."

Jane with a mouthful of toast nodded, clearing her mouth before she said.

"In truth I suspect it happens frequently, and I suspect that there must be more unscrupulous people in London and in business than honest ones, I know as I have met quite a few myself. If you're going to buy the property do so, but be fair to Mrs Allen and to yourself."

Celina continued reading the letter as Jane returned to her breakfast. Mr Jones had also stated that he thought two thousand pounds would be more than adequate; and indicated funds of that amount could be made available from her account within twenty-eight days, that was if Celina required them.

Celina arrived at the office of Mr Ellis on the stroke of three and was immediately shown inside. Mr Ellis was nothing like what Celina had imagined him to be as he moved a chair fussily into place for her.

"Now Miss, it is miss is it not?" he asked. Celina responded with a smile as she said.

"Yes Mr Ellis it is."

"Now Miss Carvel, Claire has spoken glowingly of you, and I have really been looking forward to meeting you."

"Thank you Mr Ellis," Celina replied. "I have heard a lot about you too from Claire. It was very good of you to take her in while her parents are abroad, as without your help I would be missing a valuable member of my staff."

"Thank you Miss Carvel that is most kind of you, and I do assure you we do enjoy having her. Now about this loan, what worries me about this is the security on the two thousand pounds other than the property you will have. Do you have any other security?"

Celina with a smile opened her purse and took out an expensive-looking embossed card followed by a letter. Holding them away from Mr Ellis she said.

"Before I show you these you must realise that what you are about to see is highly confidential, and what I share with you now must go no further than you and this office." Mr Ellis's eyebrows rose as he replied.

"I think anything said or shown in this office is most definitely private and certainly confidential on my part." Celina then passed him the card first.

Mr Ellis took a quick look at it and then a longer second look. The family crest and the name Lady Celina Carvel was what he found embossed into the card as his eyebrows almost disappeared from his forehead.

"I…. I did not realise," he stuttered. "I never thought…. I just never, please forgive me; I should have recognised the name." Celina laughed.

"I'm living rather incognito at present as no-one other than my family and my father's solicitor knows that I am in London. This is a secret hobby of mine, and it gives me something to do. Believe me being the youngest daughter leaves you with a lot of time on your hands, and embroidery, well it can get very boring."

"Well Lady," he began.

"No please, not Lady," Celina said interrupting him. "Just call me Miss Carvel; I would find it most inconvenient if you mentioned 'Lady Celina, or Lady Carvel' to the wrong person, especially Claire."

"Very well Miss Carvel," he agreed. "However, I am still curious as to why you cannot use your London account from your normal bank."

"Like I said I am incognito, if I go about giving drafts on my London account it would soon become common knowledge that I am in London, so I need a discrete account I can use anonymously." Mr Ellis nodded and said.

"Very well let's see what we can arrange."

That night once again Claire and her uncle Philip had a long talk about the shop, about Celina and about things in general. Her uncle let it be known to his wife and niece that he fully approved of Celina and of Claire working for her. He said he would also put a small note in with Claire's next letter stating this, as he felt sure that this would set her parent's minds at rest.

Saturday 14th December 1861.

This evening we all went to see the fireworks; it was my treat as the servants had worked hard since we came to London. It was I must admit the best display I have ever seen, and with the bands and street entertainers it made a wonderful night out.

~~~

A brutal murder

A flash lit up the window of the storeroom followed by a loud bang; the young man looked up. 'Fireworks' he thought as he continued his search. He thought of his wife and mother at the fireworks display in St James Park celebrating the recovery of Prince Albert. 'It must be good;' he thought as another flash lit up the window.

Holding the candle aloft the young man checked the line of glass jars and bottles; selecting two, he placed them into his bag. Hearing a noise from the hallway of the empty house, he felt a shiver run up his spine as he turned towards the door.

"Who's there?" he called. There was silence as he moved into his surgery where the door into the hall stood open. As a noise came from the hall the young man held his hand up to shield his eyes from the light of the candle as he peered into the hall.

Something big was moving and as it moved closer, it gradually became visible. His eyes opened wide in terror at seeing two large yellow eyes materialising out of the darkness. He opened his mouth to scream as in the light of an exploding rocket, he saw hands and a trunk like mouth reaching down towards him, but the sound was lost in the noise from the park.

Monday 16th December 1861.

Today, there is another report of a murder in the papers and this time quite near the house of Mrs Allen.

The last of Lord Hamilton's Egyptian order arrives today so I have to be at the shop early.

~~~

Lady Celina Carvel thundered down the stairs in her most un-lady-like manner; her skirts held high showing an indecent amount of stocking and a flash of bare flesh above the knee. She greeted Jane breathlessly with. "Please Jane; I need your help with my hair."

Jane seeing that Celina had a number of pins out of her hair took the brush and comb from Celina as she seated herself. It only took Jane a few minutes and with a final stroke with the brush, Jane pushed the last pin into Celina's hair as she said. "There it's done now, are you coming for breakfast?"

Taking up the morning paper and reading the headlines Celina said.

"I see we have had another murder; a doctor found dead in his own house. It says here that a Dr Jones was found by his wife and maid yesterday morning." Jane looked down over Celina's shoulder.

"That's this side of St Paul's," she noted. "It's one of the houses off the Strand; you could make a detour and pass it on your way to the shop." Celina considered it, if the area was close to where Mrs Allen lived it was an excuse to see where Mrs Allen's house was.

"That's strange," Celina mused aloud. "It makes the headlines but the paper doesn't really say a lot about it, just a 'foul murder' without any details. Usually with a murder you get all the gory details," Celina turned a page looking further. "No, nothing else," and then looking up she asked. "You did arrange for my cab to be early today didn't you?"

"Yes Celina I did,"

"Well let's hope it's not late as I have to be open very early this morning. It's today that the last items for Lord Hamilton's collection are due to be delivered, and at six hundred and fifty guineas they have to be correct." Jane's eyes widened with surprise.

"Six hundred and fifty guineas?" she asked incredulously. "Will he pay that for them?"

"Yes and possibly more if these are as good as they are supposed to be." Celina replied looking and sounding very pleased. "These are very rare and they will be the centre-piece of his collection."

Outside a cab hissed to a stop, and the cabbie could be heard ringing his bell. Jane took the breakfast things and returned with Celina's coat case and gloves.

Outside Celina explained to the cab driver the route that she wished to take. Nodding his acceptance the cabbie raised a finger to his cap, and with a hiss of steam and a slight roar from the burner the cab moved off around the Square.

The cab slowing to a walking pace and a knock on the front of the cab was followed by the driver's announcement.

"This is Temple Bar, and that is the street you wanted to see," roused Celina from her paperwork. Looking out of the window, she studied the houses in a road off to her right. She could see where a little further down the street a constable was standing at the door of one of the houses, and as she watched a man and two police officers in uniform were admitted.

"There was a murder there Saturday night," the cabbie told her. "They say there was blood and bits of the body all over the house."

Celina continued to look as more people were admitted to the house, including what looked like a clergyman.

"It looks to be quite a crowd in there," she called to the cab driver as the cab increased its speed. Putting the matter from her mind, Celina returned to her paperwork while the cab continued along the Strand. Then as they turned into Chancery Lane Celina looked out to her right where she could see a large house with extensive but ill kept gardens.

Celina watched taking note on the rundown appearance as they passed; only turning back to her reading as they continued their journey towards Church Street.

Arriving at Rarities, Celina found a steam cart was stood waiting hissing quietly outside the shop while two men stood looking at the display in the window.

"Good morning," the two men said touching their caps. Celina returned their good mornings as she stood looking up at the cart studying the three wooden boxes. There were two large boxes at the front of the cart, and a third smaller one lay at the back. Seeing the size of them Celina asked.

"Can you take them around to the back please; as there is a back door into the alley that I will open for you?" The men climbed back aboard and the steam cart quietly chugged around the corner and into the alley. Going through the shop, Celina had the back gate open and ready as they arrived.

"There's ten shillings to pay my lady," the driver said. Celina counted out five florins and then added a further shilling in small change saying. "That is for the early delivery."

"Thank you Miss," the driver said raising a finger to his cap. "Do you want us to take them inside as they're heavy?"

"Thank you but I think in the yard will do." Celina watched the deliverymen struggle with the two larger boxes as each was lifted off the back of the steam cart and put onto a wheeled platform. They were then pushed into the yard and unloaded, being left one upon the top of the other.

Next the small one was carried in and placed on top. Touching their caps again the two men left. Celina now stood looking at three stout wooden boxes bringing to mind a pyramid made of wood, and with every one of them far too heavy for her to lift, and all left in the middle of the yard. Celina stood thinking to herself. *'I should have asked them to lay them separate, but it's too late now.'*

Celina first checked outside the front of the shop to make sure neither Marcus nor Claire was likely to disturb her. Then returning to the yard she took out her wand and with a quick lift and a push the smaller box rose from the top of the pile and moved in front of her into the back room. Then it was the second one's turn to be moved.

Celina lifted it off the top of the largest box and placed it closer to the door, leaving it there as it was much too large to go through into the storeroom. Just as she turned to the third box, she heard the shop doorbell ring as Marcus arrived. *'Just in time,'* she thought leaving the box where it was. Quickly, sheathing her wand she called to him. "Marcus I'm out here, and I need a hand when you're ready."

Marcus kicking the packing from the first box out of the way stood back still holding the nail bar in his hand as Celina lifted the second box's lid and pulled the packing away.

"Perfect" she breathed. Marcus looked over her shoulder and said.

"When I was in Egypt you couldn't give these away, and now they're worth a fortune, that is if you can get them out of Egypt at all. The English aristocracy seems to have gone mad."

"Well we shall be thankful for that won't we," Celina said half turning and digging Marcus in the chest with her elbow before saying. "As we have done quite well out of it."

Tuesday 17th December 1861.

<u>Jane</u>

It had started as a bright sunny December morning, Jane had called to see several importers of Chinese and Indian goods, and there had been one in particular that had really impressed her, but now she was late heading back to Rarities.

As the afternoon had progressed, dark clouds had rolled up the Thames until they fully obscured the sky, turning the day cold and miserable.

Jane had closely watched the sky as she made her way towards the north side of the river. Now as she crossed the river rain had started to fall from the leaden clouds that promised it would soon be raining heavily. As the rain began, Jane decided Belgrave

Square would be a more sensible destination than going back to Rarities.

It was as the rain became heavier that Jane hurriedly crossed the road to where a nearby shop offered tea, coffee and also shelter. Pushing open the door she looked in to find she had not been the only one caught unprepared for the rain, as she found every table was occupied. In a corner, a table for two had a gentleman who sat alone reading. Making her way across to his table Jane stopped and asked.

"Is this seat available?"

The gentleman younger than she had thought looked up and then around. Seeing for the first time how crowded the shop had become he looked up at Jane smiled and said.

"Yes I usually have this table to myself, but please do feel free to join me." Jane pulled out the chair and sat across from him saying.

"I take it that you come in here regularly then?"

"Yes," he replied. "I teach at the school across the road, and usually it's very quiet in here at this time." Jane looked around for a waiter as the man raised one hand asking. "Is it tea or coffee?"

"Tea please," Jane said as he held up two fingers and then again, two fingers as Jane watched somewhat perplexed.

"Two fingers for tea and one for coffee," he said seeing her confusion. Jane smiling said.

"So I take it that is two teas, let me introduce myself; I'm Jane Cooper and I've been chased in here and trapped by the rain." For the first time the man looked out of the window where he could see the rain that was now bouncing off the road.

"So I see, well I'm William, William Bowden, and I teach science and mathematics at Christ Church School just across the road on Kings Street, how do you do?" He now having formally introduced himself to her rose and gave a slight bow. Jane had to stifle a laugh as offering William her hand she said.

"As I said I'm Jane Cooper, and I work as a buyer for Rarities, a shop in Church Street just of Holborn Hill, how do you do." At that moment, their pot of tea arrived, tea that William insisted on paying for.

"You say you come in here often then?" Jane asked.

"Usually about half past four. That is after my class of thirteen-year-old little terrors," he chuckled. "It's their last year, and they know it." Jane thinking of some thirteen-year-olds she had known replied with a laugh.

"I think I know what you mean." Then it was William's turn to ask her.

"You say you're a buyer, what exactly is that?"

"I make my way around London calling upon various warehouses and importers looking for wholesale items to purchase, items that we can sell from Rarities, which is our shop." William frowned slightly as he said.

"That is if you'll forgive me very unusual work for a lady isn't it?"

"Yes I suppose it is, but I enjoy it; I meet some very interesting people, and I see lots of thing's other women never would."

Thanks to the rain Jane found that she had spent slightly over an hour in William's very pleasant company. It was as they left the shop that William turned to Jane and said.

"If you just happen to be passing around four of the clock to half past during the week, my table is always available, and I'm partial to interesting conversation." Then with a small bow from William they parted.

Jane continued back towards Belgrave Square thinking about the afternoon, and by the time she arrived she had decided that she would definitely call in the coffee house again, probably about four to four thirty.

****

Spring ~ AD 190.

The sun was still below the horizon as Merlin surveyed the many dead. He'd never seen anything like it before, men women and children. The whole village was dead with their bodies looking as if they had been slowly baked and dried out. Food for their first meal of the day was still fresh, and the hearths were still smouldering. He wished Morgana was here feeling she was the one for this sort of thing. He considered his surroundings again and then decided it had been long enough, and now he needed Morgana.

Certainly, this was not a normal happening and knowing he needed advice he reached into his belt fumbling until he found the hidden fold; and from it he pulled out a small square of stitched leather containing a lock of Morgana's hair. Holding it in his hand, he closed his eyes while sending out a single thought: 'Morgana.'

As he waited, he turned one of the bodies with his staff looking closely but taking care not to touch it. "It's not a disease," he murmured under his breath. "No animals here," he said aloud while looking around. He stood silent, listening. Finding only the sound of the wind, there was silence. Nothing, no sound of life not even birdsong.

Merlin threw a shield around himself as something moved in a doorway; as it moved out of the gloom, it took on a form similar to an ant. Moving towards him it continued looking more and more like an ant until it stood upright on two legs and in doing so becoming almost as large as himself.

As it continued to move towards him two more appeared and then a fourth, all of them now moving menacingly in his direction. Merlin started backing away. 'Morgana,' he sent his thought out again but there was still no response. 'She's blocking,' he thought as he sent her a final, 'Morgana.'

A noise coming from behind him made him look over his shoulder. There was now one behind him less than three feet away. Merlin froze as he watched in horror as what it had as hands started to reach for him. While at the same time its mouth started to elongate in a tube-like extension towards his face.

Merlin finally breaking the spell of fear and horror whirled, pointed his staff and used the first cast that came into his mind. He sent a heat strike into the creature's head and watched as it dropped.

Turning around he found the others closing on him rapidly. Pushing the lock of Morgana's hair back into his belt, he whirled his staff in a blaze of light as heat strikes flew between him and the creatures. It was as the last one dropped that he heard a hissing sound almost like laughter.

Turning he found himself facing a hideous red monster far larger than himself. It was only about thirty paces away and coming towards him. Merlin struck one heat strike after another but the monster merely hissed and brushed away the strikes as if brushing away flies. It was now only a few paces away as Merlin reshaped his shield pushing it forward between himself and the monster.

Reaching Merlin's shield it hesitated, and then with apparent ease it started to push through it. Merlin quickly backed away with his legs shaking and weak finding that the effort he had used with the strikes had taken its toll on him.

He delivered another strike, and again the creature brushed it aside. Merlin was now panicking as his power was fading fast. Killing this way was something he had no experience of until today. Merlin had never before used his power to kill like this, and he needed something different, something deadlier but that used less power.

Thinking quickly and remembering Morgana's lessons on healing he desperately reached out with his mind feeling for the creature and pushing into it. Using what Morgana had taught him about living things he now wondered was it possible he could use her teachings to kill.

He tried looking for organs in the body. Finding something resembling a heart, he tried to stop it but found he just slid off it having had no effect.

In desperation, Merlin pushed deep into the body, searching and finding the living parts that made up its body. Merlin pushed his mind deeper; he was now looking for and finding the living things that made up the smallest parts of its body, only to find they resisted him in the same way as the heart.

Then pushing deeper still, he forced his mind further into the creature looking for the very smallest parts, the non-living parts that couldn't exist alone. Eventually, he found them grouped in infinitesimal clusters.

Using what power he had left he tried to pull them apart. It was hard as they resisted, but he could feel them giving. Merlin's head was spinning with the effort; he knew he had to pull them apart whether he was weak or not. Finally, all his power went into it, and still they remained whole.

He dropped his protective shield first, and then as he felt himself reaching the end of his power, he dropped the last and most important of his shields. The shield that kept him whole, kept Merlin, Merlin.

He stood swaying gathering the little power that he had left, and then he tried again. He could no longer see; he could no longer hear, and he could no longer feel.

From somewhere he suddenly gained power, power started to flood into him, and soon he found he had more than enough power. At last, one of the tiny pieces came apart, and then another. Once started there was no stopping them as they all started to melt away.

Merlin watched through eyes that hardly saw as the monster came suddenly to a halt. It shimmered, rippled and then began distorting and finally as if made of smoke it started to drift away on the wind until only a memory of it remained. As his awareness returned, Merlin found himself down on his knees and his shields open.

Desperately, he created his internal personal shield, the shield that kept him private and whole, protecting the part of him that was truly 'Merlin.' It was only then with his mind protected that he discovered he had been filled with strength.

Now strengthened he quickly pushed his external protective shield back into place. Feeling incredibly strong, he looked around at the dead once more, and then with a wave of his staff, he buried the dead villagers. Turning to the insect things, he burned them, and still he was left with a feeling of strength like never before.

****

Wednesday 18th December 1861.

Today was a day I would sooner forget. I stared death in the face, and how I survived is a miracle the answer to which is known to God alone.

~~~

Using the fact she was a tenant in one of her properties Celina arranged a meeting with Mrs Allen. Determined that their transaction should be entirely fair; Celina even went so far as to suggest to Mrs Allen that it might be to her advantage to have her solicitor present, if only to confirm that what Celina was offering was genuine, and to Mrs Allen's advantage. The meeting was arranged to take place at seven of the clock on the night of the eighteenth.

Marcus on hearing where the meeting was to take place insisted that Celina should be accompanied, as he said.

"It is only last week that a murder was committed yards from that very road." Celina felt she was quite capable of dealing with any common thieves, but she accepted Marcus's offer if for no other reason than to have a friendly face there if Mrs Allen had arranged for her solicitor to be present.

Taking a cab from the shop, they arrived to find the door opened by the maid mentioned in Mr Jones' letter. They were then shown into a sitting room on the ground floor where Marcus introduced himself and Celina to a small elderly lady. It was as Mrs Allen said.

"Please do sit down," that Celina caught the feeling that the rest of the house was probably closed off, and possibly the furniture sold. Leaning lightly she found nothing to dispel this feeling, and also that Mrs Allen had not arranged for a solicitor.

Mrs Allen waited until Celina and Marcus were both seated before saying. "I understand that you have something to ask me about the property I lease out." Celina took a deep breath to calm herself before she said.

"I understand that you have a contract with a Mr Simms to run all three of your properties." Mrs Allen agreed as she said.

"He's a very nice gentleman, and I've dealt with him for many years."

"Well I also know that this last year you received less than one hundred and twenty pounds in rent." Celina watched as a startled Mrs Allen looked up and said.

"Mr Simms explained all about the work that had to be done and how much it cost."

Celina could feel herself getting angry; she looked at Marcus, who was sitting there stiff upright and tight-lipped. Celina didn't need to lean to know that having now seen for himself how Mrs Allen was being forced to live; he was fuming.

"Surely the repairs didn't cost a great amount?" Celina asked watching closely as Mrs Allen replied. "Oh yes they did; they were just over three hundred pounds."

Now Celina leaned forward saying. "I do know that last year he spent just over one hundred pounds on repairs."

"Oh no he spent far more than that, I have it all here." Mrs Allen having said this picked up a large brown envelope. Celina with her eyes still fixed on Mrs Allen's face asked.

"Do you know how much he takes each month in rent from the three properties?"

"About thirty pounds," Mrs Allen replied, "I have it all here in his statement." Then from the large envelope, Mrs Allen produced some papers and passed them across to Celina.

Celina looked at each of them and read through them several times to work out how he was manipulating the figures he didn't want Mrs Allen to find, and how he had made it all add up to the amounts he wanted. Then she passed them to Marcus.

All the figures were there even if they were twisted and distorted, and reading it Celina had to admit it looked as if all of it was correct, that was if it was all taken as it was read. Mrs Allen had only been due to twenty pounds a month, and from that she was expected to pay part of the repair costs for the last twelve months.

Celina waited and then found herself being shocked as Marcus swore. She had never heard him swear before, and it surprised and shocked her. Mrs Allen also looked startled and disapproving at the same time.

Finally, as he handed the papers back to Celina Marcus said.

"That man wants flogging…. No, that's too good for him."

"I agree," Celina said. "Though you have to admit all this has been very cleverly done." Then turning to Mrs Allen, she explained.

"He is taking in eighty pounds a month; that's nine hundred and sixty pounds a year in rent."

"Oh no look," Mrs Allen said as she took back the papers. "It says here he only gets thirty pounds." Celina moved across to sit beside the elderly lady and painstakingly went through the accounts with her. After she had finished Mrs Allen looked close to tears. Celina now took both of Mrs Allen's hands in hers.

"I don't like cheats," Celina said bluntly, "and looking at the accounts he sends you won't get any honest answers, and as you accepted his statements, I cannot see you getting anything back from him. Mrs Allen I have a proposition for you.

I would like to purchase from you these three properties of yours on Church Street." She paused as a startled Mrs Allen looked up at her. "I have had the three properties valued at two thousand pounds."

Mrs Allen's eyes opened wide. Two thousand pounds would clear all her debts and leave a very tidy sum remaining.

"If you accept and the sale is complete before the tenth of January, I will pay for you to employ a solicitor of your own costing up to twenty-five pounds, and I will even give you a bank draft to cover this now."

Once Mrs Allen had accepted Celina had no remaining worries about this, as by holding Mrs Allen's hands Celina could do a little discreet leaning, and in doing so she could feel that Mrs Allen would no more consider the breaking of such a bond than fly. It was at this point Celina took out a bank draft for twenty-five pounds and gave it to Mrs Allen.

Mrs Allen took the bank draft and sat staring at it. The twenty-five pounds alone would clear one of her most pressing debts. Celina watched tears start to fill Mrs Allen's eyes as she looked from the piece of paper in her hand to Celina's face. Then almost as if she was unable to believe Celina, she slowly nodded.

Celina put her arm around her as the elderly lady fell sobbing on to her shoulder whispering.

"Thank you, Thank you."

It took some time for Mrs Allen to regain her composure, but with a cup of tea and a small brandy, she was soon much calmer and relaxed. Celina was very discreet about the brandy as she borrowed Marcus's flask and poured a tot into Mrs Allen's tea.

It was getting late, and the clock had chimed ten some time earlier as a far happier Mrs Allen herself saw them to the door still thanking Celina for making her dream come true.

As Celina and Marcus turned to leave, and looking down the steps from the door, they found that a fog had rolled in off the river. The fog looked like a rolling blanket of dirty silver completely covering the iron fence and gate, with the full moon only adding to the ethereal look of it.

Once on the street Celina and Marcus found seeing any distance through it was almost impossible.

By the time they had walked a little way down the road, the fog had thickened to the point where they were unable to see more than a few feet in front of themselves, prompting Marcus, who was now feeling worried about being out at night in the area of the murders to say.

"I do believe there is a place where cabbies rest; it's a little further down the road, about a half a mile I think. Will you be all right?" Celina gave him a withering look as she replied.

"Why not, come on the sooner we get there the better." They had covered barely half the distance when Celina suddenly froze. She felt the hairs on the back of her neck stand up and goose bumps began covering her skin.

Something out in the fog was searching, not searching with its eyes, nose or ears, but with its mind and Celina knew that in her, it had just found what it was searching for. Not only that, Celina could feel that whatever it was, it was not human.

She struggled to form a block not just around herself but also to include Marcus, and at the same time with both her eyes and her mind, she was searching for somewhere to hide. Getting a hold of Marcus's arm, she pulled him to a halt and whispered.

"Stop, be quiet." Then as he started to turn she said. "Don't move." Celina stood frozen her eyes and mind carefully searching deep into the fog.

Marcus could feel Celina trembling as she stood unmoving, her eyes and mind totally engrossed in looking for that hidden something.

"What is it?" he whispered.

"Shhh" was her reply; Celina's searching mind had found an alley between two large buildings. Still holding his arm, she pulled Marcus into it only to find it blocked ten yards down by a high wall.

Celina looked around in the dark for doors or windows, finding she could see nothing other than a beam that reached out above them, and the outline of a large door some twenty feet up the side of the building.

She looked up at the vague outline of these in dismay; they were no good to her at all.

By now and feeling desperate Celina unsheathed her wand, it was still coming, and despite her block she could feel it knew where she was. Celina was struggling to maintain her block and at the same time hold a shield across the alley.

Knowing that it was useless, she decided to drop her block and concentrate on holding her shield halfway between them and the alley entrance.

Marcus had just started again to ask what was wrong, when he fell silent as an enormous form slowly materialized out of the fog. Seeing it magnified through the fog, whatever it was seemed large enough entirely to block the entrance to the alley.

"My God what's that?" Celina heard from a horrified Marcus while at the same time he was trying to push Celina back in order to shield her with himself. The fog swirled slightly, and Celina felt

Marcus freeze in shock as he saw clearly for the first time what was now in the alley.

Celina felt her shield, and what she now recognised from old pictures as a demon meet. She felt it push against her shield, and then push again before to her horror, it came through her shield as if it never existed.

Celina knew that no single talent had ever fought and beaten a demon before, and for the first time in her life, she felt real fear.

Everything she knew was probably going to be useless. Celina shook her head whispering under her breath. "No it can't end like this; it just can't."

Marcus felt the hair on his head rise; he felt cold, and his stomach had twisted into knots. Instinctively, he reached for the gun he always carried whenever he was abroad only to find that he was unarmed.

Celina had now pulled him back hard against the wall. Marcus found he was shaking and for the first time ever in his life he felt terrified and helpless. The fog lifted slightly, and Marcus found he could see the shape clearly; it was a creature that was at least ten feet tall.

The head was enormous, with a rounded shape and the sides rising to form two curved horns, and it was looking at them with a pair of large glowing yellow eyes.

Celina roughly pushed him to one side making Marcus turn to her in surprise, and then look again.

Marcus could see a thin glowing rod held in both her hands that she was pointing at the monster, and as he watched several short bright white lines flashed between the rod and the monsters head, one two and three of them.

Pointing her wand and drawing all her strength Celina cast a heat strike at its head and then a second and a third. She might as well have thrown Lucifer's into a bowl of water as she found that what she had been told worked for wraiths left a demon unaffected.

The demon was now making a hissing noise that sounded like laughter. She tried to push it away, but all that did was press her back harder against the wall.

Gritting her teeth she pushed still harder, but as she did so, she could feel that her strength was waning. Pushing against an immovable solid object drained an enormous amount of energy. *'I'm fading;'* she thought, *'and there's nothing I can do'.*

Celina struggled to hold the demon back while at the same time trying to think of something else she could use as a defence. A bind did nothing as she might as well have tied it in cobwebs. She tried to lift it off its feet but her lift just slid off it.

She could feel her heart pounding while the mist had become a red fog in front of her eyes encircling the demon. A thought flashed through her mind…. *'I'm going to die; we are both going to die.'* She struck repeatedly sending strike after strike. *'I can't; I am not; I won't give in,'* the thought repeatedly circled through her head.

Celina eventually found herself giving up her last defence; the block had long since gone and so had her shield. Now as Celina directed the last dregs of what little power she had left against the demon, the shield that kept Celina, Celina fell.

She had cast the hottest tiniest heat strikes she could manage one after the other. As her power diminished her strikes faded until her last strike was so weak it would not have ignited a Lucifer.

By now, all feeling had disappeared as she had gradually become numb, not even able to feel the wand in her hand, now she couldn't see; she couldn't hear; she couldn't feel, and she had absolutely nothing left.

Her power was completely drained, and the last of her defences was down and gone. Celina now stood helpless held pinned against the wall by the demon's power, while her mind floated in a sea of darkness waiting for death.

Marcus stood watching as whatever it was came slowly towards them.

What had passed between Celina and it had not slowed its advance.

Looking at Celina with her arms stretched out in front of her body, Marcus could see that she still had the thin rod held in both her hands.

Looking carefully he could see an almost invisible dark purple line that joined the end of the rod with the creature.

A hiss like steam escaped from the end of the alleyway and drew his eyes back to the creature. It stopped and shook itself as a dog might, and then it began to advance again.

As Marcus watched the line grew thicker and brighter while the creature extended its hands as if pushing the end of the line back.

Dark lines now appeared in the purple moving away from the monster towards Celina, bunching up as they neared her and making dark gaps in the line of light. Celina's eyes were closed, and her dress was pressed back against her body and spread out against the wall as though it were in a high wind.

Celina looked as if she was pinned like an insect to the wall with her feet off the ground, though Marcus refused to look down afraid of what he might see.

Marcus could clearly see her arms shaking as if under a tremendous strain. He forced his eyes away from Celina to the monster and then back to the glowing purple rod, the line of light was gone but then flashes of light leapt between the rod and the monster's head, one after another.

As Marcus watched unable to pull his eyes away, the flashes gradually dimmed. Five or six sparks flashed from the rod to the creature's head with the last barely visible, and then the line was gone. With it went the glow from the rod, and Celina's arms dropped and the rod disappeared.

The alley darkened with just the silver moonlight through the swirling mist illuminating it. The monster hesitated. Marcus, finding he had stopped breathing forced himself to breathe as he watched the monster move slowly forward.

Five feet and then four, until it stood a mere three feet from Celina, now it started to reach forward to seize Celina and savour its triumph.

Through his fear, Marcus felt sick as he watched the creature's head start to elongate into a tube not unlike an elephant's trunk that it extended towards Celina.

The creature's mouthparts were now reaching for Celina's face, while it bent slowly forward as if to give her an obscene kiss.

Marcus wanted to scream, something, anything to distract it, but he found he had no breath as he had stopped breathing again.

He took a deep breath to scream, only to have his scream lost in Celina's scream.

It was as if from a thousand years away that words came to her, strange words that now floated through her mind. It was a woman's voice saying, *"At last she's let me in,"* followed by, *"use Merlin's dissipation."* Only two words made sense to Celina. 'Merlin's dissipation.' Celina tried, but she had no power left.

Again there came a woman's voice in her mind. *"No you silly girl not like that, you do it this way."* Like a long-forgotten memory, it suddenly came together in her mind. Celina tried again and found a trickle of power coming from somewhere. She used it to look for the demon with her mind. Finding it, she pushed her mind into the advancing demon.

Celina pushed deep into it, feeling with her mind and looking for the parts it was made of, until she found the smallest living parts.

Then forcing her mind to look deeper into a living thing than she would have thought possible, she found them, parts that couldn't exist alone. Celina found herself struggling as she looked for a way to pull them apart.

At last, Celina understood. Suddenly, from somewhere it was all there wavering in and out in her mind, but it was there. Celina forced it into her wand as sounds screamed in her mind, or in her mouth, she couldn't tell, and if in a language, it was a language she didn't understand.

She felt a power; power like she'd never known before run through her. Celina could feel it burn down her arms and into her wand and then out.

In her mind, Celina could see the tiny parts that made up the demon start to come apart. First one, and then another broke up until at last it had gained enough momentum to continue on its own, more and more, faster and faster.

Celina felt the demon start to drift away like smoke from a fire, and for Celina everything went black.

The rod was back in Celina's hand, and she was screaming a string of words; words unlike any Marcus had ever heard before, sounds he never would have believed a human voice could produce. Then the thin purple line was back and clearly visible, rapidly growing brighter and whiter until it lit the alley almost as bright as a sunny day.

The creature seen clearly now was like something from a nightmare. Heavily built, it moved on oddly jointed legs that ended in unusually large feet. It stood frozen just a few feet away from him with its hands and mouth still reaching for Celina.

Marcus found himself rooted to the spot shielding his eyes from the light as the creature hissed and then hissed louder. Throwing its head around and backing away from Celina while its hands clawed the air trying to push back the line of light but failing. Marcus could hear a sizzling noise like boiling fat filling the air.

The lines brilliance now caused Marcus first to close and then to cover his eyes though he still watched squinting between his fingers. The creature's body began contorting as it screamed a horrible sound.

Powerful as a steam whistle, the scream came again, again and again. Then as if composed of steam or smoke from an extinguished fire, it slowly started to dissolve.

Coming apart twisting and distorting as if seen through water it rapidly faded into the mist until it was gone. For an instant, all that remained was a wisp of denser mist that faded away, leaving just the faint glow of the moonlight shining through the fog.

Marcus heard a soft rustle; turning while blinking and rubbing his eyes, he found Celina lying crumpled on the ground. He dropped to his knees and lifted Celina's head before he lifted her off the wet ground and settled her across his knees.

Was she breathing? He put his finger on her throat and found a steady pulse. Moving his cheek near her nose, he felt her breath. At first, he shook her, and as he gently slapped her face. Her eyes fluttered and opened looking blankly up at him for a moment, and then taking hold of his arms; she tried to pull herself up.

"Marcus," he heard Celina croak, and then in a stronger voice. "We have to be away from here; it's not safe."

She tried to get up again and this time with Marcus helping her; she managed to stand. The rod she had held in her hand had disappeared, but as Marcus watched Celina shook her hand, and as he blinked, the rod was back, held firmly in her hand again.

Now Marcus found she was shaking and unable to stand without him supporting her, as they both stood leaning against the wall gathering their strength.

"We have to go," Celina said. The words echoed in his ears and as Marcus looked at her once more with his mind slowly starting to work again, he wondered. 'What in God's name was that thing, and what was Celina', he knew he had to know; and know now. He looked at her as he held her and supported her. The woman he worked with, a woman he liked and trusted, what was she?

"What was that?" he finally demanded. "Who are you, or what are you, and what did you do, and what language was that?" Celina looked at him.

"Later," she managed in a whisper. "It's…. It's too dangerous here…. We must find somewhere safe." She struggled pushing the rod into her skirt as he watched.

"No I want to know now. Who are you…. what are you, and what was that?" he pointed towards the alley entrance. "That monster?" Celina took a deep breath.

"Very well if you must, my name is Celina Carvel, Lady Celina Carvel. I am the youngest daughter of Lord and Lady Carvel of Ripon, as for what I am, I am a Knight of the Church, what you would call a witch, and that. That was the nearest you ever want to get to Hell." She took a deep shuddering breath. "That creature was what you would call a demon, and as for the language, what language?"

She shook her head and winced putting a hand to her temple as she said. "Now we need to find somewhere safe, St Paul's preferably."

Marcus looked uncertain. A witch…. Celina a witch, he didn't believe in witches. Furthermore, he had worked with her for nearly two years, and she was one of the nicest people he knew, and now she was claiming to be a witch, not only that but asking to be taken to a church.

He must be out of his mind, or she must be, but that was no creature he had ever seen or heard of before, he had to make up his mind. Celina had always treated Claire and himself well, and now with his arm supporting her; he couldn't believe Celina could be evil. He looked at her again and came to a decision. He liked and trusted Celina.

Throwing Celina's arm over his shoulder, they started out of the alley. They had only taken a few steps when he became aware of an obnoxious choking smell that made his eyes water and stomach heave. Moments later thankfully they were out onto the road and in the fresher air. Making their way through the fog with Marcus feeling sure they looked like a couple of drunks, and as he hoped moving toward St Paul's.

The fog had grown thicker, so thick at times that Marcus wasn't even sure that he was still going in the right direction, with only the edge of the pavement to keep him from becoming completely lost. A glow in front of them made him stop; something clinked and snuffled and from down the road, he heard the unmistakable sound of a horse. A swirl of the fog and he could see a small shelter with a light and a cab just visible for a moment or two.

<u>George</u>

George looked over the roof of his cab into the night. The fog was the type that rolled along at ground level, and sitting high on the driver's box he could see the shelter's roof above the fog. George pulled the cab up in front of the shelter and lifted the driver's box lid searching. He found the last of the carrots that had been in the box. Jumping down he gave his horse Molly a quick rub between her ears before giving her the carrot saying.

"Here you are Molly; that's the last one." George stood rubbing Molly's head as a steam whistle sounded somewhere out in the fog. Molly's head came up pulling away from George's hand as she stood ears forward looking up the road. The steam whistle sounded again and then continued to sound repeatedly making shivers run up George's back.

Reaching out to Molly, he found her trembling with all her attention focused further up the road.

"It's all right Molly." George reassured her, though having heard the sound he felt in need of a little reassurance himself. George gave Molly a pat before he turned to the shelter feeling decidedly nervous; he had to admit the sound had been strange.

The shelter was a rectangular building partially open on the front, roofed with slates and kept warm by an old cast-iron stove standing in the middle of the floor. George picked up a piece of straw from the floor and opening the door on the stove; he took a light and reached up to light the candle in the lantern hanging from the roof. With the candle lit he looked around feeling a little better in the familiar surroundings.

As he turned towards the front, he was surprised to see Molly had moved closer to the shelter, although her attention was still focused further up the road. "It's all right Molly" he said feeling a cold shiver run up his back.

"It's all right; it was just a steam ship on the river," though as he said it George was aware that the river was in the opposite direction.

"Mick and old Tom will be here soon; I'll put the kettle on." Around three walls ran wooden benches for seating, with three lockers fitted under them. Taking a bunch of keys from his coat pocket George opened one of the lockers and rummaged in the bottom.

Pulling out a kettle, three tin mugs and a packet of tea and sugar mix, he then used the tap on the horse trough to fill the kettle. Once it was on the stove, he settled back and warmed his hands. Outside Molly began thumping her rear hoof on the ground prompting George to say again.

"It's all right Molly; it'll only be Mick or old Tom." He settled back again warming himself but Molly still seemed restless tossing her head and snuffling. George finally got up and going to her began soothingly rubbing her nose.

He could see that Molly's ears were up, and her attention was still focused on something that he couldn't see further up the road. It was a slight movement in the air that brought the sound of footsteps to his ears. A swirl of the mist, and two figures could be

142

seen through a hole in the fog, with one clearly supporting the other.

"It's only a couple of drunks," he told Molly. Yet Molly still watched intently as the fog swirled between them. George was about to turn away when the fog cleared again, and a second look sent him running up the road to give aid.

It was a man who was supporting a smartly dressed woman, who looked as if she was barely able to stand, and as George drew close he found that the man looked only a little better himself. Thoughts of the recent murders ran through George's mind, and reaching them George's first words were.

"E'er have you been attacked or robbed?"

The man looked up; George was shaken by the man's face looking back at him. Horror showed there. George knew the sick look of horror on a face having seen some of the terrible accidents in the docks, but the look on the face of the man made his blood run cold. Feeling a shudder run through him he said.

"Look I've a fire and some tea on the go just down the road," pointing back the way he had come. The man looked at him again and then as if seeing for the first time the cabby's badge on his coat, he seemed to pull himself together saying.

"No, no can you get us to St Paul's as fast as possible?"

"Well I can if you're sure," George replied uncertainly. The man looked at him and silently nodded.

"My cab's just down the road," George jerked his thumb over his shoulder and then turning to Celina, he said. "Here let me take the lady."

George was a large and strong man having worked twelve years on the docks before inheriting Molly and the cab; so he easily gathered Celina up in his arms and turned to head for the shelter. As he turned, he was stopped by Molly's warm wet nose full in the face.

Molly had followed him, her night boots and the rubber tires of the cab wheels making little sound on the cobbles. Molly was now stood with her ears pricked forward looking at the woman in his arms.

"Here now Molly don't do that," he said. Then pushing her nose away with his shoulder, he carried Celina to the cab door as Marcus opened it.

"You get in first and then the lady," George said nodding his head towards the door. With Marcus inside the cab George lifted Celina in, and then the two men managed to ease her on to a seat, where Celina sat with her head resting back, and her eyes closed.

Marcus was still shaking with a jumble of thoughts running through his head. Celina, he thought he knew her, but now he wasn't so sure. What exactly was a Knight of the Church, and if Celina was a witch, surely a demon wouldn't attack her, it would aid her? Something from hell attacking a witch, and what about the church and witchcraft, he shook his head it just didn't make sense.

George closed the door and swung up onto the driver's box. Molly didn't wait for the reins; she was already turning the cab and had set off back at a fast trot passing the shelter before George had the reigns sorted. Turning into Church Yard where she rounded the Cathedral and continued before stopping by the steps leading to the doors of the south transept.

George jumped down and opened the cab door, and then with Marcus helping Celina stand George lifted her out of the cab, where she stood leaning against the wheel as Marcus climbed out.

"Thank you, you saved our lives," Marcus said as he put his hand in his pocket. "How much do we owe you?"

George, with the murders fresh in his mind put his hand on Marcus's arm and replied.

"Nothing, I could see you and the lady were in trouble, and I'm glad to be of assistance." Marcus blinked at him seeming unsure and then taking his hand out of his pocket reached into his waistcoat and withdrew a card.

"Well take this and please call and see me tomorrow.... no the day after as I am sure the lady would like to thank you herself." Marcus pushed the card into the cabby's hand, and then taking Celina's arm across his shoulder; Marcus started up the steps.

George watched for a moment and then ran to assist them. Reaching the doors, he held open the smaller door for the two of them to enter the Cathedral.

As George climbed back onto the driver's box, his mind was in a whirl. There was something quite strange about the whole episode, and it rather frightened him. Certainly, Molly had known as she had been nervous and agitated before the two had even come near.

She had followed him when he had gone to aid them as they first appeared in the fog. She had taken them to St Paul's as if she knew it was urgent and without any direction from him. He had to admit at least to himself that he was a little frightened.

The cab stopped as Molly stood before the shelter, and George heard voices calling to him from inside.

"Tea George," he could see old Tom standing near the entrance, and then he heard him calling again. "Where you bin? You left the kettle on." Then there came another voice.

"You nearly let it boil dry."

"I had a fare," George said, and then he paused feeling unsure before saying. "I think." Old Tom looked up.

"You think; just what kind of an answer is that?"

"I don't know," George replied. "It was so strange I didn't even charge them."

"You what, you didn't charge them?" old Tom said as in his surprise he almost missed the tin mug he was pouring boiling water into. Then warming himself by the fire, George told them of the night's happenings. Mick looking up said.

"You're not going to see them again are you? They sound weird to me, what with the murders and all; well I'd stay clear if I was you." Old Tom sat nodding and thinking that he could only agree. Fingering the card in his pocket George heard himself reply.

"I think I will; I want to see them in daylight." He was frightened at the thought, but his curiosity was winning.

Marcus.

As the cabbie left Marcus eased Celina onto a back pew and sat with her not knowing what to do or say.

"Is someone there?" a voice called. Marcus rose to his feet to see a man in clerical black standing under the dome and holding

145

up a lantern, seeing Marcus the man hurried across saying as he drew near to them. "I thought I heard someone come in."

"Hello Dickie," a quiet voice said. The man almost dropped the lantern as he saw Celina.

"Celina whatever has happened?" the man asked obviously shocked to see Celina in the state she was.

Marcus looked at the man; it was clear to him that the man knew Celina and knew her well. Celina's eyes opened again as she struggled to sit up.

"Dickie," she whispered. "What are you doing here?"

"Never mind about me, what happened to you?" Celina managed a slight smile and then winced.

"I think I came off best with a demon," she said weakly. "Though the way I feel at the moment I'm not sure." The man sat down hard rocking the pew.

"A demon?" he asked sounding to Marcus as if he found Celina's statement unbelievable. "Here in London, are you sure? We've been looking for a wraith."

"Please Dickie not so loud," Celina whispered putting her hand to her head. "My head really hurts; this was a full-grown demon and it had us cornered."

The man stared at Celina; Marcus still didn't know whether in shock or disbelief.

"How did you get away?" the man finally asked.

"I think I dissipated it, oh, and this is Marcus my assistant. Marcus this is the Reverend Dr Richard Bird, better known to his friends as Dickie."

Dickie looked from one to the other his gaze finally stopping with Marcus as he said.

"I think you had better tell me what happened, but first I think we should get Celina home, and then I can speak to you later my Lady, that is when you've recovered a little." He took a small bell out of his pocket and rang it, causing Celina to wince. A young man in a black cassock arrived within minutes.

"Please find a cab and arrange for this lady to be taken home, and then make sure you accompany her to her door; oh and see she enters her house before you leave." The young man with a small bow to Dickie helped Celina to her feet and watched by the two worried men; he helped Celina walk back towards the doors.

"Will she be all right?" Marcus asked.

"A lot better after a good nights rest," Dickie said turning back to Marcus. "Now I think its time we retired to somewhere more comfortable; might I suggest my rooms as they are just over the road?"

Recovering in Dickie's spacious rooms over a glass of brandy, Marcus told him of what he had seen. Dickie then continued to put Marcus's mind at rest about Celina by explaining about the order of the Knights of the Church and their oath. How in 530 A.D. King Arthur had come to the throne and had set about unifying the land. Then in 535 A.D. King Arthur and Merlin set off on a grand tour to see his Kingdom and people.

It was toward the autumn as they approached the Abbey at Glastonbury that they came across the first of several deserted villages, until eventually reaching one where they found the bodies of the villagers. They were in a terrible state, dry and hard as if they had been dried over a fire. When they reached Glastonbury, they found other villagers seeking sanctuary inside the walls of the Abbey.

There the Abbot having greeted them asked for their assistance in slaying the fearsome beasts terrifying the villages around the Abbey.

Dickie seeing Marcus with an empty glass refilled their glasses before he continued the story saying.

"The Abbot and a thirteen-year-old novice along with two sisters from one of the villages had been keeping the beasts away from the Abbey. It seems that they were unknowingly using what we call 'the talent.' It was Merlin with the help of the Abbot and the two sisters; along with King Arthur and his sword Excalibur who managed to destroy a demon and several of the creatures we call wraiths."

Excalibur, Dickie then explained being the only mortal weapon ever found to be effective against creatures from the underworld. Marcus sat listening knowing that without seeing what he had seen Dickie's story would have been unbelievable.

Dickie continued with his tale saying. "King Arthur then set Merlin a task to find others with the talent. It took Merlin five years to find eight, seven women and a boy of fifteen. The women were afraid of being burned as witches, and only with the protection of the church would they come forward and be known. Seeing them,

King Arthur commanded a great table to be made with twenty-five places. There was to be a place for himself, Merlin and twenty-three others. He then called all the known witches and warlocks as they called themselves to Glastonbury. They now had a grand total of fifteen including Merlin, so it was in 547 A.D. that King Arthur formed the Knights of the Church, with the original fifteen headed by the newly formed post of High Abbot of Glastonbury."

Marcus thinking over the night's happenings now asked. "Celina was using something when we were attacked, something that she held in her hand, what was it?"

"That," Dickie explained. "Was her wand, it directs her power as without it when she uses her power it scatters all around her so most of it is wasted, and only a small proportion is directed to where she wants it. The wand concentrates and directs her power so all of it goes to where it's needed."

Dickie now pulled his chair closer and sat facing Marcus as he said. "There are two more things I must tell you. When Celina reached sixteen, she became eligible for a wand. Once she was chosen, she took a binding oath that she cannot break, it is an oath to protect people and with that oath she is incapable of using her power to harm any human being.

The second is that now that you know about the Knights of the Church; you will not be allowed to speak or inform any other person by any means. You will only be able to speak of this to one who already knows about the Knights of the Church."

Marcus sat looking into the fire as he said. "I think I can see the reason in that, yes I understand, and I will accept that restriction willingly." He thought for a moment and then asked. "What if someone overhears?"

"They won't hear it," Dickie replied. "Nor could they see the written word so the secret is safe. It's all part of me telling you about the founding of The Knights of the Church. If you were in a position where you were given permission to speak of this, then the telling of it would place what we call an inhibition on that person to stop them from telling it further just as I have with you."

Dickie had retired to bed leaving Marcus trying to sleep in front of the fire, watching the flames and thinking about Hell as he ran over the night's happenings in his mind.

Yes, he knew about the church and its involvement with medical matters. The fact that the churches' healers had been achieving a higher recovery of patients than conventional medicine had only been recognised in the last hundred years. Marcus knew that after years of derision that the church's doctors and nurses were now held in high esteem.

What he had seen this evening, the church actively involved in fighting creatures from Hell itself had shaken Marcus to the core. Marcus laid there with his mind in turmoil.

Celina a woman he thought he had known, only to find that she was in fact from a high family, and not only was she a Lady, but she was also part of an army fighting these demonic creatures. Not only fighting them, but fighting them with what Marcus could only see as magic. It was with thoughts of magic and visions of a Hell full of enormous demons that Marcus eventually fell into a troubled sleep.

Upon Celina's return home, Jane who was horrified at the state of her put her directly to bed, and then sat by her bedside for the rest of the night, and in doing so, earning a gentle reprimand from a very weary Celina the following morning.

Thursday 19th December 1861.

Someone told mother, so she is coming down. My but I feel terrible. Even so I am still alive, and I think that must be a miracle.

~~~

The following morning and much to Jane's relief word was received that Celina's mother and father would be arriving later that evening, having heard of the recent events from Dickie. The word came just as a very weak Celina was informing Jane that she was getting up and going to Rarities. Jane absolutely refused to let her go saying.

"If you go you'll go in your nightdress as I will not bring you your clothes, and as for your hair, well it looks a mess. If anyone is going in this morning it will be me, you my Lady will stay a-bed until I get home, do you understand?"

Celina who had been secretly thinking it would be near impossible to get out of bed let alone go out quietly agreed.

Both Marcus and Jane arrived late at the shop that morning, with Jane looking pale and tired after a near sleepless night watching over Celina, while Marcus was just tired. Marcus quietly explaining to Jane that he had spent most of the night talking, and then what was left of it trying to sleep in front of the fire in Dickie's apartment.

Marcus persuaded Jane to go home at lunchtime having horrified her by telling her in full and gory detail all about the night's happenings, including the chivalrous cabby. Once Jane had left Claire pounced on Marcus wanting a full explanation of why the two of them were in such a state.

Marcus stretched the truth somewhat, explaining that last night they had been in an 'incident,' one that may have had to do with the murders in the area of Mrs Allen's house.

He insinuated that he and Celina had been up most of the night helping with inquiries, inquiries about things the people investigating the murders didn't want made public yet. He was quite proud of the fact that he had managed to infer without actually saying so that it was the police they had been with.

When Jane arrived home early the Cook insisted she rest until their parent's arrival, and to this end Kate brought their meals up to her and Celina in their rooms. It was just after six of the clock when Dickie entered Celina's room smiling and asking.

"Are you feeling better?" Celina smiled back.

"Much," she said. "But do tell me why you are here in London." Dickie having pulled a chair across said.

"I suppose you have been reading about these brutal murders, well we were under the impression it was a wraith. A portal opened about six weeks ago, and we never found it. It was sealed again before we could but something had come through it, and we have been running around London chasing it ever since."

He scowled at Celina in mock annoyance saying, "and then you go and find it without even looking. Now tell me how did you destroy this demon and who helped you; as it wasn't your friend Marcus I do know that?"

"I didn't have any help," Celina shuddered at the memory. "It just came at us out of the fog, and I had to do something." Celina hesitated before saying. "It was looking for me; I could definitely feel it searching and then its elation at having found me. No, no that's not quite right; it was not just that it had found me, but that it had found the one it was sent to find." Dickie was now starting to look worried as he asked.

"Are you sure? After all why would it want you?"

"I don't know," Celina replied with a shrug. "I just know that's what it felt like."

"What did you do next?"

"I tried to put up a block, but it still found us."

"Did your block include your friend too?"

"Yes it covered us both, and then we tried to escape down an alley. Only the alley was a dead end, so I shielded the alley entrance but it came straight in; it just pushed right through my shield." Celina shuddered again as she remembered that moment. "There was no way I could stop it."

"What did you do next?"

"I tried everything I could think of but nothing touched it. I had put everything I had at it, and I knew I was going to lose. Toward the end, I was fading and fading fast," Celina shuddered again at the memory.

"No I had passed that; I had reached the point where I had absolutely nothing left. Then it came to me like someone saying words in my head, 'Merlin's dissipation', and it just happened, suddenly I knew how to do it, and I felt it work." Celina could see doubt on Dickie's face.

"Yes Dickie," Celina insisted. "I could feel it working, and the next thing I felt was as if something; some power was pouring into me and then through me and into the demon. I felt the demon weaken, and that's the last I remember until I saw Marcus." Dickie sat silent for a few moments before saying.

"Marcus says you were shouting something in a strange language." Celina thought going through the night's happenings once again in her mind trying to remember; finally she said.

"I don't know; I don't remember a thing about that." Dickie then told her.

"No single talent has ever destroyed a demon before, did you know that? Not only that no single Knight has ever been able to perform Merlin's dissipation, it usually takes three or better still four, so I think the Abbot will have to have a full report about this." Then Dickie taking her hand said. "I've told your father." Celina looked at Jane before answering.

"Yes I know," and then she smiled as she said. "My mother and father are on their way now, and knowing my father he will be pushing that broom of his as fast as it can fly. Are you going to stay to see them?"

Dickie joining Celina in smiling at the idea of Celina's father pushing his broom said.

"Yes I'll be back to see them later, but for now my Lady; you get some rest."

Celina's mother arriving at her room found Celina apparently asleep with Jane sitting watching over her. Jane putting a finger to her lips said softly.

"She's asleep and still very tired but a lot better." Celina opened one eye.

"No I'm not," she declared in a sleepy voice. "Asleep" and rolling over in order to see them better. "I'm awake, hello mother it's good to see you."

152

Lady Mary sat on the bed as Celina with an effort pulled herself up and allowed Jane to force a shawl around her shoulders as her mother said.

"Well I hear you had quite an adventure last night, and your father and Dickie are most puzzled, as Dickie says you seem to have done the impossible." Celina pulled a face as she said.

"I don't know about the impossible, but I certainly wouldn't like to do it every day. I'm still not sure what I did or how I did it, as I don't really remember much beyond being terrified." Her mother frowned at Celina's reply as she said.

"Your father wants a word with the young man who was with you, so Dickie has arranged for him to be brought around in a cab, and he should be here shortly." Celina pulled herself upright as she said.

"Jane I need my clothes, I want to be dressed and up if Marcus is coming around." Jane looked at her mother and seeing a slight nod of her head; sighed at having to give way to her mother's superior medical knowledge, but entirely resigned to that fact she went for Celina's clothes. It was as Jane helped Celina to the bathroom that Celina said.

"Jane I need a word with Marcus before my father sees him, will you watch for him and let me know before Kate answers the door?" It was about an hour later when Marcus arrived, and though still pale and a little unsteady on her feet Celina met him at the door, telling him.

"My father wants a word with you, so please don't tell him about buying the shop, that is unless he asks, and don't try to hide anything.

Just tell him we went to see the owner of the shop about alterations, and if he wants to know why you came with me.... Oh tell him you didn't like the idea of me going out to that area alone at night, as he will be able to tell if you deliberately try to hide things; so keep to the truth but not necessarily all of it, and just keep it simple." Marcus looked at Celina and nodded his agreement.

"That would be the truth after all," he reminded her. "It was because of the danger that I insisted I go with you." Marcus hesitated before asking. "I take it your father is, well like you?"

"Yes and my mother too," Celina whispered as she took Marcus into the study to introduce him before collapsing into a chair to listen. Marcus did exactly as Celina had said, and kept as to why they had been in that area down to a minimum. It took only the mention of the recent murders to justify his presence.

It was past midnight when Marcus left, and Celina insisted that he did not come into the shop until after lunch saying, as she had spent the entire afternoon asleep, and with Claire's assistance, she would be perfectly able to manage the shop during the morning.

Friday 20th December 1861.

Celina arrived at the shop that morning obviously not yet fully recovered; knowing this Jane settled her in the office and went to make them both drinks. Claire arrived and was horrified at the sight of Celina, and finding Jane in the back room she asked.

What happened to Celina, she looks terrible and where's Marcus?" Jane considered what to tell her and finally said.

"Celina will tell you more of the detail as I only know her side, but I understand they had some trouble after leaving Mrs Allen's as they were the victims of some form of an attack, but everything's all right now and Marcus will be in later."

As the morning wore on Celina could feel curiosity burning in Claire, so calling her into the office she implied but without mentioning the police that they had been assisting with inquiries until the early hours of the morning, and then again yesterday evening. Once more she gave the impression that Marcus had remained there long after she had left and that he knew a lot more than she did. Claire seemed almost though Celina knew not fully satisfied.

Marcus arrived just in time for Claire to take lunch, and at the same time a cab arrived outside the shop. Looking rather nervous the cabby opened the shop door and looked in. Marcus smiling went to greet him taking his hand and shaking it enthusiastically as he said.

"Come in, Miss Celina will be most pleased to see you." Taking the cabby back toward the office where a much brighter looking Celina seeing them approach opened the door for them. Pulling a chair out for the cabby and seeing him seated Celina began by expressing her gratitude.

"I must thank you for the other night; I was much shaken and you were a real Knight in shining armour." The cabby looked embarrassed as he said. "It was nothing my Lady."

"Oh yes it was, and Marcus has told me you refused the fare. Now you can't be doing that, are you married?" Something rang in her mind prompting Celina to ask.

"Do you have children?" He nodded. "Well if you keep refusing fares, just how are you going to feed them?" Celina watched as he looked down embarrassed at her words.

"I'm sorry," she said suddenly feeling a little ashamed. "I should be more grateful and not be chastising you as we owe you far more than you realise." Celina smiled and then leaned just enough to calm his nerves.

"Look if you won't take payment…." Celina thought for a moment. "Well if you won't take payment I must at least give you a nice little present for your wife, and as for your children. How many are boys and how many are girls, and how old are they?" Celina found once again that something ringing in her head; she felt fear from him in the way he shied away from certain thoughts, but she had caught a memory. The cabby looked up and replied.

"We have two little girls." He was clearly frightened, and Celina could tell that he didn't want to mention the children, but she had already caught his memory of a pencil turning in mid-air, and a small girl laughing.

She didn't have to lean, he was so close and it was all there almost shouting at her. He was thinking now of a woman possibly the child's mother who was also frightened. The cabby radiated both love and fear just at the mention of his family as he said.

"One is ten and the other is twelve." Celina thought; *'I have to get those girls here; Claire is off tomorrow afternoon so that will be perfect.'*

"How about tomorrow afternoon?" she asked with a smile and a little gentle leaning. "I want you to bring your wife and daughters here, and I will see that they each receive a nice little gift from out of the shop. Now no arguing, I owe you a lot…. an awful lot." Celina took three sixpences out of her purse and pressed them into his hand leaning at the same time to make him take the money.

"That is the fare for your wife and children; I have found you to be a good and honest man, and I feel that once having accepted the money you will do your best to earn it." She smiled again leaning lightly to calm him and ease his worries. "Now I want to see you all tomorrow." The cabby looking bemused started to decline.

"Well I…."

"No, no arguments now." Then going to the door she called for Marcus. Marcus came back into the office where she handed the cabby over to him saying.

"He is coming back tomorrow afternoon, and as he won't take anything in payment. I am going to see that his family receives a little something from the shop, just a small gift." Marcus explained more to the cabby as he walked him through the shop.

"I'm afraid that Miss Celina…. well, she hasn't fully recovered yet; she was very badly affected the other night, and I know she wants to thank you properly." The cabby started to protest again, but Marcus stopped him by saying. "I know it's important to her, and she feels very strongly about it so please do come back tomorrow."

Climbing back onto the driver's box George shook his head totally bemused. He'd accepted the sixpences so now he felt a responsibility to earn the fare, and he knew that he would return tomorrow, something, curiosity was driving him. Marcus came back into the office, stood looking at Celina for a moment, and then asked.

"What's happening and why ask him to bring his wife and family?" Celina pushed a chair towards him as she replied.

"As you now know so much about us you may as well know a little more, when I mentioned his family, I had a distinct impression that he was hiding something. I felt he was actually frightened, and then when I asked about his children, I felt the same thing again."

"Well?" Marcus asked.

"So the next time when I asked about the children, I was ready; I think his children or even possibly his wife has talent."

"Talent?" Marcus asked.

"Yes that's what we call what we do, our ability." Marcus looking at Celina felt there was still something he had to know as he asked. "How many of you are there?" Celina had to think as she wasn't all that sure.

"Well I'm not sure but the last time I heard; I think it was something like two hundred." Marcus was stunned.

"I had expected thousands," he said.

Ixcte ~ 2

Ixcte raised a head out of its hood. A food/slave/pet was approaching stopping every nine steps and prostrating itself for the required nine heartbeats. It stopped and lay in reach of one of Ixcte's major feeding tentacles waiting.

"Tell me of the fate of the black. Tell me." Ixcte's thought hammered into the mind of the slave and then Ixcte waited. The food/slave/pet lay still. "Tell me," Ixcte pressed more insistently. When further silence followed Ixcte moved a major feeding tentacle toward the body.

The head came up, and the Cesdrik said. "That which we sent found the black, but it did not return. It failed." The food/slave/pet now lay trembling in terror. A major feeding tentacle was immediately plunged angrily onto the body.

The food/slave/pet then arched in agony as dissolving fluids were pumped into its shell. Ixcte tasted not just the agony but the fear and the dissolving tissues as the food/slave/pet slowly succumbed to death.

Saturday 21ˢᵗ December 1861.

I awoke again last night from a strange dream. All I remember is images of red sand and a feeling of hate and dread. It's unusual for me as I usually sleep the night through. Jane stayed with me for the rest of the night again.

Today I found two little girls with talent. As far as I can tell, they both could end up as full Knights of the Church.

~~~

The cabby arrived with his wife and children all looking very smart and dressed in their Sunday best. His wife was as small and petite as he was large and powerful, while the two girls who were shy and nervous were hiding behind their mother. Celina rose and went to meet them saying.

"Thank you for coming as it means so much to me." Having decided that the office would be rather cramped she said. "I think it will be better in the back room as the office is a little small for all of us, so this way please."

Seated around a table in Celina's storeroom Celina looked at them one at a time with her gaze finally stopping on the wife.

"I don't know how much your husband has told you, but Marcus and myself can almost say he saved our lives that night." The cabby began shaking his head as he said.

"No it wasn't that bad, by the time I saw you your friend had things well in hand." Celina turned her attention back to him as she said.

"Later I will let Marcus explain, and as he will tell you it was a lot worse than you think, but first I must meet these two young ladies and then I will let you into a little secret about myself." Celina then turned her attention to the two little girls and leaned slightly for their names.

"Now your name is Molly isn't it, and you're the little girl who likes to play with pencils aren't you?" Celina could see that this had startled the whole family with the man and his wife blanching noticeably.

"What do you mean?" the mother asked looking from one little girl to the other and then back to Celina. Her husband half rose to his feet as Celina calmly held out a pencil to Molly.

The little girl recoiled back with her face turning white, shaking her head and looking at the pencil as if it were a snake. Celina placed the pencil in front of her and then taking another pencil; Celina balanced it on one-finger saying.

"Now this is my little secret." Then the pencil lifted into the air and spun just as she had seen in the memory, and then while closely watching Molly's face Celina said. "Now you've seen my little secret." Celina let the pencil fall back to rest on her finger as she asked. "There now can you show me your little secret?

Molly looked at her mother as her father rose fully to his feet with his fists clenched. Celina leaned slightly on Molly calming her, as slowly and without taking her eyes off her mother Molly picked up the pencil and placed it on her finger. It lifted just off her fingertip, and then it started to spin slowly at first and then faster. Celina clapping said.

"That's very good Molly, and now we're even, I know your secret, and you know mine. Now what is Alison's little secret?"

Alison now not to be outdone by her younger sister took the pencil from her, and then without taking her eyes off Celina's face, she placed the pencil on her fingertip where it lifted and then spun faster and faster until it was just a blur.

Their mother now with tears starting in her eyes took hold of her husband's hand as he collapsed back onto his chair asking.

"What are you going to do now, turn them over to the police or something?" Celina found herself leaning on the four of them helping to ease their fears as she said.

"Going to the police, no, nothing like that." Celina leaned again this time pushing trust and belief as she said.

"Just because ordinary people would call us witches does not mean that we're evil or in league with the devil. In fact, it's just the opposite, so this is what I am going to do. I'm going to get these two a grant, and then have them enrolled in a special church school to develop their talents."

"Talents?" their father asked. "What do you mean talents, special church school, and what do you mean by a grant? Just what is this all about and who are you anyway?"

"Children, in fact all people like us are very valuable to the church and as such the church looks after us." Before Celina could explain further the cabby interrupted her asking.

"Us, people like us are valuable to the church, how and why?" Celina leaned to find their names.

"George, it is George isn't it and…. Molly?"

"Yes, yes this is Molly my wife," George said impatiently. Celina now found herself explaining about the Knights of the Church, meeting first disbelief and then amazement with George looking constantly back and forth between his wife, Celina and his children.

By the time Celina had finished telling them about the Knights of the Church, George who was looking much more comfortable turned to his wife his look asking her consent before he turned back to Celina to explain.

"When it first happened with Alison, we were so afraid; we thought that she would be taken away from us, and then little Molly started doing the same things as well." His wife Molly interrupted him saying.

"We loved them so much that we tried to hide them and make them stop doing it, but they couldn't, every so often they'd do something new, and now you say there are others?"

Celina pointed up at the gaslight saying. "Watch," as the gas turned down and then up. Allison, who had been watching in wonder as Celina gave her demonstration of talent. Now to Celina's surprise she turn the gas down, and then with a giggle back up again; prompting Celina to say.

"I definitely think they will be a very valuable asset to the church, especially if they can do things like that with no training at all. Now I think its time for the presents I promised you."

"First though what use does the church have for them?" George asked. Celina looked first to his wife as she replied.

"Many uses, for instance, my mother is a church doctor," and then turning back to George. "While my father, he is a church surgeon."

"Surgeon, doctor?" George asked her.

"Yes just think a surgeon who operates without knives and a doctor who can see inside her patient. Other thing's Talents can do range from helping the police to engineering. One of my tasks is to find others with talent as well as to protect ordinary people. Marcus will explain about that later, but now back to the presents."

Celina taking a box from the table took out a chain with a silver cross inlaid with black jet which she placed around Molly's neck. Then she took two chains with smaller plain silver crosses that she gave to the two girl's. Finally picking up a leather pouch Celina turned to George only to find George shaking his head and saying.

"No Miss, I didn't do anything special."

"Yes you did," Celina insisted. "Later I will let Marcus tell you just what you saved us from, but first this." Celina opened the leather pouch and took out a silver hip flask engraved with a cross and offering it to George she said.

"This is for you, to keep you warm on cold nights. I decided that after you'd heard about me being what you would call a witch, and especially if I was mistaken about the children that you might be sceptical about receiving a gift from me, so as you see they all have the sign of the cross in one way or another.

Now I am going to ask Marcus to tell you what happened the other night, and by the way, he is perfectly ordinary, the only talent he has is honesty and being a very nice person. Then after you've heard from Marcus I want you to think over my offer for the girls and let me know."

Marcus was surprised to be allowed into Celina's store, but when Celina asked him to tell them about the happenings of that night he quickly settled into Celina's chair to tell them. Celina took the two girls into the office where she entertained them with sweets and her favourite childhood stories about King Arthur until Marcus returned.

George and Molly came back into the office with both of them visibly shaken but wanting to thank Celina, with Celina's breaking of protocol by taking Molly's hand as she said. "Please think about it." Molly looked up at George as she said.

"We will; we shall have a good talk about it, and George will let you know on Monday." George reached out and gathered the two girls into his arms pulling them close as he said.

"Thank you, we both feel a lot better now knowing there are others like Alison and Molly."

Monday 23rd December 1861.

True to his word George arrived promptly as Celina was opening the shop on Monday morning. In the office, Celina poured a cup of tea for him before asking. "Have you decided?"

"We had a long talk over the *weekend," George replied, but to Celina he still looked troubled though his voice became more certain as he said. "If for no other reasons, it's protection for the children. You know how some people can be, and well, you must know.... so we decided yes, yes to all of it."

Celina feeling both relief for the two girls and pleasure for herself at his reply said. "You won't regret it, and now I'm going to ask Dr Bird to write to you. You'll like Dr Bird; he was my teacher when I was Molly's age." George, even after having heard this still felt a little worried as he asked. "Where is this school that you talked about, and do the girls have to go away or something like that?"

"The school is wherever Dr Bird is, and at the moment I think it will be in one of the church houses across from St Paul's."

"That close," he replied with some relief before he asked. "How many children will there be there?"

That evening arriving home Celina found an envelope on her desk; opening it, she found it was from the Abbot of Glastonbury.

"He wants to see me tomorrow morning," she told Jane.

"Tomorrow morning that's short notice?" Jane said looking over Celina's shoulder to read the letter herself.

*Weekend used to describe Sunday as a day of rest and attending Church, though slowly starting to include Saturday in some sections of the population

"Well if it's that urgent I'd better go tonight so that I can see him first thing in the morning, so can you pack me my overnight bag please? As Jane turned to go, Celina said.

"Oh and Jane I think it's going to be cold up there, so can you look out one of my heavier winter dress's and my thick coat for me." Celina found Jane giving her a worried look as she left to pack her things.

"I have some appointments to keep in the city tomorrow morning,"
Jane called back as she made her way up the staircase. "If you want I can call in the shop first and let them know you will be away for a day or two."

Celina wearing her heavy riding coat, hat and gloves pulled open the old stable doors to find her broom looking a little dusty where it was racked along one side of the stable. The broom resembled nothing more than a nine foot long three-inch diameter pole, that was flared out over the last two feet to a flattened oval about twelve inches across.

Across the pole, two padded wicker seats were positioned one behind the other, with footrests fixed below the pole to provide support for the feet and a comfortable sitting position, while in front of the first seat was mounted a crossbar for the hands to hold.

The same type of bar was attached to the back of the front seat to give the rear-seat rider something to hold on to. Celina fastened her overnight bag to the front seat, and then as the broom lifted at her touch, she eased it off its rack and then with her foot she kicked the rack up and out of the way.

Floating the broom out into the yard Celina swung a leg over the centre pole and settled herself into the rear seat. Once settled she adjusted her coat and skirts to either side of the centre pole before pulling the lap strap tight and buckling it. Jane standing well back and watching said.

"Just be careful, and Celina, please call me as soon as you can."

"Don't worry Jane, I will call you on the Telson as soon as I can, or at least before I set off back." Jane watched as Celina pushed down and the broom rose vertically into the air. Having

163

given a last wave as Celina disappeared into the night sky; Jane turned and made her way back to the kitchen where Cook was ready with a hot drink.

"She's gone then?" Cook asked passing a mug to Jane as she settled by the fire. Jane nodded as she wrapped her hands around the hot mug saying. "

Yes, and for once I don't envy her; it's going to be cold up there." Cook rolling her mug in her hands warming them said.

"Rum doings I say, I didn't expect anything like this in London." There was silence for a moment or two before she asked. "Are you all right working in London, I mean going around seeing all these people and what not?" Jane sat looking into the fire thinking and then said.

"Yes I really enjoy it; I didn't think I would, but I do; I'm seeing people and places I never thought I'd see and I've met some very nice people…. and some not so nice.

There's a lot of walking to do, and sometimes it can be hard work for the feet but it's usually enjoyable. How about you, how do you feel being here in London?"

"Oh it's not so bad," Cook replied. "It's much better than in the house up north, me Thomas and the maid, we manage fine. The house looks after itself most of the time, keeps itself clean. It's just odd bits like the fires needing attention and other little things."

Then settling down deeper in their chairs they sat comfortably with mugs in hand looking into the fire, sitting watching dragons at play until Kate came in to make mugs of cocoa for Thomas and herself.

Marcus

Marcus sat with his feet up on his desk feeling at peace with the world.

He had gotten over the shock of Celina being a witch; although he had to admit he was more comfortable with the title Knight of the Church. His burial urns no longer adorned the desk and the money from them had paid the few debts he had been left by his mother. He had even been left with a tidy sum in the bank. He had

164

found his work enjoyable, and it was bringing in more money than he had expected. Indeed, life was good.

His thoughts now turned to Elizabeth, a nurse whom he had recently met. He had started calling in the little tearooms across from the shop for an evening meal as it was easier than Cooking for himself at night, and thanks to his work at Rarities, he could easily afford it.

At first, the nurse had just been another customer there, but after a few weeks of passing the occasional comment with her; they now shared a table whenever their working times coincided. She had told him how she was working at the new St Bartholomew's hospital, and sometimes it was easier for her to obtain a meal at the tearooms than at home. He smiled to himself again; yes, life was looking good.

Claire.

The letter to her parents was taking longer to write this week as it seemed to Claire that her mind insisted on straying. She had told them many times before how much she enjoyed working for Celina so that would be old news. Instead into this letter she put what she knew about Celina's meeting with her uncle, and how Celina was buying the shop.

She still hadn't let them know that as generous as their allowance was her salary now exceeded it, as Celina certainly showed her appreciation for hard work with an ample salary. She did tell them that sales were up, and that she missed them. Then she sat and chewed the end of her pen and thought. *'I'm happy; really happy, things are so good.'*

Celina.

Celina had pulled the broom up over the clouds; she loved flying with a good moon. This one though just half full still illuminated the cloud tops and made them into billowing silver mountains and dark valleys, making her realise how much she had missed flying.

Now high above the clouds she pulled the broom around and pointed it toward the southwest thinking. *'Glastonbury here we come.'* Celina didn't push her broom too hard; though cold to Celina it was an almost perfect night for flying.

It was about half after the hour of eleven when she dropped back through the clouds to find the Abbey tower's guide-light about a half a mile in front of her. Reaching the Abbey she dropped into the stable yard and floated her broom into the stable reserved for visiting Knights.

A sleepy novice took charge of it and then directed her to the building reserved for church visitors and Knights. There she had to wake the night guard who assigned her a room for the duration of her stay.

Celina pushed the door open and looked at the room; it wasn't much of a room as to Celina it seemed more like a cell. *'Not like our rooms at Fountain's Abbey,'* she thought. Looking around as she found herself in a plain stone walled room twelve feet by ten. It contained a cot with very little in the way of covers. A chest of drawers and a small table along with a washbasin that was fixed under a tap for cold water, and to make it even worse there was no mirror.

"Well," she said aloud. "I suppose it will do for one night." Returning from the washroom area reserved for ladies, she quickly undressed and slid into bed, shivering in a room that must have been just above freezing. Burrowing down under the thin eiderdown, she reminded herself. "This is how the other half live."

Tuesday 24th December 1861.

I woke with the memory of a strange dream, though it was not disturbing like the other ones. I seem to remember a strange woman who was calling me her daughter. It wasn't my mother though as her hair was a darker red, more like mine. I do remember that she was trying to tell me something, something about my abilities. She wanted to tell me about something here at the Abbey, a warning I think. It was all so confusing but not like the hate and fear of the other dreams. I felt love from her. I think it was very strange, and I hope she comes back.

~~~

Breakfast was better than Celina had expected. Celina found the small refectory for Talents to be pleasantly warmed well-furnished and even a little luxurious. The food was excellent and more than made up for the deficiencies in the rest of the accommodation, and so fortified she headed to the Abbey offices to meet the High Abbot.

It was the Abbot himself who following her knock opened the door, and Celina found he was totally unlike anything she had imagined him to be. For a start, he was younger than she had expected, probably about thirty-five to forty. He was also small and bouncy with a round face topped by a ring of bushy black hair, and to Celina's surprise, he was wearing a monk's habit.

He welcomed Celina into his office with a smile and an elegant wave of his hand. Celina found a woman of about her own age waiting with the Abbot, a woman who Celina recognised as having been at breakfast sitting with an older lady. The Abbot pulling out a chair at the table for her said.

"Lady Celina, I am very pleased to meet you, and I am only sorry it has to be under these unusual circumstances, now let me introduce you to Lady Elizabeth." Celina and Elizabeth touched hands briefly in greeting. "Coffee?" the Abbot asked. As a silver coffee service and cups were already on the table, Celina helped herself as the Abbot said.

"Celina I'm sorry that I had to request your presence on such short notice; I have received a full report from Dr Bird but after what has happened, I still felt we should meet as I would like to hear your side from you personally."

Celina started to explain how after their visit to the shop's owner. Celina then had to stop to explain to the Abbot the reason for the visit to Mrs Allen's, and only then could she continue to describe how they had been walking back for a cab when the attack happened.

The Abbot sat quietly occasionally drumming his fingers on the tabletop until Celina finished her story. Celina waited watching the Abbot as he sat thinking before he said.

"Most unusual and frightening, I will be the first to admit, and as for you being the one it was looking for are you certain of this. After all there hasn't been a demon attack in, oh three hundred years, and apart from that why should you be a target for a demon? Have you any idea?" Celina had to admit that she was completely in the dark as to why she should be its target saying.

"All I can remember was its feeling of elation at having finally found the one it was sent to find."

"Is there any way the feeling could have been directed at your companion?" the Abbot asked.

"No it was definitely directed at me."

"Well is it possible that someone who knows you could have summoned a demon and set it on you?" Before Celina could answer, the Abbot shook his head saying.

"No I can't believe that if they knew you were in London; they could have found you easily. No they wouldn't need a demon to spend weeks looking for you, and apart from that I know of no-one who still knows how to summon a demon so that's not the answer." The Abbot then turned to Elizabeth and said.

"Elizabeth here works as a doctor at St Bartholomew's hospital and her time away from London has to be limited, and so I'll let her tell you what she can, Elizabeth if you would please."

Elizabeth who had been in the process of pouring herself another cup of coffee now began to relate her experience.

"Six months ago I was working one night when just after one in the morning I felt something. I didn't know what at the time, as it was only much later that I found out it could have been an underworld portal that had opened. The feeling was something new to me and very strange. Whatever it was it didn't last long only about two or three minutes, but it was long enough for me to feel its direction.

While it was open, I felt two or possibly three of what I can only describe as ripples. It was hard to tell just how many ripples there were, and it was later that I was told that the ripples could have been something coming through the portal."

She stopped and looked at the Abbot as she said. "I suppose it could also be that two came through and only one went back." Celina was looking at Elizabeth somewhat bemused, and the Abbot seeing Celina's expression explained.

"We have found Elizabeth is very sensitive to changes such as portals opening, and we think she may also be able to sense beings from the underworld, but not having a live one we can't really be sure."

"Yes," Elizabeth said as she turned to Celina. "But having read some more about them, it seems they can either hide from us better than they once did, or else we have lost some of our abilities as I need to be quite close to sense them."

The Abbot looked first at Elizabeth and then at Celina as he said.

"Also very worrisome is that it appears that they may have found a way to come into our world un-summoned." Looking pensive, he said to Celina. "I wonder if one was left in our world, and if so I wonder if it is the one that attacked you."

Neither Celina nor Elizabeth felt they had an answer, both remaining silent as the Abbot poured the last of the coffee for them; after taking a sip the Abbot said.

"I would like you two to work together; Elizabeth has a broom so use your brooms to fly over London and see if you can sense anything. If you do, don't try to deal with it yourself, just try and find its source, and then we can deal with it. Or better still we can keep a watch on it." He took another sip and made a face before he added even more sugar to his coffee.

"It will be better if we can keep them under observation without them knowing it as we may learn more that way. Celina, going back to the attack on you as this worries me a great deal; you say the demon was looking for you?" Celina now beginning to feel she wasn't being taken seriously replied.

"Yes I definitely got the impression it had found the one it was sent to find."

"Why you?" the Abbot asked again. "Why pick you?" he looked at Celina his eyes finding hers as he asked. "Also are you sure you used Merlin's dissipation?"

"As I have said, I have no idea why it was looking for me; I only know that it was, and as for Merlin's dissipation well that's what I tried so I think that must be what I did."

"So," the Abbot summarised. "Not only do we need to know why a demon should be looking for you, but we also need to know how you destroyed a demon using something that has always taken at least three strong talents. I think we shall have to gather our research team to have a word with you about this but not just now."

He then looked sternly at Celina and wagging a finger at her said. "Don't try it again, do you understand?" Then with a smile to take the sting out of his words, he said. "Stay away from demons."

Celina could only say. "I didn't want to try it the first time, and I certainly wouldn't recommend it."

The Abbot leaned back in his chair and looked at the two of them; then after a moment he said. "I have arranged full clearance for you to use the inner library of the Abbey, and there I want you to look at what, and I regret to say what little is known about the underworld and its occupants. I'm sorry it isn't much, but it may help." Then he ended their meeting by saying. "Good luck to you both and good hunting, now off to the library with you."

As the Abbot spoke, he stood to open the door for them. It was as Celina reached the door that she remembered the cabby. Turning back to the Abbot, she said.

"I almost forgot; I've found a family of talents for you." The Abbot stopped and turned towards her saying. "Interesting, a family two or possibly dare I hope for three?"

"Two at least," Celina replied. The Abbot looking pleased asked.

"Does Dickie know yet?"

"He should by now as I've written to him," Celina replied and then asked. "By the way, may I suggest something?"

"Feel free." Celina watched carefully the expression on the Abbot's face as she said.

"It may be we are missing a lot of talent by looking at a small proportion of the population. I think it is a mistake for us to concentrate only on the middle and upper classes of the population, as the families I found are working-class people and the girls have quite a strong talent even untrained as they are."

"Working class?" the Abbot asked thoughtfully. "Well the original Knights were from poor village stock so maybe we should try to remember that. I shall bring it up at the next meeting of the High Abbots, yes you could be right Celina; you could be right." The Abbot then touched their hands and watched as they left walking across the grass.

As they turned towards the refectory, the two women looked at each other as Elizabeth said. "Well Lady Celina, I must admit I am pleased to meet you. You certainly are going to cause a stir what with destroying a real demon, and now finding the Abbot two new Talents."

Celina who had been looking towards the refectory suggested. "I think we should go and have a drink before we visit the library and get to know one another better. I have to say that the Abbot likes his coffee stronger than I do." As she said this Celina gave a shudder at the memory.

Over a pot of tea, Celina and Elizabeth swapped life stories. Elizabeth was surprised to find Celina came from what was said to be the richest family in the land. She laughed to find that Celina was in London incognito and didn't want the fact made public, and in general she found herself liking Celina more and more.

Celina found Elizabeth Gibbard, to be twelve years older than herself, Oxford-trained as a church doctor and that she had been working in London for the last two years. Her ability to sense activity from the underworld had only become apparent about six months ago as Elizabeth explained.

"It was on a Sunday night at around two in the morning while I was attending a rather ill woman. It was something very strong that pulled at me inside my mind; it's hard to describe as I could feel the direction, but at first I didn't know what it meant. It wasn't until I saw a report in the paper about a murder that I worked out it had occurred from the very same direction that I had felt it pulling at me, so I told Dickie a friend of mine."

Celina interrupted her asking. "Do you mean Dr Dickie Bird?"

Elizabeth agreed saying. "Yes I believe you know him."

"I certainly do," Celina said. "He was my teacher and he is still a very close friend."

"Well it was Dickie, who told me it was a wraith and that it had killed a museum guard. At least, that is what we thought then, but we now know differently don't we. Dickie also informed the Abbot, and I've been keeping in touch with them ever since."

Finishing their drinks they made their way over to the Abbey itself and then into the library, and as the Abbot had said, the Abbey library was extensive. However, all that was known of the underworld was on one shelf in a single locked room holding about twenty shelves of books.

Being admitted to this area was a rare occurrence and a privilege, so they both took the opportunity to look up many other things held by the Abbey as secret, or too dangerous for general knowledge.

First however, they took pains to read all they could find on Merlin's dissipation and all other possible means of defence and attack that they could find. As it was they were both sorely disappointed at the availability of any means for defence or for that matter, attack against demons.

"It looks like one demon by itself outnumbers us by at least four to one," was Elizabeth's sobering comment as they continued their search.

The two of them searched through one book after another until Elizabeth reaching the end of another dusty shelf said. "What we have found up to now that is of any worth could be written on the back of a small envelope."

Celina, who had grown more and more despondent as the day wore on, eventually misquoted part of one of her father's sayings, saying to Elizabeth. "We know more about a cold than we know about the underworld."

"The common cold, we know almost nothing about colds," Elizabeth answered.

"That's just what I mean," Celina said as she pushed a large book back on the shelf.

After a day of shuffling old musty books and scrolls on and off shelves, both Celina and Elizabeth felt like they needed a bath, but neither of them felt like experimenting with the antiquated baths of the Knights lodgings. With both being of the same mind, they decided that following an early evening meal in the refectory Celina and Elizabeth would reclaim their brooms and head back to London.

Flying close so their shields could overlap, and they could discuss tactics made it a pleasant flight back to London where a quick spin over the suspect area found nothing, and so it was agreed that unless something happened, they would resume their patrols after Christmas.

It was a very annoyed Jane who greeted Celina's arrival home, complaining to Celina as she racked her broom in the old stables.

"What happened to my Telson call? I've been worried sick and so has the rest of the staff."

"I'm so sorry Jane, but the only Telson is in the Abbot's private rooms and I never had the opportunity to get out of the Abbey, so let me get out of these clothes have a hot bath, and then I will tell you all about it." Jane relented enough to bring a drink up to Celina in the bath and sat on the edge of the bath as she listened to Celina's story.

Wednesday 25th December 1861.

Christmas had arrived, and with all that was and had happened Celina felt unprepared for it. Indeed if it hadn't been for Jane, Celina would have wished it cancelled entirely. As it was Jane had found things on her travels around London that Celina could never have found on her own. She also bought presents for the staff, both at the shop and at the house. Jane had also collected Celina's and her own presents from Marcus and Claire, and so it was that there were presents for all of them to open.

Thankfully, Celina had managed on a last minute impulse to buy a silver hatpin for Jane. It was in the shape of a sword with a jewelled cross guard and pommel. On opening the box Jane just sat and stared for a long moment.

For some reason, the image of a sword resonated in the back of her mind, pulling at her and stirring strange and unknown feelings. Then holding it tightly in her hand, she embraced Celina and as tears threatened in her eyes, she told her. "It's beautiful."

Celina next contacted Claire whose uncle had recently had the Telson installed to wish her and her aunt and uncle a very merry Christmas. She also explained to Claire a little about her sudden visit to the Abbey, and that she was sorry she hadn't been able to get back until late the previous night.

Then it was Claire's turn to tell Celina that a letter had arrived from her parents for her and her aunt and uncle containing some bad news. Her father's tour of duty had been extended, and he was now going to be staying the full two years in Africa instead of the hoped-for original abbreviated tour of duty.

Celina knew Claire was upset as they talked, and also overhearing her later in the shop saying to Jane. "It was not the best Christmas present I could receive, but at least they are safe and well, and that's the most important thing."

Then Celina tried to contact Marcus even going so far as to get Thomas the footman to fire up the steam carriage, whereupon a delighted Thomas was sent around to his address with his present, only to find that he was not at home. Celina reluctantly decided that Marcus would have to wait for his present.

Lord and Lady Carvel arrived in the early hours of the morning of St Stephen's day with presents for the family and staff, along with presents for Jane and Celina from the Coopers. It was literally a flying visit, as Lord Carvel had to be back up north early the following morning.

Friday 27th December 1861.

Celina and Jane arrived early at the shop on Friday morning; Jane was making a drink as Marcus arrived looking very pleased with himself as he offered Celina a cheery.

"Good morning and a belated merry Christmas to you," before he went through into the back room only to find Jane had already made the tea. Picking up two cups, he returned to the office and putting a cup down on the desk, he asked.

"Did you have a nice Christmas?" Celina catching something in his tone of voiced looked up at him as she replied.

"Yes very nice how about you?" Marcus suddenly looked slightly sheepish as he said. "Very nice, I spent it at a friend's parent's house."

Having noticed Marcus's expression Celina now enquired. "Would it be a young lady's house?"

"As it so happens, yes," Marcus replied with a most superior emphasis on the 'Yes.'

"What's this tilting your cap at a young lady?" Jane asked as she stood in the doorway. "Who is she then?"

"Oh a nurse at St Bartholomew's," he replied.

"Come on," Jane prompted. "Who is she and how did you meet her?"

"Well her name's Elizabeth and she's a nurse, and I met her in the tea room across the road a few months ago."

"What's this?" a voice came from within the shop where Claire had entered unnoticed and was now joining the conversation.

"Leave him alone," Celina said seeing Marcus was starting to blush, although a feeling had just materialised in the pit of her stomach as the name caught up with her.

There must be plenty of Elizabeth's at St Bartholomew's, and this Elizabeth couldn't be 'the' Elizabeth Gibbard. After all he'd said she was a nurse not a doctor, and that he'd been to her parents' house. No, it couldn't be the same Elizabeth, of that Celina felt certain.

"I'm sorry I wasn't here before Christmas, as I had to go to the Abbey on urgent business." Celina didn't say more intending them to assume that it was shop business. Then taking two boxes from her bag and handing one to each of them she said. "So here are your presents now." Opening them revealed a bracelet for Claire, and one of the new fountain pens for Marcus.

Saturday 28th December 1861.

Saturday brought a letter from Mrs Allen's solicitor accepting Celina's offer, a letter that Celina immediately passed to Mr Jones and within the week Celina, or rather Fountain's Abbey had become the proud owner of three properties in London.

It was the following week as Celina was serving in the shop, and Marcus was out assisting Jane that Mrs Allen looking much younger and happier came to see her. Taking Celina's hand and with tears in her eyes she said.

"I want to thank you; you have changed my life; I have decided to put the house up for sale, and as you know it's a very large house in extensive grounds, and it's all far too big and costly for me."

She gave Celina a knowing look as she said; "and they tell me it is worth over one thousand five hundred pounds, so I'm moving out of London to my sister's home in Surrey." Celina guided the elderly lady into the office and then personally made a pot of tea, after which she sat while Mrs Allen told her about Mr Simms.

"He arrived the other day with the papers to sign for the contract on the shop, and do you know, he told me how hard it is right now to let property in central London, and how low the rents were.

Then when I said I couldn't sign he was most upset, especially when I said I had sold the properties to an anonymous buyer. Do you know he was really angry, and I thought I was going to have to call a Bobby, but my neighbour's gardener over the road heard him and threw him out for me."

Celina who was having trouble smothering a bit of justified laughter simply said. "It couldn't happen to a nicer person; I should think he's lost at least half his income."

Mrs Allen was very disappointed not to see Marcus, and as she left she was still to Celina's embarrassment thanking her. Later Claire coming into the office asked.

"Was that the old lady who owned the shop?" Still feeling a little embarrassed Celina replied.

"Yes, she wanted to thank us all for helping her."

"Helping her?" Claire asked.

"Yes, I think it was for getting her out of the frugal lifestyle she had fallen into."

Over the next few week's workmen started alterations in the shop, while Celina and Elizabeth continued with their nocturnal patrols. Finally, after two uneventful weeks had passed they decided to wait for further developments. As the days passed the shop settled into a comfortable routine with Jane regularly returning with samples and new ideas.

Jane returning one afternoon with twenty beautifully made Chinese silk and lace fans, saying as she put them on the desk.

"Just look at the quality of these pieces." Marcus picked one up opened it and whistled as he acknowledged.

"That really is well made, and I must admit; it's as good as any I've seen, and the ivory work is exceptional. Where did you find them?"

"I found them in a little workshop run by a Chinese woman on the other side of the river. Her mother makes them, and she sells them to the local shops at three shillings and six pence, so I bought all her stock. I paid her two shillings and nine pence each and promised her that if her mother did us fifty as good as these, then we would buy them all, and that there would be more orders to come."

"They are certainly worth it," Marcus said spreading one to examine the sturdy binding. "I'm sure we could sell these at more than twice that price."

"After I'd seen the fans, she took me to see some other silk products that may be of interest to us when the shop is larger," Celina heard Jane say as she left them to discuss future opportunities while she went back into the shop serving customers with Claire.

Despite the interference of building work to enlarge it the shop continued to prosper while on the demon front, things remained quiet.

Friday 10th January 1862.

Now it is not only Marcus who knows my secret. I'm afraid Claire has also found out and rather dramatically, but now that she knows I think I am relieved. I have done something, something I don't understand.

~~~

Celina had arranged to meet Elizabeth on her afternoon off, and now they had just finished a cold but pleasant walk in Hyde Park discussing the latest developments on the demon situation. As they were about to part Celina asked Elizabeth. "Do you know if anyone has thought to check for manifestations over the rest of the country?"

The question was initially little more than an after-thought but once Celina had said it aloud, she found that it now seemed important.

"Do you know; I don't think anyone has thought of that," Elizabeth replied. "I think you should ask the Abbot." It was approaching closing time for the shop as they parted so as Celina made her way towards Rarities she decided. *'As I'm almost at the shop, I may as well call the Abbot from there.'*

Crossing Church Street, Celina watched as two of the workmen who were working on the shops alterations opened the shop door and walked in. It was as she drew closer that she found the sign on the door had been turned from 'open' to 'closed'.

Inside the shop, Marcus turned as two workmen came in. At first, Marcus took them to be two of the men working on the alterations; however, a moment later he found that he didn't recognise either of them.

Once inside the last man in turned and closed the door, putting the bolts across to lock it before turning the sign on the door from open to closed. Marcus turned back to the first man who had come in with his hands in his jacket pockets, only to find he now stood with a gun in his hand. Claire returning from the back storeroom froze in fright.

"Here you, fill this with the money," the one with the gun said taking a leather bag from his accomplice and thrusting it at Marcus; the other man now moved down the shop and opened one of the display cabinets where he started to fill a second bag with jewellery.

With the gun pointing at him Marcus went to the office and started to fill the bag with the part of the day's takings that were still in the cash box, about six pounds in all. Returning he then gave the bag back to the man. Turning the man thrust the bag towards Claire.

"You, put that silver stuff in as well," he said pointing to the central display cases before pushing the bag into Claire's un-responsive hands. Before Claire could move there was a click from the bolts on the door sliding back, and then the bell jangled as the door opened.

Both men spun around; Claire screamed, and Marcus felt his heart stop as the gun went off pointing directly at the door.

Celina stood in the doorway with her wand in her hand and not six feet from the man with the gun.

Celina could feel the momentary horror in the mans mind at what he had done, and then his relief, as calmly she reached up and took from the air an object that was held immobile not six inches away from her left breast.

Celina's attention was now on the man as she watched the expression of relief quickly turn to face and mind-congealing terror, as his mind registered what his eyes were seeing.

Celina never took her eyes off the man with the gun, as she held the two men frozen, locked in a bind, unable to do more than blink as the door swung closed behind her, and the lock clicked.

Marcus hearing a noise turned to see that Claire, who as white as a sheet had with a bump slumped down on to the floor and now sat there.

At first glance, it seemed to Marcus as if she had fainted, that was until he saw the terror in her eyes as she sat looking at Celina. Turning back to Celina, Marcus found himself grinning like an idiot.

Celina examined the remains of the bullet and then looking at the man standing frozen with the gun still pointing at her said.

"Marcus take that thing off him will you, and then get rid of this, but be careful it's hot." She held out the bullet.

Marcus pulled out his kerchief and took the lump of metal from Celina's fingers, and then taking the gun from the man Marcus turned to Celina, and for the first time looked into her eyes. He was shocked at what he saw, and as he would describe it later. "Her green eyes looked colder than Arctic ice."

"Now," Celina said looking the two men up and down. "What should I do with vermin like you?" Though unable to move themselves, the two men were visibly shaking. Celina looked them up and down again as she walked around them.

"I suppose I could turn you into something rodent like," there was a hesitation and then Celina said, "possibly rats or mice." Celina now walked around them a second time as if deep in thought tapping her wand against the palm of her hand.

Unbidden the vision of a strict schoolmistress came into Marcus's thoughts, one holding a cane in her hand and looking disapprovingly at two naughty boys.

"I wonder if you would like to spend the rest of your life as rats," and then Celina shook her head before saying. "No I don't think so, no, I wouldn't want to inflict something like you on the rodent population." She shuddered and turning to Marcus she asked. "I hate rats don't you?"

"Not the most pleasant of creatures," he replied surprised at how calm his voice sounded. Celina walked around them once more still tapping her wand on the palm of her hand, as Marcus with a twinge of amusement, noticed a dark spreading stain on the front of the gunman's trousers. Celina continuing to walk around them said.

"First I think I shall make sure that neither of you two hangs. You may not thank me now, and you certainly are not going to like what I am going to do to you, but later you may be grateful. Now first I must show you what will happen if you ever think of stealing again."

With a flick of her wand, both men fell to their knees clutching at their heads. The faces of the two men who had been white now lost what little colour that had remained, as with faces contorted in agony they began rolling and twisting on the floor. Their mouths were open as if screaming but not a sound passed their lips.

Marcus himself was now standing ashen-faced while Claire, who still sat on the floor was shaking, and had covered her face with her hands.

Celina snapped her fingers, and the two men ceased moving lying like limp rags on the floor, although Marcus could now hear them moaning.

"Get up," Celina ordered, and then after waiting a moment she said. "I said, get up, now!" The men slowly and shakily rose to their feet.

"Now both of you listen and listen very carefully to what I say. Should you ever think of trying to tell anyone about this…." Celina paused giving each one a look hard enough to break glass. "Or do any acts that will hurt anyone or any of a criminal intent." Each statement was emphasised by sharp prods in their direction with her wand. "Or a dishonest action you now know what to expect." She looked both men full in the face now seeing more than fear there, indeed there was absolute stark terror.

"Next time," she said almost prodding the gunman in the chest with her wand. "The pain, it will last twice as long, and each time it happens it will get longer, now do you understand?" There was a vigorous nodding of heads.

"Now go, and from this day onward, see that you behave." The door then clicked and swung open, it then became a fight as to who could exit the shop first. Marcus watched as the door slammed behind them and locked itself again. He turned back to

Celina as she turned and made her way into the back room, hearing her say.

"Marcus can you help Claire up," and then in a more pleasant voice with what Marcus took to be a slight hint of a laugh she said.

"You had better take Claire into the office and explain while I get us a drink, I think it may come easier from you."

When Celina returned with three cups and a small bottle of brandy, Marcus was still explaining to Claire how Celina had saved their lives that terrible night.

As Celina put the drinks down Claire drew back from her obviously still unsure, so Celina took her drink into the shop leaving them alone. Looking back into the office, she could see Claire still looking fearfully at her. *'Well,'* she thought; *'I might as well do it my way now.'*

Taking out her wand, she first put a blind* on the window and door making it so no one would want to see in, or if they did look, they would see only the normal shop.

Then she started replacing stock back in its place the easy way. Marcus seeing the expression on Claire's face stopped his story for a moment to look. Then with a big smile he turned back and continued his tale but now with many an enjoyable glance through the office window.

It didn't take long to replace all the stock back in its respective showcases,"

Celina deliberately made a show of it with a cup of brandy in one hand and her wand in the other, walking around the shop, and flicking things into place with a flourish.

Finally, sheathing her wand Celina picked up the two bags and returned to the office, saying as she put the two bags on the desk.

"I think we may show a profit on this little episode," prodding the bags with her wand. Claire, who still looked to be very nervous, was now looking at her wand with big round eyes.

*Blind or blind block as used by Celina. Thought by Celina to be a form of leaning suggesting to an observer to see what the observer would expect to see rather than what was really there.

"Is it true you're a real witch?" she asked tearing her eyes off the wand to look at Celina.

"We prefer to be known as Knights of the Church," Celina replied and then asked. "Has Marcus told you anything about our history?"

Claire shook her head, so Celina recited the history of how the Knights of the Church came into existence. Claire sat and thought deep and so long that Celina could almost see the wheels turning in her mind until Claire eventually asked. "You're not evil then?"

"No under oath we cannot harm a person in any way."

"What about what you did to those men, didn't you hurt them?" Claire asked. Celina shaking her head replied.

"Hurt, no I just put the idea into their minds, and their imagination did the rest; they hurt because they expected to be hurt but I in no way harmed them, in fact I may have saved their lives."

"Saved their lives, how?" Claire asked.

"If it had been you walking into the shop you would have died from their gunshot, and then they would have committed murder, which is a capital offence." Claire sat thinking. *'Here it comes any time now.'* Celina thought.

"Could you really change them into rats?" Claire asked. Celina shook her head as she replied. "No, though sometimes and with some people I wish I could."

It was then that Claire's curiosity overcame her as she blurted out.

"Do you dance at the full moon, you know how I mean?" Celina laughed out loud but not at Claire's question. She had been watching Marcus for his reaction before replying.

"No it would be too cold most of the year, and it would serve no purpose."

Claire looked sheepishly up at Celina and said. "I'm sorry; I shouldn't have asked that."

"Most women do." and then looking at Marcus Celina said. "Men usually ask if we ride a broomstick."

Marcus looked startled and confused as he said. "I never thought of that." and then he asked. "Do you; I mean have a broomstick?"

"Yes I do fly a broom," and then with a smile in Claire's direction. "I usually wear rather warm clothing and a hat, and I must say not a pointed one either, and as for my broom, it looks nothing like a sweeping broom. You certainly wouldn't get far cleaning with it."

"Is it true about the other night?" Claire asked.

"Yes I'm sorry to say that it is." Celina replied. That night as Jane was seeing to her hair, Celina said.

"Jane I'm worried; something happened today that I don't understand." Celina then told Jane about the entire attempted robbery, including what she had done to the two men, and finally said.

"Jane I put an idea into those two men's heads, and then I made it happen." Celina took Jane's hand as she said. "I don't know how I knew how to do it. Jane, it was just there in my head; I had no idea what to do with those two men, and suddenly I found myself doing this to them."

Jane sat thinking and then said. "It must be something you either read or heard at some time. What about what you looked through at the Abbey. Do you know what I think, I think you probably just glanced over it and then forgot it until today?"

Celina knew Jane was wrong; she knew she had never read anything like that or about what she had done to hide her activity in the shop as she replaced the displays after the robbery, still feeling even more puzzled a worried Celina decided to put them out of her mind.

The following afternoon Claire finding Celina sitting in the office, decided that now was the time to ask certain questions, woman-to-woman. Her questions were about things that she and Marcus had discussed while Celina had been out for her lunch.

Celina who had been sitting thinking over Jane's suggestion about what she had done to the two men had finally concluded that it just didn't fit. Celina having thought long and hard about it was certain she had never ever heard or read of any of these things. Then seeing Claire approaching the office, she decided. *there is nothing more I can do about it for now.'*

184

Claire entered the office, and Celina waved her to the chair saying.

"Please sit down, as I have the feeling you want to talk to me or perhaps ask me something." Claire was taken by surprise; so much so that the questions she had wanted to ask went right out of her head. Instead, she found herself asking the first thing that came into her mind.

"Can you read my mind?" Then blushing Claire quickly said. "I'm sorry." Celina interrupted her saying.

"No I did not read your mind, but I can sense when someone has something on his or her mind, or if they are disturbed.

What I sense are their emotions and feelings not their thoughts. I can also tell if a person truly believes what they are saying, or if what they are saying is not necessarily true. Actual thought though is difficult, and not always possible."

Claire paused for a moment considering Celina's reply and then said.

"What about those two men, you said you couldn't harm them but what if they…." She stopped.

"Like I said," Celina almost broke talent protocol by taking Claire's hand. "I cannot cause permanent harm to anyone even if I wanted to. The oath I took at sixteen when I became a Knight will not let me; it's not a choice that I can make. I gave them the idea of pain and because they expected to feel pain they felt pain, but I did it only to stop them from being hurt later.

"If he had shot at you, you would probably have died. Then the men would have been hanged. Which is worse a little pain in the head or actual death?"

Saying all this brought back to Celina that nagging little worry of where she had gained that knowledge of how to do what she had done. She pushed it out of her mind as Claire pondered over what she had heard until eventually she said.

"Yes, I think I understand, but you can make people do things?"

"Nothing they wouldn't normally do, I can sort of nudge or push someone or persuade is perhaps the better word to do something or not do something, but I can't make someone do or not do something totally against their wishes or nature. Those two men somewhere had some good in them, so I just let it take over."

Having heard this and with a shy smile Claire asked. "Can you really fly; I mean on a broomstick?" Then with a changed and softer expression on her face, she said. "It must be wonderful?"

"Yes I can, and it is wonderful." A calm and distant expression now came briefly over Celina's face as she said. "On a night high above the clouds with the moonlight lighting the tops of them.... well it's like another world. Someday if we can I will take you and show you." Claire stood to go and with a look of relief clearly showing on her face, she said.

"Thank you, I feel a lot better now." As Claire turned to go Celina said.

"Ask me anything if you need to, both you and Marcus as it's going to be a lot easier for me now that you know my 'secret'."

More than anything that had been said, it was the lingering memory of Celina's expression as she described flying above the clouds that reassured Claire.

Tuesday 14th January 1862.

<u>Jane.</u>

Jane had heard just the day before that the Chinese lady had finished the fans, and they were now ready to be delivered after payment, or picked up with payment. Having finished her morning tea Jane picked up her case and set off on her rounds, calling out to Marcus as she left the office.

"Will it be all right if I see you about two this afternoon?" Celina looked from Jane to Marcus and back to Jane again as Marcus replied.

"Yes I would think that would give us plenty of time."

"Sorry," Jane said. "I forgot to tell you that the Chinese fans are ready to be picked up, and Marcus said he would come along as a pack mule." Celina was delighted saying.

"They're ready then are they? Well it's about time; I am really looking forward to seeing these incredible fans."

Jane arrived back at Rarities just after two in the afternoon, and then with Marcus in tow she set of across London, Marcus found it was a good hour's walk to what turned out to be a house in an older part of London. It was a small house situated in an area of narrow winding streets and overhanging roofs that in its day had been an area of shops and drinking houses. Now it was a home to part of London's large immigrant population.

A small Chinese lady opened the door to Jane's knock greeting them with a traditional Chinese bow, to which Marcus automatically replied in a like manner. It was as the woman spoke to them in a mixture of mostly Chinese, and a little English that Marcus found to his surprise that he understood some of the words, and in broken Chinese, he haltingly asked her where she originally came from.

Her face lit up, and a stream of words followed. Marcus stood there listening understanding about one word in ten. At last she slowed down, and Marcus repeated his question in English, explaining that he knew only a little of her language.

Her reply this time came at a much slower pace and then with many repeats she told him how she came from a little village on the outskirts of Shanghai.

From then on Jane was left out of most of the conversation. A conversation conducted in a mix of Chinese and English. Later and to the delight of Marcus, they were served with tea and food in the traditional Chinese style.

To Marcus, the afternoon's visit brought back pleasant memories of his office and his staff, and then later as they were about to leave, to his surprise and pleasure the lady invited him to call back any time he was in the area, saying that he could practice his Chinese.

By the time they left it was early evening, and walking back towards the river with the only light coming from the occasional nearby window, or the odd torch outside a drinking establishment, the road was dark and forbidding. They had almost reached London Bridge when three men wielding lengths of wood blocked their path.

"Well what have we here, I be a thinking we've caught a couple of right toffs," a big thickset man in the middle sneered. Then on his right, a little skinny man with a broken toothed grin said.

"Let's be a looking at your pretty jewellery me pretty lady, and what's you have in that pretty little bag." He then raised his cudgel and for emphasis smacked it in the palm of his hand; while the one on the left sidled up toward Marcus, menacingly swinging his cudgel like a police constable would his baton. Once more Marcus wished he had the gun he normally carried when abroad.

"Let's have a look in the box then," the big man said as he moved toward Marcus. The man after Jane's jewellery tried to look menacing by lifting his cudgel as he stepped forward, and in doing so bringing him within reach of Jane's hands.

Catching the man by surprise Jane's left hand flashed out and grabbed the cudgel, pulling it and him towards her. At the same time, lunging forward herself, she plunged her right fist full into his face.

Marcus said later that he had heard the crunch of breaking bones as blood splattered and the man went over backwards, falling to the ground where he sprawled full length in the road making strange noises, and with blood running across his face onto the cobbles.

Jane was now left with a weapon; holding it like a broadsword in both hands, she turned towards the big man who raised his lump of wood and made a wild swing at her.

There was a crack like a pistol shot when the two pieces of wood met as Jane, without loosing her momentum turned with the swing ducked beneath his arm and then brought the back end of her cudgel down and around, pushing it deep into the man's stomach. He doubled over as Jane continued twisting her body out of his way. Then straightening up she felled him as she brought the cudgel hard down on the back of his head.

The third man seeing the plight of his two friends decided to forget about Marcus's box and took off at a run. All this left Marcus standing open-mouthed and looking at the carnage on the road. One man was now kneeling dripping blood from a crushed nose into a rapidly spreading pool on the ground, while the other one lay unconscious on the cobbles making strange wheezing sounds.

Marcus looked across at Jane where she stood prodding the one lying in the road with her foot.

"Remind me never to upset you," he said and then asked. "Where did you learn all that?"

"From my older brothers," Jane replied and then looking around she said. "There may be others, come on let's get away from here."

Jane dropped the cudgel and looking at her hand said. "God I think I may have broken my hand."

With Jane supporting her hand they hurried on their way over the river. It was as they crossed the bridge that a stray thought ran through Jane's head. *I've done it again; I've rescued a little boy; well maybe not so little. Why is it always me?'*

The shop was closed when they arrived, but a light on in the office indicated that someone was still there. In fact, both Celina and Claire were in the office when Marcus opened the door. Once inside the office Marcus breathed a sigh of relief as he put the box down, having found it had grown steadily heavier all the way back.

"Well let's have a look at them," Claire said as she opened the box, and then taking out several of the fans she flicked one open. The silk and needlework really was beautiful.

"Oh they are wonderful," Claire exclaimed turning one and fanning herself as Celina asked.

"What kept you, we were getting worried?" Jane in mock disgust said.

"Our seasoned traveller here knows the area our Chinese lady comes from," and then with a sidewise nod towards Marcus. "He speaks the language." Then holding out her hand she said. "Celina have a look at my hand, I think I may have broken it."

"You've what…. broken it? How did you do that?" Celina asked.

"It was a street brawl." Marcus said quickly jumping in with his reply. "I've never seen anything like it, well not since that fracas in a street market in Cairo, Jane was brilliant." Celina looked at Jane asking.

"All right what happened?"

189

"Nothing much," Jane replied with a shrug, "just three ruffians who wanted the box."

"Nothing much, she was almost as good as…." Marcus paused and then said. "Well like I said she was brilliant. I've not seen a punch like the one she threw since, since, and fencing she fences like…."

Marcus suddenly stopped as he looked from one to the other. Claire already looked shocked and had turned quite pale; but to Marcus's surprise, Celina hadn't turned a hair.

"Brawling again is it?" Then she laughed and said. "Marcus you should know there's more to our Jane than meets the eye. You may not believe it but her brothers lived in fear of her punch, and if ever you need a Shire horse shod, Jane here is your woman. I would say she's almost as good a blacksmith as her father.

There's many a time I've seen her with a horse's hoof between her knees hammering the nails in, not to mention sorting the village lads out." This time it was Marcus who looked bewildered.

"A blacksmith?" he asked incredulously looking at Jane. Jane shrugged and said.

"Well I used to help my father."

"I don't think it's broken," Celina finally said letting go of her hand. "It's just complaining a bit; next time don't hit as hard."

Later that evening a call came for Celina on the Telson. Elizabeth had sensed something that could be a portal opening saying to Celina. "If it is a portal its open now, so can you meet me at the usual place?"

"I'll be there in ten minutes," Celina replied. On her arrival Celina swung her broom across to fly alongside Elizabeth's.

"It's still open and in that direction." Elizabeth said pointing northwest over London, "possibly about a mile or slightly more." Together they cruised over the dark streets straining to see anything suspicious. It was as they crossed over a small park that Elizabeth called.

"We've passed it." Turning her broom, Elizabeth looked down into the darkness below saying. "It's in that park," and then swinging her broom down low over the trees she called out.

"It's somewhere near that building." Elizabeth was pointing at the small bandstand in the centre of the park. Celina swung her broom around having a look at the ground below as she circled back to Elizabeth to say.

"We could land there by those trees." Celina pulled her broom around in a slow circle until she finally dropped to the ground in front of a group of trees and waited still mounted as Elizabeth landed.

"Here put the brooms under the trees," Celina said as she turned her broom to point away from the bandstand and towards an open space. "That way if we need them in a hurry they'll be easy to get at."

The two moved nearer the dark and uninviting bandstand until crouching down in the shrubs by the side of the path they waited.

Celina was very much aware of her heart beating and the hollow feeling in her stomach, as peering between the shrubs, she could see that the far side of the bandstand seemed to have a faint red tinge to the woodwork. Celina pointed saying.

"Look over there; do you see where it's red? Come on let's get closer." Keeping off the gravel path and with the low-growing shrubs between them and the bandstand, they worked their way around. As they rounded the curve in the path, what started out as a dull red oval slowly turned into a circle. Celina estimated it to be about eight feet across and about a foot or so above the bandstand's wooden floor.

For a moment, they just stood looking until Celina said. "Come on we need to be closer," cautiously they climbed up the steps into the bandstand. As they reached the bandstand's floor Celina pulled her wand from the sheath on her belt and let it lock itself to the wand safe.

"Is that it?" Elizabeth asked taking out her own wand.

"You tell me, you're the one who can sense them," Celina replied as she moved so she could see through the circle.

"Look is that sand, red sand?" Elizabeth asked pointing at what looked like a desert of red sand visible through the circle.

Celina couldn't speak; she felt as if ice was running through her veins and goose bumps now covered her skin. Looking through the circle, she knew that desert landscape and that red sky. Oblivious to Celina's shock Elizabeth was saying.

"It looks like a desert, all rocks and sand, and that sky just look at it." The sky was dark red and though no stars were visible, it still gave the impression of being the night. Something like a moon but twice the size and with no visible features hung just above the horizon. Celina having recovered from her shock moved closer and said.

"It's hot, just feel that wind. Elizabeth came up beside her and nodded asking.

"Is it Hell do you think?"

"I don't know but if it is, where are all the souls in torment? All I can hear is that wind, but it certainly seems hot enough." A gust of hot dry air smelling strongly metallic blew around them.

"What's that?" Celina asked pointing at two rods stuck in the sand forming a V, while on the top ends of the rods there was what appeared to be a five-pointed crystal star split down the middle. It looked to Celina as if a sharp knife had cut it through from top to bottom, and then possibly right down the centre of a single rod leaving the two halves of the crystal spaced about three feet apart.

"It's coming back," Elizabeth hissed. Celina looked in the direction Elizabeth had turned asking.

"How far away is it?"

"A hundred yards or may be a bit less, it's over that way." Elizabeth pointed toward the dark outline of London's buildings, where in the dark a shape could now be seen approaching. It was definitely a demon shape. Quickly turning they both ran down the steps and hid in between the shrubs.

As it came closer Celina could see it was smaller than the one that had attacked her, perhaps seven or eight feet high, and that it had something clutched in its hand, something about the size of a small saucer. Holding it close to its body it ran up the three steps into the bandstand, hesitated and then giving a curious little jump it leapt into the circle.

As the two stood looking the demon ran to the rods in the sand. It did not cross in front of them but took obvious care to go around them where it placed the object it had been carrying carefully down on the sand. Standing and putting a hand either side of the V it then proceeded with some effort to push the arms of the V together. As it did so, the circle shrank until it was gone.

The two looked at each other as Celina said. "I think the Abbot had better know about this tonight don't you?" Then as they made their way towards their brooms, Celina asked. "Are you coming?"

"It's three hours to the abbey," Elizabeth said as she floated her broom clear of the trees.

"Well we can leave your broom at the shop, I can fly faster than you do and I can manage it there in a lot less time than that."

It was only minutes later, two brooms dropped down into the yard at the back of Rarities. Then with Elizabeth having tucked her broom up close to the wall she climbed onto the front seat of Celina's broom. Seated there Celina insisted that she fasten the safety strap before she lifted the broom above the rooftops. Above the rooftops, Celina pointed the broom at an angle upwards and southwest, and then throwing her shield forward she pushed hard.

Elizabeth had never experienced anything like it as the acceleration pushed her back into the seat, and the wind whistled around Celina's shield as London became a blur under them. At one point, a terrified Elizabeth found herself screaming as they hurtled toward what looked like a solid wall but turned out to be just clouds. Then almost before Elizabeth knew it, they were through.

Once above the clouds speed ceased to have any meaning as they found a clear starlit night with just a few high clouds well above them. It was a little over two hours later when they again dropped below the clouds to find the guide-light on the towers of the abbey in front of them. Celina circled looking for and finding the High Abbot's lodgings where she dropped quickly down to land outside them.

Elizabeth slowly climbed off the broom, and pulling off her hat, she turned to look at Celina and asked.

"On the way back can I ride the back seat, and can we go slower? Hurtling through the clouds at that speed does nothing for my bladder. I hope he's in; I need the closet." With a quiet chuckle, Celina knocked on the Abbot's door.

The Abbot himself in his dressing gown opened it, blinking sleep from his eyes as he stared at his unexpected visitors before asking.

"Celina, Elizabeth has something happened?" then quickly saying. "Come in come in." Once through the door Elizabeth having asked the Abbot for directions to the outside closet took a candle and left, leaving Celina to recount the happenings of that night.

"So it looks as if our worst fears are true," the Abbot said looking worried. "If they can now cross into our world un-summoned then we are in grave danger." Elizabeth returning and taking a seat asked.

"Did Celina tell you the demon brought something back and took it through the portal?"

"Yes, and it's a pity we don't know whether it carried it with it when it came or obtained it here."

Elizabeth hearing this looked across to Celina for support before saying. "To me it looked like an object about the size of a small saucer." Celina agreed as she said.

"I think it could be a piece of jewellery, possibly a bracelet or large brooch or something of that description." Then remembering her discussion with Elizabeth in the park Celina asked. "Do you know if anything was stolen at the other murder scenes?"

The Abbot looked pensive as he answered. "I haven't heard but I will find out in the morning." Celina then asked.

"Have the murders or portals been confined to just London? There haven't been any other strange happenings in other parts of the country have there?"

"Again I will have to make some enquiries and I will let you know." The Abbot sat drumming his fingers on the table thinking before saying. "I find the idea of jewellery intriguing." The Abbot rose and crossed to his collection of books; looking along the shelves at them, he took one out. He then leafed through the pages until he finally found what he was looking for before he passed the book over to Celina and Elizabeth.

Together the two women read from the book. It was a section on the Stars of Destiny, or as they were alternatively known, The Jewels of death. Celina started to read the descriptions aloud.

"A belt buckle or clasp shaped as a five-pointed gold star having a ruby on each of the points of the star. Combined with five other objects these being in order of size, a clasp, a bracelet, a brooch, a pendant, and a finger ring. All are made in gold, and all have five rubies on the five points of a pentagram. It is said that if all of them are brought together at the right time and the right place," she turned the page. "That it will bring the end of the world," she looked up at the Abbot.

"Please continue," he said.

"The clasp being the largest is the best known of these," Celina looked up at the Abbot and then read on. "It has been in the possession of the church for many years. All the rest of the items have been lost and found many times over the centuries. A seventh item has been mentioned, the Ring of Blood, but it has never been found and is thought not to exist. How they all fit together is not known." She stopped and looked up at the Abbot.

"You don't think, do you?" Celina began and then fell silent as the Abbot said.

"I don't know, but what I do know is that the items we possess have been kept separated and under lock and key for many years."

"I wonder, do you know how many murders there have been?" Elizabeth asked.

"Twelve, I do know that; now are you staying the night at the Abbey?"

"No we have to get back," Celina replied.

"Well then you must have a hot drink before you go just to fortify you on your journey." He gave Elizabeth a wink. "I know how Celina flies."

"Well," Celina said indignantly. "I fly as well as anyone."

"Faster than most I should think but not as fast as others," the Abbot said with a further wink at Elizabeth.

The quick drink turned into a night long discussion over several drinks before they set off on their return journey.

Wednesday 15th January 1862.

The sky hadn't yet started to lighten in the east as Celina lifted her broom and turned towards London, saying. "I'm sorry but I will have to push hard if we're going to get home for breakfast, will you be all right?"

"I think so," was the uncertain reply from the back seat so Celina again pushed hard and flew fast. It was just before eight with the sky starting to show some light over London when Celina dropped into the back of the shop.

"Do you want to leave your broom here for now?" Celina asked. "I have a room that we can put it in, and then you can collect it tonight."

"I think that would be best. I don't want to start rumours about witches now do I?" Elizabeth said laughing as she said it.

Opening the back door into the storeroom Celina said. "Let's get it inside then before my manager arrives, though he shouldn't be here for at least half an hour yet." Between them, they started to manoeuvre Elizabeth's broom through the back storeroom and towards the private storeroom. They had managed to get it as far as the passage and had just decided that it wouldn't make the turn into the storeroom door as the shop door opened and Marcus walked in.

Seeing Celina he said. "Good morning Celina." Then before he could say more Elizabeth had turned and exclaimed. "Marcus!"

Marcus in the process of taking off his gloves looked up in surprise and said. "Elizabeth, what are you doing here?" Then his eyes took in the strange object in the passage. Finally leaning back against the wall he asked.

"Is that a broom?" Elizabeth just looked at Marcus without answering until Marcus said. "You two know each other." It was only then that Celina remembered what Marcus had said after Christmas.

"This is your Elizabeth?" she asked him. Marcus ignoring the question and pointing at Elizabeth said.

"You didn't tell me you were a witch," before quickly saying. "I'm sorry a Knight of the Church." Elizabeth looked from Marcus to Celina as she asked. "He knows about us?"

"He does," Celina admitted. "He was the one who was with me when the demon attacked me. I'm sorry Elizabeth; I think I must be tired and not thinking, there was no reason at all for us to struggle moving the broom as we could have left them both in the yard. Give me a hand please Marcus."

Marcus looked back at Elizabeth and then rather gingerly as if he was expecting something to happen, he took hold of one end of the broom and with Celina's help returned it to the yard. Returning to the storeroom, they found Elizabeth sitting at the table and not looking at all happy. Looking up at Marcus, she asked.

"Does it make any difference me being what I am?" Celina caught the sound of a plea in her voice.

"It doesn't to me does it to you?" Marcus asked. "I have no problem with you being a Knight of the Church. In fact," he said almost coming to attention. "I'm proud to know that you are."

The bell on the front door rang as Claire came in prompting Celina to exclaim. "Is everyone going to be early today?"

Claire stopped in the doorway looking at the group in the storeroom. Celina pulled two chairs out from the table and pushed one in Claire's direction before sitting down herself and saying.

"Hello Claire, this is Elizabeth a friend of Marcus, oh and by the way; she's a witch." Then looking across at Elizabeth, she amended her statement to, "sorry a Knight of the Church."

Elizabeth looked even more shocked as she asked. "Does everyone here know?"

"Well it's hard to keep it a secret when you work so closely with people." Celina replied, and then without getting up or even looking; Celina lit the gas ring causing Claire to jump slightly. Marcus stopped looking for the Lucifer's and put the kettle he had filled on the gas ring to boil.

Over a drink of tea, the two Knights told the story of their night's adventures. They told of how they had flown nightly over London without success until last night.

Marcus was very interested in the description of what for want of a better word was described as Hell had actually looked like. Some of the many questions that followed were whether it was night or day. Or for that matter, was there even such a thing as night and day, and if it was daylight was the daylight normally very dim, and what was causing the metallic taste to the air? Could the red sand have been rust, and how big had the object been that the demon had carried until Celina called a halt saying? "It's time the shop was open."

Claire who had remained very quiet throughout the story of the star of death rose and went to change the sign on the door, and open the shop. When she returned she was carrying an old book on the occult.

Sitting in the office and leafing through the pages, she found what she was looking for. It was a detailed drawing of what had been named the Jewels of Death, showing all six and giving a history right up to 1735 when the book had been published. It even mentioned the curse supposedly placed on them by an ancient god after they were stolen from him.

There were also stories of how they had been seen on and off since ancient times, and always with fatal results for their owner. The author then cited various tales of the gruesome deaths of the owners. In the last paragraph, there was a mention of the Ring of Blood, and the fact that it had never been proven to exist.

It was at this point Claire threw a very disturbing possibility into the discussion by asking.

"What if the reason that the Ring of Blood has never been found is that the demons already have it, and have had it for centuries?" Everyone went quiet after that. Then the doorbell jangled causing Claire to jump again.

"I'll go," she said getting up quickly.

The man waiting in the shop wasn't old but his hair was totally white. The two of them spoke for a few minutes, and then Claire shook her head. A few more words were exchanged before Claire returned to the office to ask Celina.

"Have you ever heard of 'The Book of Days,' supposedly written by Merlin?" Celina and Elizabeth risked a quick look at the man then at each other.

"I'll see to him," Celina said as she rose and went into the shop with a cheery. "Good morning, I understand you are looking for a copy of 'The Book of Days?" The man slowly nodded his head.

"Yes have you heard of it?" he asked.

"Yes I do know of it, but I understand it's very hard to obtain." Then Celina hesitated, feeling a shiver run up her back along with a growing reluctance to say more and ended up by saying. "I could get hold of a copy for you, but it would be expensive and possibly take some weeks."

"I'm prepared to wait and the price," he shrugged, "is of no consequence." The feeling was back; Celina hesitated again wondering just how much to tell him. Finally, she decided and said. "You do know that there are only twenty copies from the sixth century in existence?"

"Yes I have been told that," he acknowledged. Celina considered her next words carefully before asking.

"Do you also know that no two are alike, and that they all have differences on almost every page?" His gaze had been moving slowly around the shop but now his head came sharply around to look at Celina as he asked.

"Every one is different; surely there must be an original?"

"There may be but which one is the original? Apart from the damage they have suffered over the years they are all the same age and look the same, yet they all have differences in what they say."

He looked at Celina for a moment and then abruptly as if having just made a decision he said. "I will have to have words with my master about this; you have my thanks." Turning sharply he walked out of the shop.

Celina watched him go and then returned to the others who she found were still discussing demons. Elizabeth turned to Celina and asked.

"What did he want with The Book of Days?"

"I don't really know," Celina replied looking through the office window into the shop. "He was very deadpan, no expression at all, and he didn't seem to know an awful lot about it. I believe he was shocked when I told him of the twenty books that exist that there are no two the same. Then he wanted to know about the original."

"Did you tell him?" Elizabeth asked.

"What that even the one thought to be the original one may be a copy? No I didn't." Celina looked back into the shop as she said. "I don't know why, but somehow talking about it, well it just didn't seem right."

"So what did he say then when you told him?" Elizabeth asked. Celina still looking into the shop, and with a puzzled frown replied.

"He said something very strange; he said he was going to have to have words with his master. To me, he looked more the master type than a servant."

Celina sat down and feeling a shiver run up her spine again looked into the shop as she said. "I don't know why but he sent a shiver up my spine, and there's something about him that I don't like." Celina turned back to the others as Marcus asked her.

"What is this Book of Days or shouldn't I ask?"

"No there's no real secret about it, it is a book that Merlin supposedly wrote before he disappeared. When the Abbey eventually had it copied, they found that though the scribes claimed that they had faithfully copied it every copy they had was transcribed somewhat differently.

The strangest thing is that after they had finished the copying no-one knew which one was the original. Anyway, after a lot of arguments it was decided that the one with marks on the pages was the original, so that one was kept in the Abbey's library."

"Have you read it?" Claire asked.

"Oh yes my father has two copies, and one copy that he had made that has been fully translated into English. Some Talents say Merlin was the most powerful Talent ever, while others having read the Book of Days say he was not." There was silence until Elizabeth with a yawn said.

"Well powerful or not I don't know, but me; I'm going to bed for an hour or two." Then turning to Marcus she asked. "Will I see you on Sunday?"

"I don't see why not," Marcus replied. "By the way, what will your mother and father say about me knowing that you are a Knight of the Church?" With a laugh, Elizabeth replied.

"Mother will be relieved as she's talented herself, and father he will probably be pleased to have someone to discuss us with."

Having seen Elizabeth on her way home in a cab Celina stayed another hour explaining to Marcus and Claire about the two brooms in the back. Claire was more than a little disappointed that they didn't look like the witch's brooms of stories, but as Marcus said.

"Think about it Claire, how would you feel after sitting on a one-inch thick stick for any length of time, and would you ride it side saddle or astride?" Claire didn't take much convincing that something truly resembling an ordinary broom would not only be uncomfortable but also unworkable.

Celina returned home to be chastised by Jane about being gone all night without leaving word. Then after a late breakfast that was really more of a lunch where Jane heard all about the night's happenings Celina decided a little sleep was in order.

It was a shorter sleep than Celina would have liked as it was interrupted by a call from the Abbot asking if she could return that evening along with Elizabeth. Also that she would be required to stay overnight and possibly the following night. Celina asked Jane to pack a bag for her while she took a bath to help wake herself up.

Celina, who had been brooding about what she had seen the previous night; and how it had matched what she had seen in her recent dreams, sat watching Jane as she packed her clothes for her. Celina eventually halted Jane's packing as she said.

"Jane about those dreams I have been having." Jane who had been sorting Celina's nightwear turned sharply as the tone of Celina's voice began ringing alarm bells.

"I've seen it," Celina said. "I've seen the actual place, and it's Hell."

"Seen it, seen what?" Jane asked as she pushed the bag aside and sat beside Celina on the bed listening.

"Last night when we found the portal it was open and we could see through it. There was all this red sand, a whole desert of red sand and a red sky just like in my dreams."

Jane didn't know what to say as she sat wondering how Celina could dream about a place she had never seen.

"Are you sure that it is the place that you dreamed about, and it is Hell?" Celina shrugged as she said.

"Well it's hot and there was a hot dry wind blowing from it through the portal, and you could hear something a sort of moaning. Either souls in torment or possibly just the wind blowing, I don't know." Then she paused before she asked. "Jane how could I dream about a place I have never seen?" Jane was silent for a moment then she asked.

"What did the Abbot say?"

"I never told him, I didn't even tell Elizabeth. Jane I'm frightened, what have I done to them for them to want me dead?" Jane put her arm around Celina only to find Celina shaking.

"I don't know, but I do know this…. You destroyed a demon and that is something no other Talent has ever done alone, and since then I have a feeling that you have become even more powerful and better able to defend yourself. I think the demons should be more afraid of you than you need to be of them. Now let's get you dressed."

For a moment Celina felt comforted by Jane's words, but then Jane broke the feeling by saying. "I'm sorry Celina, but I have a bad feeling about this meeting. Somehow I think it means trouble."

Jane's words sent a shiver down Celina's spine as she said. "Well I shall know by tomorrow, or the day after and then I can tell you."

Elizabeth's house on the outskirts of London took some finding in the rain, and with open fields to the back the unbroken wind made landing in the dark difficult. Racking her broom, Celina knocked on the door.

The man who opened it looked startled to see a young woman in a heavy overcoat standing there; recovering he called out. "Sally I think it's for you."

"No Mr Gibbard, I'm Celina, and I need to see Elizabeth." Just then a woman appeared behind Mr Gibbard, who introduced herself as Elizabeth's mother and said.

"You must be Celina, if you want Elizabeth I'm afraid she has been called urgently to the hospital." Disappointed Celina apologised saying. "I'm sorry to have disturbed you at this time of the night; I'll let you go in as its cold."

Celina mounted her broom and then throwing a shield in front of the broom against the wind and rain; she lifted the broom to clear the hedge, and as Elizabeth's parents watched Celina turned the broom, pointed the front up toward the clouds and then pushed.

Until Celina cleared the clouds, she was flying blind as the rain was a solid wall in front of her shield, but once above the clouds Celina found the stars were like diamonds and flying became a joy again.

When Celina arrived at the Abbey, the novice taking charge of her broom directed her directly to the Abbots lodgings, saying that the abbot was expecting her. Celina found the Abbot waiting for her and as the refectory had closed at eight, she welcomed his offer of a hot drink. It also gave her chance to air Claire's theory about the missing jewels.

After Celina had left, saying to the Abbot. To claim her cell, it was a very worried Abbot who retired to bed. He took with him a large drink of brandy expecting a troubled and sleepless night thinking over what he knew, what Celina suspected, and in dread of what tomorrow's meeting might bring.

Celina booked in for a cell, opening the door and looking in she murmured. "It hasn't got any better." Quickly undressing and once in her nightclothes Celina dived shivering into the cot, pulling the blankets and eiderdown up around her chin.

Polly

After three days in the cellar, the afternoon's sunlight in the orphanage yard was blinding. Polly stumbled as the chains wrapped around her ankles caught on the step, and she would have fallen if Mr Jackson hadn't taken hold of a hand full of her hair and pulled her back to her feet. Then delivering a slap across the back of her head that caused her to stumble again, he said.

"They're here to take you to be burnt witch." Polly squinting in the bright sunlight could see a large box on wheels at the gate, and a man dressed in black taking a large padlock from the door at the back. Polly in desperation looked across the yard to see the watching girls, most of whom were crying, but two who were standing with a small girl, and seeing Polly looking their way nodded before each deliberately placed a hand on the girl's shoulders.

Another push sent Polly staggering towards the box, again almost falling beneath the weight of the chains around her ankles and wrists. Mr Jackson taking hold of her picked her up and roughly bundled her through the door and into the box before slamming the door. Polly winded lay on the rough floor in the dark as she heard the padlock snap and the key turn, followed by Mr Jackson laughing as he called through the door.

"Burn witch, go burn in Hell," and then with a jerk the box started to move.

Polly was startled to find light flooding into the box, and looking up; she saw a dark-haired woman in green removing the wooden boards from the windows. Hearing a sob, she turned to see on seats either side of the box were two more women both dressed in black.

Thursday 16th January 1862.

My flight home this evening was drastically interrupted, and I again came close to losing my life. I wish I knew why I have been singled out like this, and I must admit I'm starting to feel frightened.

~~~

After a good breakfast, Celina reported to the Abbot whose secretary directed her to a meeting room where seated alongside Dickie, she found a number of strangers already assembled.

Looking around she was surprised to find that the Abbot and Dickie where the only men present, while the other four were women. Celina took a chair leaving one spare.

She had hardly settled herself down when a short elderly woman entered seating herself across from her. The Abbot rose and looking around them said.

"As there are strangers among us, I would like to introduce first, The Reverend Dr Richard Bird. Who has been hunting a wraith around London for several weeks, and then going around the table we have. Dr Teresa Martin, Lady Anna Richmond, Lady Maria Jennings, and…." Turning to the small woman who had followed Celina in, he introduced her as, "Dr Julie Harris."

Then obviously for Celina's benefit he said. "Who all have specialised one way or another in demonic subjects, and finally let me introduce Lady Celina Carvel."

The Abbot looked again around the table as he said. "I must apologise for calling this meeting on such short notice, but after my earlier meeting with Lady Celina and Lady Elizabeth, I felt it necessary.

Regrettably, Lady Elizabeth has been urgently recalled to the hospital where she works and thus cannot be here today. Regardless of this I have made some inquiries as suggested by both Celina and Elizabeth." He turned to look at Celina and said.

"Celina you were right; manifestations have occurred at other places, in fact, quite a number, though I think there are only three that we will have to review today as it is just three objects that have been stolen."

He was looking at Celina as he said this, Celina, hearing the Abbot now felt that her stomach had slunk down and was hiding in her boots.

The Abbot turning back to the others asked. "How many here other than Celina have heard of the Star of Destiny?"
It was Dickie who nodded and said.

"I have, and the other jewels linked with it." No-one else answered as the Abbot looked around the table until his gaze came back to Celina; he gave a nod as he accepted the fact she had before he turned back to Dickie and asked.

"Would you please tell us what you know about the Star of Destiny?"

"Certainly, although I must admit I don't know a great deal about any of them, but from what I have read the Star of Destiny is a gold five-pointed star with a central ruby, with each of the five points of the star being tipped by a small ruby.

No-one knows where it came from or how old it is, but as far as it is known it has been around for centuries. Early legends have it belonging to one of the Greek gods while other legends associate it with the end of the world, and that's about all I know." The Abbot resuming his stance said.

"Thank you Dr Bird, that sums it up very well, and the Star of Destiny is one of the objects that have disappeared. Now does anyone else apart from Dr Bird know anything about a finger ring called the Stones of Death, or the Death Stones?" There was no reply to this inquiry.

"No-one?" the Abbot asked. "What about the Ring of Fire which is a bracelet?" The Abbot waited again looking around the table. "All right what about a brooch called the Gift of Blood?" A woman whom the Abbot had introduced as Lady Julie Harris now nodded and stood to speak.

"It is a gold brooch with five inset rubies, and it has been associated with bad luck to its owner. I understand it is reputed to have demonic connections and that several of its owners have met with untimely ends."

"Correct," the Abbot replied. "Now, a pendant called the Tears of Blood." Again, as no one answered the Abbot continued with his explanation as he said.

"All these items have been associated with bad luck to any individual owner and invariably and ultimately with death. Two other items have boded similar misfortune for their owners. One is a clasp called the Five Stones of Fate."

He paused looking around the table and then said. "All these items have two things in common," after which he paused again to see if anyone noticed what he had just said, or rather not said. Celina felt sick. The Abbot looked around the table again before continuing.

"One is that all of them are gold, and two that they all have five rubies arranged into the form of a pentagram. There is a very old legend that says if they are all brought together at the correct place and time that it will bring about the end of the world." He hesitated for a moment and then continued saying.

"There is a second legend that refutes the first, and which indicates rather than bringing about the end of the world, that a permanent way from the underworld into our world will be created, bringing damnation upon the world."

He stopped and waited looking at his audience before saying. "We have reasons to believe that they are all being brought together by underworld demons, and we can assume the reason." He looked at the surrounding faces all showing shock disbelief and horror.

The small woman Julie Harris pulled herself together and said. "It appears that they only have three of the five items; where are the other two and can we stop them from getting them?" The Abbot turning to her replied.

"The other two items have been lost for centuries and where they are is totally unknown." He paused and then looked at Celina.

"Celina put forward a theory when I spoke to her last night, one I don't like but one I feel may be correct." He then turned back to Celina saying. "Celina if you would please."

Celina, pale of face looked up at the Abbot, having only now come reluctantly to accept Claire's theory as being correct, and then looking around the table and feeling sick she rose to her feet, seeing a blur of faces watching her. Finally, she blinked them into focus and said.

"I think the reason they have never been seen for so long is…." She hesitated again looking at the Abbot for support before she said. "Because the demons already have them, and only needed the last three to make the full complement of seven." Silence followed, and Celina was suddenly aware of everyone looking at her.

"Seven?" Dickie queried. "I thought the Abbot said five."

"There are seven," Celina replied. "There are seven if you include the clasp called the Five Stones of Fate, which the Abbot mentioned only in passing, and the Ring of Blood." The Abbot rising to his feet and with a small bow in Celina's direction said.

"Celina is correct. The Ring of Blood is mentioned several times though it has never been described nor is there any record of it. We have no idea what it is or what it looks like. We can only assume again that it also has five rubies arranged in a pentagram." The Abbot then took up a book from the table and passed it to Dickie. It was the book Celina had seen the night before.

Dickie read the relevant passage and then on a following page marked by the Abbot he reviewed the list there.

The Star of Destiny, a gold five-point star with a ruby affixed on each point.

The Stones of Death (or Death Stones,) a finger ring.

The Ring of Fire, a small bracelet.

The Gift of Blood, a brooch.

The Tears of Blood, a pendant.

The Five Stones of Fate, a clasp.

The Ring of Blood, an item of an unknown description, if this item exists where it fits into the pentagram is not known.

He studied the drawing of the six known items showing all of them arranged with the star of destiny as the centre of the pentagram, after which he passed it on to Dr Teresa Martin. From her it was passed around the table until the book was returned to the Abbot. The Abbot looked around the table and asked.

"Has anyone any comments or questions? Lady Jennings," the Abbot acknowledged. Lady Jennings stood first looking around the table and then back at the Abbot.

"Are we sure that the stolen items are…." The look on her face gave the impression that she thought naming trouble could bring it about. She struggled for words. "Well the ones mentioned."

"I think we can safely assume so, Dr Bird has identified all the items stolen from drawings and eyewitness descriptions." Then turning to Dickie the Abbot asked. "Perhaps you could elaborate please Dr Bird?" Dickie looked around the table, decided against standing and then sitting forward in his chair he began.

"The items stolen have been in the keeping of the church for many years, and for security they have all been separated and kept in supposedly safe places. The Star itself was kept in the vault of the Museum of British Art, a place as secure as any known." Dr Harris interrupted Dickie by asking.

"How was it stolen then?"

"We don't know; the vault appeared intact and unopened, if it hadn't been for the two guards it could have been days or even weeks before the theft was discovered."

"The guards discovered it then?" Dr Harris asked.

"No the guards were at their station inside the vault, and both were dead, and that is where Lady Elizabeth is right now assisting with their autopsies."

"How did they die?" Lady Jennings asked.

"We don't know yet, but the report from the guards who found them says they had seen nothing like it before." Dr Bird fell silent as he looked solemnly around the table before he said. "We need to know how they died, and who or what it was that killed them." Dr Bird now grew quiet sitting looking at the Abbot and waiting.

The Abbot stood and looked across to Dr Martin and said. "Dr Martin is our top authority on demonology." The Abbot looked around the table before looking back to Dr Martin and saying. "That is our small variety of known underworld creatures, and what little we do know of them she will now tell you."

Dr Martin then rose to her feet looked at the faces around the table and said.

"As the Abbot suggests we know little about actual demons. Now wraiths are the most common underworld creature, so we know more about them than any other, and these creatures are the ones I wish to discuss first.

Outwardly, they look like insects, but they have many features that differentiate them from actual insects. For example, insects don't breathe by way of lungs while wraiths do. Their lungs are not like ours as theirs work continuously rather than intermittently.

Specifically, air enters through their mouths or nostrils, just as we draw in air, but instead of exhaling as we do. The air is forced down through their lungs and out by muscular contractions to exit. Though we believe this direction is reversible, below what would be on an animal the back of the rib cage through what have the appearance of gill slits. We believe both the gill slits and their nostrils can be opened and closed, to restrict the entry of foreign bodies.

They also differ in the way they create audible sounds. Unlike the air-breathing creatures of our world that create sound by passing air over vocal cords, wraiths produce sound by way of a ring of tissue under their mouthparts. This tissue is vibrated using special muscles to produce sounds.

Their blood to us looks black and is highly corrosive. It is also rich in iron, making it capable of carrying and storing far more oxygen than human blood.

"Now the way they are made, they don't have skin or a bony internal skeleton, and in this way they are very much like insects. Their external skeleton is formed from a material more like chain mail. While it is strong and difficult to penetrate like chain mail, it differs in that it is flexible only in one direction, in contrast to being flexible in all directions. This is why their external skeleton or exoskeleton is so hard to penetrate.

Internally their skeleton is similar to that of some fishes, namely the shark being composed of a material similar to cartilage.

"Nevertheless, it is known that they have specific points of weakness at what could be termed their waist and neck making them the only demonic creature that can be killed, though I must say with difficulty by conventional weapons.

"Wraiths are reasonably easy to kill with talent; it just takes a heat strike as you would use to heat a kettle or to start a fire directed through the wand and aimed at the head.

"Demons we think look on them as intelligent dogs and use them as such. The last specimen of a wraith we have was obtained in 1690, and is held at Roche Abbey, so what little we know about them is mostly derived from this one specimen."

Dr Martin looked at the faces watching her as she waited for any comments. As there were none forthcoming, she continued.

"Now demons are another matter as we have practically no information on them at all. We are told conventional weapons are ineffective against them, though we know conventional weapons at that time were the bow and arrow, spears and swords. Talent used by a single individual acting alone is always insufficient resulting in the death of the attacked.

Because demons normally attack and successfully kill persons even those with talent there has been little if any opportunity to obtain first-hand information. To kill a demon using talent has always taken at least four Knights working together. When a demon is destroyed it is totally destroyed, and nothing is left to examine, which I have to say has further limited our knowledge of them.

"Now as I said the destruction of a demon has always required four Knights working together, and I have to say that the last demon destroyed in this way was three hundred years ago, and it took four of the strongest Knights living at the time." By now she was looking directly at Celina as she said.

"Until now…. The latest demon to be destroyed was destroyed by one Knight alone. Celina would you please tell us all what happened to you?"

Celina sat shocked for a moment at this unexpected request. At first, she started to her feet but then changed her mind and as Dickie had done, remained seated. Sitting she recounted the story once again of what had happened that fearful night. Then she passed the narrative on to Dickie for him to tell them what he had learned from Marcus.

It was during a short break for coffee that the four women attending the meeting pounced on Celina with questions she couldn't answer. They prodded for details that she felt unable to provide. Specifically, they wanted to know the how, why, what and where of her encounter with the demon.

To most of their questions, Celina could offer little in the way of explanation. How she had managed to dissipate it; she didn't know. Why it had worked for her? She had no idea. She knew only that if it hadn't she wouldn't be here now. As to how it had unfolded, all she could say was.

"I was thoroughly beaten and barely conscious, and I knew I was about to die and then it was an idea that came into my head almost like words, 'use Merlin's dissipation.' That's what I tried to do and as far as I know that's what I did."

It was now that Dickie, who had been sitting silently listening, rejoined the conversation saying.

"That night back in my rooms Marcus said something about Celina shouting what could have been words in a strange language. It was one he couldn't place or understand, and I must admit I'm fascinated.

In the old records about Merlin and the earliest Talents, it was often said that they would direct the power of their talent using for want of a better word verbal spells. In some cases they would even shout out words in an unknown tongue, especially when using a difficult or powerful cast."

This information provoked considerable debate, but Celina could only reply to their questions by saying. "I don't know," or. "I don't remember."

After the adjournment of the formal meeting, the informal one continued again over lunch. Then it was back to the Abbot's rooms where Celina told them about the portal in the park and describing 'Hell' in as much detail as she could, telling them about the demon and how they had seen the way it closed the portal. Considerable further discussion ensued over this, and it was well into the afternoon before the group split up.

212

Now having some quiet time alone Celina and Dickie then discussed her latest find. The two young girls she had sent to him whom he said showed a lot of promise, and he was expecting Allison the older girl to be acceptable to a wand on reaching her sixteenth birthday, and then teasingly, very likely Molly as well. Celina was delighted. It appeared there could be two new Knights for the church.

Then Celina finding she wouldn't be required to attend the following day decided it was to be a hot drink and an early flight home.

It was just starting to get dark as Celina lifted her broom into the sky. Above the clouds in the east, one or two bright stars were now showing, and in the western sky, the last sliver of sun was shining a brassy yellow. Celina was less than five miles from the abbey when either instinct or a premonition made her pull sharply round to the right.

A black object hurtled past her, just missing her broom by a few feet. Looking down, Celina could see in front of her an object that appeared to be about the size of a large dog, and with its wings a-blur was climbing rapidly back toward her.

Whatever it was it was moving considerably faster than she was, and coming out of the west against the sun made it difficult for Celina to see.

As it rapidly closed from her left, it assumed a more and more insect-like appearance. Celina swerved and twisted before throwing all her strength into her shield on that side.

The insect if that's what it was hit her shield where it seemed to hesitate for an instant before forcing its way through, but by then it had lost momentum and missed.

Celina turned her head to see it as it passed behind her, and then watched fascinated, as it started to climb until high above her it turned and dived.

Celina slowed as fast as she could while at the same time pulling the front of the broom sharply upwards. In doing so, she found herself thrown forward hard against the safety strap, almost hitting her face on the back of the front seat.

The insect made an incredible twist in flight and slowed rapidly. Celina watched as it passed so close in front of her broom that she could see the mouthparts of its long pointed mouth working, and the two frighteningly large black composite eyes of an insect looking at her.

The legs folded back under the shiny black body, while held out of the way along its sides were two crab claws. It was an insect from a nightmare; an insect like she could never have imagined.

Celina pushed hard, her stomach felt queasy with fear as she looked around. Where was it? Then she saw it coming at her again. Without realising it, she found her wand was out of its sheath and had attached itself to the wand safe on her wrist.

Twisting the broom to one side and pushing as hard as she could the broom continued to accelerate. With a flick of her wrist, the wand was in her hand.

She cast first one heat strike, then a second towards the creature, but the thing was just too fast for her to follow, and she missed.

She tried again with two more heat strikes and missed with both. It had twisted to follow her and now was coming in fast from behind and to one side.

Celina pulled the broom sharply around hearing an alarming creaking of the seat and safety strap, only to find that they were now flying directly towards each other. Taking aim, she cast another two quick strikes. 'Almost,' she thought as one of the strikes passed just above it.

As it turned to dodge her cast's she lost sight of it. Celina swung out and down before swooping up again, and found it now coming in towards her right side. Strengthening her shield on that side, she turned the broom toward it so the insect hit her shield at an angle.

Again, the insect slowed as it came through her shield and passed behind her so close, Celina felt a bang on her broom as some thing knocked against the broom's tail.

It was too fast; she twisted down in a corkscrew to dodge and then looped up trying desperately to get behind it. Although she was momentarily behind it, it turned and Celina lost it in the gloom, only to find it appear in front and coming directly at her again.

At the last moment, Celina pushed the front of the broom down hard and tried to cast a heat strike upward as it passed above her, but it had twisted away and was lost to view.

Pushing the broom to her limits and using heat strikes was now taking its toll. Celina was feeling the strain; she needed something that took less energy.

She tried casting a bind at it, but either she had missed, or as like with the demon it didn't have any effect.

Pulling the broom up and over brought her down behind it, and two quick heat strikes almost got it. Celina blinked, as it was lost in the gloom only for her to find it coming at her from the side.

Celina pulled the broom's front up and slowing rapidly while sending another two heat strikes at it as it passed under her; she missed again. With the light failing, she looked around desperately.

"Where is it?" she found herself shouting. Panic was now settling in; it was just too fast for her. She hauled her broom around in a tight circle so sharply that the safety strap cut into her, but she couldn't see it anywhere.

"Where are you," her scream echoed in her ears, and then seemingly from nowhere it was there in front of her and to close to dodge.

Weak disorientated and terrified, panic overwhelmed her. Wishing for an impossible pain block on herself, she dropped her shield for a last desperate cast.

It was now that everything went wrong. The front of the broom came up, and the broom lifted but then started to fall.

The bug was to close, and in her panic, it wasn't a cast she sent projected forward through her wand, it was the pain block. With no shield to slow it, the bug came straight at her. Something clipped her left shoulder and for Celina, everything went black.

Pain brought Celina back to her senses. At first, she thought her shoulder had been broken but then the pain subsided to a dull throb.

Celina found herself falling, spinning and tumbling, like a wind blown autumn leaf, held in her creaking seat by the lap strap and not even sure which way was up.

With a struggle, she brought the broom under control to find she had fallen at least five hundred feet. Desperately, she found herself looking around for the bug, searching until at last she saw it, finding it was still falling and now well below her.

As she watched, its wings started to beat slowly at first and then faster, with its wings turning into a blur as it started to rise coming up towards her again. Celina watched desperately trying to think, asking herself what could have happened to affect the creature for it to have fallen like that.

'A pain block?' she thought. *'A pain block, I was wanting a pain block, could I? It must be; I must somehow have hit it with a pain block but how?'* Celina's wand flicked from the wand safe back into her hand as she waited for the bug to get closer.

It was as she gripped the wand that the idea came to her; some how she must have pushed the pain block at it through her wand.

Unsure if it would work Celina waited until it was about fifty yards away, and then using her wand to direct the block she sent a broad pain block towards it. Not just a narrow beam as with casting a bind or a heat strike, but instead an ever-widening unseen cone.

The creature flew straight into it; Celina held her wand pointing it in its direction and watched elatedly as its wings stopped beating, and it started falling.

Just for an instant, it disappeared as Celina lost sight of it in the gathering dark. She found it again just as its wings started to beat, and she dived after it. Celina pushed her broom hard closing the distance between them until she was close enough to hold it once more in a pain block.

At first just taking a rough aim with her wand, and then narrowing her pain block as she closed the distance between them.

As the gap closed Celina watched as the insect's wings ceased to beat, and it started to fall. With the air howling against her shield, Celina found herself pushing her broom into a near-vertical dive while not daring to ease the pain block and trust it to hold as she would with a human.

As she dropped below the clouds, Celina was surprised to find that the fight had taken them back over the Abbey gardens. She

216

watched holding the pain block until the insect crashed into the paving by the side of a glasshouse. Then she almost screamed in delight as she watched the dark stain spreading across the stone slabs.

Seeing the insect motionless on the ground Celina spun her broom to lose the speed she had gained in the dive.

Then over the soft soil of the garden, she forced the back of her broom onto the ground, digging it in, in order to slow her before letting it slide to a stop.

Now once again things went wrong for Celina. With the tail of her broom pressed down and ploughing a deep furrow in the soft ground, it passed over something hard. The back of the broom lifted, and she lost control with its front dropping and digging into the soil turning her over.

Pulling one-handed to release her safety strap, she fell out of the seat. Rolling away from the broom, she tried to get to her feet. Only to find not just her legs trembling and weak, but that she was shaking all over with fatigue. Swaying she stood with her head pounding and the world swirling around her.

With her wand still pointing at the insect, she looked around. In the failing light, her eyes picked out one of its claws torn off and stuck in the soil by the impact.

Then to her horror, her searching eyes found a long stinger, or something stinger-like that was protruding from the back of the body. It was pointed and over a foot in length.

Celina seeing a man in a lay-monk's habit running in her direction, and hoping that her voice was loud enough, shouted,

"Go, go fetch the high Abbot," The monk took a quick look at what lay on the ground and then set off at a dead run across the gardens.

It was then that the smell hit her, and she retched; it took all her self-control not to be sick. Retching she swayed her way upwind until she could prop herself against the greenhouse.

With her head spinning and leaning against the structure, she took deep gasping breaths as she tried to get her breath back and settle her stomach.

Celina had dropped the pain block, as she was almost certain the insect was dead, or if it was not that it was in no condition to move rapidly, although she still had her wand held in her hand and pointing at the mess.

Celina pushed her wand back into its sheath, and then letting her legs give way she slumped down with her back against the greenhouse wall.

It was several minutes before Celina saw the Abbot and two women carrying acetylene hand lanterns running toward her across the garden. Running up to Celina, he gripped her by her shoulders pulling her to her feet and hugging her as he asked.

"Are you all right?" His words almost had Celina laughing hysterically, and it was only with an effort that Celina gained a grip on herself and nodded.

Celina watched with a kind of fascination as the younger woman moved closer to the creature's body, illuminating it with the brilliant white light of her lantern, and then doubling over, she was noisily sick.

Dr Martin coming around to Celina picked up a rake and prodded the creature's hard body. With a cloth over her mouth and nose she declared.

"What a God awful smell." Then turning to the Abbot, she apologised saying. "Oh I am sorry my Lord."

"It is dead isn't it?" Celina asked. Dr Martin looked up and responded with a shudder saying.

"Was it ever alive? I've never seen an insect this size before. That's if it is an insect, I think it has lungs look here, it definitely has nostrils." She pointed the rake at its head and turning it over with the rake; she exclaimed. "My word fangs, and I think it's poisonous too," as she looked at the yellow liquid oozing from one of the fangs. Then running her light along its body she said.

"And by the look of it, it's poisonous at both ends. If that's a stinger it's a stinger and a half." Then looking at it again she said. "Or I think could it be an ovipositor, where on earth did this thing come from?"

"Not from anywhere on earth," the Abbot corrected her and then said. "I think we had better get it out of the open."

Straightening up and wiping her mouth the other woman who by now had emptied her stomach came closer and said.

"I never did like insects especially large ones, and what an awful smell." Then looking towards the Abbey buildings she said. "Here come the porters." pointing towards four men running toward them.

With the use of a couple of spades, the creature's body was loaded into a wheelbarrow and Celina watched with relief as it was taken to the mortuary.

The High Abbot insisted that Celina visit the infirmary to be seen by a doctor, while at that moment all Celina wanted to do was to sit down before her legs gave way. However, she soon decided that lying on a stretcher, though it swayed like a ship in a storm was even better.

Resting in a bed in the infirmary with her eyes closed her head slowly ceased its spinning. A church doctor who examined her eventually decided that there was no damage; just that she was suffering from extreme exhaustion.

The Doctor then quietly and so as not to distress Celina started to quiz her on her latest encounter, putting her through every little detail.

"For the High Abbot," she repeatedly said. Then she proceeded to tell Celina that under no circumstances was she to attempt to return to London that night. The doctor even threatened Celina with instant sleep if she so much as thought about it. After the doctor had left, Celina found that the ceiling had started slowly to revolve again. Closing her eyes, she decided that lying there in the infirmary was definitely the best idea of the day.

It was later that night Celina was informed that the Abbot had assigned two Knights to escort her home the following morning, and that they were to leave before first light.

Friday 17th January 1862.

Today I met a young girl who flies a broom better than anyone I know. I learned a lot from her in just one flight.

~~~

The following morning Celina and the Abbot were standing in the pre-dawn of a windy and overcast day. A two-seat broom was dimly visible approaching across the grass from the far side of the Abbey. The Abbot turned from watching its approach as Celina asked. "What's happening with the bug?"

"Oh that, I've arranged for a medical research team from Roche Abbey to collect it for examination and dissection." Then the Abbot surprised Celina by asking.

"Just how many casts did you say you made?" Celina hadn't said, but it made her think, she had been using heat strikes fast and furiously.

"I don't know maybe six or seven," she replied and then asked, "why?"

"I was just wondering," the Abbot said with a shrug. "I think Celina that it's imperative we get you back to London as soon as possible. In fact, the sooner you are in London the more I will like it. There have been two deliberate attempts on your life already." Celina spun around to face him asking.

"Yes, but why me?"

"I don't know but the first time the demon attacked you, you said it was looking for someone and you said that someone was you. Then last evening that attack had all the appearances of a pre-planned attempt on your life."

He took a look at the approaching broom as he said. "I wish I knew why too; that's why I've arranged for you to be escorted back to London. I want you to fly as fast as you can, and from what I hear you can really push that broom of yours." The last was said with a smile and twinkle in his eye.

"Heat strikes," he mused out loud, and then asked again. "Was it six, seven or more?" Celina had a feeling it was more, and she was certain she had used far less on the demon, yet here she was almost fully recovered in just one night. She shook her head putting it out of her mind. *'Later,'* she thought.

The broom came to a stop in front of them; sitting in the front seat was a woman who Celina had seen at breakfast yesterday morning, while in the rear seat was a young girl.

The young girl, well Celina decided if she was older than sixteen it would be a surprise. The woman had swung her leg over the broom shaft with a total disregard for modesty or the Abbot and now stood waiting for them.

Walking across to meet them the Abbot introduced the older Lady as Lady Marjory, Knight of the Round Table. Feeling a little awestruck at this introduction to a Knight of the Round Table, Celina held out her hand for a quick touch.

"So you're the famous demon killer are you?" there was a quick touch of hands as Marjory chattered on. "Pleased to meet you, I'm to ride wand for you and Polly here," she turned to the young girl, "is going to get me back afterwards."

Then without giving Celina a chance to reply Marjory continued to chatter on. "I saw the remains of that one yesterday, an ugly brute wasn't it?" She would probably have continued if the Abbot hadn't butted in saying.

"Marjory if you don't mind I think you had better be off before it gets too light." He then took Celina by the shoulders and looking her straight in the eyes said.

"Remember; fly as fast as you can, I'm going to contact your maid now and let her know you've set off, and I want you to let me know as soon as you arrive back in London. You won't forget will you?"

Celina looking at him and seeing the worry on his face said. "I will, and I won't forget," and then turning to Marjory and indicating her broom she said. "Would you mind taking the front seat?"

Settling into her seat and fastening the lap strap tightly Celina could see in front of her Marjory doing the same. Then with a wave to the Abbot Celina lifted the broom and rose into the predawn sky. Once above the trees she turned the broom and headed for London.

The young girl Polly drew into about ten feet on her left matching her every move. Breaking through the clouds, Celina started to push faster and then faster, while out of the corner of her eye she watched the other broom.

To her surprise, Polly sat looking relaxed and comfortable with just the odd glance across to check her position. Marjory called back over her shoulder.

"Don't worry about Polly, you just push as hard as you can and she'll stay with you." Celina pushed hard on the broom and felt the acceleration push her back into her seat, but just as before Polly remained about ten feet away and still showed no signs of strain.

The wind howled around Celina's shield as she began to feel the strain herself. She was really working, pushing harder than she ever had before and yet Polly just sat there.

"Don't worry you'll not lose our Polly," came Marjory's cheerful voice over the sound of the wind. Celina now began discreetly to study Polly, how was it that she seemed to match her speed so effortlessly?

Celina herself began to worry thinking. *I don't think I'm quite as recovered as I thought, at this rate I'll be worn out long before I reach home'.*

Looking more closely Celina slowly became aware of Polly's shield, or rather the apparent lack of it. Then with further care and concentration, Celina finally saw the difference in their shields, and at last it struck her. It was so obvious she wondered why she hadn't thought of it before.

Polly's shield wasn't positioned as a wall in front to protect her pushing the air aside as they moved forward. Instead, it started as a point just in front of the broom and smoothly swept around to cover Polly before it tapered away to the back. Celina cursing herself for a fool immediately saw the advantage to be gained from a shield of that shape.

Concentrating Celina pushed her own shield forward trying to match the shape. It took a few tries but once Celina had accomplished something resembling Polly's shield she found flying became truly effortless and almost silent.

With the wind resistance gone, Celina's broom leapt forward taking Polly by surprise. Polly recovered almost instantly and pulled back to her original position on Celina's left. Celina was startled as the young girl flashed a smile at her while still sitting as relaxed and comfortable as ever.

It was awe-inspiring as the cloud tops just flew by, and in what seemed to be a surprisingly short time Celina found it was time to drop below the clouds.

Under the clouds, it was raining, a fine misty cold rain that cut visibility down to about fifty yards. Peering through the rain, Celina managed to pick out the stable yard and dropped thankfully to the ground.

Marjory slipped off the broom and turning to look at Celina, she smiled and said.

"They said you were a fast one, and it certainly looks like you are." Polly crossed over to them and stood looking at Celina before saying with just a hint of approval.

"I can see you're a fast learner too." The kitchen door flew open and Jane ran down the steps only to halt looking at the other two visitors in surprise.

"This is Jane my companion," Celina explained and then turning to her escorts. "Jane this is Lady Marjory, and Lady Polly." After a quick touch of hands, Jane said.

"Come on in the Cooks got hot drinks ready, and you must all be cold." Jane then ushered them in, taking their coats and hanging them in the cloakroom as she passed, while Celina took them into the day room where she intended to entertain her visitors.

Polly was awestruck at the interior of the house. Never before had she seen such opulence, it overwhelmed her. While Lady Marjory sat at ease, Celina could feel the unease that Polly radiated. It was only a few minutes before Jane brought in the tea things saying.

"There's breakfast shortly if you wish." Both Marjory and Polly declined Jane's offer as Celina poured and served the tea herself, and at the same time watching the visitors while paying special attention to Polly, who appeared to be getting more nervous by the minute. Celina who had seated herself next to Polly finally broke the silence as she said.

"Jane I've finally found someone who can fly a broom faster than I can."

"Never," Jane said as she turned to Marjory. "You know I've met people who absolutely refuse to fly with Celina."

"Not Marjory, Polly," Celina declared. "Polly here makes my flying look slow."

"It's all a matter of technique," Polly murmured quietly sipping her tea. Marjory reached across to take Polly's hand as she said.

"Polly here is already the most skilled Knight I've ever come across flying a broom." Polly who was already looking uncomfortable and now having heard Marjory's praise looked to be getting more so with every minute. Celina made a guess that Polly was not from a high-status family and found being in her home possibly an unpleasant experience. Looking at Jane Celina drew her eyes to Polly.

Jane who had been watching Polly had herself come to the same conclusion. Sitting and sensing Polly's discomfort Marjory came across to sit between Celina and Polly, and putting her arm around Polly's shoulders she asked.

"Polly, do you mind if I tell Celina and Jane a little about you?" Polly shook her head still looking down.

"Polly has been with us less than a year." Marjory took Polly's hand and gave it a squeeze as she said.

"Before that she was in a church school for just over a year. She was originally taken from a kind of orphanage or workhouse. It was a bad situation for her and the other girls as beatings there were a daily occurrence. Then after they found her using her talent to protect one of the younger girls they said she was a witch." Polly looked up indignantly saying.

"They locked me up." Marjory's arm tightened around her shoulder pulling her close as she said. "Would you believe it? They threatened to have her burned, they actually asked the vicar of the church to arrange it." Polly's eyes looked from Celina to

Jane and then back again, and Celina could see the tears starting there.

"It was only the fact that a new vicar had recently started, one who knew about talent that it was brought to the notice of the Abbey. It's hard to believe I know, but he had to have her taken away in chains as that was the only way they would let her go." Marjory gave Polly another squeeze as she said.

"Since then she's been with me." Celina slid to the floor and knelt in front of Polly putting her hands over Polly's as she said.

"Polly, remember you're not just Polly any more." Celina pointed to the wand at Polly's side as she said. "When you were chosen you ceased to be the Polly of your past; you became Lady Polly.

Lady Polly with all the privileges and responsibilities that entails, so hold your head up with pride and look everyone in the eye because whether they like it or not you have rank, rank as high as a Lord in Parliament or his Lady." Polly swallowed and said.

"But I'm just Polly; Lady Polly doesn't sound right." Celina was at a loss. It was Marjory, who spoke up saying.

"You may say you're just Polly and only seventeen, but you fly a broom better than anyone I know." She turned towards Celina to say. "Not only that but at seventeen, she has been brought in as a research assistant to the round table the youngest ever." Then she said with a knowing look towards Celina.

"Polly here has developed three new casts that would probably interest you. All of them are deadly to living creatures and possibly to demonic creatures as well, and then there are two that are totally destructive. I've seen her turn a wall three feet thick and six feet high into a pile of sand." Polly hung her head not looking up or saying a word.

"Polly." Celina said as she reached out and gently lifted Polly's chin. "I think after what the High Abbot told me this morning I could do with you teaching me something like that. I take it that you already know about yesterday." She didn't have to go any further; Polly nodded and said.

"Yes the Abbot spoke to me about teaching you, but he has to get permission from the Round Table first." Celina sat back surprised at Polly's mention of the Round Table.

"You didn't tell me." Marjory said indignantly.

"I'm sorry Marjory but I haven't had chance to tell you, and I'm not supposed to tell anyone else yet not about that or about Merlin's dissipation."

"Merlin's dissipation, what about Merlin's dissipation?" a startled Celina exclaimed.

"Well I know how you did it as Merlin intended, I worked it out after hearing about you." Celina sat stunned for a moment and then said.

"You worked it out, well just how did I do it?

"I'm not allowed to tell anyone yet. I shouldn't have said anything." Polly sat looking down at her hands clasped on her lap. Celina looked across at her and then stopped; her question left unspoken as she suddenly said.

"Damn I forgot; I have to call the Abbot." Polly smiled shyly, and Marjory laughed while Jane just looked from one to the other.

Celina returned after a few minutes to ask. "Now where were we? Oh yes Polly. Polly please believe this, you are no longer just Polly, but you are now Lady Polly. You are Marjory's and my equal and by the sound of it; you are a very talented young woman who I hope will consider me to be one of your friends. After all that I've just heard I really would hate to be grouped with those you consider not your friends.

Now can you tell us about the other casts you've developed? I think we may need something like that as up to now there hasn't been much you can do about most demonic creatures. Normal weapons don't work, and talent has never been destructive enough to do any real damage."

"Well beyond a wraith anyway," Marjory said, and then turning to Jane she asked. "Did you hear what happened with the bug yesterday?"

"Bug what bug?" Jane asked turning suspiciously towards Celina. With this Celina recited the whole story as Jane became visibly more and more agitated until finally she had to say.

226

"I told you, I told you I had a bad feeling about the Abbey. Next time I say I have a bad feeling you should take notice."

Polly who had been sitting and thinking now interrupted saying.

"Yes I wonder if it's possible fully to combine a block or a bind with your shield."

"It would take a lot of concentration so think about it when we get back." and then getting to her feet Marjory said. "It's starting to get light, and we should have been on our way back ages ago."

Gathered back in the old stable yard and while Marjory was saying good-bye to Jane. Polly, who was already to go beckoned Celina across and shyly said.

"You got the shape nearly right, think of a fish and how it uses fins and tail to bank and turn." Then having waited for Marjory to take the front seat and push her skirts either side of the broom's shaft, Polly lifted her broom into the air.

Celina watched carefully and saw how instead of the broom lifting up and then going forward it all happened as one smooth movement, forward and up with a constant and steady increase in speed.

As Polly made a turn over the yard Celina could see how the broom instead of sitting flat leaned into the turns while accelerating, and again it was all made in one continuous movement while Polly's shield remained smooth and unbroken, covering both herself and the broom from front to back in a sleek shape just like a fish.

Celina watching the broom disappear into the rain decided Polly's skill on the broom was nothing short of remarkable.

Ixcte ~ 3

Ixcte raised a head out of a hood aware that a food/slave/pet was approaching. Stopping every nine steps and prostrating itself for the required nine heartbeats, the food/slave/pet finally drew near and stopped. It lay in reach of one of Ixcte's major feeding tentacles waiting. "Has the Lovan returned and is the black dealt with?" Ixcte asked. The food/slave/pet lay still not moving. "I asked a question, I expect an answer." Ixcte's thought bellowed in the Cesdric's mind.

The food/slave/pet raised its large head, its yellow eyes clouded over with fear as it finally acknowledged. "It has not returned it has failed." Ixcte twisted a small part of its massive bulk into a better position to strike. "Has another Lovan been prepared?" Ixcte asked.

"One is shortly due to rise, and once it is ready to lay, it will be imprinted with the black's matrix," the food/slave/pet replied.

"How long?" Ixcte asked. "One more rising until mating and then one to laying,"

"It must not fail," Ixcte's thought screamed back. "The black must not be allowed to stand between Ixcte and more food."

One of Ixcte's feeding tentacles moved towards the food/slave/pet. Ixcte now knew that everything was ready. The native food/slave/pet on the other side had all the talismans necessary, and the time approached. Now the only barrier remaining between Ixcte and more food was the black, the black who had withstood Ixcte twice in the past.

"The next time the black must die." Ixcte's thought was driven into the Cesdric's mind as the feeding tentacle struck and the food/slave/pet stiffened in agony as digestive fluids were pumped into its body and started to dissolve its internal organs. Even while the food/slave/pet died, Ixcte fed on its pain.

Discarding the empty shell, Ixcte watched as two more food/slave/pets advanced to remove it. Ixcte's feeding tentacles twisted and poised to strike but disquiet held them back.

Finally Ixcte flexed into a more comfortable shape. "Next time," Ixcte thought. "The black must die. Time is growing short."

Ixcte turned an eyestalk to look back along its entire length. It could see the thousands of food/slave/pet that were attached to its feeding tentacles. Others waited to take the empty shells away and then to take their place. Food was getting scarce as Ixcte was feeding faster than the food/slave/pet was breeding. New food/slave/pet sources must be obtained. Ixcte retracted its head back into its hood. Leaving just its eyestalks showing as it rested not fully satisfied.

228

Early winter 1862.

January turned into February, and alterations to the shop were drawing to a close. Celina had taken on two more young assistants to work under Marcus and Claire who would soon be heading their own departments.

Celina had surprised herself by taking on two very young girls when she had originally been looking for two young men of about fourteen or fifteen years of age. Having spoken to these two girls Celina found they seemed ideally suited to her needs, and now she found herself more than satisfied with her choice.

The nightly patrols over London had proven fruitless, so Celina and Elizabeth had decided to wait for further developments.

Monday 3rd February 1862.

Celina and the foreman of the builders were looking around the first floor.

"Just one or two bits of painting left to do down here now me Lady. Then there's a bit of the woodwork on the top floor still to paint, but it should be all finished for you by the end of the week."

Celina looked around and in her mind's eye she could see the display cabinets in place, the gaslights lit and the shop full of customers.

"Thank you Mr Smith" she said, and then asked. "I wonder if I could prevail upon you to help us just a little more? If I arrange for the display cabinets and furniture to arrive on Friday afternoon, could you and your men bring them up here for me?"

"That would be a pleasure me Lady," he replied.

"Thank you Mr Smith, that's very good of you and it is greatly appreciated." With that Celina hearing footsteps turned to find Claire coming up the stairs.

"Celina that gentleman has returned about that book, The Book of Days." With a last "thank you Mr Smith," Celina turned and followed Claire down the stairs to find the white-haired gentleman was still standing waiting for them where Claire had left him. Upon seeing Celina, he gave a small bow and said.

"Good afternoon, I was making enquiries about The Book of Days." Celina despite the shiver that ran up her spine smiled as she replied.

"Yes I remember, and I have made some enquiries for you. One is available on seven days notice; I can't say that it's the original as after the copies were made the original was mixed in with them. What I can say is that this is a sixth-century copy of that I am certain."

"I think I must ask you to get it for me," the gentleman said. "Do you know the price?"

"The gentleman who owns the book is asking one hundred and eighty-five guineas, and then there will be a cover charge for obtaining it. That would bring the total to one hundred and ninety-five guineas." The gentleman inclined his head in acceptance as he said.

"The price is quite acceptable. If I give you a bank draft for that amount now will that be satisfactory?" Celina graciously accepted allowing the gentleman the use of the office until the financial transactions were completed.

Once he had left the shop Celina immediately called Mr Jones at his office, and with the gentleman's calling card still in her hand she asked.

"Do you know of a Dr Bernard McDonald of Lownde's Square?" Mr Jones hesitated and then responded with.

"May I ask why you are enquiring?"

"Well he has just given me a bank draft for one hundred and ninety-five guineas." There was a brief silence and then Mr Jones asked.

"Can you describe him?"

"Pure white hair is his most distinguishing feature," Celina replied.

"That is Dr McDonald," Mr Jones confirmed. "He has rooms and a surgery In Lownde's Square, and a very select clientele; I do believe the draft should be good."

Celina leaned back in her chair reached down and from the bottom draw of her desk; she withdrew one of two slim volumes. Both were her father's copies of The Book of Days. One an original he had bought and the other a copy he had ordered to be made.

"Thank you Mr Jones you have been most helpful," she said replacing the Telson. Celina sat tapping her finger on the book as once again, the thought ran through her mind.

'If Dr McDonald is a wealthy doctor living on Lownde's Square, just who is this master whom he refers to? Most strange.' For some reason, a shiver ran down her spine again.

Pulling the Telson closer she lifted the earpiece. When the controller answered she asked for Dr Elizabeth Gibbard and also gave the Telson controller her home address. It was Elizabeth herself who answered the call.

"Hello Elizabeth, it's Celina. I think I may need your help so would you be free at lunchtime?"

"Does this have something to do with you know what?" Elizabeth asked. By general agreement, certain things were no longer addressed directly over the Telson as the Abbot had said.

"It may be the Telson Company's instructions to its controllers not to listen to a conversation, but you never know."

"I'm not sure but it may be," Celina replied. "If you call in the shop about lunch time I'll treat you to lunch."

"That sounds wonderful," Elizabeth said. "So I'll see you about one." As Celina put one of the two books away, she looked up and found Marcus standing in the doorway looking worried.

"It's not starting again is it?" he asked.

"I don't know, lately things have been very quiet, too quiet".

"That man with the white hair do you have suspicions about him?" He asked.

"Dr McDonald? I don't know," Celina mused in reply. "But why would he want a copy of The Book of Days? It's no good to him."

Celina turned the book on her desk around and pushed it towards Marcus asking. "Would you pay one hundred and ninety-five guineas for that?" Marcus settled into a chair and opened the book. For several minutes he flicked through the pages stopping to read a paragraph while now and then struggling with his mostly forgotten schoolboy Latin. Finally, he looked up at Celina who was still watching him and said.

"Even if I had talent I don't think I would pay money for this. It might be more interesting to Claire than me, what with its old herbal cures and remedies. All this talk about magic doesn't really tell me anything, and all this."

Marcus tapped his finger on a page. "About strange beasts," he then shrugged and said. "Even now having seen a demon it doesn't mean that much to me. Then there is this part about the ending of the world. Well…." He passed the book back to Celina and said.

"And most of it I can't even read as it's written in a foreign language." Celina putting the book away asked.

"Do you think Claire can manage over lunch with just the two girls? I've invited Elizabeth to have lunch with me, and I would appreciate it if you joined us."

"Well thank you yes I would, and yes I do. I must admit the two girls seem to be settling in a lot better than I had expected."

Marcus paused and looking at Celina, he said. "I just hope they don't get a baptism like we did." Celina looked at him horrified as she said.

"Oh no, no we don't want that again do we?"

Once their lunch had been served, Celina told Elizabeth about the return of the white-haired gentleman. Only at the last did she mention his name and occupation. Elizabeth put down her knife and fork, and then deep in thought she picked up her glass. Twisting it, she looked frowning at the contents.

"Dr McDonald," she finally said. "How very strange…. I know he came to London from Edinburgh perhaps five or six years ago. Once here he set up a practice where he seems to have developed a good reputation. All I can really say is that as a Doctor he is well known and highly regarded in professional circles."

She paused and took a sip from her glass thinking for a moment before saying. "I have heard that he is financially very secure. Though I have also heard rumours about him being rather reluctant to open his purse, but as for him having a master…. well that I don't understand. When I get back to the hospital, I shall try to make some inquiries. Oh and by the way, did I tell you the results from the autopsy, you know on the museum guards?"

Celina straightened in her seat, and as she leaned forward she said. "No what killed them?"

"It's hard to say as we couldn't find any parts of them large enough to do a proper post-mortem. It looked as if they had been exploded from the inside."

On Friday at lunchtime Mr Smith took Celina around the first and second floors of the shop pointing out various little items that he was especially pleased with. On the top floor, he pointed out several places where the paint was still wet saying.

"I'm afraid the paint is still too wet for the final coat, so I have arranged for the painters to be back first thing tomorrow morning, and they'll work until it's all finished." He looked around obviously pleased with the work his men had done.

"We shall be lifting your things in this afternoon, and then the painters will sheet over the top of everything so they can paint tomorrow, and so by Monday you will be able to use the entire building." Celina turned to Mr Smith saying.

"Thank you Mr Smith, I must give praise where praise is due. The shop has been greatly improved, and the quality of the work that you and your men have provided is much appreciated." Celina then broke with talent protocol by extending her hand to Mr Smith for more than a touch before he left the building. Back on the ground floor, Celina called Marcus and Claire into the office.

"I need to ask a favour of you," she said looking from one to the other. "Could you both stay after closing on Monday just for an hour or two to get the sales area upstairs sorted out? If you can I'll treat you both to supper down the road."

"Yes that will be fine with me," Marcus replied.

"What about you Claire?" Celina asked.

"I shan't be doing anything special so that will be fine with me too."

"Good we shall have the whole two upper floors clear of the builders by Monday morning, so I can arrange for stock to be delivered during the afternoon."

Saturday 8th February 1862.

Today is our birthday. This year it was Jane's turn to buy the present, and I will provide the meal.

We decided to invite Marcus and Claire given all the work they've done, and the support they've provided both in the shop and in other ways.

Marcus asked if he could invite Elizabeth as well as his guest. I told him to bring her but explained that her being there as his guest was out of the question as it was my treat for the dedication that they had shown. It will be nice to share this day with her too.

~~~

It had been arranged to meet at an establishment on the corner of Gray's Inn Road and High Holborn at eight of the clock. Elizabeth had accepted Marcus's invitation but then raised the question of Marcus being the only man among four women, saying.

"It hardly seems right for him to be so outnumbered." Hearing this Celina turned to Claire and asked.

"Have you a friend and preferably a man who could keep Marcus company?"

"I don't really know anyone in London, only you and my aunt and uncle." Hearing Claire Elizabeth asked.

"My younger brother is home this week so could I invite him as my guest." Celina turning to Claire asked. "Do you feel comfortable with this?"

"Yes that's fine; that is if it's all right with you." Claire replied before saying to Marcus. "I'm sure he will be fine company for you Marcus."

"That's settled then, but as for paying it's my treat, so I shall be the one paying, Jane do you want to bring anyone?"

Celina had asked not expecting a yes, but looking directly at Jane and seeing her face she knew instantly that there was. Jane shook her head saying.

"No no-one." After the others had left, Celina called Jane back to say.

"Jane if there is someone you want to ask, ask. You won't be hurting me, and I won't be upset in the least." Jane looked a little embarrassed as she said.

"Well I don't think he would be able to come anyway." Celina sat looking at Jane waiting. Finally, she had to ask.

"Come on then you can't stop now, who is he?" Jane blushing said.

"Well his name is William, and he teaches science and mathematics at Christ Church School in Westminster." Jane stopped obviously wanting to end the conversation there and then, but Celina was having none of it.

"Keep going," Celina said with great interest. "How and when did you meet him?" Jane was now looking even more embarrassed, but as it was Celina who was asking she had to be told.

"It was during a rainstorm; I had to take refuge in a coffee shop in Westminster and we had to share a table. The shop was full and his table had the only place left to sit so. Well, we enjoyed talking and, well I sometimes see him there."

Celina took Jane's hands and held them as she said. "Well Jane if you want to ask him please do so." Jane shook her head saying.

"No it would make me uncomfortable asking a man and it would leave you on your own." Celina gave her a hug saying.

"Don't worry Jane, someday I will find someone, it's just that the right man hasn't shown himself yet."

Elizabeth's brother turned out to be a rather nice young man of twenty-one by the name of Terrence. He was well spoken and had a ready wit along with impeccable manners. In all he was a pleasure to dine with; a fact Celina noticed wasn't lost on Claire. Indeed the two seemed to be getting along extremely well.

Monday 10th February 1862.

At last, the alterations to the shop have been completed, and we have moved the stock in. Marcus and Claire stayed on to complete the alterations so that we could open the new rooms tomorrow. I had promised to take them for a meal after we finished, but some wraiths had other ideas.

~~~

The first thing Celina did Monday morning was to use the Telson to call Dr McDonald and inform him that the book was ready for collection at his convenience, or that it could be delivered. Dr McDonald said he was happy to collect the book himself but not until Tuesday as he was about to leave London for the day.

The first delivery of new stock arrived early at ten of the clock and Marcus took charge of getting it up and installed on the upper floors. Jane arrived next in a cab that was in turn closely followed by a man with a cart overloaded with the first of several deliveries of packages from the Abbey.

By closing time most of the upstairs stock was loosely in place and just required a final sorting and pricing to complete the first floor. On the top floor, one room was to be used for books and the other smaller room for Celina's talent goods, this freeing the ground floor completely for more fashionable sales.

The packages Jane had brought contained beautiful handmade silk garments that had Celina and Claire enchanted. There were silk dressing gowns, housecoats, wraps, shawls, and scarves with as Jane said, "more to come." These items were to be prominently displayed in one of the first floor rooms.

The outdoor and sports clothing from the north was to be exhibited in an area at the top of the stairs while the rest of Jane's purchases filled what was left of the first floor. On the ground floor, new glass fronted display cases down the centre and sides held jewellery and other small goods from the north. By seven of the clock the four of them had things in good order in the new display areas.

At last, everything that could be done had been done. Celina looked around and felt she was finally satisfied and looking forward to tomorrow. The gas for the upstairs lights had been turned off, and the three women and one man were now more than ready for some food.

Claire had just collected the tea things and taken them into the back room. Jane was taking the screen down between the old shop and the new staircase while Celina and Marcus were in the office when a scream from Claire in the storeroom sent Marcus and Celina racing along the passage.

Celina's wand was already in her hand as they burst onto a scene that to Marcus was nothing short of a nightmare.

Claire was trapped between the sink and some sort of advancing monstrosity that to Marcus looked like a five-foot ant that was walking on two legs. The sight stopped him frozen in his tracks only to find himself pushed aside from behind by Celina. A sharp forward thrust of her wand threw a streak of light between the wand and the creature.

The sharp burst of white light struck against a dark pointed head that snapped back on its thin neck. Marcus watched as the creature dropped like a puppet whose strings had been cut.

A scraping sound from the doorway turned them to see the arrival of another creature. It was just stood there apparently having trouble climbing the steps. Another cast from Celina's wand jerked this one back in the doorway, though something like hands were still locked to the doorframe. It swayed for a moment and then fell forward across the threshold blocking the door.

Letting go of her wand for it to swing back and trusting it to lock onto its wand safe Celina grabbed the yard brush and ran to the door. Using the brush, she pushed the remains of the creature off the steps.

It was as Celina was pushing the creature from the doorway that she looked up and found that between the back door and the gate, there was a red circle hanging in the air.

"Wraiths," she called out to them all just as Jane came through the door from the shop.

Jane seeing Claire slowly collapsing by the sink ran across and caught her, and then found herself standing supporting her feeling helpless.

Standing in the yard Celina could see through the portal three more wraiths. Two were approaching from across the red sand, while one had already started to climb through the portal. Celina waited until both its feet were on the paving stones before dealing with it. It fell backwards where for a moment it was left hanging half in and half out of the portal before the edge of the portal cut it in half.

Celina looking through the portal could see two rods with half a star on the ends that pulsed with a white light; Celina tried a strike through the portal directed at one of the stars only to find that on reaching the portal the strike disappeared. Celina turning to see Marcus standing in the doorway said.

"Marcus the gun from the robbery it's in the bottom desk drawer. Get it quickly Marcus, quickly."

Marcus turned and dived back into the storeroom, but he went only as far as the door to the corridor. There he took down a leather bag from the shelf over the door from which he withdrew a gun and ammunition, returning to Celina gun in hand and already loading it. Celina glanced at it seeing something that to her looked more like a cannon than a handgun.

"It's one of my service revolvers," Marcus explained. "I used to carry one of them all the time when I was abroad." Celina pointed at the portal and asked.

"Can you see those two rods with half a star on the ends?"
Marcus nodded asking.

"Sort of glowing is that right?"

"Yes that's right, do you think you could hit the stars before the other wraiths get here?" It looked about fifteen possibly twenty yards to the stars inside the portal, and the light on the other side of the portal was bad. Marcus now saw that a demon and five more wraiths had appeared approaching the star from across the sand.

238

Leaning back against the wall, Marcus grasped the gun in both hands and took careful aim.

An enormous bang made Celina cover her ears while from the other side of the portal, a line of white light hung in the air for a moment before it disappeared clearly showing the flight of the bullet. They watched as a wraith staggered and dropped hit by the stray bullet. Marcus shook his head.

"Strange," he murmured. "It seemed to be deflected to the right; I missed by about a foot." He then stared in amazement as the shot wraith climbed back to its feet again and started toward the portal. Taking aim once more, Marcus pulled the trigger. The right hand star didn't just shatter. Celina and Marcus had time to see it explode into a cloud of glittering dust before everything went white.

Celina and Marcus were blinded as the portal blazed with brilliant blue-white light while at the same time being deafened by the sound of a horrific explosion. Celina stood blinking and peering towards where the portal had been and finding a large round red shape burnt into her eyes was all that she could see, while her ears were ringing like church bells. Turning she vaguely made out the shape of Marcus standing there alternately rubbing his eyes and thumping the side of his head.

As her sight returned and looking around Celina found that despite the flash and noise there had been no actual blast and no damage. Only the bottom half of the wraith remained lying in a pool of black blood on the paving stones to say that a portal had been opened there.

Marcus pocketed the gun and taking Celina's arm helped her back through the door and into the storeroom. Inside the storeroom, Jane was helping Claire towards the office where the Telson was buzzing insistently. Jane picked it up saying.

"Hello." A worried voice came back over the Telson.

"Jane, it's me Elizabeth; a portal has opened again in a new place; it was only open for a few minutes and then it abruptly closed, nothing like a normal closing."

"We know, and you'd better come over here fast, land in the yard behind the shop but be careful as there are some bodies out there."

"You mean the portal was at the shop?" a shocked Elizabeth asked.

"Yes in fact it was almost in the shop." Celina who had now joined Jane in the office and heard the last of the conversation put her mouth close to the sound collector and asked.

"Can you arrange to have the bodies collected? They are smelling out the shop something terrible."

"I'll be over with a team in about five minutes," and then there was a click and she was gone.

"This is getting to be a habit," Celina said as she reached into the bottom drawer of her desk and took out the small bottle of brandy saying. "Marcus if you please," as she held up the bottle.

"We need something to drink out of; I don't fancy drinking straight from the bottle." Celina held the bottle up and looking at the level of the liquid, she said.

"The way we keep hitting the brandy, we'll be giving Claire bad habits." Then with a small laugh, she said. "She'll be turning into a drunkard along with the rest of us." It was as they laughed at Celina's words that the tension was finally broken.

Elizabeth arrived with a passenger and landing at the back of the shop she came in holding her nose. Following her was a man carrying a large canvas sack over one shoulder.

"You're right; it is smelly out there," Elizabeth declared. "Come on then tell me what happened?"

"Hello Mr Gibbard," Marcus said standing up and helping Elizabeth's father with the bag. "I see you've brought your photographic engine."

"Elizabeth thought it might be a good idea," Mr Gibbard replied as he placed the sack on the floor. Then as he started to unpack his photographic engine, he said. "Elizabeth says there are no actual photographic records of any of the demonic forms so this will be a first."

"Where's the team you were bringing to get rid of the smell?" Celina asked.

"They'll be here soon; they're bringing a steam cart as horses don't like the smell of wraiths."

"Wraiths?" Claire asked.

"Yes wraiths," Celina replied. "That's why I could deal with them. If it had been a demon things would probably have ended quite differently."

"You managed last time," Marcus said supportively. Celina turned to him saying.

"Last time was last time, and I'm definitely not saying I could do it again. What I want to know is why they were here and why tonight?"

"Yes how did they know you were here?" Elizabeth asked as she pulled her heavy coat off.

"You know that's a good question." Marcus said as he looked around. "I believe the only ones who knew were our staff."

"What if they didn't know we were here?" a very pale Claire asked, and then finding everyone looking at her, she said.

"What if they expected the shop to be empty?"

"If that was so what would they want in the shop?" Elizabeth asked. Claire pointed at Celina's desk drawer.

"Perhaps one of those books," she said as she turned to look at Celina. "You called Dr McDonald this morning, and he couldn't come to collect the book, and then these creatures turn up this evening. Possibly he was greedy and wanted the book without having to pay for it; a little suspicious isn't it?" Mr Gibbard picked up his photographic engine and said.

"Look I can't help you with this so I'll just go and take my photographs, that is if that's all right with you Elizabeth."

"Yes father, but be careful if you need to move them. Use something like, like that brush that's out there. Don't under any circumstances touch them yourself, and especially that half of one."

It was about twenty minutes later when a hissing in the alley announced the arrival of the steam cart. Marcus took the key and went to open the gate passing Mr Gibbard, who had tied a wet cloth over his nose and was taking his last photograph and feeling very relieved to have finished. He had found the acrid smell of flash powder mingled with gunpowder and dead wraiths, burned his nose, stung his eyes and turned his stomach.

"Do they always smell like this?" he asked Marcus as he packed his photographic engine away.

"You'll have to ask Elizabeth as it's the first time I've ever seen wraiths." Then moving to one side the two of them stood watching as two men in heavy leather aprons and gloves began to clean up the yard. The men placed the remains of the wraiths on to large India rubber sheets and wrapped them tightly before loading them onto the back of the cart.

"When is this doctor of yours due to pick up the book?" Elizabeth asked.

"Some time tomorrow and I intend to be here when he does," Celina replied.

"If I was you, I would have a good rummage around inside his head never mind whether it's permitted or not." Claire hearing Elizabeth came instantly to her feet looking anxiously from Elizabeth to Celina as she blurted out.

"You said you couldn't read minds." Celina shook her head as she replied.

"No I said I didn't read your mind and nor would I, and certainly not without your permission, and even then I can't think of any circumstances where I would. It's not something we like to do."

"She's telling you the truth," Elizabeth said. "Our oath stops us except in extreme circumstances like this. If Dr McDonald is innocent Celina will be compelled to stop by the oath. She has no choice it's part of the oath's power."

Marcus having locked the gate was making his way back towards the storeroom door. Reaching the door he held up the lantern he was holding and stood looking around a yard that even after all the bodies had been removed still smelt of wraiths.

Between the gate and the door Marcus noticed that there was a small pile of what looked like reddish rusty sand missed by the wraith's blood. Back in the storeroom, Marcus found the dustpan and brush, and then carefully avoiding the wraith's blood he swept up what he could of the red sand from the flagstones.

An empty tin tea box from the storeroom made a suitable storage container, and Marcus tipped the sand into it before putting the lid on and pressing it tightly down. Next taking a bucket, he swilled water over the yard washing away the blood before finally taking the tin into the office where he held it out asking.

"Elizabeth do you think a sample of Hell will be of interest to anyone?"

"A sample of Hell what do you mean?" she asked. Shaking the tin, Marcus said.

"Well some red sand from the other side of the portal was left on the flagstones outside, so I swept it up and put it in this tin."

The two Knights looked at each other in surprise, and then Elizabeth said as she took the tin.

"The people at Glastonbury may make you an honorary Knight for this; I think I should drop this off at the hospital on my way back, and then they can send it off to be analysed tomorrow." Looking up at the clock Elizabeth said.

"Where is my father, I must get him home as mother will want to know all about tonight." Celina looked at the clock and laughed saying.

"I'm sorry about this, but I think our dinner is off, as by now the tea shop will be closed not to mention the problem of our smelly new perfume."

Tuesday 11th February 1862.

During the first hours in the shop, Celina and Jane were kept busy running between floors and moving forgotten items about. Things that hadn't sold previously were suddenly selling briskly, and like Claire said.

"It could be the display units and the new way things are being displayed."

Dr McDonald's coach arrived just after midday, but to Celina's disappointment, it was a young man who came into the shop. He introduced himself as the doctor's Butler, and then apologised to Celina for Dr McDonald's absence as he explained.

"Dr McDonald has been detained overnight, and we are not expecting him to return to London until later this evening."

Celina taking him into the office found him more than ready to sit and talk as they waited for Sally to wrap the book. Eventually the carefully packaged book was signed for and transferred to his safe keeping, and then as a final and courteous act Celina herself escorted him to the door. As Celina watched the coach being driven away Jane joined her at the window saying.

"Your Dr McDonald didn't come then."

"No he didn't; and it's strange. His footman is worried about him."

"Worried, how do you mean worried?" Jane asked.

"Well he feels that over the last four years or so he's changed. Somehow he's different, and his servants don't feel he is the same man. He disappears for days or even weeks at a time and then when he comes back he locks himself away."

Celina turned to walk back to the office saying. "He's frightened too. He's frightened of his master and frightened that his master is doing something illegal." A surprised Jane asked.

"You managed to get all that leaning?"

"No he told me most of it, in fact, it seemed as if he wanted to talk to someone and I only eased his conscience by leaning a little and lending a sympathetic ear."

"Is it worth calling the Abbot?" Jane asked.

"I don't suppose it would hurt," Celina replied as she reached for the Telson. She gave the answering controller the direct number for the Abbey, only to be told by the Abbot's secretary that the Abbot was unavailable, and that he would arrange to have the Abbot call her back.

Celina had almost given up hope of the Abbot calling her back when the buzz of the Telson called her into the office. After filling in the details of the previous night and their thoughts on Dr McDonald, Celina then confessed to leaning slightly on the footman and revealed what she had learned. The Abbot after gently chastising Celina went on to compliment her on her handling of the wraiths, and her handling of the footman.

It was as Celina was about to put out the oil lamp in the office that the Telson buzzed again. This time it was the Abbot's secretary asking Celina if she could see the Abbot later that evening. Reluctantly, Celina agreed thinking to herself of another long flight and a late night.

Polly

Celina arrived home that night to find Jane waiting with another message for her.

"It isn't much," she said, "just the Abbot's secretary cancelling your meeting and asking if we could put up a guest until further notice."

"A guest, who can he mean, and is it a man or a woman?" Celina asked.

"He didn't say, so we made ready the guest rooms above your rooms." They both turned to find Kate stood in the open doorway knocking and saying.

"Please Miss the Abbot has called. Your guest has just left the Abbey and he says to expect her in about an hour or so, and the cook is asking if she should hold dinner?"

"Tell the cook thank you yes hold dinner." Celina then turned to Jane and said.

"I guess that narrows our guest down to one of two, either Marjory or Polly." Jane with a puzzled frown asked.

"How do you work that out?"

"Well apart from me who do you know who can get here in less than an hour and a half?"

It was just under an hour later when a broom arrived. Jane who was looking out of the kitchen door sent Kate for Celina as a small man several inches shorter than herself dismounted and lifted a large travel bag from the front seat. He was dressed in baggy trousers, a jacket and a close-fitting hat held in place by a scarf. Jane went out to greet him as Celina arrived at the door.

Turning to Jane the visitor pulled off the hat and shook out a head of light brown curly hair, and only then did the visitor smile broadly at the two of them. The smile stopped them both in their tracks. It wasn't a man smiling at them; it was a young girl who stood there.

"Polly is that you?" Celina asked uncertainly. Still smiling Polly said.

"Of course it's me. Who else would it be arriving by broom at this time on a night?"

"Well come on in then," Celina said. "The cook has held the dinner for us." Seeing Thomas in the kitchen Jane dropped the bag in his arms saying.

"Would you take that to the guest rooms please and then put Polly's broom away for her."

Thomas who could hardly take his eyes off Polly in trousers backed out of the kitchen and as the door closed all four women burst out laughing.

"Well I must admit." a laughing Celina managed to say. "That you look more like a gamekeeper than a Knight of the church dressed like that." Polly looked down at herself and said.

"I usually wear this when I run courier for the Abbey. It's far better for flying in and not nearly as draughty as a dress, or as embarrassing as you can't catch your foot in your skirt getting off and fall off."

Jane looked at Celina and smiled as Polly took off the jacket to reveal a man's thick woollen sweater, a sweater that was definitely on the large size for her, pulling at it, she said.

"I've got my normal clothes in the bag so can I go and change? It gets a bit warm in these things when I'm inside."

"Come on then," Jane said as she took charge of escorting Polly up to the guest rooms, and passing a round-eyed Thomas on his way down. As they walked into the sitting room Polly stopped. It was as opulent and beautiful as the rooms below, and in daylight it had a view from the windows the same as Celina's. From there Jane found herself having to pull Polly through into a bedroom with an attached bathroom just the same as Celina's on the floor below. A horrified Polly turned to Jane and said.

"I can't have these rooms. These rooms are for a lady not for the likes of me." Jane put her hand on Polly's shoulder and looked at her, while through the hand contact feeling just how insecure Polly felt. Jane quietly said.

"Polly you are a Lady now, you are Lady Polly and in this house, you will be treated as Lady Polly. These are your rooms for whenever you stay here, and they are just the same as Celina's." Polly looked around the bedroom looking as if she wanted to run until turning back to Jane she said.

"Jane I can't," and then looking around the room again she said. "What if I do something silly and make a fool of myself? I'm no Lady, you heard Lady Marjory I was a workhouse drudge, and I don't know any of your fancy ways."

Jane turned Polly fully towards her and taking hold of her hands she said.

"That's why I'm here to teach you and help you. Celina won't laugh at you; she's not like that. If you need anything or any help, we are both here. There are only three servants other than myself and all of them are here to help you." Polly looked shocked.

"You are a servant? You're a Lady, a Lady and you have talent a lot of talent." Polly looked down at Jane's hands holding hers as she said. "I can feel it when you touch me."

Jane pulled her hands away saying. "Polly I have no real talent; I only have a small amount that's very erratic and that's all."

Polly now took hold of Jane's hands again feeling the flow of energy just under her skin. It was now Jane's turn to be shocked. Suddenly, it wasn't the young girl called Polly that she knew standing there. She found herself looking into the palest of blue eyes. They were the eyes of a Lady standing strong and assertive, even if she didn't come up to her shoulder.

"Jane you do have talent," Polly said firmly. "You're one of the strongest I have ever come across." Jane pulled her hands away and sat down on the bed looking a picture of misery.

"I know I have something," she said tearfully. "But there's something wrong and I can't seem to use it. It's just that it's all there inside me and stuck. Please Polly don't tell anyone, especially Celina." Then wiping her eyes she said. "I'm not a Lady, I'm just Celina's companion friend and maid, and I will be yours too." Polly stood for a moment undecided before she said.

"I promise I won't tell anyone that is if you promise to let me help you." Then she took Jane's kerchief from her and wiped away the rest of her tears as she said. "First though I have a job of work to do on Celina, and I think I had better include you too."

Having changed her clothes and still feeling a little embarrassed at having Jane help her, it was a slightly nervous Polly who came down to the dining room for her first meal with her new friends. Over dinner, Polly explained the reason she had been sent in such a hurry.

"I was told just after the Abbot came out of his meeting that all restrictions on me showing you defensive spells had been lifted, and I was to get over as of yesterday, and so here I am."

"What do you mean by defensive spells?" looking first at Polly and then Jane. Celina then asked "and what exactly do you mean by spells?" Polly picked up her glass and after taking a drink she began.

"When Merlin and the first warlocks or wizards and witches were using talent; it is believed that they used spoken spells or words. Marjory says we believe it was to help them concentrate their thoughts." She giggled as she said.

"Marjory keeps teaching me long words," she took another sip before continuing.

"Over the years and as talent was used more and more, spells became what you might call ordinary things, and speaking them became unnecessary so it gradually dropped out of use." Polly leaned forward and said.

"Do you realise we have no new abilities? Merlin could do everything we can do now, and probably more." She paused and looked at Celina, who appeared deep in thought as she said.

"Do you know I think you could possibly be right, we may have improved slightly on some of them, but basically, we do the same things that were done in Merlin's day."

"Good," Polly replied. "Now I have been sent here to teach you magic." Celina and Jane both looked at Polly as if she had used a swear word.

"There's no such thing as magic, it's just a myth." Celina said though having heard this from Polly, Celina was not feeling quite as sure as she sounded.

Polly looked at them quietly for a moment before getting to her feet where she stood holding her empty glass in one hand. Then after licking one finger, she circled it around the rim of the glass creating a high-pitched note. As they all watched the note became higher as the glass filled with water.

"I don't think I'm good enough for wine yet," she said looking at her astonished audience.

"That's magic?" Celina asked as she rose to her feet and came around the table. First taking the glass off Polly she sniffed at it, and then took a drink. Polly winked at Jane as she said.

"Yes it really is water." Celina returned mystified to her seat and said.

"Polly if I hadn't seen that with my own eyes, I would never have believed it. Can anyone with talent do?" She hesitated, "magic?"

"I think so that is if their talent is strong enough. Marjory has managed that one and she can move things like this…." Suddenly, Celina's glass moved so fast that if Celina hadn't been looking at it, it would have appeared to disappear, only to reappear at Jane's elbow, and before Jane could react back again to Celina.

It was seeing the glass move like it had that prompted Celina to ask. "Has your ability to push a broom like you do anything to do with magic?"

Polly with a shake of her head replied. "No that's just hard work and knowing a few tricks."

It was Jane who asked. "Can you do anything with magic, like possibly turn one thing into another?"

"No. In fact I didn't create that water. I just moved it out of that bottle over there in little tiny bits but ever so fast so that you couldn't see them." Polly pointed at the decanter as she spoke.

"You were so busy looking at the glass that you didn't see the water in the bottle go down, in fact none of it was truly magic." Then giving them both a shy smile she said. "It was all trickery, but it shows what can be done with talent."

It was at this moment that Kate came into the dining room to enquire about dessert, only to find the dinner half-eaten and cold. Over dessert, it was decided that the actual lessons could wait for tomorrow as Polly had to admit she was ready for bed, having had very little sleep over the last two days.

Wednesday 12th February 1862.

Jane took Polly under her wing the following morning having heard from Kate, who had found when assisting Polly dressing that she possessed as far as clothes were concerned, little more than she stood in, and precious few of those. Celina readily agreed that lessons should be put back a day for something as important as shopping, at least in this case.

Going around London with Jane was a terrifying experience for Polly as she was fitted out with dresses, underclothes, hats, day and nightwear along with other assorted apparel that Jane thought necessary.

What with the prices and quantity of the clothes being bought Polly was left in a state of shock, and Jane was left to make arrangements for Polly's purchases to be delivered to Belgrave House. Lunch was taken with Celina and it was at this point that Polly broached the subject of the cost, and who was to pay for everything. Celina and Jane looked first at each other and then at Polly before saying in perfect unison.

"The Abbot of course, who else," and then to Polly's horror they both burst out laughing.

"He'll go wild," Jane spluttered trying to contain her laughter as Celina said.

"Well he should have made sure a Knight had decent clothes, after all it's his duty to see that a Knight in his employ is suitably attired and looked after in fulfilling her duty." Polly was aghast.

"What if he wants me to pay for them? I haven't any money and they cost over twenty pounds."

"Only twenty pounds?" Celina declared looking shocked. "Jane you had better take her back and buy her something better, or at least some more of the same." Polly now looked close to tears as

Celina said. "Polly, it's truly all right. When did you become a Knight?"

"When I was sixteen,"

"Right, and how old are you now?"

"I've just turned seventeen," Polly said still sounding a little unsure of where Celina's questions were leading.

"So I would say that in your church account, you should have at least eighty pounds of your own money. Didn't any one tell you that when you became a Knight you started to receive an allowance which is banked through the church for things just like this?"

Polly shook her head and then her eyes opened wide as she realised just what Celina had said.

"You mean I…. I have money of my own?"

"Yes," Celina assured her. "You are a Lady now, a Lady of the Church, but on a project like this it's the Abbots responsibility to see you are suitably attired and provided for, so I think he will end up paying for at least some of these things from church funds."

Then Celina gave Jane a sly look as she said. "Do you think we can put this meal down to the church?"

Jane appeared to think for a moment and then said. "No I don't think we ought to."

After lunch and with for her unusual bravado Polly asked Jane.

"Do you think I could get proper flying clothes in London? Ones that fit me instead of those cast-offs I've been using, if I have money that's what I would like." Jane considering her request said.

"You say you fly courier for the Abbey?" Polly nodded. "Well if that's the case yes we can; I'm not quite sure where to go but we can certainly look around."

As providence would have it, the cabby that was to take them home was able to suggest a suitable establishment that he knew. The establishment he recommended specialised in cold weather and hunting apparel, and so at Jane's request he turned the cab around and took them there.

A young man approached them as they entered the shop. For some reason he made the mistake of assuming that it was Jane who was requiring hunting or riding clothes and that Polly was her maid. Jane put him right with her first words.

"My friend Lady Cavendish is in need of some rather specialised clothing and you have been recommended." With something of a start the young man gave a small bow to the two of them asking.

"Specialised clothing for riding or hunting?" Jane looked at Polly asking.

"I would say both wouldn't you?" Polly looked around the shop surveying what was displayed before she said.

"I think so, in fact something like this might work quite well." As she spoke she walked over to a mannequin wearing corded trousers and a heavy leather-riding coat reaching down to the knee. "Something like this only it needs to be suitable for a much colder place."

"I assume that the clothing is for a young gentleman?" the man asked.

Polly turned away from the mannequin and putting on a look that even impressed Jane she said. "No, it is for myself, is that going to be a problem?" The man looked aghast.

"Trousers?" he said and then again. "Trousers?" Finally he said. "I'm sorry you did say for yourself." Polly who was several inches smaller than him suddenly did the impossible. She went from looking up at him to looking down her nose at him as she said in a voice that broached no argument.

"Yes for myself, and as I have said, is there a problem?"

"No Miss, no," the young man quickly replied. "I will just have to call Mrs Johnson as it would not be acceptable for me to serve you." Jane finally had to laugh as the young man made a hasty retreat to the back room.

"You're doing brilliantly so now keep it up," she told Polly. The young man returned a few moments later with a stout woman dressed in severe black, and introduced her as Mrs Johnson.

"I understand you wish hunting apparel?" Mrs Johnson asked Jane. Jane stepping to one side so the woman could see Polly said.

"No, Lady Cavendish here is the one who requires your assistance." Mrs Johnson now looking at Polly replied.

"Oh I am so sorry; I thought this young woman was your daughter."

Polly who happened to see the look on Jane's face promptly stepped forward to stand between Jane and Mrs Johnson saying.

"Yes, I require something rather special for riding and hunting, and I'm afraid normal skirts would be out of the question. Also where I shall be it is usually very cold so I shall need something that will keep me warm. Trousers, a warm coat, boots and gloves come to mind. Oh yes and possibly some form of a hat."

For a moment, Mrs Johnson looked shocked. Then pulling herself together and taking a deep breath she said.

"If the Lady would come with me, we will see what can be done." Jane followed Mrs Johnson and Polly into a small room with a large mirror hanging on the wall.

There Mrs Johnson turned up the oil lamp, and then after asking Polly to remove her dress and underskirts she proceeded to take what to Polly seemed a lot of intimate measurements, while having frequently to leave to consult the manager as to what measurements would be required for men's garments.

In the meantime, Jane sat quietly fuming in a corner, absorbing the insult of Polly being taken for her daughter. Gradually though and as Jane's temper cooled, the funny side of the situation started to become apparent to her. Sitting and watching, Jane noticed that as the measurements were taken, her so-called daughter became gradually redder in the face, and as she did so, her back became straighter and her chin rose higher.

Eventually the funny side of Polly having measurements usually taken for a man started to take hold and Jane's sense of humour started to take over. At last, Mrs Johnson stood back and looked at her slate saying.

"The trousers are going to be the problem, if you don't mind I will just bring a few things for you to try on," and with that she left the room. Jane looked at a Polly who was now bright red in the face and managed to say without laughing.

"Well you did ask for flying clothes." That started Polly giggling as she said.

"Yes Mother and it's a good thing I had a bath and put on clean under-things this morning." That set Jane off giggling, and it was only Mrs Johnson returning, that silenced the two of them.

Mrs Johnson returned laden down with clothing. Shaking out a pair of boys riding trousers she said.

"These should fit you if you would like to try them."

Polly started without much success to struggle into them. Mrs Johnson finally pointing at Polly's borrowed fancy drawers said.

"I'm afraid those will have to come off." Jane almost bursts with the effort to suppress her laughter as Polly, who was growing redder by the minute divested herself of a pair of Kate's best and extremely lacy drawers before pulling on the trousers.

"They're a bit tight, especially in the leg and around the knees." Then patting her rear end she said, "and here."

"Yes I thought that might be the case," Mrs Johnson said with a smile. "We don't get many young ladies asking for trousers." Then as she changed some of the measurements on her slate, she said. "There seems to be a slight difference in measurements.

Now while you have them on, try this coat." Mrs Johnson offered Polly a coat made from thick Scottish wool. Polly shaking it out found it quilted inside, and definitely warm looking.

"It's made for our Scottish customers, and this one is made for the ladies," she said giving Jane a knowing look. Polly put it on and buttoned it up to the throat.

"Oh yes," both Polly and Mrs Johnson said together. "I thought that would be just right," Mrs Johnson then handed Polly a pair of boots saying. "Now try on the boots." Watching Polly pulling on the boots Mrs Johnson said.

"I think we shall make the trousers wide enough to go over their tops so that when it rains the water will not run down into them." Polly pulled the boots on and then Mrs Johnson gave her the gloves saying. "Again these are made for our Scottish customers."

Jane was thoroughly impressed. The coat obviously styled for a lady reached down to the knees. It was beautifully made and a perfect fit. The boots were sturdy but smart-looking while the gloves were well padded to be warm but not so heavy as to be cumbersome. Polly now looked in the mirror and apart from the trousers, the fit and look was perfect.

"Now for the hat," Mrs Johnson said holding out a hat that was stylish and elegant but made to keep the rain off the wearers face. "What about something like this?" and then looking at Jane she said. "This one is made especially for the ladies." As she shook it, two straps dropped from inside ready to be fastened under the chin.

"Yes," Polly said. "I like it."

It was arranged for Polly to return in seven days for a fitting of the trousers, and then when everything was ready it would all be delivered to Belgrave House. Polly thanked Mrs Johnson, who said it had been a unique experience and a pleasure.

Jane forgave Mrs Johnson enough so that as they left the little room she pressed half a crown into her hand. "Just for Polly's sake," as she later said to Celina. Outside the shop the cab was still waiting.

That night after Polly's new clothes had been unpacked and put away; Celina was treated to the full tale of Jane and her 'daughters flying clothes. Then it was time for the expenses to be totalled up, when Celina included Polly's specialised flying clothes Polly was horrified at the additional expense, but as Celina said.

"The Abbot will pay for these. He may spend a week in church praying for forgiveness after the language, but he will pay."

Thursday 14th February 1862.

The following day, after a hot bath and with her hair arranged by Jane, along with clothes provided by various sisters of Celina Polly looked every inch a Lady as she arrived for breakfast.

After breakfast and in accordance with the Abbot's strict instructions. Polly insisted that Celina have her first lesson in the full use of her talent. With this being the case Jane was dispatched to look after the shop for the day, and Polly took Celina to her sitting room.

Polly still seemed very shy and uncertain about herself and in the use she had of the rooms. Celina could see that the schooling was to be a two-way affair. Polly and Celina chose to sit in the window seat, and with Polly radiating uncertainty Celina decided it was up to her to break the ice by asking.

"Who taught you to do these things or how did you find out how to do them?" Polly looked down obviously troubled. Then giving Celina the impression that she had come to a very difficult decision she started to explain, though not quite in the way Celina had expected.

"I was put in the workhouse not long after my mother died; they said I was about five years old and…." Polly hesitated. Celina remained silent waiting as Polly struggled to say what she wanted to say while not sure how to begin.

"You don't know what life was like there. They got you up before first light and put you to work for as long as three or four hours before we had anything to eat, and then it was only thin watery gruel. Some of the girls died of starvation, or if it wasn't starvation it was from the beatings or both, it was horrible. If I could have done then what I can do now, I would have burned it down.

"It was so bad after one beating that one of the girls I slept with stopped eating and starved herself to death; and another girl, she was only seven, and she never came back after a beating, we heard tell the guardians buried something that night.

"For me it was the beatings that did it. That's how I learned to what you call shield. I think I was about eleven when I found that if I kept sort of pushing with my mind that I could stop the cane from touching me. Only that made it worse because they thought I was hard and unreachable." Celina sat listening in horror at what Polly was saying and wondering how such a place could exist.

"Then I found how to make it so that I could feel the cane but not let it hurt me. I would scream when they hit me as it made it better for me if they thought they were hurting me. Then I tried to teach one or two of my friends how to do it, but it wouldn't work for them. Later, I found that I could do other things…." Polly stopped, and Celina could feel that there were certain things Polly didn't want to talk about. Then Polly started speaking again.

"It was after Mrs Tomlin had beaten little Mary to death; I hated her for it, and afterwards I prayed at night for her to die. It was one afternoon not long after Mary died, we were scrubbing the big hall and Mrs Tomlin just started screaming at us; it was then that I...." She paused again and then shook her head before saying.

"It was when she started lashing out with her cane at Emily; she was hitting her really hard, and I couldn't stand it. I reached out with my mind and I found I could feel her heart...." Polly shuddered.

"I could feel it was beating so fast with the excitement of beating Emily...." Polly stopped speaking. Her eyes seemed unfocused as if living her memories over again. Then Polly started speaking as if she had never stopped.

"I could feel that she was enjoying it, her heart was beating so hard and I wanted it to stop. I reached out and, and I took hold of it and, and . . . I just stopped it.

I held it until I had stopped it beating. I could feel her excitement turn to terror when she felt her heart stop. I knew she thought she was dying and then when she fell down I was frightened and I let it start again; she never came back to the workhouse."

Polly looked up and said. "I'm not sorry I did it. I wanted her dead, but I couldn't kill her."

Celina was feeling that she had heard enough about the horror of the orphanage for now and decided to see if she could change the subject slightly.

"How did they find out about you?" she asked.

"It was little Nancy; she was only something like three when they brought her to the orphanage, and she cried every night for over a week, so I let her sleep in our bed." Polly sniffed. "I really miss her; it was the day she dropped some plates that it happened...." Polly sniffed again as tears welled up in her eyes.

"They were the really heavy ones, plates the guardians used for their meals." Polly stopped and looked down. Celina could see her twisting her fingers together.

"I think she was only seven, and it was when the cook pushed her that she dropped them. The cook well she had a terrible temper." Celina could now see real tears in Polly's eyes as she said. "Cook was really angry at Nancy even though it wasn't her fault, and when I saw the cook reach for her stick, I knew she was going to beat Nancy...." There was now a big sniff from Polly.

"Cook had a thin square metal rod that she used to poke the fire or pig swill, and other things. It was about a yard long and when she beat a girl with it most of them died from infection." Polly looked at Celina.

"I couldn't let her do it, so I shielded Nancy. I'd never shielded anyone else before and when cook found she wasn't hurting Nancy; she called her a witch and said you have to burn witches and, and then she threw her into the fire. I didn't know if my shield would protect her from the fire and, and I screamed...."

Polly fell silent then with a shake of her head she said. "They said I screamed I don't know, but then I, you know what I mean; I threw the cook across the kitchen and pulled Nancy out of the fire. They all saw what happened and that it was me...."

She stopped and sat looking at her hands silent for a moment and then in a whisper she said. "I was bad; I deliberately broke both cook's arms when I threw her."

Celina could see Polly was now really crying so putting her arm around her shoulders and wiping the tears away she said.

"I'm not going to blame you, if it had been me I would probably have done worse. What did they do then?"

Polly looked up and said. "The cook was screaming with the pain, and others were shouting that it was witchcraft. Then they called for Mr Jackson; he was a simpleton." Celina wiped Polly's eyes again.

"He was really brutal to us, especially the little ones. He was the one who got hold of me and locked me in the cellar." Polly sniffed again.

"They said they would get the vicar to have me burned...." She stopped Celina had a feeling it was as if she was remembering something that was to her horrible. Then with a shudder she said. "They left me in the cellar for three days, three days in the dark; that's how I learnt how to do this."

Polly held out her hand. On her palm appeared a ball of golden sunlight about two inches across. Gently, she tossed it into the air where it hung giving light and gentle warmth.

Celina was amazed; she'd never heard or seen anything like that before. Polly closed her hand and the light disappeared.

"They didn't bring our vicar; he had been taken sick or something and so another one came. They brought him down to the cellar and there was Mr Jackson, the matron and two guardians with him…." Polly sniffed.

"He had a large bag with a bell and a Bible and a candle inside." Celina wiped Polly's eyes and face again as with another big sniff Polly said.

"He took them out of the bag and set them on the floor, and then he lit the candle. Then he told the others to go. He said he couldn't hear my confession if they were there. When they had gone he put his ear to the door and listened to them leave. I was frightened but once they had gone, he changed. He took some bread and cheese out of his bag and an apple; I hadn't eaten for three days, and all of it was for me." Polly looked up at Celina as she said.

"I remember the food more than what he said. While I was eating he sat on one of the sacks and asked me a lot of questions…." Polly sniffed again. "Then he told me not to worry. He said he would be coming back the next day to take me away somewhere safe. I could tell, you know how that he meant what he was saying, and then he told me about Merlin and the Knights of the Church.

"He said he was going to take me to them, and they would look after me and keep me safe. After he went the guardians came, and they locked the door again and then they told me that he was coming back with iron chains to take me away to be burned." Polly wiped her nose on the back of her hand; Celina gave her back the kerchief as Polly said.

"I didn't know what to believe, but they came back the next day and they put me in chains, big thick iron ones so heavy I could hardly stand. The whole orphanage was there to watch; I was crying, and some of the girls was crying too. I could see Nancy with two of the other girls, and she was crying. My special friends pointed at her and then to themselves, so I knew they would look after her. They put me in a big black coach with no windows."

Polly wiped her eyes with the back of her hand." Celina took the kerchief back and wiped Polly's eyes and face again as looking at Celina Polly said.

"Inside the coach there were two sisters and a woman. As soon as we were out of the orphanage, they started taking the chains off me. Sister Annabel and Sister Margaret were both crying. The other woman was Lady Marjory, and I've been with Marjory ever since." Celina giving Polly her kerchief back went to the bell pull to call for Kate, who was given an order for tea.

Once tea had been served, and Polly had recovered slightly, Celina asked.

"Do you know what has happened at the orphanage since you left?" Polly shook her head.

"No I would like to know about my friends and especially Nancy. She was like my sister and…. well, I really miss her and she will miss me." Celina who had been thinking of ways to get news of the orphanage for Polly said.

"Dickie, he's a friend of mine and I wonder if he could help. You finish your tea while I call him and see what he can find out."

Celina called Dickie on the Telson and after giving him a shortened version of Polly's story found she had to talk him out of finding and going to the orphanage himself. Eventually, she persuaded him just to make inquiries and find out what if anything was being done.

Returning to Polly's room, Celina found a far more composed young woman. Polly had obviously taken the opportunity to wash her face and was now pouring them both another cup of tea. Celina resumed her seat beside Polly asking. "Now how do I create a light like you did, is it hard?"

Polly opened her hand and the little sun was there again. Then as she closed her hand and the sun disappeared, she said. "No it's quite easy but first you have to find where your power comes from. Normally with Talent's, it comes from inside you, and when you do something with your power a little of what you have is used. That's why if you do something hard using talent for a long time you feel tired and weak. It takes time for your body to reabsorb energy again." Polly giggled. "That's Marjory again giving me big words." Celina feeling puzzled asked.

"How do you mean to absorb energy? Absorb energy from what or where?"

"Let me explain." Polly said. "What you have to do is look outside yourself and feel the source of your power. It's all around you, so open your mind and push your awareness out and see if you can feel something like a hot fog."

Celina closed her eyes and sat still, focusing her mind until finally she said. "Yes it's there but I can't hold it; it comes and goes."

"Don't try to hold it." Polly said encouragingly. "Just feel that its there." Celina remained very still, and then said. "Yes I see what you mean; if I chase it, it's as if it runs away."

"That's it." Polly said. "Now relax your mind and just watch how it surrounds you, never quite reaching you."

Celina sat perfectly still and then said. "Damn I've lost it."

"That doesn't matter." Polly said. "The reason it never quite reaches you according to Marjory is that we all have a personal internal shield. It's the shield that keeps us ourselves, but at the same time it keeps the energy away, and that's why ordinary people can't do what we do."

Celina again not quite understanding asked. "How do you mean?"

"Well according to Marjory our internal shields are leaky and let more energy through than ordinary people's shields. It makes us more sensitive to the energy and being aware of it allows us to use it, the surplus that is. If we use too much we feel weak and have to wait for more to seep in."

Celina thought it over remembering how she felt after destroying the demon.

"Then if we could weaken that shield of ours we could use more.'" Celina shrugged, "talent and not feel so weak?"

"That's it, and now we just have to teach you how." For the rest of the lesson, Celina struggled to relax her internal shield alternately succeeding and failing, and finally ending up with a splitting headache making her wish she could place a pain block on herself.

News from Jane upon her return in the evening helped Celina to feel somewhat better. The new shop layout was working. Sales were up and the silks were doing particularly well, but even better for Celina was that the products from the north were selling so fast they were in danger of selling out.

Then just before dinner, there came a Telson call from Dickie asking if he could come over that night, so with the invitation having been extended the Cook was asked to provide another place for dinner. After dinner, Dickie took Polly aside and told her what had happened after she had been taken from the orphanage, Polly listening in silence as he said.

"The Reverent Martin had contacted his Bishop and a full investigation by the police was ordered. What they found was horrifying." Dickie looking at Polly's face could see the hope and fear in her eyes as he continued.

"They found the remains of fourteen children buried in an un-consecrated area within the grounds." Polly sat still not making a sound and just looking at him, so he continued saying.

"They found other children in a state of starvation and with marks of excessive beatings. It all ended with two of the guardians and eight of the staff both present and previous being charged." Dickie had been carefully watching Polly, who now sat looking at him with her face completely devoid of expression, so Dickie continued.

"The ones that I know of that were charged with murder were two of the Guardians along with Mrs Green the cook, Mrs Gillesby the matron, Mrs Tomlin, and then there were five others on lesser offences. They were all tried at York Assizes where the ones found guilty of murder suffered the usual punishment.

The others including the two guardians found not guilty of murder, but guilty of other offences received sentences from fifteen to twenty-five years with hard labour." As Dickie fell silent Polly in a whisper asked about her friends.

Dickie hadn't asked about any of the girls in particular, so he couldn't help there, though he was able to tell Polly that the orphanage was now run as part of an estate and was kept under close supervision.

Celina watching as Polly listened to the news from Dickie could see that he had only partly answered Polly's need. Celina decided there and then that she would have to find some way of helping Polly find the rest of the answers she sought. Celina reached across the table and gave Polly's hand a comforting squeeze. It was later over coffee that Dickie remembered about the bug saying.

"Oh, and that bug have you heard the results of the dissection of it?" Celina had to admit she hadn't, but as she said.

"I haven't had chance to see anyone from the Abbey, and the Abbot hasn't said anything over the Telson." So Dickie settled back to tell the three of them what he had heard.

"It isn't truly a poisonous creature, as the venom, if you can call it venom only paralyses its victim while it lays its eggs inside its victim with its ovipositor." Then Dickie added for Polly's benefit.

"That long sharp-pointed part Celina thought was a sting. According to the report, it would be a truly horrific way to die as its offspring would eat you alive from the inside out, and when they opened the bug up, they found the demon equivalent of eggs, over a dozen of them and all ready to be injected."

Celina knew she had paled but looking at Polly, she found Polly was now looking definitely sick as she said.

"I'm glad you told us that after the meal rather than before. I don't think I could have faced eating thinking of what could have happened to Celina." Jane looking at Celina just said.

"I told you I had a bad feeling about it didn't I?"

There was then silence until Dickie asked. "The thing is. Why was it attacking Celina and what is the reason for these attacks, and why now?"

Dickie looked at Celina as if expecting her to have an answer for him, but all Celina could say was. "As I told you all I have absolutely no idea, and I wish I knew myself?"

Dickie looking at Celina and knowing the reaction he would get said. "I've saved the best news for last; Roche Abbey is going to try to incubate some of the eggs." To which a horrified Celina said with a shudder.

"Oh God no never, please Dickie just keep them away from me." It was Jane who said. "Aren't we having enough troubles with demons without growing our own?"

To which Dickie replied. "I have been assured by the Abbey that any bugs that are produced will be kept securely contained, and we do need to know as much about demons as we possibly can."

Saturday 15th February 1862.

Today was Jane's turn to keep Polly company while Celina had a day in the shop to see for herself how things were working. It was just after eleven when a Telson call came for Polly saying that the trousers were ready for a first fitting.

Hearing this Polly and Jane took a cab into central London. On their arrival, Mrs Johnson was called while Polly and Jane found themselves being shown into the same small room where Mrs Johnson bringing a package with her came to join them. Opening the package, she said.

"The gentleman who makes our specials was so intrigued that he decided to have your order filled immediately." Mrs Johnson then unfolded a pair of riding trousers made of leather and held them up against Polly. Mrs Johnson looking at them and by her expression obviously disapproving of ladies in trousers started pulling at the legs, and as she did her expression eventually softened as she said.

"Yes I think they may be about right; if you would try them on please." Jane assisted Polly in removing her skirts only to find again that even with the looser-fitting legs of the trousers, she couldn't get the trouser legs over her new and excessively lacy drawers. Removing her drawers, Polly sat blushing furiously as she started pulling the legs over her feet. Watching her Mrs Johnson said.

"I see you've worn trousers before, and possibly on a regular basis." Polly looked up at her replying.

"Only occasionally but these are a lot less baggy and will be the first ever made just for me." Standing up she fastened the trousers noting with interest the double fitting on the front.

"I'm told it's like that to stop the rain from driving in when riding," Mrs Johnson who was now looking more relaxed about Polly in trousers volunteered. Polly pulled on the boots and then walked around before sitting back down on the chair.

"We have a saddle if you would like to try a riding position," Mrs Johnson offered. Polly looked at Jane uncertainly.

"You might as well," Jane said. Polly turned a number of the men assistant's heads and thought she heard a few remarks as she walked through the shop wearing her new trousers and the coat to cover her bodice. While to Jane's surprise, she heard a whispered, "ignore them," from Mrs Johnson. Reaching the ladies saddle that was mounted on a wooden horse Polly said.

"Side-saddle; no I don't think so," and crossed to the gentleman's saddle where putting one foot in the stirrup, she surprised Jane by swinging up and astride as if it were something she did every day. Jane as an experienced handler of horses had to admit to herself that she couldn't have made it look easier.

Polly had to admit the fit was good as Mrs Johnson took a few more notes and insisted that a few minor alterations were needed to stop the seams from pulling. Then looking over her notes, she concluded that another fitting would not be necessary, and everything would be ready in just a few days. As they left the shop, Jane asked.

"Have you ridden a horse before? You seemed quite familiar with that saddle."

"No," Polly replied with an impish grin, "but I used to be sent out to help with the local hunt, in other words, cleaning up the mess afterwards, and I watched."

Monday 17th February 1862.

I finally managed it; I managed to drop my personal shield and absorb energy directly. Not only that I created a glow in the palm of my hand. How I feel I just cannot put into words.

~ ~ ~

Celina spent a frustrating morning. Her ability to relax her internal shield came and went. At times she felt she had full control and at other times it seemed she had none at all. It was after lunch that Celina found she had achieved a breakthrough. She found that she was doing the small tasks that Polly set her and without thinking about it her mental shield had been allowing the flow of power through whenever her talent needed it.

As the afternoon progressed Celina found herself becoming less and less conscious of the reduction of her shield, until at last she reached the point where she almost ceased to be aware of her action altogether.

Once Celina had reached this point Polly started Celina's lessons in her talent starting with as Polly had named it a 'glow globe.' Following the successful creation of a glow, Polly now told Celina to put her wand away and practice several moves that normally required a wand, and quickly followed this with a warning about how painful it could be to try a full cast or strike without a wand.

It was at this point that Polly brought up the use of spells, and for the first time she took out her own wand, a dark red one and Celina noticed an apparently unlettered one.

"No-one is entirely sure what was meant by spells; it's only from old manuscripts that we know that Merlin and Morgana-le-Fay used them."

"Morgana-le-Fay?" Celina asked.

"Yes it has been said that she was a great Welsh sorceress, and the legends say that she was the equal of Merlin. Some say she was Merlin's sister, others Merlin's lover and there were some who even said she was Merlin's sworn enemy, but apparently she was very powerful.

Like I was saying they both used spells. It is thought that they would say or even shout out spells to focus and strengthen their talent. Legend has it that both Merlin and Morgana wrote down all they knew before they disappeared. Merlin wrote in The Book of Days and Morgana in a book that was lost."

"The Book of Days." Celina laughed. "I've read it but it doesn't make sense."

Polly nodded her agreement as she said. "I know; I've struggled through it too, but that's all legend and long in the past and anyway no-one can be sure until an old spell is rediscovered."

"Well have you discovered any old spells?" Celina asked. Polly put on a glum face as she replied.

"I don't know; I've found some things but whether they're new or old I don't know, but you need to practice pulling in and holding your power. When you gather it inside it's possible to cast most of it out all at once, that's how I blew up a wall."

"You blew up a wall?" Celina asked intrigued having previously heard Marjory mention the fact.

"Yes I was practicing pulling in power and holding it," Polly gave Celina a shy smile as she said. "I guess I over did it, it felt like I was on fire so I just threw a cast at an old wall. Marjory says I pointed my wand at the wall and then I screamed something, and the wall blew up. It left great piles of sand all over everything, and it scared Marjory and me." With a chuckle, Celina replied.

"I don't think we'd better try that here my father might object if I damage this house. I'll tell you what though, I have to visit the shop tomorrow, but I can get away for a few days after that.

How do you feel about flying up to my father's estate in the evening? We can spend a few days there and we can see if we can find a spot on the moors where a bit of noise isn't going to matter, and then you can show me some of those noisy casts." Celina found Polly smiling and nodding enthusiastically.

267

Wednesday 19th February 1862.

I have invited Polly to stay a few days with my mother and father. Being up here means we can find a quiet spot on the moors where a little noise will not matter.

~~~

Celina and Polly arrived at Brimham Hall just after eight of the clock giving Celina time to introduce Polly before having a late dinner. As they ate Celina was able to fill her mother and father in about the latest wraith attack. Then later after Polly had retired, Celina over a glass of sherry told her mother and father all about Polly and the orphanage, going into all the horrific detail she could remember.

Lady Mary was horrified at hearing what Celina was saying and the instant Celina finished she turned to her husband and said.

"James I am going down there tomorrow, you can have the hospital as your pet project but I think I shall make places like that mine."

"Are you sure Mary?" Lord James asked. "After all what reason would you give to explain becoming involved? You can't just turn up demanding to be let in."

Lady Mary considered for a moment and then said. "I shall use the fact I am a doctor and I will offer medical advice and help for charitable reasons."

"It will take a lot of your time." Her husband replied looking rather doubtful.

"James, I have the time on my hands, as now that the new doctors have started at the hospital I only take surgery two days a week. I also have the advantage of speed; I can visit more places in a day than…. well than you know who can in a week." Celina burst out laughing.

"All right," her mother asked. "What's so amusing?"

"Mother if you want speed I might be of some help to you there. Do you know how long it took us to get here from London tonight?" Lady Mary hesitated before answering.

"Perhaps four and a half or five hours, what do you think James?" Lady Mary looked across to her husband as Celina looked expectantly between her mother and father waiting for his answer. After thinking it over her father said.

"Knowing Celina, more like four." He looked at Celina for confirmation.

"Well," Celina found herself smiling. "To be honest we took it fairly steady. Polly could probably have taken half an hour less than I did. She flies faster than I do."

"Faster than you?" her father retorted in surprise. "That little slip of a girl." Her father laughed as he asked. "Just how old is she?"

"She's seventeen," Celina replied.

"Go on then how long?" her mother asked. Celina buffing her finger nails replied.

"One hour and fifty-five minutes."

"Come on how long?" her father asked incredulously.

Celina looked up from her nail-buffing as she replied. "Polly can manage the one hundred and forty miles from Glastonbury to London in just under fifty-five minutes, possibly even a little faster," causing her disbelieving father to say.

"You must be joking; that's nearly one hundred and fifty miles an hour. No one can push a broom anywhere near that speed. In fact, that's almost twice as fast as an express train." Celina found it no surprise to see her father had a look of total disbelief on his face.

"She can and she has," Celina replied firmly. "Not only that she's shown me a number of ways to improve my ability talent-wise, including how to more than double my fastest speed on my broom with no extra effort on my part." At this, her mother put her hand over Celina's saying.

"Whatever you do don't let your father find out how. If he learns to fly that fast I promise I will never fly with him again."

"I'm sorry father," Celina said turning towards him. "The Abbot has my promise not to show anyone what Polly is teaching me, but I can tell you how to increase your speed considerably if you want." With paper pen and ink, Celina drew a broom with a fish-shaped shield around it before adding a tail for stability. Celina then explained how this reduced air resistance and how you could change direction without losing speed simply by modifying the shape of the shield.

Celina then went on to explain about Polly's way of letting the broom lean into turns while using the tail shape of the shield to give extra stability and steering.

"Getting the shape right takes some practice and concentration, but it's worth it." Celina told her doubting parents.

Thursday 20th February 1862.

Today I didn't just learn about talent; I also found out a few other things, things I find most disturbing.

~~~

Celina and Polly brought their brooms to the courtyard early the following morning, and having received a well-filled picnic basket from Cook, they were soon heading east toward the North Yorkshire moors.

The day rapidly turned into one of those beautiful February days that didn't just promise spring, but gave a foretaste of summer with the day being both sunny and warm. They soon found a small rocky hollow on the moors miles from anywhere. Then sitting in a warm sunny spot Polly began to explain what she knew about the use of words in a spell.

"In the early days' people with talent, let's call them magicians or warlocks as its easier were supposed to use spells. We think it helped their concentration, but the problem is no one seems to have thought to write them down. In fact, no one seems to have recorded anything about them, so it leaves us just guessing.

Marjory says when I turned the wall to sand she heard me shouting something. I can't remember myself, but she says that if it was a language that it was a language she had never heard the like of before."

"That's strange, Marcus says I shouted something when the demon attacked us, but I can't remember either."

"Don't worry about it; I don't think it was a language. I think it was probably just an exclamation or something like that, I know I'm sure mine was." Polly looked around and then said.

"Now let's start with that small rock over there." Polly flicked a head-sized rock about a foot into the air for Celina to see the one she meant. "Now see how high you can lift it without your wand." With an obvious struggle, Celina managed to lift it about half a yard before she dropped it.

"Now use your wand," Polly instructed. Following Polly's instructions and using her wand, Celina was able to lift and keep the rock in the air without any obvious effort. Polly looked around again and then seeing a rock easily as large as Celina, she said. "Now lift that one."

Celina pointed her wand, and the rock wobbled into the air, three and then four feet before she dropped it. Polly then took out her own wand, and lifted the rock smoothly up and swung it from side to side moving it over the bracken under perfect control. Finally, Polly put it back in its original place saying.

"Now to control a large object like that rock you will need to open your shield and let the power flow through you, and straight into your wand." Celina concentrated, feeling the power run through her arm and then into her wand as the rock leapt into the air.

"Careful," Polly cautioned. "Not too hard you're not trying to throw it; you just want to move it." Celina swung the rock back and forth and side-to-side amazed at how easy she now found it, finally she lowered it back into its original place.

"Now can we try some other things?" Celina asked excitedly as she turned around to look across the moor for something larger and heavier. Turning back to Polly, she found Polly was smiling at her as she said.

"Let's just keep practicing on various sizes of rocks and then you can move on to bigger and harder things."

Celina was starting to feel warm; she felt like she had been shifting rocks for what seemed like hours. Though it wasn't particularly hard anymore she was definitely feeling hot and sticky. With the sun now well up in the sky Celina looking around found a large flattish rock that faced the sun, and seeing it looked ideal for them to sit on she said.

"Let's have a rest as I'm getting a bit warm, and I think it's about time to eat."

Celina opening the basket of food turned to find Polly who was sitting next to her had kicked off her shoes pulled off her stockings and now sat wiggling her toes at the sun. Then Polly exposed her legs by pulling her skirts and drawers up well over her knees before leaning back on the dried bracken saying. "That sun feels lovely." Celina kicking off her shoes joined Polly and leaning back against the bracken with her eyes closed she asked.

"Why is it I get so hot when I don't seem to be working all that hard?" Polly thought for a moment before she replied.

"According to Marjory it's because though you aren't doing much work yourself, when you channel the power to move the rocks through your body, she says it's like some of that power gets stuck as it goes through you, and you get warm. Does that make sense to you?"

Celina having put the basket between them decided to copy Polly by pulling off her stockings and exposing her legs to the sun. Now as she laid back into the bracken, she said. "Mmm yes in a way."

"You do know we are in trouble don't you?" Celina heard Polly's words and thought them over before she opened one eye to find Polly propped on one elbow looking at her, as she said.

"Three of the Abbots were discussing it before I came to see you."

Celina still looking one-eyed at Polly asked, "in trouble why, what have we done now??"

"No it's not just us; it's all of us; you know everyone." Celina had been lying on her back with one eye closed, but now she opened the other, and turning on to her side she looked directly at Polly to ask. "How do you mean?"

"Well you know that there have never been enough Knights to fill the Round Table since it was made?" Celina sat up pushing the picnic basket towards Polly as she said.

"There must be enough, there are lots of Knights, I know I've seen the list." Polly shook her head and explained.

"That list includes all Church trained Healers and Doctors as well as Knights, in fact, just about everyone with any talent at all. Knights however are different from others with talent. Knights are Talents who are able fully to use a wand, and there are only about sixty Knights living and not all are eligible to sit at the table.

Take your mother and father, they are both medically trained, and for some reason that inhibits them in some way so, they cannot be called to the Round Table even though they are both Knights with wands. That means there are still only fifteen places taken at the Round Table." Polly rummaged through the picnic basket as she waited for Celina's reply.

"That just can't be right; there are more than twenty-five Knights."

"That's right." Polly said interrupting her, "but again not all Knights are strong enough Talents or emotionally suitable to be called to sit at the Round Table. When the demons were unable to enter our world unless they were summoned, it was possible for the Knights to control them. Now if they can open the way themselves, and if any number can enter instead of just one at a time, well we won't stand a chance." Celina felt shocked to her bones as she listened to Polly.

"Not only that but nearly half of all the Round Table Knights are around one hundred years old, and I think five are even older. They say one is over one hundred and fifty; that's why you have to learn as much as I can teach you."

"What about the research that they do at Glastonbury?" Celina asked.

"Do you know how many there are doing research?" Polly asked in return. Celina shook her head.

"Before I joined the research team there was only one, Lady Marjory. Very few Knights have the talent required for research,

273

and that's probably why no new magic or spells or whatever has been found in over five hundred years."

Celina who had thought the Abbey had a large research department found herself staring speechless at Polly until she finally said. "But some new," she hesitated over the word. "Magic must have been found."

"Again in Marjory's words, all Talents have been trained by other Talents who thought they knew what was possible and what was not," Polly giggled and said. "Then I came along. I was never told what was possible and what was not, I just had to do it.

Marjory says when I do what others do I do it differently, and I've done what others thought was impossible because I didn't know it was impossible as no-one had told me, so I just did it. In Marjory's words again, ignorance is bliss."

Polly looked around and found a fist-sized stone about fifty-feet away. Then she took out her wand and with a casual wave, the stone with a sharp crack exploded. She waved her wand across the bracken, and it was as if a scythe had crossed it cutting it down.

She looked around and finding a large bolder sticking up out of the moor several hundred yards away; Polly pointed her wand. The line of light from her wand was dazzling as it connected with the rock and then the rock exploded so forcibly that the blast almost knocked them off the rock they sat on.

"I'm sorry about that," Polly said apologetically. "I got carried away, but you see what I mean. I'll need to show you all these things and how to do them." Celina was shocked into asking.

"Why me?"

"Because Celina I'm told that you're the only one known who may have a strong enough talent, and If I can't teach you, well I'm going to look extremely lonely standing there facing a horde of demons all on my own." Celina who had stood up briefly now sat down again saying.

"There's Elizabeth and Marjory, and what about Dickie?" Polly shook her head as she said.

"Again like your parents Elizabeth is medical; she has a wand but her ability in that direction isn't much more than flying a broom or other minor things. Marjory can do some, but she is limited in how much power she can channel, although I think that it's more her not believing she can than her not being able to.

About Dickie, well he teaches, but he doesn't really have a great deal of push. That leaves you, and the fact that you managed Merlin's Dissipation by yourself."

Celina interrupted her by asking. "How did I do that, you said you knew how?"

"I think you tapped the energy without realising it but only after your own energy had been totally depleted." Celina sat quietly thinking as Polly continued to say.

"I think when you had used up all your energy reserves, and you had reached a point where you couldn't hold a shield any more. Because you wouldn't give in, and you still kept trying without a shield of any sort to hold it away, you accidentally tapped the external power directly. Then after you dissipated the demon and the power started to flow back into you, the first thing you did was put up a shield."

Polly closed her eyes and leaned back again saying. "You're unusual you know; I heard the Abbot say he's never come across a talent like yours before, and do you know he's also a little frightened of you."

Polly giggled again as she said, "and of me too. You know back in the orphanage when I first did things I did them and then I had to find out how I did them. You were told how to do things, and then you learned to do them as you were taught. I think that's the difference, I do many things in a completely different way from you because I learned them on my own."

They sat quietly for a while and then Polly said. "Marjory says that when I do things I always use energy from outside, I just never knew any other way, but when you do things you always use your internal energy, and then you have to wait for it to trickle back.

She says that's why I can do so much. I have all the power I need immediately available. Does that make sense?" Celina nodded as she sat still thinking about that night in the alley and how she had known what to do; finally, she decided to tell Polly about the voice in her head.

"Polly about that night I dissipated the demon, well there's something I've never told anyone. I'm not even sure it happened but just before I tried to dissipate the demon I was totally exhausted. I had used every bit of power I had left. I had…. well I had given in." Celina was now hugging herself and shaking at the memory as she said.

"I was ready to die, and then there was a voice, a woman's voice that came into my head into my mind." Celina stopped sorting out her memories.

"I think what she said was. 'At last she's let me in', and then she said. 'Use Merlin's dissipation'. Well, I tried it and at first I failed. Then she was there again that same woman's voice in my mind saying. 'No you silly girl not like that, you do it this way,' and even as she said it there it was all there in my head, and I suddenly knew how to do it." Polly shook her head as she said.

"Don't worry it was probably just a memory of something you had heard years ago and forgotten." Celina wanted to contradict her remembering what she had done on the afternoon of the robbery, but instead, Celina putting her shoes and stockings on stood up shook out her skirt and said.

"I know what does make sense, if you don't want to be a very, very lonely Knight you'd better teach me all you can and fast."

It was getting dark as Celina and Polly dropped down into the courtyard of Brimham Hall where a groom appeared to take their brooms. Celina gratefully handing hers over to the groom and by now aching all over and feeling as if she'd done twenty miles on a horse, she made for their rooms, saying to Polly as they entered the house.

"I smell worse than a pig, and I want a bath." Polly fully agreed with her, though she felt it would be impolite to say so.

Polly and Celina were sharing adjoining rooms with a common bathroom, with Polly's rooms normally being Jane's. Polly gallantly allowed Celina the first bath after which she retired for a soak of her own.

Bathed dressed and feeling much better Polly returned to Celina's room to find a maid putting the finishing touches to Celina's hair.

"Well how did I do on my first day of lessons?" Celina asked as soon as they were alone.

"Better than I had expected," Polly replied. "You're much more flexible than Marjory, and you have managed to thin your shield far easier than she did. In fact, you've just about stopped using your own power, and you are drawing it from around you most of the time. Yes, I think you did well. Now we'll see if you do as well tomorrow."

"Tomorrow you mean I have to go through all that again?" Celina asked as she dropped into a chair.

"No," Polly replied. "Tomorrow you will learn how to fight. Today was just how to move, manipulate and destroy."

"What do you mean by 'fight'?" Celina asked. "I thought that's what I was doing today." Smiling Polly answered.

"No tomorrow, you learn to punch, kick, claw and use your power as a sword or spear. In other words, you learn to do some of the dirty thing's children do in an orphanage, and I assure you; children can be really nasty."

Friday 21St February 1862.

Low clouds over the moors greeted them as they dropped into their secluded spot. "It's not as nice as it was yesterday," Polly commented.

"In that case, I might not perspire as much." Celina replied, and then she asked. "What am I doing today?"

"Today you learn how to punch and also how to break things at the same time. There's one thing that I forgot to tell you yesterday, and it's very important." Polly looked straight into Celina's eyes as she said. "I mean it's really important. Never try to use the external power you've gathered with your shield in place as it will just bounce back at you. Now think about it and describe to me why."

Celina didn't need to think about it. She could easily imagine what a full-power cast coming straight back at her from inside her shield would do.

"Now Celina," Polly said taking out her wand, "a push or a punch."

Celina rapidly understood the theory and watched carefully as Polly demonstrated on a bag of straw that they had brought for the purpose. "Now you try it," Polly said. Celina without the use of her wand knocked the bag about fifty feet.

"Now bring it back," Polly said assuming that Celina would go and bring it back. Instead and to her surprise the bag flew back from a reverse punch.

"I never thought of that," Polly said laughing. "It could be useful; most people expect a punch from the front not from the back. Now another thing I must warn you about. When you punch, but especially push or pull you must do it in both directions at the same time."

"How do you mean in both directions at the same time and why?" Celina queried. Polly looked around. About fifty yards away stood a stunted tree.

"Come on," she said as she set off pushing her way through the bracken. As they drew close to the tree she turned to Celina saying.

"Stand here and face the tree, now put the palms of your hands on the trunk and then push." Celina didn't even bother as she said.

"All right I get the idea, if I push against something stronger than me I will be the one who moves, especially if I am using power directly."

"That's right and the same can be said of a really powerful punch. Marjory says that for every action, there is an equal and opposite action, something to do with a man called Newton. It means when I push backwards on my broom the broom moves forward."

"Yes Polly I am aware of the theory, now tell me how do I push both ways at once?"

By the time they stopped for lunch Celina had developed a total disregard for her modesty and a grudging respect for the cushioning qualities of heather and dead bracken. With Celina having ended up several times either sitting down heavily or flat on her back, and even twice on her front, but she had finally mastered the technique of the simultaneous push.

Over lunch, Polly explained the technique used to form a spear or sword from her shield, and then it was time to experiment with Polly explaining.

"The sword is really only a modification of your shield." She demonstrated on a rotten log cutting it in half effortlessly.

"The difference between this sword and a steel sword is that it has no weight and is infinitely sharp. Another one of Marjory's words," she said with a giggle. Then and with Polly's help, Celina formed a sword with her shield.

"Don't make it too long and don't forget that only you know where it is. Oh and keep a tight hold on your wand. Lose your wand and you lose your sword." Then Polly demonstrated how to cut straw only it was bracken cut with a long blade swept across the moor.

Watching Polly Celina decided that the first thing she was going to obtain for Polly when they got back to London was a wand safe. Having used her wand as a physical weapon, and now seeing what else could be done with a wand had made Celina realise just how essential having a wand safe was.

"How did you learn all this?" Celina asked.

"Oh here and there," came the reply. "Mostly it was scrubbing floors pushing barrows, doing washing, polishing, cleaning chimneys. Just the ordinary everyday things you do in an orphanage." Celina made a face.

"No really" Polly said. "They are only alterations to things I used to do, like stone floors; you take a thin sliver off them, and then they sweep up lovely and clean. It saves hours of scrubbing. Pushing barrows you can see is similar to pushing a broom. Doing the washing and cleaning chimneys it's all push and pull."

Celina just couldn't believe it. "You mean living in the orphanage taught you all this?" Polly laughed.

"I don't suppose they intended it, but yes it did."

Arriving back at the Hall Celina made straight for the bath. She knew she smelt, and she needed to get clean. Also she wanted to examine her cuts and bruises.

279

Later during dinner Celina's mother revealed that she had visited the orphanage, and she brought news for Polly about her friends.

"Polly you wouldn't believe the change in the orphanage, the new guardians appointed by the Bishop have changed everything. It's a Mr Philips and his wife who run the orphanage now, and they welcome visitors. I have been shown around the orphanage including the school rooms, kitchen and the dormitories for both the boys and the girls."

"Boys, they have boys there as well now?" Polly asked.

"Yes but in separate areas. The only time they are together is in the garden or dining hall."

"What's the food like?" Polly asked.

"It's very good, the staff and children all eat the same food in the hall together. I had a look around the small farm that they have attached to the orphanage, and now most of the food they have comes from there."

"Did you get to see Nancy?" Polly asked.

"Yes I did; she's training to be a cook, and Mrs Frost the orphanage cook says she should be able to find a place for her with ease."

"One day I shall visit them," Polly announced wistfully.

Saturday 22nd February 1862.

I have suggested to Polly that we could see Jane's parents as I haven't seen them myself for some years. Polly enjoyed her visit but on the way home I found out a number of disturbing and upsetting facts about Polly.

~~~

Polly spent the morning with Celina going over the last two days lessons and meeting Celina's younger brother Robert.

Robert was two years older than Polly and Celina was really surprised to find that he turned quite shy on meeting her. It was after lunch as they sat finishing their coffee that Celina asked Polly. "Would you like a walk into the village and meet Jane's family?" Polly who had developed a great liking for Jane was delighted with the idea and accepted it enthusiastically.

Upon their arrival Mrs Cooper welcomed them in first giving Celina a warm embrace and then when introduced to Polly, she almost smothered her too with a hug so tight it crushed the breath out of her before saying.

"Sit thee down at yon fire and get thee warm, whilst I put a kettle on, Peggy," she called, "Where is thee lass?" Celina turned as a young girl came into the kitchen.

"Peggy go tell thee granddad that Celina's here, and I've put the kettle on. That's our Albert's youngest," Mrs Cooper said as she filled the big black kettle and put it on the range, then taking a blue and white teapot off the dresser. It was the teapot that Celina knew to be her best rather than the old chipped brown one that saw everyday use. Jane's mother started to gather the tea things together and then with a laugh; she turned to Celina saying.

"Do thee know? It's so long since yon's been here I'd forgot. Here warm the kettle for us will thee lass?"

Celina laughed and without even bothering to point her wand, she pushed heat into the kettle, and after a few moments the kettle started to boil.

"Eee lass that's smart," Mrs Cooper said. "I've not seen yon do it that way afore." Then wrapping her apron around the handle, she poured a little water into the teapot to warm it.

The sound of boots outside the door turned Polly's head in time to see a tall slim man coming in the door.

"Hello lass," Mr Cooper said seeing Celina. "I don't suppose our Jane came up with you did she?"

"No I still can't get her up on a broom; though I do keep trying."

"Never mind lass," he said, "some a day maybe." Celina put her arms around her second father and gave him a kiss.

"Now then lass you be getting them fine clothes of yours all mucky. Look I'm all covered in muck from the forge." Celina laughed looking down at her clothes.

"It'll not be the first time I've been in trouble from going home from the forge black bright. I'll wash and as for the clothes, well." Celina waved her hand down them and the little dust and muck that was evident flew off. Mr Cooper now turned to Polly and with a broad smile said. "Now who's this bonny lass, another witch I'll be bound?"

"Mr Cooper," Celina said turning towards Polly. "This is Polly a friend of Jane and myself. Polly this is Jane's father and now we all know who we are."

"That's a good telling lass," said Mrs Cooper as she took the kettle of the range and filled the teapot. Then turning to Celina and nodding toward the dresser she said. "Will thee get the mugs lass?" Celina took three mugs and a very large one commonly called the guzunder in the Cooper household for Mr Cooper, into which Mrs Cooper heaped sugar and then poured milk.

"Polly lass, do thee take sugar and milk?" Mrs Cooper asked as she fussed around serving them all.

After Mr Cooper had finished his tea he returned to the smithy saying he had work to finish. Mrs Cooper then entertained Polly with 'Tales of the terrible three,' as she called Celina Jane and Jonathan.

Polly was delighted enjoying not only the way she told the stories but also hearing her strange country accent. While Celina was horrified at just how much Mrs Cooper knew about their exploits, and at times finding it more than a little embarrassing, especially when it came to the village boys. Thankfully for Celina, one exploit involving a broom and a tree that Mrs Cooper knew about wasn't mentioned.

Walking home at first Polly was full of Mrs Cooper along with her accent and motherly ways, and having seen Jane's parents had made Polly realise just what she had missed in the orphanage.

As time and distance passed Polly gradually spoke less and less, until Celina finally coming to the conclusion that Polly's silence was more than nothing to say turned to Polly to find she was quietly crying. Catching hold of Polly's arm Celina pulled her to herself and holding her asked. "Polly what ever is wrong?" Polly then really started to cry, as in between her sobs she said.

"Oh Celina I can't remember my mother. You and Jane don't know how lucky you are; your mother and Mrs Cooper are just as I always imagined my mother to be. I miss my mother and I'll never know her, not even her name or what she looked like." Celina pulled out her kerchief and wiped Polly's eyes.

"Do you realise," Polly sniffed. "I don't even know my real name, and it may not even be Polly." She then gave another big sob as she said. "I do know my last name is not Cavendish because that's Marjory's, and she said I could use it." Celina found herself holding the sobbing girl and not knowing what to do or say.

"I never had any brothers or sisters," Polly sobbed. "I never had anyone I could call mine. That's why I loved Nancy so; she was like my own little sister, I looked after her and then I lost her."

Celina held her tight thinking that Nancy was still at the orphanage training to be a cook. Maybe her mother could think of something, after all Polly looked as if she was going to be someone very important in the Knights of the Church. Celina was certain something could be done, and she was sure her mother would know what to do.

Celina held Polly close until she had cried herself out, and then with a small shy smile Polly said. "I'm sorry; I am being a cry baby, but it just got away from me and I couldn't help it."

"Polly if you want to cry again, or if you just feel melancholy you can always talk to me or Jane as we'll both listen." Then arm in arm they slowly made their way home.

It was dark when Celina and Polly finally arrived at the large front doors of Brimham Hall. There they found a footman stood waiting especially to let a worried Lady Mary know that they had arrived. Polly saying she had a headache made her way directly to her room, while Celina went to explain to her mother. Seeing her daughter Lady Mary greeted her anxiously asking.

"Celina where have you been, I've been worried sick? I had visions of you being attacked again."

Celina dropped into a chair and pulling her boots off, she threw them aside as she said. "No mother I think it was worse than that. I learned a few more things about Polly." Her mother patted the seat beside her and then moved to make room for Celina.

"Go on then tell me the worst," she said as she pulled the bell cord to call for tea.

Celina, for some reason found herself feeling rather embarrassed sitting next to her mother and thinking about just how much Jane's mother knew about them. Suddenly, she found she was not sure how or where to start, so gathering her thoughts together she decided to start with Polly and started, saying.

"Coming home I found out that Polly doesn't know anything about herself. She knows nothing about her mother, or even if she has any brothers or sisters. She doesn't even know her own name or even if Polly is her real Christian name. The only thing she knows is that her surname isn't Cavendish. That was Lady Marjory who told her to use her surname if she needed to.

"She also told me the reason why she's so upset about Nancy. In the orphanage, she grew to love her like a little sister, looking after her and protecting her. Then she lost her and it broke her heart."

Celina dropped from the chair onto her knees in front of her mother and asked. "Mother do you think we can do something for Polly and Nancy?"

Her mother sat and thought before saying. "We certainly can and we will but what? I shall have to think about it."

They fell silent each with their own thoughts as the maid brought in and served the tea. Over the tea, Celina broached the other subject that was now troubling her. If Mrs Cooper knew about most of the exploits she and Jane had been involved in. Did her mother too, it turned out that she did.

Some she had laughed at, others had made her shake her head in disapproval while a few had left her shocked. Having heard it all again from her mother left Celina a very embarrassed and blushing daughter, until finally her mother burst out laughing saying. "If you could only see yourself, didn't you know mothers always hear about these things, and thankfully you outgrew these exploits?" Then with a smile, her mother said. "I hope."

As their conversation ended, Celina was easily persuaded to join the family for Church on Sunday, as she was also hoping to hear that her mother had come up with an idea about Nancy.

It was after church on Sunday morning that Lady Mary drew Polly and Celina aside saying. "I've been in touch with the orphanage by Telson, and the matron suggests that Polly calls in to see Nancy.

I've also put forward the possibility of funding for Nancy to take special schooling. The matron says she is a very intelligent child and well advanced for her age. She also told me that Nancy says she enjoys cooking and would like to cook for a large household." Seeing her mother use her kerchief to wipe the tears from Polly's eyes, Celina found herself almost as emotional as Polly.

Arriving back at Belgrave House they were greeted by Jane who was hungry for news. She devoured every word about the visit to her parents as well as news about the orphanage. Equally Celina was hungry for news about the shop. It was a jubilant Jane who told her that sales were so good that Marcus and Claire were now ordering up to four weeks in advance, in order to obtain deliveries from the Abbey as and when they were needed.

It was after supper that Jane told Polly about the two large packages that had been delivered on Saturday for her. Jane went to find Thomas and it wasn't long before the two returned with the packages.

Polly was so excited she had to be assisted to open them. Once they were unwrapped, Polly's flying clothes were revealed. To Polly they looked wonderful and it was all they could do to stop her getting changed in the study there and then. As it was all three of them carried the remains of the packages into Polly's bedroom where she insisted that she should put them on herself as she said.

"After all, there's no-one to help me at the Abbey." Once dressed in her new clothes Polly standing in the bedroom doorway shyly asked. "Are they all right and do you think they fit?" Celina and Jane both fought for words with Jane eventually managing to say.

"It's disgusting." but then she said, "but I think it might work."

"Celina." Celina walked all around Polly carefully studying the apparel. The jacket was lined in a warm quilted material that fitted closely but not too tight, allowing ample freedom of movement before dropping to knee height. The gloves Polly had tucked into the belt out of the way but where they could be easily retrieved.

The trousers in soft dark-brown leather emphasised Polly's legs enough to look indecent on a woman, but loose enough to give room to sit comfortably and bend at the knees. The trouser legs also had enough width below the knees to be pulled over the tops of her sturdy boots.

"Try the hat," Celina said. Polly pulled the hat over her hair and then tucked her loose hair into the back. Celina turned her around again.

"Sit down," Celina said watching as Polly feeling very self-conscious gingerly lowered herself onto a chair. "How do they feel?" Polly wriggled a bit.

"The trousers feel funny like all trousers do, tighter than my others but what do you think?" Celina laughed.

"If they work for flying you never know you may start a new fashion." Polly was all for a flight there and then but as the time was long after midnight; indeed it was fast approaching one of the clock she was persuaded that Monday night would be soon enough, and as Jane informed her, the leather would need plenty more goose grease to keep it supple before Polly used them.

"I don't want to damage them by having an accident falling off landing in all this rain either," Polly said running her hands down her jacket. Jane looked at Celina who blushed.

"What's all this about falling off?" Polly demanded. "Every time I mention something about falling off you two look at each other and you," she said pointing at Jane. "Have a wicked smile on your face and you Celina, you always blush. What does it mean?"

"Well," said Jane with a smile still on her face. "It's like this."

"Don't you dare tell," Celina stuttered. "If you do I…. I… well I'm going now." Celina hurriedly came to her feet and walked regally but rather quickly out of the room. As she closed the door she heard Jane saying. "When Celina was about fourteen, and even before she had a wand she took her mother's broom for a ride…."

Monday 24Th February 1862.

Celina arrived early at the shop to find both Marcus and Claire already there sitting in the office leafing through a sheaf of posters. Looking around the office Celina found a number of framed pictures stacked all ready for hanging. Picking one up for a closer look, Celina found they showed men and women wearing various items that were for sale in the shop. Celina picked one out and asked. "Where did you get these from; they're very good?"

"Sally has drawn them." Claire said as she picked up a drawing of a woman wearing one of the riding outfits from the north, and passed it to Celina saying. "It seems Sally is very good at portraits so I got her to do one or two just to see what they looked like. Impressive aren't they? I had these framed as permanent displays and these," Claire pointed to the smaller one she had given to Celina. "To put up while our stocks last."

Marcus then opened a heavy wooden box that had been fixed to the floor saying. "Have a look at these." Lifting some of the contents out he passed Celina a black velvet-covered tray.

"The Abbot has sent these samples from a small workshop that does some beautiful dress jewellery in silver. Just look at them," he said offering a tray of teardrops in silver and various semiprecious stones to Celina. "If we keep on like this I would recommend getting a safe." Celina looking at the trays of jewellery in the box and remembering the attempted robbery said.

"Marcus I think I agree with you there; I believe there is a firm by the name of Roberts who supply safes. Would you contact them please and arrange something?"

Next Celina took a tour of the shop with Claire and Marcus seeing some of the changes they had made during her absence. Celina had to admit that she could not fault the alterations and found she was more than pleased with their efforts.

It was as she finished her tour of the top floor that Celina came to a decision deciding to implement something she had been considering since the enlargement of the shop. Calling Marcus and Claire into the office, she seated them and saw them settled comfortably before she said.

"With what has happened in the past, and now having had a look around the shop and seeing the work you two have put in...." Celina's gaze moved back and forth between the two of them. "Especially over the last few weeks...." She paused considering her next words before saying.

"I've come to a decision; I have to say that I will be spending less and less time here, so I am officially offering you the post of manager and manageress in your own departments. Marcus is to be in overall charge with Jane available if there are any emergencies or disputes, now are you interested?"

Marcus and Claire looked at each other before Marcus said. "Well I know we work comfortably together, and I want this shop to succeed so I'm more than happy to accept. What about you Claire?"

Claire who had been watching Marcus now turned back to Celina to say. "Yes if you're not going to be here we shall have to pull together. Between the four of us, we've put a lot into this shop and I for one have enjoyed the work; I don't want it to fail now, and apart from that I owe you such a lot." Then with tears starting in her eyes she gave Celina a heartfelt. "Yes."

"Good," Celina said. "I take it that I don't have to tell you that I intend to make it worth your while salary-wise. When I opened this shop, it wasn't just to make a lot of money, if it did that was simply a bonus. Its main purpose was to provide employment for workers in the north.

If you haven't already guessed Fountain's Abbey put a lot of money into this venture, and I'm happy to say they are very pleased with the results. I will also say that this venture has grown and changed beyond my original idea, and as for making money, well it has achieved both in the class of its clientele and quantity of its sales far more than the Abbot or I ever expected, and I intend to pass a lot of the credit on to you two.

As I said the shop was opened to promote northern goods and tradesmen here in London so that must always be our first priority." Celina turned to Marcus saying.

"Now Marcus your salary how does an extra fifty guineas a year sound to you?"

Marcus gave a good impression of a fish out of water. Then finding his voice he squeaked. "That's a fortune."

"If the shop takings just stay at their present level that is what I propose to give you. If they increase, then your salary will increase. If they go down your salary will of necessity reduce. Is that fair?"

Marcus pushed his fingers through his hair as he said. "More than fair, it's more than I ever expected."

"Claire," Celina said turning to her. "On the same terms I propose." Celina stopped noting that Claire's eyes were shut.

Celina looked closer and said. "Marcus would you get the smelling salts please; our Claire has fainted."

Once Claire had recovered Celina continued. "Jane will be around although not as often as usual to make any major decisions. She will also be able to get hold of me if necessary. I think you already realise why I have to be away from the shop more now."

"I take it that it is the demon problem?" Marcus asked.

"I can't tell you too much," Celina said. "All I can tell you is that certain people are very worried."

"What about your other stock?" Claire asked. Celina considered for a moment or two before replying.

"Take names and make arrangements for people to come on the last Friday of the month at five, or if it's urgent see Jane. I will obtain keys for both you and Marcus to the room so as that any new stock can be put in there on its arrival. In addition, I hope to get a girl from one of the church schools who would be in a position to demonstrate, that is if she needs to. Now any more questions?"

Marcus and Claire thought for a moment before Marcus said. "If we have any we can ask you later, but I haven't for now."

"I can't think; I'm still dazed," Claire admitted.

"All right then now back to work," Celina said with a smile. Celina informed Jane over dinner of her decision and after thinking it over Jane came up with a question.

"How is it that they get paid and I don't?" Celina sat there somewhat surprised.

"Probably for the same reason I don't," she replied. "After all I consider the shop as much yours as mine. To which Jane responded sarcastically.

"Thank you, but it was you who put up the idea and some money in the first place." Jane again making Celina think before she could reply.

"If you spend any money, where does it come from?" She finally asked.

"From you of course,"

"Well if the money you spend is mine it must also belong to you otherwise you wouldn't be able to spend it would you? Therefore, the shop is as much yours as mine so that settles it." Jane laughed as she said.

"I've been manipulated all ways haven't I?"

Saturday 1ˢᵗ March 1862.

Jane had advised Cook in the morning that she would be late arriving home, and a late dinner would be in order. Dinner was in its final stages of preparation as Celina and Jane were sitting together taking tea and talking over the day when there came a knock on the door.

Kate entering announced rather than dinner being served that it was Elizabeth on the Telson for Celina. It was an apologetic Elizabeth who said. "I'm sorry to call you just now; I expect you're in the middle of dinner?"

"No not yet," Celina replied. "We're having a late dinner, why?"

"Well Marcus has just solved a problem for me. You know how the portals are only opening for a short time now, and we can't find where? Well, he's suggested a way to."

"Don't say any more," Celina interrupted her and then asked. "Have you eaten yet?"

"No Marcus and I were going to eat out tonight; we were just about to leave when Marcus came up with this idea."

"Well if you and Marcus can get a cab and come over I'll have Jane have a word with Cook and arrange two extra places."

"Are you sure it will be all right," a doubtful Elizabeth asked.

"Of course Cook always cooks for ten as she's used to cooking for a large household, so don't be long."

Elizabeth wasn't long in arriving, it was less than ten minutes later when she landed in the stable yard on her broom, along with a wild-eyed and excited Marcus on the front seat. As they came into the hall from the kitchen, Marcus couldn't wait to say.

"I can see why you love flying, its marvellous; I only wish we had been able to see the stars and cloud tops as you've described them, but there are a lot of high clouds tonight, and the new moon is hardly there at all."

Celina laughed as she said. "Marcus I'm sure Elizabeth will oblige, but I hope you realise that if Claire finds out she will want me to keep my promise to take her for a flight?"

Marcus's reply to Celina came with a sly smile as he said. "Well you'd better get planning then." There was a knock on the door and this time it was Kate, who announced that dinner could be served. Over dinner Marcus explained his recent idea.

"It's so simple: Elizabeth carries a compass with her all the time, and whenever a portal opens she takes a bearing on its direction." Marcus looked across at two uncomprehending faces looking back at him and decided to continue anyway.

"When she gets home she puts that bearing on a map." Marcus paused and looked at their still-confused expressions and tried again.

"Look it's like this," he said as he held out his hand for Elizabeth's compass. He laid the compass on the table and then reaching for the saltcellar; he tapped it and said.

"Let's say this is the portal and this," he reached across for the pepper and moved it closer, "is Elizabeth. Now whenever Elizabeth senses a portal, she takes a compass bearing like this by turning the compass so that north lines up just so, and then she looks along the points in the direction of the portal, or the saltcellar here and look it's almost exactly due east.

Then when Elizabeth gets home, she takes a map of London and puts the compass on the map at the point where she was standing, and then she turns the map so north on the compass is the same as north on the map and draws a line just off due east exactly as she saw it before. Now she knows that the portal opened somewhere along that line."

"I can see that," Celina said. "But how far along the line?

"Well the next time a portal opens," Marcus moved the pepper to one side. "Elizabeth takes a reading again and then puts that one on the map. Now if she does that several times and from different places, and she finds that the lines all cross at one point she will know that's where the portal is opening. Or if it's at a different point or at several different points so long as it opens twice at the same place that place will show up on the map."

"Do you understand that?" Celina asked Elizabeth.

"Yes after you see it on a map it's very simple, and all I have to do is carry a compass and a notebook so I don't forget when and where I was, and what direction it was in."

Marcus seeing the doubt on Celina's face said. "Look if Elizabeth does this every time a portal opens, very soon you will know a great deal more about where the portals are opening. This may also tell you more about what is being sought and where you need to be most careful."

Saturday 15Th March 1862.

I have kept my promise to Claire she had her ride on a broom for about three-quarters of an hour. I left her outside her aunt's house just after ten of the clock.

~~~

Marcus and the two girls were just leaving and Claire was putting on her coat when Celina called her into the office.

"Sit down please," Celina said waving her to a chair. "I suppose Marcus has told you about Elizabeth taking him on her broom." Claire frowned not really understanding the reason for the question as she said.

"Yes he told me all about it."

292

"Did he say how good it was and how much he liked it?" was Celina's next question.

"How good," Claire exclaimed. "He hasn't stopped telling me about it for the last two weeks."

"Well I promised I would take you for a flight sometime didn't I?" Claire nodded as her eyes widened with excitement.

"Well if you're not in any hurry, I'll treat you to a meal and then I will take you home by broom. It's a full moon tonight over the clouds, and it should be beautiful." Celina couldn't help it; she had to smile with amusement having watched the various expressions on Claire's face as she had been speaking.

Claire was a bundle of nerves as Celina fastened the strap across her lap before she arranged Claire's skirt and coat for her over the broom's shaft. Then Celina slowly lifted the broom until it was well above the rooftops before she pushed for any speed.

To Celina, it was a near-perfect night for flying. The sky had cleared leaving some broken cloud and an almost full moon. Once above the clouds London was spread out below them with just the occasional cloud drifting slowly under them. The black white and silver panorama spread below was so beautiful it took Claire's breath away.

Celina took a slow circular route around the outer edge of London. At first Claire sat stiffly in the seat but with the beauty of light and shadow on the cloud-tops along with the sight of London spread out below them, and with the wonderful dome of stars above them. Celina felt her gradually relax and knew that the wonder of flying had reached her.

They had been flying for about half an hour when Celina veered off to one side as she caught sight of another broom flying above and to one side of them. Celina pushed harder until she came along side the second broom surprising the riders when she called out.

"It's a nice night for courting." Elizabeth and Marcus both jumped as they had been so totally engrossed in the view that they hadn't noticed Celina's approach.

"If the sky gets any more crowded I shall have to start a new hobby, like, well, fishing." Elizabeth called back.

Marcus seeing Claire called across. "Hello Claire, what do you think of flying, and you have to admit it; it is a beautiful night for flying?"

"Words can't describe it," Claire called back. The two brooms pulled in close and hovered briefly before continuing flying together.

"How high are we," Marcus asked.

"About four thousand feet I think give or take a couple of hundred," Elizabeth replied.

"Look at the river," Claire said pointing down. "It looks just like a silver snake from up here," and then she asked. "Where is the shop?"

"Somewhere down there," Marcus said pointing generally downward.

"I know that," Claire called back with just a hint of exasperation. "But just about where down there?"

"Somewhere by that bend," Celina replied pointing. Before turning and pointing further to the North saying. "And your aunt and uncle's house is over there."

"Every thing in London looks so small from up here," Claire said looking down.

"It gives you a totally different perspective on things doesn't it," Marcus replied. As they slowed to a hover again he asked Elizabeth.

"How long can you hover like this?"

"Not much longer I'm sorry to say as I have to be back at the hospital soon," was her disappointing reply.

Celina chose a quiet moment to return Claire home, landing hidden by some small trees in her front garden.

"Well did you enjoy it?" Celina asked.

"It was wonderful," Claire whispered. The look Celina could see on Claire's face told her that she had shown Claire something she found too beautiful for words.

"Well be careful when discussing it with Marcus in the shop," she cautioned. "Our young girls most certainly have sharp ears, and I'm not sure whether this will be covered by the inhibition."

"I'll be careful," a grateful Claire assured her as she turned and made her way to the front door of the house.

Monday 12th May 1862.

Over the last two months I have made regular trips over to Glastonbury to see Polly. I am learning and teaching at the same time. Between the two of us and with Marjory's help, we have developed three new very destructive casts, one of which we nearly killed ourselves with. That one is only for use as a last resort. Our main worry is still the lack of Knights able to drop their shields. Marjory has finally accepted that it was only self doubt that inhibited her, and she is now getting quite proficient.

~~~

Thursday 15[Th] May 1862.

It was just before dinner when Kate announced that Polly had arrived and was putting her broom in the old stables.

"Ask Cook for an extra place at dinner will you please Kate," Celina asked. It was only minutes before Polly arrived in the hall with Thomas carrying her bag.

As Polly came into the day room, Jane who had been studying her in her flying clothes asked. "Well how are they working out?"

"All in all, not bad, the coat and things are perfect."

"But?" Jane asked.

"Well the trousers tend to ride up and rub in a tender place when you are sitting for some time on a broom." Polly admitted pulling the tops of the legs downward. "They really dig in and eventually it gets quite sore." Jane looked for a moment and then bent and pulled at the trouser legs, thought for a moment and then said. "Wait here I think I know just what you need."

Jane left the room leaving Celina and Polly wondering where she was going. It was only a matter of minutes before she was back and holding something folded. Shaking it out she said.

"I think these might work; they were Robert's when he was about thirteen, but I think they should fit you." Jane then held a pair of boy's cotton under trousers up against Polly.

"Yes they'll do," she confirmed. "Come on you've just enough time to clean up and change before dinner." Then taking a bemused Polly by the arm, she led her out of the room.

When Polly returned she looked clean and fresh dressed in a green gown that made her look every inch a lady.

"Well do they fit?" Celina inquired. With no more ado, Polly lifted the front of her skirts to reveal a pair of boy's underclothes that fit perfectly, though possibly a little tighter than they had been on Robert.

"How do they feel," Celina asked. Polly tried to look down over her skirts as she replied.

"They're comfortable enough and they're a lot less bulky than draws so I can wear them under my trousers. I'll try them when I go back and let you know." It was after dinner that Celina gave Polly a small flat box saying. "I think you will find this to be useful." Polly opened the box and took out a plain gold bracelet.

"It's a bracelet," and then as she started to fasten it on her left wrist she said. "Thank you Celina but you shouldn't have."

"It's for your other wrist," Jane told her. "It's a wand safe."

"A wand safe," Polly asked. "What's a wand safe?" Celina taking out her wand held it out at arm's length before she let it go. Instead of falling, the wand snapped sharply back and attached itself to the wand safe on her wrist, where the wand remained held attached to the gold band while pointing backwards along Celina's forearm. Celina shook her arm, and the wand remained held firmly in place by the wand safe.

"It stops you losing your wand when you're being very active." Celina demonstrated waving her arm about. "Just touch your wand to the wand safe to attach it for the first time, and then it will work every time.

After following Celina's instructions Polly found her wand had swung back and now pointed backwards along her arm. Polly then tried shaking her wrist before saying.

"It's marvellous." and then she asked. "How do I get it back?" Celina showed her the quick flick of the wrist and explained the mental push that brought the wand forward into her hand. Instructions and demonstration over Polly and Celina fell to discussing what had been developed over the last months.

Jane sat quietly listening while at the same time exploring and comparing her own awakening abilities. The power was there but it was vicious raw and trapped. Jane felt frustrated at being unable to get it out feeling it fill her, and then it would seem to stop at her skin.

She could feel one hundred feet tall and able to pick up mountains, but she just could not do it. The conversation had gotten around to spells, and Jane began wondering if that was her trouble. Perhaps she needed spells.

Silently pleading under her breath and then demanding she tried to create a glow globe. The power reached her skin where she could feel it welling up, but then it seemed to bunch up and stop. Something was wrong, and the power couldn't get out. A question from Celina brought her attention back to the conversation.

"Has anyone worked out why they're coming into our world?"

To this Jane quickly asked. "Is it only to England or are portals opening elsewhere?"

"Well." Celina asked looking at Polly. "Has anyone worked it out?"

"No I don't think so, and until we can get a live demon. I don't suppose anyone can ask. As for portals opening in other countries, I think there is something about the position of England, something to do with two spheres only being able to touch at one point, but I don't really know. Anyway here we are talking about an invasion and trying to prepare defences against something that may never happen."

Jane looked at Polly as she said. "Well I for one will be more than pleased if it never happens." Polly looking at her nodded her agreement as she said. "Yes but I'd sooner be prepared even if it is only a one-demon invasion."

They all laughed with Jane saying. "I'll admit that's best, I only wish I could help, but I feel sort of like a hanger-on here able to give moral support and nothing else."

"No Jane," Polly said. "When the time comes I think you will be a very valuable member of our small," she looked at the two of them. "Too small a team," Polly then rose to her feet and walked over to Jane, and as she put her hands on her shoulders she said. "In fact, I can feel it," as she gave Jane's shoulders a squeeze.

Polly saying she was worn out having flown courier the previous night decided to retire early with Jane following her to assist her in her preparations. As Jane brushed Polly's hair, they discussed Jane's problem until Polly said. "I think I will have to sleep on it; I'm a bit lost at the moment."

"How long will you be staying?" Jane asked.

"Well for a few days at least, as I don't like flying when…. you know women's things."

Jane thought for a moment and then said. "Oh you mean…." Polly nodded.

"Yes it's so awkward. Most of the places I go to have no facilities for women." Then with a little laugh she said.

"Some won't even speak to me let alone let me in the door." Jane who had been sorting and putting away Polly's clothes had now stopped and turning to face her, she asked. "You mean no-one's told you?"

"Told me what," Polly asked.

"One of the big advantages of being a Talent as strong as you are is you don't have to have this happen; you can stop it."

"Stop it stop what?"

"Your monthly bleed," Jane answered and then said. "I think I'd better get Elizabeth to have a word with you, after all she is a doctor." Once back with Celina Jane told her of Polly's predicament.

"Well I suppose I could explain as my mother is a doctor too."
Then Celina paused and said. "No I think its time we heard from
Elizabeth. It's been too quiet for my liking and the back of my
neck's starting to itch."

Elizabeth was delighted to be invited along with Marcus for
dinner. She said she would bring her map for Celina to see what
progress she had made in plotting the portal openings, and while
she was there she would explain to Polly in non-technical terms
the advantages of being a powerful talent when it came to
women's matters.

Friday 16th May 1862.

After dinner and with the table clear, Elizabeth spread out her
map. Six lines crossed not at one point but almost and most
important to Celina at or near Lownde's Square. Celina found this
to be particularly significant as she ran her finger along the map
and then said.

"Damn! The lines cross too high up, in fact they could be on
Charles Street, and his rooms are lower down in the Mews."

Turning to Marcus she asked. "Have you had a look what's in
this area?"

Marcus leaned forward to look over the table at the map as he
replied. "Yes it's either a small hotel or two private houses but I
haven't been able to find out who owns them yet. I did make some
enquiries from the kitchen staff at the hotel but all they could say
was that both are owned by elderly people who aren't seen very
often."

"I was so sure," Celina said and then paused. "No I still am; I'm
certain he has something to do with it. It's too big of a
coincidence; he lives in that area and the portal opens along this
street." Celina tapped the map, "but why would he want that
book?"

"Have you got a copy of the book here?" Marcus asked. Celina
went to her father's library and returned with a book putting it on
the table. With the four of them going through the book they were

still unable to see why Dr. McDonald would want or need a copy of the book of days, as Marcus said.

There is nothing of real importance that I can see, unless it is hidden somewhere in some of the strange wording."

Before they left that night Celina and Elizabeth decided that on Monday night, they would have a look at the three suspect buildings first from the air and then land and see if they could see anything suspicious behind them.

Monday 19th May 1862.

As it was a beautiful morning I took an early morning constitutional through Hyde Park and found that Elizabeth had the same idea. We decided to have a look at Lownde's Square. Unfortunately, events conspired against us, and we were not able to visit that area. Due to this misfortune, I discovered the incredible power of a glow globe.

~~~

It was just after ten of the clock, and Celina was sitting in Hyde Park enjoying the morning sun, when a shadow falling across her face made her open one eye to find Elizabeth seating herself on the bench saying. "Good morning, I thought you were asleep sitting there with your eyes closed."

"No just enjoying the sun as it's such a beautiful morning," Celina replied. Elizabeth leaning back on the seat alongside her said. "I think it's going to be a really warm day too, in fact, to nice to work indoors so I decided that as I have nothing pressing at the hospital I would have a walk this morning. What about you?"

Celina laughed and feeling much the same way she replied. "No I had nothing that couldn't wait so like you; I decided a nice walk would do me a power of good."

Elizabeth closed her eyes enjoying the warmth of the sun as she said. "By the way, has Claire mentioned my brother?"

"Mentioned your brother, no why?"

"Well I do know they were out together the other night along with her aunt and uncle, and he said something about the theatre." Elizabeth opening one eye gave Celina a sideways look while she waited for a response.

"Good for her, its time she found something to do other than work. All work and no play makes' Claire an old woman," Celina said misquoting the old maxim to fit the situation.

Elizabeth starting to get to her feet asked. "Should we take a walk and see what we can see of Lownde's Square, if we go out the side gate that will bring us out right at the middle of Knights Bridge."

Celina moaned and then getting to her feet said wistfully. "It was so nice just sitting here." A steady walk to the end of the lake and once across the little bridge brought the gate into view.

It was an annoying whine that made Celina look back. Across the lake, a black dot floated in her vision. She blinked, and it was much larger. She blinked again and then with all her strength she pushed Elizabeth to the ground diving herself in the opposite direction.

A large black object passed through the space where they had been standing with a deafening whine. Celina catching a glimpse of it as it passed them so fast it was hard to believe it was possible.

Celina rolled over and looked up; it was a bug, and it had already turned and was on its way back flying low over the grass. Celina's wand was digging into her trapped under her weight, struggling to free it from the folds of her skirt Celina looked up. It was too late; the bug was less than a hundred yards away and the wand was still trapped.

Celina's mind froze as instinct took over, her shields fell, and she pulled at the energy around her for all she was worth until she felt as if she was going to explode.

Without a wand to direct a cast anything she did would have a terrible effect on her as the power was directed through a part of her body, or affect everything around her as most of her power was dissipated into everything and everyone.

301

Celina didn't have time to think, seeing the bug so close and unable to act there was only one thing that she could do that was not a cast but could be contained and directed.

Celina made a fist with her hand and pointed her arm toward the black object now less than fifty yards away. She vaguely remembered opening her hand and someone screaming something as the world turned hot and white.

Somewhere in the back of Celina's mind had been the vague intention to distract the bug by throwing the biggest and brightest glow globe she could produce at it. She succeeded beyond her wildest dreams.

When she opened her fist what left her palm was not a two-inch globe of light, but a miniature sun. A sun that was so bright that it outshone the real sun in the sky. In less time than it took it to travel across twenty yards it had expanded to a blue-white sphere four feet in diameter. Before it even met the globe, the bug was dead and completely incinerated, while the globe continued to expand until its lower edge met the turf where it exploded.

Celina felt something had happened to the earth under her. She had just started to wonder where the earth was when it hit her hard. She rolled and lay flat with her ear's ringing, and her eyes blinded and finding herself unable to breathe. Then she blinked and found that she was not blind or suffocating, it was just her face and nose pressed into the soft damp earth of a flowerbed. She rolled over seeing great blue blotches slowly fading in front of her eyes.

Blinking and looking across the grass she could see where Elizabeth was lying about ten yards away. She watched as Elizabeth rolled onto her stomach and tried to get up on to her hands and knees, failed and then tried again. Celina turned her head to look across toward the gates.

As the last of the blue blotches faded, Celina found she could see a crater about five or six yards across directly in front of where they had been standing. The grass burned to an ash now formed something looking like a large black arrow pointing to the place where they had stood.

Dragging her skirts from under her, Celina managed to get to her feet, almost fell and then wobbled over to help Elizabeth, helping her to her feet where they stood supporting each other.

From the gate, a policeman was running in their direction with a crowd following him, and from further away a park gardener was running still carrying his spade.

"Are you all right," the policeman asked puffing and wheezing. "What happened was it a gas main explosion or something?" He looked alternatively between Celina Elizabeth and the hole, while Celina and Elizabeth just looked at him as if dazed and not understanding.

"Are you sure you're all right?" he asked again. Celina nodded as she replied.

"A little shaken but that's all thank you constable." It was then that the gardener followed by a number of other park attendants arrived.

"Did you see it?" the gardener asked throwing his spade down, "it was ball lightning and just fantastic." The gardener then hurried over and looked down into the crater, saying to all and sundry. "That's going to take some filling in." The mass of people that had followed the policeman now stood looking on as the other gardeners all made their way over to look down into the hole.

The policeman now noticed that the crowd that had been milling around them had started moving towards the hole, so he quickly guided Celina and Elizabeth to a seat before he hurried over to assist in keeping order.

As soon as the policeman had left them Celina caught Elizabeth's hand and pulled her to her feet saying. "Come on let's get away from here before someone starts getting too curious and asking sensible and awkward questions."

Pushing their way through the press of people approaching from the gates she hurried Elizabeth through the incoming mass of people, and out onto the pavement. Elizabeth looking back at the gathering crowd in the park said. "We'd better take a cab back to Belgrave."

Celina quickly corrected her saying. "No, not from here, if they start asking questions some cabby is going to remember us. We had better take one to St Paul's and then hopefully George will be around, and he can take us home from there."

"George?" Elizabeth asked.

"Yes the father of the two talented girls I found, he drives a cab." Celina looked around and noticed a little further down the road a cab with its driver standing on top of the driver's box so that he could see into the park.

Pulling Elizabeth behind her Celina ran towards the cab and opening the door, she pushed Elizabeth up the step and into the cab, and then quickly climbed in behind her. Only then did she call out. "St Paul's please cabby."

Not a word was spoken in the cab as Elizabeth sat white-faced and occasionally glancing at Celina sitting beside her. Once at St Paul's Celina and Elizabeth found an empty bench where they sat in silence, both occupied with their own thoughts.

They hadn't to wait long before a cab pulled up across the road and stopped, then it turned and crossed the road to come to a stop directly in front of them. The driver dropped down from the box and approached, taking a seat on the bench next to Celina saying.

"Good morning," then looking first at Celina's soil-smudged face and Elizabeth's white face, and then seeing the torn lace on the front of Elizabeth's dress he said. "Don't tell me it's happened again and this time in broad daylight. What is it this time?" Celina looked up.

"Hello George, how are the girls?" George didn't answer as having seen the state the two were in. he simply said.

"Come on get in the cab, I take it that you need to go somewhere."

"Thank you George," Celina replied. "Belgrave Square will do nicely." As Celina and Elizabeth settled back in the cab's seats, George opened the flap in the roof and looking in he asked again.

"Well what happened this time?"

"Yes what did happen?" Elizabeth asked, "I remember you pushing me down and then a loud whining noise followed by…. well, I don't know what. Someone screamed something I couldn't understand and then everything went white. The next thing I know I'm flying through the air. What did you do?"

"I'm not sure but I saw a bug…." "A what?" came from the roof interrupting Celina. "I suppose you could say it's the demon equivalent of a wasp. They are about the size of a large dog and poisonous, and they move so fast that I don't think even Polly could out-fly one."

"Who is Polly?" came from the roof, and Celina had to explain to George who Polly was before she could continue.

"It was coming back for me, and I couldn't get to my wand as it was all caught up in my skirt, so I had to try to distract it. All I could think of that might do it was to make the largest hottest and brightest glow globe I could. Celina paused before saying. "I think I over did it."

"I'll say you did, and what the Hell is a glow globe?" Elizabeth asked. Celina concentrated for an instant and then opened her hand, and a two-inch globe of light lit up the inside of the cab.

Elizabeth's eyes grew round in amazement as she watched the glow lift off from Celina's palm, and immediately asked. "How do you do that?"

George looking through the flap in the roof followed her question closely with. "That could be really useful on a dark night." George dropped them off at Belgrave House, and once again he refused payment from them insisting he owed Celina more than she owed him.

Jane

Polly and Jane decided after breakfast that as Celina had taken herself off into the city, that they would find a spot in the square and continue Polly's exploration of Jane's stalled ability. As they walked around the small lake, Jane tried again to explain her problem.

"I can feel the power, so I know it's there. I can also channel it to where I want it, but it just won't leave my skin. It's as if my skin is an iron wall that holds it in."

Polly frowned and asked. "Can you feel this wall or see it or well, anything?"

"No I can feel my skin, and I can feel the power, and I can direct it to where I want it, but after that it just seems to bunch up and stop inside my skin." They came to a seat not far from a beech tree and sitting in the dappled shade neither in nor out of the sun, they relaxed and enjoyed the warmth of a beautiful early summer's day. Jane closed her eyes enjoying the sun while Polly remained deep in thought.

It was then that Polly decided to try an experiment. Very quietly and as gently as she could, Polly leaned on Jane pushing the idea that Jane should open her eyes and look around. Polly just wanted to see how Jane might respond but the result was very unexpected.

Polly knew she wasn't very skilled at leaning as she tended to be rather heavy-handed at it, so she was even more surprised at the result.

First Jane just remained sitting with her eyes closed, and second Polly found that her efforts at leaning on Jane simply went through her. As far as leaning was concerned it was as if Jane wasn't there at all. Polly tried again, and this time she also looked for Jane's shield or block. To her surprise, she was unable to find either.

At this point, Polly was entirely flummoxed, she had never heard of anything like this. Polly knew leaning on a Talent was bad manners so it just wasn't done. Polly also knew that if a more powerful Talent caught you, they would slap you down rather painfully mentally speaking, and someone with less talent would still feel your push and at the very least tell you it was bad manners; Jane couldn't be leaned on at all. As far as leaning was concerned Jane just didn't exist.

Polly now decided to risk a little more and go beyond 'not very nice'. Taking her wand, she tried to attract Jane's attention by burning Jane's arm. It was intended to be only a hot spot just to see how Jane would react. To Polly's amazement, Jane didn't react.

Polly could see the hot spot she had placed on Jane's arm, but it wasn't reaching Jane's skin, something was protecting Jane.

Polly now became even brasher and decided rather bold action was in order, so she gave Jane a push. In fact, she gave her a good old-fashioned dig in the ribs with her talent elbow, not enough to do any damage but enough to be very noticeable.

"What was that for?" Jane immediately asked.

"I wanted to see if you were real,"

"Of course I'm real. What did you think that I was…. a statue?"

"Well," Polly said as she pointed at Jane's arm. "Right now that little hot spot should be burning you." Jane looked down and saw a distinctive white spot glowing on her arm. Jane lifted her arm for a closer look, and as she did so Polly kept the hot spot in place so that Jane could easily inspect it.

Looking at it, it seemed to the two of them that the hot spot actually stopped short of reaching Jane's skin. Looking closely they found it was just possible to see the slightest gap between it and her skin.

"Well I never…." Was all Polly said as she joined Jane in the study of the hot spot. Polly now confessed, "I lent on you and you never felt a thing, and as I'm not very good at leaning you should have felt it."

"No I didn't feel a thing. I can feel when Celina tries to lean on me but it doesn't work, and I can feel when other people are being leant on." Polly lent on Jane again causing Jane to frown and say.

"Yes you are there but only just, normally I wouldn't even notice."

"It's not just that I can't lean on you Jane. If I shut my eyes, I can't even feel your presence, it's as if you don't exist. I had to give you a dig in the ribs to see if you were alive."

"Well I am," Jane said rubbing her side, "and as for burning me." Jane held out two immaculately manicured hands for Polly's inspection as she said. "Look, even after all those years working with my father at the forge, not a burn or a mark."

Polly took one of Jane's hands, at first she just visually inspected it, and then she closed her eyes and pushed her awareness into her fingertips while at the same time asking Jane to try to do the same. For the next few minutes to any passers by they must have looked an odd couple sitting there holding hands with their eyes closed. Jane could feel Polly holding her hands and even feel Polly pushing against her skin. It felt strange but not unpleasant, not like it had been with a wand, or as it was with a broom.

While holding Jane's hand Polly could feel Jane's power surging just under and into the skin, but not beyond the skin. It was strange; it seemed as if the power was part of her skin. It seemed as if Jane and her power were one and inseparable. Jane's power seemed to be purely defensive protecting her and nothing else.

Polly reached out and ran her fingers along her hair. It was just the same, in the skin and hair but not beyond. She would be protected but not her clothes or anything external.

Jane sat and listened in silence as Polly described what she had found and what she thought it meant until Jane finally asked. "You mean I may have a permanent and impenetrable shield?"

"Very nearly and certainly as far as leaning and talent go," Polly replied. By the time they returned home, they found Celina and Elizabeth were already there and bursting with a story to tell. Making it quite easy for Jane and Polly to say nothing about their day, they simply listened to Celina and Elizabeth tell about theirs.

Celina

Returning early, Celina first sent Kate for tea and then settling comfortably in the day room, Celina started teaching Elizabeth how to produce a glow globe.

After several attempts and to the delight of them both Elizabeth managed to produce a pea-sized globe of light attached to the palm of her hand. In fact it was so attached that no amount of trying by Elizabeth would persuade it to lift into the air.

When Jane and Polly arrived back, Celina and Elizabeth told a horrified Jane and a mystified Polly the tale in full of what had happened in the park. When Polly heard about a glow globe having been created powerful enough to do so much damage, she was most intrigued, with both Polly and Jane immediately wanting to go and see for their selves.

It was only with Celina mentioning that Elizabeth had created a glow globe that Polly decided to postpone her visit to the park long enough for a demonstration by Elizabeth.

Elizabeth concentrated and then opened her palm to reveal a small ball of light.

"Well that's amazing," Polly said glancing at Celina. Celina knew exactly what she meant. To create a glow globe without lowering her shield meant that Elizabeth was using only the power she had in her body.

"Can you send it off your palm," Polly asked as she opened her hand and with a gentle toss threw a globe of light into the air. "Like that?"

Elizabeth tried throwing the globe of light off her palm but without success, and then once again this time a little harder, but the glow remained firmly stuck to her palm. Elizabeth paused to consider her efforts.

Frowning in thought, she brought her hand to her mouth where she gently blew the globe of light off of her palm. They all watched as it floated slowly up and then over her head.

"That's really different," Polly said and then tried it herself with the same result.

With the two globes of light floating above them the room was now illuminated so brightly that Celina felt the sunlight from the windows had paled. Comparing the two glows, Celina could see that Polly's globe was not only larger by a considerable amount but also whiter and possibly hotter.

Looking closely at Elizabeth's globe Celina decided that it was slightly larger than the ones she had created earlier, but with a softer and warmer light than the one created by Polly.

"What made you think to blow it?" Polly asked.

Elizabeth looking at her glow hesitated for a moment before saying. "It's just that if you're careful you can blow a candle flame off the wick and still have it burning, so I thought I would try it."

"Well." Jane said comparing the two glows. "It worked."

Celina who had been sitting studying Elizabeth's glow globe now felt certain that it was larger than her earlier attempts. Celina wondered that if Elizabeth could do it how many others could, and how many Knights could be taught totally to drop their personal shield. Celina decided there and then that Polly should be persuaded to bring Elizabeth into their select little group as soon as possible.

After a late dinner Celina and Elizabeth decided it was time to start out for their nocturnal visit to Charles Street.

Racking their brooms at the back of the first house in the alley, Elizabeth finding it was as black as a coal mine proudly created a small glow globe, and blowing it off of her palm she asked.

"Where do you intend to start?" Celina looking back along the alley at the large wooden doors to the hotel decided on the gate to the first house.

"I think here is as good as anywhere." Trying it and finding it locked she said. "It's locked." Celina ran her hand down the gate feeling for the lock on the other side of the door, finding it was a padlock; she deftly turned it and lifted it away. By the light of Elizabeth's glow, they looked into a garden.

"Disappointing isn't it," Celina said looking at what was a medium-sized and very neat garden. Making their way further into the garden, Elizabeth climbing on to a large plant tub looked over the wall into the back of the hotel.

"Quite a lot of rubbish," she reported, "but no demons." Back out into the alley Celina re-locked the gate, and then opened the gate into the second garden. Again, a neat and tidy garden greeted them.

"Well its not here either or is it in one of the houses?" Then Celina turned stood still and began sniffing before asking. "Can you smell something?"

Elizabeth crossed over to the next garden's wall sniffed and said. "It's this way and further up I think."

Letting themselves out and re-locking the gate, they sniffed their way further up the alley.

If it hadn't been for the glow globe they probably would have walked right past it. Propped up lengthwise in a junction on the opposite side of the alley was a four-foot long matt-black box that looked rather like a coffin. Only it was not made of wood but made of some very light and hard material. The two of them stood looking at it propped there with the top open and the pungent smell of bug making their stomachs churn.

"So this is where it came from." Celina said as she poked at the box with her foot. "I think we should get this to the Abbot don't you?"

"How?" Elizabeth asked. Celina looked back down the alley and said. "I think I saw a clothesline in the last garden, we can use that to tie it on my broom."

Back in the garden Celina started to take down the clothesline only to be stopped by Elizabeth saying. "You can't do that it's stealing." Celina stopped and giving it some thought said. "I can always return it in the morning.

"What if you forget or just don't do it, then it will have been stolen."

"All right then." Celina said looping the clothesline over her arm as she had seen Kate do. "I'll pay for it." With the clothesline neatly coiled Celina fumbled in her purse tilting it towards Elizabeth's glow to find some halfpennies, and giving them to Elizabeth said.

"Put them where they can be seen in the morning." Celina watched as Elizabeth put the coins on the back doorstep before saying. "All right then, and now can we continue?"

With some difficulty and the help of the clothesline that had almost been stolen out of the garden, the box was eventually fastened on the back of Celina's broom, Celina saying to Elizabeth as she took the front seat.

"I am not having a bug-smelling box sitting in front of me." It was an unsteady and shaky journey to the Abbey with Celina having to stop and refasten the box twice. Arriving at the Abbots lodgings they had to knock loudly to rouse him as he had long ago retired for the night.

After having examined and smelt the box, the box was at the Abbots insistence moved down wind and well away from his door ready for collection by a team from Fountain's Abbey.

"This object is really more their domain than ours, and then there's the smell, we certainly don't want that do we," the Abbot asked holding his nose to emphasise his point.

Once inside his lodgings the Abbot placed a note on his secretary's desk to contact Fountain's Abbey's research team first thing in the morning.

Then as they all settled down in the Abbot's study with a glass each, the Abbot found himself listening to another, and despite Celina and Elizabeth's objections, "fisherman's tale," as he insisted in calling them. Fisherman's tale or not he sat through the story so engrossed that he forgot his drink.

"It looks as if Polly has become as good a teacher as Dr Bird," the Abbot mused. Then turning to Celina, he said.

"Back to the bug, I still want to know why they keep targeting you and why do you seem to be their main goal? Yes, I know you are a remarkable and talented woman but so is Polly.

Both of you are very powerful, and it looks as if you're both getting more so every time I see you." He hesitated and then changing the subject he said. "I wonder how many others could benefit from Polly's teaching. I take it that you've heard Dickie has altered quite a lot of his curriculum to take into account Polly's methods."

Celina decided that this was the best time to reveal more, saying. "Elizabeth would you show him the glow?" Elizabeth first held out her closed fist and then opened it to reveal a glow globe. To Celina, it looked like it was not only larger but also brighter.

"It looks like practice is all that's needed." Elizabeth said looking very pleased with herself. She then gave a slight toss with her hand and to her surprise, the glow globe floated free to hover between them.

"Well I never," Elizabeth said and then with a look of delight upon her face, she swung the globe of light around the room saying. "That's easier than I thought." Closing her hand the glow disappeared.

Turning back to the surprised Abbot she said. "I'm sorry my Lord Abbot, but we had better be getting back as I have to be at the hospital later this morning." Celina held back as Elizabeth led the way to the door to say to the Abbot.

"I think Polly should open her training further." Celina inclined her head toward Elizabeth's back. The Abbot nodded saying.

"Well having seen that I think I shall have to have a word with Lady Polly myself, the Abbey candles are costing me a fortune." The Abbot then walked them to the door stopping them at the door to say. "Now be careful as you all mean a lot to me." As the brooms lifted into the night sky, Celina called across to Elizabeth and asked. "I wonder what that last remark really meant."

Tuesday 20th May 1862.

Jane greeted Celina the following morning waving the paper and saying. "Here you are in the headlines, look." She started to read aloud. "Ball lightning strikes in park, and then under it, it says miraculous escape for two young women."

She continued over her breakfast to read out a lurid and totally fictional description of how two women. Who by the grace of god had miraculously escaped a fifty-foot sphere of ball lightning that had struck from a clear sky in Hyde Park.

This was followed by varied eyewitness accounts prompting Celina's comment of.

"The only truth in any of it was the clear sky bit; after all it was a beautiful day." Polly was determined to see the damage done to the park so after breakfast Polly and Jane took a walk to the park gates. Inside the park, a small crowd was gathered around a roped-off area. Polly with no ceremony at all elbowed her way to the front for a better view.

"When you're as small as I am elbows work wonders," she told Jane as they arrived at the rope barrier.

Standing at the rope barrier Jane whispered. "Watch me and when I need you to, lean." Hearing this Polly, who had been looking at the hole turned to find Jane was already under the rope, so she had to follow. Walking over to the constable Jane pulled a notebook and pencil from her bag, and giving Polly a wink she said. "Good morning officer I'm with the Evening Standard."

Polly began to lean pushing belief at the policeman.

"Now sergeant…." Jane began.

"Just constable if you please madam," he said modestly declining her promotion.

"Surely you must be a sergeant guarding an important happening like this?" Then giving him her best smile Jane asked. "Now sergeant, were you here yesterday morning?"

"I'm sorry madam I was not," he replied, "but I have heard a full account of all that happened from the constable who was." From then on Jane took copious notes on an impossible occurrence as Polly wandered around examining the crater and burnt grass.

After many thanks and a shilling tip to the constable, they made their way back to the gate. As they hurried back towards the gates, Polly could see Jane was on the point of bursting with what she had to tell her. Once well away from the crowd Jane insisted they found a quiet place to sit, saying to Polly.

"We need somewhere to sit just in case either of us collapses with laughter." They found a seat in the sun where Jane opened her notebook saying. "Listen to this," and then she began to read her notes.

"At approximately eleven of the clock police constable Brown was patrolling outside the gates of Hyde Park when he heard a loud noise passing overhead. Looking up he saw a ball of fire a hundred feet across and trailing smoke and sparks as it moved at an incredible speed across the sky, until it fell into Hyde Park where a horrendous explosion followed.

Upon entering the park he could see through the flames and smoke a hole some twenty yards across, and beyond it he could see two women lying unconscious on the grass. Having approached the two women police constable Brown assisted them to their feet and helped them to a safe place.

It was as he assisted them that they told him as how they had seen the fireball coming straight towards them where it blew them off their feet before hurling them fifty yards across the park and almost into the lake.

After ensuring that neither of the women was seriously hurt, police constable Brown helped them across to the park gates and called a cab for them. The cab driver saying he took them to St Paul's Cathedral where they said they wished to give thanks to God for their 'miraculous deliverance from the fires of Hell'."

Returning to Belgrave House where they found Celina, who having met Elizabeth at Rarities was just about to settle down for a late lunch, so it was over lunch that Jane and Polly were able to entertain them with a graphic description of what was alleged by police constable Brown to have happened in the park.

Elizabeth couldn't believe the nerve of Jane walking up to a policeman and pretending to be a newspaper reporter, and getting a story that would be snapped up by any of the papers in London.

Polly herself had to confess to being impressed by the damage done by the outsized glow globe, and going as far as saying.

"I couldn't have done better myself, and I would never have believed something like a glow globe could do so much damage, I am really impressed." Then turning to Celina, she asked. "When can we go back up north? I really must try it myself."

Elizabeth now feigning horror said. "Well if you do I for one don't want to be anywhere near. Once was bad enough and twice would be unbearable."

Celina remembering the Abbot's remark about candles said. "You ought to have had your father there with his photographic engine, as that way we could take a picture to the Abbot, and then he may change his mind about his reliance on candles."

After the attack in the park, Elizabeth noticed the frequency of portal openings dropped to one or two a month, though they were still in the general vicinity of the doctors but higher up on Charles Street. Regular checks for portals demons and wraiths were still made by Elizabeth and Celina; or by Elizabeth and Polly if Celina was unavailable.

During all this time Polly found herself getting more and more frustrated with the lack of progress she was making with Jane. Sitting in the kitchen after Cook had left for the market, Polly finally had to admit defeat saying.

"The energy or power, call it what you will is clearly there, but you have a shield of some form that holds it in." Then she shrugged and said. "Why I don't know, but until we can find some way of breaking it down we're stuck."

Polly walked over to the kitchen door and looked out. Her broom was still where she had left it racked outside the old stables.

Turning to Jane she asked. "How about we give it a rest, I may think of something, something that we can try next time I'm here."

Walking over to stand with Polly at the door Jane said. "Well I'm not making much progress am I?"

Suddenly, Polly said. "Let's have a go with the broom then," and without waiting for an answer she pulled the kitchen door fully open and was away running down the steps.

Jane hesitated uncertain and a little fearful about the idea of following her. Eventually, and feeling she had little choice in the matter she relented and followed. Standing by the broom Polly explained.

"It's not mine; I borrowed it from the utility store at the Abbey and so in theory anyone who has a wand can use it." Jane stood beside Polly looking at the broom. It certainly looked well used; the leather on one of the seats was starting to split, and a footboard had lost some of the wickerwork.

"It may not be beautiful, but it flies," Polly said. Then turning to Jane she asked. "What can you feel from the broom?"

Jane reached out a hand stopping a mere inch away from touching the handgrip. "It's like a push holding my hand away," then she hesitated frowning and said. "No it's not a push; it's me. It's more a reluctance on my part to touch it." Jane still hesitated carefully considering her feelings.

Then she said with a touch of surprise in her voice. "It's different; it's not the same as it was, not now that I can feel my skin as a barrier." Jane gritting her teeth in the expectation of something horrible happening reached out and firmly gripped the bar.

Both Jane and Polly had expected something to happen, but nothing did. The broom sat on its rack and there was no reaction at all; no sparks or flashes just a very surprised Jane. Polly seeing this whispered. "What does it feel like?"

"Strange," Jane replied. "It's as if the energy in my hand knows of the broom and has pulled back, I think…. It feels…." Jane stopped and shook her head. "It just feels very strange," she concluded as she let go.

Kicking the rack up out of the way Polly sat astride the broom, and as it lifted she said. "Now try again." Jane took hold of the front grip and still felt nothing. Lifting her skirts she put her leg over the bar and stood astride the broom's shaft. Then sitting on the seat, she lifted her feet and put them on the footboards. With a look of utter amazement on her face, she turned to Polly and said.

"I don't believe this; I've never been able to get within a foot of a broom before and now look." Sitting on the rear seat and with Jane on board Polly lifted the broom about six feet into the air.

"Well it still responds to me as usual, but I think we should stop this for now and wait until its dark." As Polly let the broom down onto the paving of the yard, Jane who found herself feeling rather frightened at what had happened was about to agree but then changed her mind and said.

"Do you mind not telling Celina just yet, if Celina knew she would want to fly with me immediately, so can we wait and see what happens first, but just being able to sit on a broom. Oh Polly it was marvellous, but I want to know how far I can go before I tell Celina as it would be terrible if this is all I can do." Jane hesitated again and then said.

"Though this is more than I ever believed I would be able to do." As she dismounted, Jane found that her legs felt like jelly, and her hands were shaking.

"Come on then," Polly said. "Tell me what actually happened, just what did you feel?"

"I don't know; like I said since I can feel the power and my skin meeting, something is different. It's like the power has changed and is more accommodating.... no more.... well I don't know how to describe it, but it's not dominating me any more. It's not controlling me as much. I've more say about it if that's what I mean.... I'm not quite sure. It's like I've reached a compromise with it." Jane shook her head feeling totally lost and bemused.

Polly dismounted and pulled the broom back on its rack. It was as Polly stepped back that Jane tentatively reached down and ran her hand along the shaft and then the hand bar with a look of wonder on her face.

Polly knew how she felt; she remembered her first experience on a broom along with the experience of being chosen by her wand. A feeling of love and joy had swept over her at the memory. Polly felt she had to touch her wand to be able to feel the warmth of it right through its protective sheath.

How would it be having a power like Jane and yet never knowing the joy at first contact with your very own wand? Polly felt tears in her eyes and gently touched Jane's hand. Jane's hand was burning hot and Polly could feel the power flowing under Jane's skin. It now felt different to her too; it was smoother and not so raw.

Touching Jane's skin, Polly found for an instant she could feel her excitement and hope, hope that someday she would be able to join Celina in the air. Polly found to her astonishment that Jane was open and very much unguarded. For that fleeting instant while touching Jane's hand, she could see all of Jane's hopes.

She saw Jane's memory of Celina's description of the moon light on clouds and her joy of flying. She knew Jane's desperate hope of one day being able to join her. She felt the unique bond between Jane and Celina; and how Jane and Celina loved each other as sisters. Polly could also sense how Jane and Celina felt each other's joys and fears as deeply as their own.

Only now did she realise how closely they shared each other's feelings as an awareness of this radiated into her consciousness during that one moment of frozen time. Polly was startled at what she was sensing, and all at once the feeling of being a peeping Tom overwhelmed her, quickly she let go of Jane's hand.

"Come on let's get a drink," Jane said as she started up the stairs. "Cook has some home-brewed ale in the pantry, and I know she hides it under the stone slab to keep it cool." Taking two glasses on her way to the pantry Jane drew two foaming glasses of ale. Returning to the kitchen the two girls settled down to talk over Jane's experience and relax.

By the time Celina returned Polly was still struggling, still only half understanding what she had felt, but now looking at Jane and Celina, she saw clearly for the first time how strong the bond between them was. It made her think of Nancy and the bond that developed between the two of them in the workhouse.

It was after dinner with thoughts of Nancy still lingering in her mind that Polly brought up the subject of Nancy. Jane had left to answer the Telson as Polly asked Celina.

"Do you think it would be possible for me to see Nancy? I still miss her so, and I'm sure she misses me." Then with tears starting in her eyes she mumbled. "She probably thinks I'm dead." It was as she said this that she started quietly to cry. Celina moved closer so she could put her arm around her shoulders as she said.

"If you want we can go north on Friday, and we can stop at the Hall overnight. If we do that, then you can see Nancy on Saturday." Jane who had answered the Telson returned to find a tearful Polly and then had to break the news to her that the Abbot was asking her to do a run that night.

Friday 23rd May 1862.

The last two days to Polly seemed to have taken forever, but at last it was time for her and Celina to leave. Despite it being a warm evening flying high and fast left Celina and Polly chilled to the bone.

Landing outside the tack room Celina was pleased to find that her favourite brother Robert was already waiting with the doorman to greet them at the door, and knowing how cold they would be flying from London; he was ready with a warming drink of brandy for Celina and a small glass of sherry for Polly.

With drinks in hand, Robert escorted them to Lady Mary's study where Celina's parents were waiting for the serving of dinner to be announced.

It was as dinner was being served that Lady Mary, who knowing how Polly felt about Nancy turned to Polly to say.

"I visited the orphanage this morning." Polly felt her heart leap as she listened with excitement building up inside her as she heard. "I saw your Nancy again, and she was telling me about how she is training one week a month in the kitchens of a hotel in Lincoln." Polly couldn't wait she had to ask.

"Is she all right and did you tell her about me?" Polly waited impatiently as Lady Mary sat in silence while the first course was served, Lady Mary eventually saying.

"Yes Polly she is all right, but I thought rather than me say anything about you it would be a nice surprise for Nancy if you visited her."

"Mother," Celina interrupted. "That was one of the reasons Polly and I have visited you, to give Polly a chance to visit Nancy." Lady Mary with a frown at Celina at having interrupted her now finished what she had been about to say.

"As I feel that the weather seems set fair for tomorrow you could take a picnic with you, and I will write you a note of introduction to Mrs Philips."

A chastised Celina, who had been quietly watching Robert's face and the way his eyes had never really left Polly since he had sat at the table now perked up and with a sudden insight asked.

"Robert would you like to go with Polly in the morning? I really ought to call and see the Abbot while I'm here." Polly had turned to look at Celina, so she didn't see the look on Robert's face, but both Celina and her mother did, and the meaning of that look wasn't lost on either of them; causing Celina to have a quiet little chuckle to herself as she exchanged a look with her mother.

Later after Polly had retired to her rooms, Celina caught up with Robert on the stairs and stopping him she said. "You be careful flying with our Polly." Puzzled at Celina saying this Robert asked.

"Why surely she's not that bad on a broom is she?" Celina laughed as she said.

"No it's not that she's not a good flyer, in fact she's probably the best there is."

"What better than you?" he asked with disbelief evident in his voice.

"Much as I hate to admit it, but yes she's not only better but she can push a broom far faster than I can."

"Never," an astonished Robert declared. "You're as fast as father if not faster."

"You'd better believe it; she is far faster than father or I am, and another thing; Polly is a nice girl so you behave yourself, do you understand." She jabbed a finger into his chest as she said. "If I find out you've hurt her in any way."

"Why would I want to hurt her? I like Polly; there I've admitted it. I've liked her since you first brought her here and even more after hearing about her life." This revelation shook Celina; Robert was actually admitting that he liked Polly. This was not like the Robert she knew and especially knowing his reputation with the girls in the villages.

Taking hold of his chin something she hadn't done since he was a child she said. "You take care of her, or it won't be an irate father you will be running from; it will be me, and I can still run faster than you remember?" Robert did remember, as children Celina had always been fast on her feet.

"Please Celina," Robert said pleadingly. "Polly is different and I don't want to spoil it, if I need your help can I count on you?" Not waiting for an answer, he gave Celina a kiss on the cheek and ran up the stairs.

A surprised Celina stood and watched him go. She hadn't leant on him in any way as it wasn't a thing you did to family, but Robert had radiated sincerity. In fact, Celina had actually felt his attraction for Polly as a woman and that level of emotional investment was for Robert very unusual.

'Yes' she thought. *'He might actually feel something for Polly. Polly as my sister? We could do worse, and being the youngest son he might have difficulty doing better.'* Celina still deep in thought and with hope in her heart slowly made her way to bed.

Saturday 24th May 1862.

Robert and Polly left early on a bright sunny morning with a well-filled picnic basket for later. Once on their way Polly chose for her a steady and sedate flying speed as she told Robert about her life in the orphanage. He had already heard some of it from his mother but hearing Polly tell of it made it seem more real to him, and as the miles passed and Polly's story unfolded; Polly found herself telling Robert about things she had never told anyone else. Things she thought too painful to speak of.

As Robert sat on the front-seat listening and hearing from Polly of her early life, he could feel revulsion, horror and anger start to boil up within.

Arriving at about nine of the clock, they put the broom under some trees about half a mile from the orphanage, and with the picnic basket over Robert's arm they walked first down a lane and then along the road.

Polly was surprised to see how the orphanage had changed. There was new paint on the building, and in a fenced-off area around the back she could see neat vegetable plots where children were working with only one adult supervising, and not a whip or a cane in sight.

Robert led the way to the front of the building and in through the main door. Once inside the door instead of the dark green and brown hall she remembered it was now brightly painted, and the walls were hung with colourful needlework samplers obviously done by the girls.

Sturdy plain chairs that she assumed had been made by the boys were arranged along one wall. A woman entered and introduced herself as Betsy Philips the matron.

Robert introduced himself and then introduced Polly as Lady Cavendish. He then asked if Nancy the girl his mother had taken an interest in was available.

Seeing the doubtful expression on the matron's face Robert handed over the letter of introduction from his mother before saying.

"My mother believes Lady Cavendish may be able to assist the young lady." Still not feeling fully satisfied with this Mrs Philips seeing them seated left to find Nancy.

It was no good; Polly couldn't rest she paced up and down until the matron returned and asked them to follow her. The matron took them into a pleasant first floor room with a window looking out over the gardens. A young girl was sitting at a table near the window with her head down and looking as if she was studying the tabletop.

"I'll leave you for now," the matron said. "If you want me just ring the bell." Matron lifted a small brass bell on a shelf by the door, and then without another word or a backward glance she left them quietly closing the door behind her.

"Nancy," Polly said with tears starting to mist her eyes. The girl didn't look up.

"Nancy it's me Polly." The girl's head slowly lifted, and she looked up. At first, she shook her head in denial not recognising Polly dressed in her fine clothes.

"Yes Nancy," Polly said. "It really is me." Nancy slowly got to her feet, and then in a rush threw herself at Polly. Robert smiling as he watched them found that he had tears threatening in his eyes.

Polly was holding Nancy as close as she could and both were crying. Robert looked around as the matron who obviously had been listening at the door opened it almost instantly.

"It's all right matron. Nancy thought Lady Cavendish was dead, and as you can see she is very much alive and well." The Matron having heard Robert stood looking for a few moments and then deciding both Nancy and Polly's tears were happy ones, she quietly left the room. By the time matron returned with a tray of tea things Nancy was sitting on Polly's knee still occasionally sobbing but smiling radiantly.

Seeing the tea things and getting a disapproving look from the matron Nancy wiped her eyes on her pinafore before taking the tray from the matron. With the tray now on the table Nancy smiled shyly at Polly as she poured the tea and asked. "Is it really you? I just can't believe it and can I still call you Polly?"

"Since when have you ever called me anything else," Polly asked with a smile.

"You're such a lady now," Nancy said as she ran her hand along Polly's sleeve. "Just look at you in your fine clothes." Then quietly she asked. "What happened? They said they were going to burn you as a witch."

"Well they didn't do it did they, and as you can see I'm still here."

Nancy for a moment went all shy again and then in a whisper she said. "The girls said you were a witch, and I said you were a good witch. I told them that good witches don't get burned, but I

323

didn't know and it was terrible." She looked up first at Polly and then at Robert before she said.

"Later after they had taken you away, these men came with lots of Bobbies and took all the others away and leaving Mr and Mrs Philips in charge. It was awful; they dug up the yard and the ground out at the back of the kitchen." Then in a cabal whisper she said. "We heard they found dead bodies."

Nancy suddenly became even shyer as she whispered. "You are a witch aren't you?" The question didn't exactly take Polly by surprise, but still it took a moment or two for Polly to pull her thoughts together before she could answer.

"Yes Nancy I am, and as you see they didn't burn me. I'm a witch who works for the church so you see I am a good witch."

A smile lit Nancy's face as she said. "We knew you were, but we kept it as our secret and no-one else had to know."

Polly turned Nancy to face her as she said. "Nancy it still is a secret just between you and me, can you do that?" Polly waited as Nancy nodded before asking. "I hear you're training to be a cook in a large hotel, is that right?"

"Well to cook at least, and I am learning in a big hotel in Lincoln. They say that when I'm thirteen I can work there." Nancy suddenly looking pleased with herself asked. "Do you know what?" Nancy waited for an answer that was obviously not coming and then said. "Since Mr and Mrs Philips came we've had schooling." Then proudly she said. "I can read and write now."

"Well I will give you my address so you can write to me in London, and I will be able to write back to you, will that be all right?" The smile on Nancy's face was all the answer Polly needed.

The visit lasted nearly two hours and then at the matron's suggestion and with Nancy as a guide, they were taken for a tour of the orphanage. At the end of the tour and with the matron's permission, they took Nancy for a picnic in the fields.

After the picnic, they took a walk along the riverbank where Nancy told Polly about how her life had changed since Mr and Mrs Philips had arrived. It was late in the evening when with more tears they said good-bye at the orphanage's door. As she was leaving Polly promised that as soon as she had her own rooms, she would invite Nancy down to see London.

It was as Polly and Robert walked back to the broom in the gathering dusk discussing the visit that Robert suggested. "I can always ask mother if Nancy can stay for a few days at the Hall when you're up this way, or she could stay with Celina when you're in London." Then with a sly smile he said. "After all transportation won't be a problem will it, as she already knows you're a witch."

It was over dinner Robert broached with his parents the subject of Nancy seeing Polly on a regular basis. "After all," he told them. "It won't be a problem getting her either here or to London and back."

"I take it that you approve of Nancy," his mother remarked giving Celina a knowing look.

"Yes mother," he replied. Then sounding a little pompous he said. "I found her to be a very nice well-spoken child." Celina looked at her mother and found just like her; she was barely managing to keep a straight face. It was after dinner that Celina cornered Robert.

"Well," she asked.

"Well what?"

"Well how did you get on with Polly?" then she asked more directly. "I take it that you still like her?"

"Yes she's a very nice girl," was his bemused response.

"Lady, a very nice lady," Celina corrected him, "and she's only a few years younger than you."

"Yes well she's a very nice lady, and yes I do like her. She's nice, yes very nice."

Next Celina cornered Polly and asked. "So, how did it go?"

"Very well, the orphanage is totally changed. I talked to some of the other girls, and it's a much happier place now, though there aren't many left who were there when I was. Nancy says she is one of the oldest there now."

"Not the orphanage," Celina said stamping her foot. "Robert." Polly looked taken aback.

"Robert, what about Robert?"

"Oh you are worse than he is," Celina said as she turned and walked off. Polly watched her retreating back totally confused. "What about Robert," she quietly asked herself while thinking. *'He is very nice for a Lord's son.'*

It wasn't until Polly was almost asleep that a stray thought brought her back to fully awake and so surprised that she said aloud. "Lady Cavendish," Robert had called her Lady Cavendish, and he was the son of a Lord. Though she was not a daughter or wife of a Lord, she was still an actual titled Lady. Polly found to her surprise that she had finally come to accept the fact that she was a Lady in her own right.

Thinking about it, she had to admit she did quite like Robert. Her last thought before falling asleep was that travel wouldn't be a problem. She was a witch, and as Elizabeth had told her being a witch had certain definite advantages. In the morning, she had vague memories of a dream, and somewhere in her dream Robert had fitted in very pleasantly.

Sunday 26th May 1862.

The morning was warm and sunny so the family decided to walk to church. Celina couldn't help smiling as she noticed that Robert was definitely keeping close to Polly. Celina walking over to join them said.

"I think it would be a good idea for Nancy to join us at Christmas. We could arrange to fly up here to pick her up and then take her back with us." Celina looked at Polly as she said. "We could then spend a few days up here after we take her back."

After church was over Polly and Celina sat in the churchyard along with Jane's mother and father while Celina told them all about the latest attack in the park.

"It's unbelievable," Polly said as she opened her hand to produce a glow globe now pale in the sun. "Celina blew a hole in the ground twenty feet across with a larger one of these, and I must admit I was absolutely amazed."

Polly then had to tell them how Jane had posed as a reporter to get past the police. Jane's father found it most amusing and was laughing as he said.

"That's our Jane." Then holding his hand over the globe, and then almost to the point of touching it he said.

"There's not much heat can you make it hotter?" Polly obliged prompting him to ask. "I wonder if you could melt steel with it."

"I don't know about steel, but it can turn soil and stones into a black glass." Celina shook her head as seeing Jane's father look at her, she said.

"Don't ask me I still don't know how I did it. I was only intending to distract the creature so that I could get to my wand."

"You didn't distract it." Polly said with a chuckle. "You destroyed it. There wasn't a trace left I know because I looked. I made a special point of looking all around for anything that might be bits of bug."

"What none at all, how far away did you look?" Polly shaking her head said.

"Sorry Celina not a trace. I looked as far as I could right past where you rolled into the flowerbed and beyond. Then I looked in a circle all around, there definitely wasn't a trace left; it was total destruction, not even a sniff of a smell remaining."

"Smell?" Jane's mother asked.

"Yes smell." Celina confirmed. "They all have a very unpleasant odour."

"Definitely eye-watering," Polly said.

"Breath-taking." Celina added.

"It clears your sinuses among other things," Polly said closing the discussion.

As they walked back to the Hall Polly finally picked up the courage to ask Celina if she really meant it about Nancy.

"Polly, if I didn't mean it I wouldn't have brought the subject up. Of course Nancy must come there's plenty of room, or we can have a small bed put into your room for a few days if that's what you or Nancy would prefer. I really think that it would be nice for you both to have a family Christmas." Celina stopped and turning she took Polly's hand as she said.

"It would be even better if we came up here but I don't know if that would be possible." Polly remained quite lost in her own thoughts for a few more yards, and then she said.

"That would be nice and not just for Nancy. Do you know I can't remember a proper Christmas before I went in the orphanage, and Christmas in the orphanage wasn't anything to write home about that I can tell you. It's only been the last year or so that I've had a Christmas worth remembering, and then it was just at the Abbey." Celina put an arm around Polly's shoulders and said.

"Well this year we shall see if we can make it something special for you both." Polly remained quiet for a time thinking, and then said.

"If it can be arranged, I think Nancy should have her own room, she never has had a room or for that matter anything to call her own."

As they walked on Celina remembered Polly's reaction to being shown the rooms in London, and suddenly Celina felt she was learning more and more from Polly, and not just about Polly but about life itself.

It was just as the sun was setting that Celina's mother and father along with Robert came down to the stables to see them off. Celina couldn't help noticing that her mother and Polly were having a quiet talk together along the way. Then it was a hug for all and a final farewell. Celina took the front seat, and as they turned toward London Polly said. "Your mother's nice isn't she?" Celina could only agree.

"She says if I have time when I'm up this way I should call on her and then possibly see Nancy, do you think she really means it?"

"If my mother says so she means it," and then having thought about it, she said. "Yes I agree with her; I think you should too." Then seeing as she was doing the flying Polly asked Celina if she would like further instructions on the art of flying. "My way," to which Celina readily agreed.

Polly decided that lessons about high speed and aggressive flying would be a good place to start, so she started by showing Celina how to hold or even increase her speed during a sharp turn

328

by allowing the broom naturally to bank into the turn rather than holding it upright. Then she took Celina through a series of twist and rolls that Polly said; "could be used to avoid an attacker."

All these manoeuvres were given with a stern warning that the safety strap must be firm or else. After one or two twists and turns, the creaking of the seat and leather safety strap reminded Celina of the bug attack and set her to thinking again about the need for something better.

Possibly, a stronger seat and something more in the way of a harness, a strap across your lap was all right for sedate flying but some of the manoeuvres Polly was doing put a lot of strain on the seat, the strap and the rider. After a particularly sudden drop, Celina found herself saying.

"It certainly lifts one out of one's seat doesn't it." Low-level flying over the Derbyshire moors was next. With Polly flying in the dark at speeds that terrified Celina, especially when Polly took the broom within feet of the moors and hugging the ground so close that Celina swore the bracken dragged at her boots.

After only a few minutes of low-level high speed flying, it was a terrified Celina who called a halt to the experience as almost sick with fright she asked. "How can you do that? I'm in the front seat and I couldn't see a thing?"

"It's easy," Polly said. "Look you take over the flying and just fly slowly." Celina pushed the broom forward at just above a walking pace.

"Right now push your shield out in front of us about five yards." Celina pushed her shield out struggling for a moment to hold its shape and forward position, until drawing power from around her; she finally mastered it and held it in the required place as Polly said.

"Right now dip the front of the broom and feel with your shield." Celina allowed the front of the broom to droop slightly and instantly felt the moor push against her shield.

"Do you feel it?" Polly asked. The broom was now moving slightly nose-down held just above the moor by Celina's shield.

Celina who was still not comfortable about looking away from their direction of flight called over her shoulder. "I understand now; you use your shield to see with."

"That's right; you feel with your shield and let it lift the broom over whatever is in front of you." Now with a better understanding and acceptance of Polly's technique Celina pushed the broom a little harder.

"Good," Polly said, but then after a sudden lift and drop almost caused her to bang her head on Celina's back she said. "Push your shield further out, the further out you push it the smoother the ride becomes."

Following her directions worked and Celina's speed gradually increased as her confidence grew. Finally, she was flying not as fast as Polly would but certainly fast enough for her.

Taking over the flying again Polly showed Celina how to bring a broom to a rapid halt. The technique involved slewing the broom sideways and at the same time leaning in. This was an eye-opener to Celina as she had always been taught to stop in a straight line, but as Polly explained there were major pitfalls to rapid straight-line stops from a very high speed.

"If you stop fast in a straight line, and you're not very careful the front of the broom can either dip, or it can pull up. If it dips you're in trouble because if its front digs into the ground, you can flip right over.

On the other hand, if the front pulls up and the tail hits the ground hard, or the tail catches and lifts over something on the ground that can throw the front down, and you are still likely to go over the front. It's far better if you have to stop fast to lean in and let the broom slide sideways. At least if you hit something you're sitting on top of it, and your shield takes the knock."

A few demonstrations showed Celina what she meant. Celina found a sharp sliding stop pushed you hard down in the seat making it almost impossible to fall off, reminding her of the tumble she had had in the Abbey Gardens.

It was as they approached London where they were flying so high and fast that Polly had to use her shield to keep them breathing that Celina asked.

"How did you learn all this, and don't tell me it was the orphanage again."

"No you're right it wasn't the orphanage this time, I simply like flying and the excitement of doing things like this." Polly laughed as she said. "I do have to confess to more than a few accidents in learning it all."

It was as they came over Belgrave Square that Polly said. "And here ends the first lesson," after which she provided Celina with one last manoeuvre. Rather than just letting the broom drop vertically under gravity into the stable yard Polly did something Celina had never quite mastered. She actually pushed the broom hard down while keeping the broom horizontal causing Celina to lift in her seat, and gasp in surprise as her stomach came up into her throat.

"If you have to fight on a broom," Polly said as she eased her downward push, "you have to fly like this or die. Remember this the next time something attacks you, you have to fight dirty just like a cat. You have to spit and claw and bite, being 'Miss Nice' only gets you dead."

Just as she finished saying this Polly pulled the broom up sharply providing them with a soft landing in the stable yard at the back of Belgrave House. Then watched by Celina, she floated Celina's broom into the tack room.

When she turned around Polly found Celina looking not just shocked but even a little frightened. This was a Polly Celina had never seen before. An aggressive and potentially combative Polly totally unlike the Polly she knew.

"Celina," Polly said in a soft quiet voice, while at the same time reaching up and cupping Celina's face in both her hands. "I like you, and I don't want to see you dead, so please for me learn what to do to stay alive."

It was Jane who opened the kitchen door and ran down the steps to welcome them home, and then having to break the sad news to Polly that she was needed to run courier that night. Though Jane refused to let Polly even think of leaving before they had all had a hot drink.

After her warming drink, Polly gave both of her friends a hug before climbing on to her broom, and then muttering a number of unpleasant things that could happen to the Abbot for sending her out again so late at night, she rose rapidly into the dark night sky.

Ixcte ~ 4.

Ixcte turned an eyestalk to follow the progress of an approaching food/slave/pet. It stopped every nine steps and prostrated itself for the required nine heartbeats before coming to rest at the required distance and well within the reach of the primary feeding tentacles. Prostrate on the ground it submissively waited. Ixcte raised its head.

"The Lovan has returned," Ixcte's thought asked.

"No Great one the Lovan did not return in the time allotted to it, it must have failed."

"Failed no!" Ixcte's thought screamed in the slave's mind. "Failure is not acceptable; the black must die. The native food/slave/pet must be instructed to deal with the black. The black must die before the time of the gate. Go and inform the native food/slave/pet that it must not fail, the black must die."

Ixcte watched the food/slave/pet retreat from the primary food tentacle that twisted unfulfilled in its need; Ixcte called for more food/slave/pets. A group of two hundred were dispatched prostrating themselves every nine steps, until Ixcte's feeding tentacles struck. The pain from the food/slave/pets felt good to Ixcte, and Ixcte savoured it as the dissolving fluids were forced into their bodies.

As the empty shells were dragged away Ixcte retracted its head back into its hood and continued contemplating the black. Long, long ago the black had hurt and twice almost destroyed Ixcte. Now the black was back; Ixcte drew its head further down into its hood remembering the fear and pain from so long ago.

Wednesday 18th June 1862.

I woke about one in the morning to find Jane holding me. I'd had a nightmare again, the same one. Red sky and sand are all I could remember apart from a feeling of hate and I feel the hate was directed at me.

Jane stayed with me; otherwise I don't think I could have slept again.

~~~

Jane

Tuesday 5th Aug 1862.

Over the ensuing months Jane had become a regular customer at the coffee house. William having finished teaching would arrive just after four, and Jane usually had drinks ordered and on the table. They found that they thoroughly enjoyed each other's company, and if the weather were clement William would often walk back to where Jane caught a cab to Church Street.

As it so happened this was one of those pleasant evenings and William was telling her about his family and his early life in a small seaside town on the south coast near Brighton.

"It's not far from the sea, in fact you can see it out of my bedroom window," he was saying as the cab shelter came into view. "I used to watch for father coming home when I was younger, and he used to fish himself."

"Doesn't he fish any more?" Jane asked. William shook his head.

"No there was an accident where my father was injured, and now he controls a fleet of.... I think it is twelve fishing boats." William shrugged. "I will probably end up running them when father gets too old to run them himself."

333

"Why," Jane asked. "Don't you like teaching?"

"Oh I like teaching well enough, but if I hadn't been one of the first to win one of the scholarships sponsored by the Prince Albert Trust and a place at Oxford I probably would be still in Brighton, as it is I was offered this post here."

They had almost reached the deserted cabstand when a commotion behind them caused them both to turn. A dray horse had broken free and was galloping towards them running wild. William quickly pulled Jane into the safety of a doorway. Jane who had seen what was happening further up the road was horrified.

Only a few yards beyond them Jane could see the road was filled from one side to the other with men women and children, all standing watching three men performing conjuring tricks and acrobatics in the road. There were far too many people and nowhere for all of them to go to safety. Jane could see amongst the crowd of people some would be injured or even killed.

Jane didn't stop to think she acted. Shaking off William's hand, and before he could stop her, Jane had stepped out of the shelter of the doorway and directly into the path of the oncoming horse, where she stood frozen and waiting. Willing herself to be as small and inconspicuous as possible, so as not to distract the horse galloping toward her.

Standing there and feeling a calm detachment come over her, she watched and waited studying the horse as it approached. Carefully, she judged her position waiting as the horse with hooves striking sparks from the cobbles came towards her, and then as instinct took over she leapt forward catching the rein in one hand and the bridle in the other. Jane threw her weight against the horse, and unexpectedly she found herself leaning heavily on the animal helping to calm the terror she could feel in the horse's mind.

Horror at Jane's action rooted William to the spot, and then to his surprise he saw Jane had not only caught the rein and bridle but had held on. With his heart-pounding William watched as Jane successfully pulled the horse's head down stopping the horse so fast that she was hardly dragged along at all.

Jane found herself leaning and pulling at the horse's bridle until she had control. Then standing at its side talking and rubbing her face against its, while she continued leaning to calm the frightened horse's fears as the dray man came puffing and blowing up the road.

He stopped beside her and doubled over trying to catch his breath as between gasps he kept repeating. "I don't believe it; I don't believe it." Others who had seen Jane's actions were also echoing his words.

As he straightened up and having recovered some of his breath, he once again looked at Jane and shook his head saying. "I don't believe it."

William now hurried over and taking Jane's arm he asked. "How did you do that?" Jane turned to both William and the drayman and replied.

"My father's a blacksmith, and I know horses." Handing the reins to the drayman and then pulling William after her, they quickly disappeared into the crowd. Now it was Jane's turn to do some explaining to a totally mystified William.

"I started helping my father when I was about five," she told him as they sat in the deserted shelter watching the crowd still milling around a little way down the road. "He let me help in the forge with just about everything to do with blacksmithing. Being a village blacksmith meant that he not only repaired and made items, but also he had to be an expert farrier, so I was shoeing horses by the time I was eleven using shoes that I had made myself."

William could hardly believe his ears. Here was a young, tall, slim woman who he had to admit was more than a little pretty. 'Yes,' he thought *'she's extremely pretty and attractive.'* Looking at Jane a sudden doubt came into his mind. She was wearing gloves and for the first time he really wanted to see her left hand. He couldn't so he found himself doing the next-best thing; he took Jane's hand in his. His heart leapt as he discovered that there was no ring.

Now he realised that Jane had come to mean far more to him than just someone to talk with after school. Looking up William found that Jane was still talking, and regrettably he had missed part of what she was saying as he heard.

"It was only after I went to live at Brimham Hall that I. Oh, here comes a cab," Jane said jumping to her feet. William helped her into the cab and then with a sudden intense feeling of longing, he watched it drive away.

Thursday 7th August 1862.

Today I received word that my mother and father are coming down to visit over the weekend. Cook is in a flap getting everything ordered food wise. Jane and Kate are opening the master suite and airing it out.

~~~

Cook was in a definite flap at times wanting Kate to be in two places at once. The master's rooms had to be ready for Lord and Lady Carvel's arrival that night, yet Cook also wanted food brought in from the markets. It was not that she was short of food in the house but like all cooks she preferred to overstock than find herself under supplied.

At last every thing was decided, and Cook set off shopping with Thomas in tow leaving Jane and Kate to sort out the master's accommodation. Celina was getting ready to leave for the shop having been told by Jane.

"Go, your only getting in everyone's way." The morning being warm and sunny Celina decided to walk into London and window shop.

As she was passing the entrance to Hyde Park, she found herself looking through the gate. In the distance Celina could see the work being done to repair the damage from the small explosion she had caused. On a whim, she decided to make a closer inspection; in place of the hole she now found a neat round flowerbed being worked on by some gardeners. Celina made her way across to speak with them.

Approaching the nearest of the gardeners who with his pipe in his mouth was stood leaning on his spade. To Celina, he looked to be contemplating his newly planted and now wilting plants. Standing there next to him, she said. "I don't remember this the last time I was here."

"I'm sorry Miss, I didn't see you," the gardener said taking the pipe out of his mouth and knocking it against the spade handle. "It's new, rare goings on it was." He then put the empty pipe back in his mouth and sucked noisily. Celina found the gurgling noise from the empty pipe bringing her out in goose bumps.

"Goings on," she asked. "Why what happened?" From the gardener, there was another sucking session on the pipe sending more shivers up Celina's spine. Then taking it out of his mouth and waving it in the general direction of the flowerbed he said.

"Rare goings on indeed, a big hole there was, yes rare big hole right here." Then he put his pipe back in his mouth for another sucking session. Celina cringed again at the gurgling sound coming from the bowl of his pipe. Finally taking out the pipe he said.

"They said it was the gas, yes, a big gas build-up under the ground." He then briefly put his pipe back into his mouth for a quick suck before he said. "I don't believe it though. No there's no gas around here. Anarchists, that's what it was, anarchists trying out a bomb." The pipe went back in his mouth and then came out again.

"A big bomb I reckons, twenty feet deep that hole was," he pointed the pipes stem at the flowerbed. Celina hearing his description privately thought that if that was the case, it wasn't a hole it was a mineshaft. The pipe made more gurgling noises and then with his head nodding as if about to fall off he said.

"Lucky escape, yes, lucky escape." Celina waited enduring more sucking sounds.

"Escape?" she finally asked. Taking the pipe out of his mouth again and prodding in the bowl with a Lucifer the man said.

"Yes a lucky escape, two women blown clean down to the lake." Celina looked at the lake over one hundred yards away and thought. *That must have been some bomb'.* He continued with a quick suck on the pipe before saying.

"Yes lucky escape, they could have been killed, mind you," he nodded towards the wilting plants. "It's made a rare nice flower-bed."

Keeping a straight face with difficulty Celina thanked him and gave him three pence for the information. Then she walked slowly around the new earth works before turning back toward the path and toward the park gate.

Once back on the path Celina almost didn't notice him. A smartly dressed man wearing a top hat was walking in front of her toward the park gate. From under the brim of his hat Celina could see his distinctive pure white hair.

Celina dropped back a little as the last thing she wanted was for him to notice her. Leaving by the gate he turned right toward Charles Street and the hotel on the corner.

Celina felt her heart beating harder. *He's walking toward the hotel,'* she thought as he crossed the road and then her heart sank as he walked past the hotel and carried on towards his rooms. It was at the third house down from the hotel that he turned, hesitated and then as Celina watched with obvious reluctance, he climbed the short flight of steps. Standing at the door he took a key from his coat pocket and let himself in.

Celina was almost jumping in excitement. *'I knew it. I knew it,'* ran through her mind. *'Now all we need is a portal to open tonight, and we'll know for certain.'* Celina was so excited that she went back to the old gardener and gave him half a crown saying.

"That's for holding me up with such an entertaining story." Then calling a cab she continued on to Church Street.

The instant Celina walked through the door Marcus knew something had happened. Instead of taking a moment to enquire about the shop Celina made straight for the office. Marcus followed her in time to see her picking up the Telson while trying to take her coat off at the same time. The call she placed was to Elizabeth who was at home and answered the call herself.

Celina couldn't wait as she said. "Elizabeth you know those two houses, the ones we looked at on Charles Street? Well, it's the third one."

There was a brief silence from Elizabeth before she asked. "The third one, what do you mean the third?"

"I've just seen Mr White let himself into the third house on Charles Street; he must own or have something to do with that house as he has a key." There was a pause as Elizabeth gathered her thoughts before she asked. "What do you suggest?"

"I think a patrol would be in order tonight, what time do you think would be best?"

Elizabeth paused to think before saying. "At this time of year I would say not before ten, so I suggest we meet at the usual place at ten of the clock."

Marcus who had been holding his ear close to the ear speaker now put his mouth to the sound collector and said. "I want to be there as well; I'm not letting you go alone."

Elizabeth didn't reply immediately but then Celina heard her say. "It looks like I've got a passenger tonight so tell him to bring a warm coat as it will be cold up there, and to be here early."

Celina replaced the Telson and said. "From that I take it that you heard it all." He nodded.

"So you were right," he said sitting down. Celina thought for a moment and then asked. "Have you still got that cannon of yours in the back room?"

"Yes, do you think we're going to need it?"

"I don't know," Celina said. "I don't know but bring it."

It was just after ten of the clock when Celina pulled alongside Elizabeth and Marcus who were hovering in place waiting for her. Calling across to the other broom she said.

"I don't think we should wait to close to the house just in case someone or something is sensitive to us, and I don't fancy sitting here half the night trying to hold a block that I'm not sure will work. How about moving over into the park?"

They turned the two brooms and moved quickly over the park so that the brooms now hovered two hundred or so feet above what Elizabeth gleefully called, 'Celina's garden.' While hovering there

Celina explained to Elizabeth more about how that night coming away from Mrs Allen's the demon had found them despite her best efforts to block herself and Marcus. Then she passed the rest of the time telling them all about her episode with the gardener and his disgustingly noisy pipe.

It was definitely getting chilly as midnight approached. Celina and Elizabeth had brought their brooms within touching distance and merged shields in an effort to keep warm. With the three of them aboard to some extent it worked.

Church clocks were just striking midnight when Elizabeth suddenly pulled her shield back and pointed.

"A portal's just opened and not far over that way." As the two brooms drifted over the roof of the third house, Elizabeth started to circle saying.

"It's definitely down there, let's go down we can land in the alley and then have a look around." Once in the alley Elizabeth started to walk up and down and eventually decided. "It's still open and it's below ground possibly in a cellar."

"Can you block Marcus?" Celina asked.

"No I can block myself but I can't manage anyone else."

"All right I'll try to block all of us." Celina turned her attention to the gate; the bolt clicked and the gate opened into the garden. "Marcus," Celina said as she pushed through the gate. "Keep very close to me." Celina pulled extra power for her block, and then making it as dense as she could she pushed it around all three of them.

The garden was dark, and neither of them wanted to risk a glow globe so they felt their way across to the house. Elizabeth leading the way angled them to one side of the building; it was as they came to the house wall that a slight red glow low down near the ground became apparent. It was coming through a very dirty window at the top of the cellar wall. Elizabeth used the hem of her dress to wipe some of the dirt away allowing them to peer in.

A dim red oval cast a glow in the cellar barely giving any light at all. As they watched a large object bent almost double under the low ceiling of the cellar moved between them and the oval. Celina whispered.

"I wish we could hear."

"We probably wouldn't understand demon anyway." Elizabeth whispered in reply as she wiped some more dirt off the glass. "Look in that corner, is that a man?" Marcus who was now lying on the ground so he could see better through the window said.

"It could be, but look at the way its hanging.... whatever it is it looks as if it's been pinned to the wall." He twisted for a better look. "Yes I think it is a man."

In a whisper Celina asked him. "Is he alive?" Marcus whispered back.

"Yes.... yes he is and it is a man; I can see his mouth moving but oh my god; he's bent something awful. He's all twisted like he's a cloth that's been wrung out." Then the object under discussion fell to the floor out of sight while the large object turned crouched low and disappeared into the oval which faded to nothing leaving the cellar in total darkness.

"What do we do?" Elizabeth asked.

"We do what we were instructed to do, we tell the Abbot of course," was Celina's reply. The three made their way across the garden and out the back gate waiting for Celina to lock it behind them.

"I'd better go wake the Abbot up," Celina said as she mounted her broom. "Marcus I may not see you tomorrow."

Celina hesitated, and then said. "Damn, I forgot about my mother and father. I'm sorry Elizabeth; I can't go. Mother and father are coming over tonight so I have to be home, so can you go?"

"It's three hours by broom and I'm not as fast as you are, so I may as well drop Marcus off at his home and then get a couple of hours sleep. If I do that I can go in the morning before it gets light."

Celina considered for a moment, she hadn't officially had permission to tell Elizabeth anything yet, but it was essential for the Abbot to Know of the night's happenings as quickly as possible, Celina looking at Elizabeth decided saying.

"All right do that," and then with another look at the sky she said. "There are some things I'm not supposed to tell you yet as I haven't received permission from all the High Abbots, but some I can tell you and this is one I think you need to know now. Polly has found a way of doubling your speed on a broom."

"Doubling it, how?" Elizabeth asked.

"At least doubling it and possibly more, all you do is change the shape of your shield."

"Change the shape of my shield, in what way?" Elizabeth asked, so Celina began to explain.

"Well as Polly told it to me, I was to imagine the shape of a fish, smooth and pointed at the front and then tapering down to a tail at the back. Then all you need to do is push your shield into that shape. That way it cuts through the air instead of just pushing it aside. Polly also says she uses the tail to help keep her stable in winds."

Celina looked around at the sky and said. "I'm sorry you two, but I've got to go." The two brooms then split up over the park with Elizabeth taking Marcus home and Celina heading for Belgrave Square. Lifting her broom towards the broken clouds where two objects high above London caught Celina's eye, it was two brooms. 'Father,' she thought at which Celina pulled the front of her broom up and started pushing hard to catch them.

Reaching them, she quietly slipped in unnoticed behind her mother's broom. Her father and his manservant Mr Ross were flying on one broom, while Celina's mother and her maid were seated on the other. Celina continued to fly unnoticed behind them until they circled to land in the stable yard.

Jane and Thomas were waiting as Lord James dismounted. Jane seeing Lady Mary still sitting on her broom hurried across to help Lady Mary's maid in assisting her Mistress to dismount, while Thomas stood steadying the broom. Celina's mother embraced Jane first and then turning to Celina; she put her arms around her and with a weak smile said.

"You should never have told your father how to modify his shield." Celina's mother was so tired Celina could feel her trembling with fatigue. As they made their way into the house, Celina found her mother increasingly leaning on her for support.

"Has father been pushing over hard?" Celina asked. Her mother gave a weak smile as she replied. "Very much so, we travelled here in just under three and a half hours with only twenty minutes' rest halfway."

Jane having passed the storing of brooms over to Thomas now helped Lady Mary's maid with the baggage. Celina managed a nod to Jane as she assisted her mother, letting Jane know there were developments on the demon front to be talked over later.

Lady Mary was so tired she retired to her bed with a hot drink almost immediately, closely followed by her husband although he was strongly denying he was even the least bit tired. With their parents gone, Celina and Jane retired to Celina's rooms where Celina told her about what they had seen in the cellar. Jane thinking about it asked.

"I wonder if he is working for the demon willingly, or is he being forced?" Celina shuddered as she replied.

It could be he somehow summoned a demon that was too powerful, or perhaps he made a mistake in the warding he set and the demon escaped his control."

"Well if that's the case not even God can save him now," was Jane's matter-of-fact reply.

Friday 8th August 1862.

Celina's father looking a little pale at breakfast the next morning informed Kate that Lady Mary's breakfast would be taken in her room,.

It was Celina who took the tray up to her mother and found to her surprise that her mother was already out of bed and in her sitting room, sitting by the window and looking very frail as her maid fussed about her. Celina setting the tray down on a side table said.

"Good morning Mother," as she pulled a chair across. "Cook was fixing you a breakfast of bacon, eggs, fried bread, devilled kidney and chops." At the mention of this food, Celina could see her mother's face turn from pale to grey, so she relented and said.

"But as I told Cook scrambled egg and some toast with a little honey would be much better." Celina poured coffee for the two of them as she said. "I know what it's like over-stretching yourself." Lady Mary took a cup of coffee with a hand that shook.

"I had words with your father last night," she said taking a sip of her coffee. "He admitted it took more out of him than he expected. All right I will admit you can fly faster and easier your way, but it still takes a lot out of you, and I'm not nearly as strong a Talent as you and your father." Celina could see her mother looking half-heartedly at the scrambled egg.

"Go on Mother," Celina said encouragingly. "You need your strength. Besides if you don't eat it Cook will be upset." Lady Mary reluctantly spread a little egg across a slice of toast, picking at it one tiny mouthful at a time. Celina sat and watched as the pieces gradually became larger as her mother's appetite improved. This was not to say that she ate all her breakfast, but she did eat most of it.

Celina sat patiently; though burning with curiosity until her mother finally pushed the plate aside and held out her cup for a refill. Refilling the cup, Celina asked.

"Well mother. What brings you and father down here in such a hurry?" Lady Mary delicately replaced her cup on the saucer before saying.

"Oh nothing much, we just thought it was time we paid a call on our wayward daughter."

"Come on mother," Celina laughed. "Why are you here?"

"Well your father wants to attend a lecture on Tuesday morning about the latest advances in talent surgery. Then in the afternoon there is a talk on hidden diseases that I would like to attend."

Celina frowned asking. "Hidden diseases?"

"Yes, diseases like smallpox polio and measles. These are diseases where we can see the damage that is happening inside the body, but not why. Professor Sykes has a theory and both your father and I are interested."

"I thought all diseases were caused by little wiggly things," Celina said as she wiggled her fingers.

"The Church did at first but some diseases don't seem to be. We can see the damage they do but no matter how hard or where we look, we can't find the cause, all we find are dying cells." Lady Mary took another sip of coffee and said.

"All we can do is help sustain the body while either it beats the disease or the patient dies." Lady Mary put her cup down and looked at her daughter saying. "We also hope to see this marvellous shop of yours that the Abbot keeps telling us about. He's so proud of you that anyone would think you personally had solved all his problems."

"Well Mother I don't think you will be up to seeing the shop today, so I recommend that you and father take it easy, and then on Monday I will show you around."

"I think that would be very nice," her mother said settling back smiling and asking. "You do remember its Robert's birthday on Friday next week don't you?"

"Yes Mother I have remembered, and both Jane and myself have bought him a present." Lady Mary taking hold of Celina's hand now asked.

"I was wondering if you were coming up for the celebration as it is his twentieth year, and he asked specifically for you and Jane. Oh and he asked for Polly to be invited too." Celina couldn't help but smile.

"He did, did he, well I never."

"Is this something I should know about?" her mother asked.

"Oh it's nothing really special; it's just that our rakish Robert has been smitten by Polly's charms."

"Well I never." Celina's mother repeated before saying. "I never thought I'd see the day, and a nice girl like Polly, just wait until I tell your father."

"All right Mother you tell Father, and I'll have a word with Jane, but remember that she still won't fly, and I can't see her taking the railway for just a weekend."

Saturday 9th August 1862.

Having tried unsuccessfully at breakfast and again at supper to persuade Jane to fly back for Robert's birthday, Lady Mary finally admitted defeat. Jane just wasn't ready to fly, and Jane herself most certainly felt a first flight of that distance was out of the question. Lady Mary then accepted Jane's offer to show her two adoptive parents around a side of a London they had never seen before.

Monday 11th August 1862.

Monday morning arrived, and Celina's parents were eager to see the shop that they had heard so much about. Arriving at Rarities, Celina introduced the shop staff to her parents and then took them on a tour of the shop, showing her mother and father some of their unique wares.

After this it was time for Jane to go on safari hunting down George and hiring him for the rest of the day. With George's knowledge of the south side of London, and Jane's travels around the street markets, Celina's mother and father saw a London of many faces.

By the time they arrived back at Belgrave house Jane had come to a surprising conclusion. In spite of considering herself to be a professional buyer, she now knew that as far as spending money was concerned, she was an amateur and Lady Mary was the true professional. Seeing to Celina's hair that night Jane treated her to an account of her mother's prodigious spending ability saying.

"She spent more in half an hour than I spend for Rarities in a week."

Jane

Tuesday 12th Aug 1862.

Jane sat looking despondently at her teacup thinking. *'Only two more sips and it will be empty.'* Her eyes burned, and she could feel the tears at the back of them. *'It's over'* she thought. *'It must have been the horse; I made it too obvious.'* She turned and rotated her cup staring into it as if trying to see the future. 'I couldn't just let it run into all those people; she thought as she blinked away a tear. *'Someone would have been hurt or killed.'*

She took a sip of the now-cold tea looking up as the clock struck the hour. She had been waiting for William since four of the clock, and he'd never been this late before. Draining her cup, she started to look in her purse for change now certain that William wasn't coming. She blinked away more tears not hearing the door open.

It was a shadow falling across the table that made her look up; William was pulling the chair out and sitting down. Jane blinked, was that look on his face relief? Hope flared within her as he said.

"I'm so glad you waited; the headmaster wanted to see me after the last lesson." He looked around to find Stefano and catching his attention, he held up two fingers and then again, two fingers. Jane covered wiping away her tears by blowing her nose before William taking her hand said.

"The other evening with the horse," he stopped for a moment looking uncertain and unsure. Then as if making a final and difficult decision he said. "When you stepped out in front of it my heart nearly stopped. I thought you would be killed or at the very least severely injured, and well, it made me realise something."

He stopped again as the waiter arrived with the tea waiting until he left. Jane sat in silence with both dread and hope fighting within her until William continued saying.

"I've thought this over-all week, and when I thought I might lose you or see you injured; it made me realise how much you had come to mean to me."

Jane put her other hand over his silencing him as she said. "Please William don't say any more. There are a number of things

347

about me that you don't know, and I think you should before you...." She stopped unsure of what to say, watching William's expression change. William sat quietly his face slowly draining of hope.

"You're not married are you, or anything like that," he finally asked. Jane shook her head.

"No nothing like that." She paused for a moment dreading to admit it even to herself and then quietly she said. "You might think it worse." Relief now showed on William's face and then was quickly followed by puzzlement.

"Worse?" he asked. "

Let's finish our tea as I can't tell you here," Jane giving the excuse. "Someone may overhear me." In reality, she just wanted to be alone with William when she explained fearing what his reaction might be. Finishing their tea they started walking towards the river, until finding a deserted spot on the embankment William took Jane's hand, and turning her to face him he asked.

"Well?" Jane studied his face trying to remember every line before she said.

"First if I tell you about myself you will not be able to tell another living soul without permission."

"If that's what you want it's all right with me," a curious William replied.

"No, what I mean is you will be physically unable to tell anyone about me or others like me."

Looking around the embankment, William found and propped himself against a bollard, leaning there looking at her and holding her hands he said. "I don't understand; you're not making sense." Jane looked up and down the embankment and then said.

"First I must tell you about something that happened over a thousand years ago." Jane then explained about King Arthur, and Merlin and how they had created the order of the Knights of the Church. William still looked puzzled as he said.

"I don't see what a story about Merlin and Arthur has to do with you." Jane looked him full in the face and said.

"It has everything to do with me because the Knights of the Church still exist, and I am what you would call a witch."

William didn't know whether to laugh or not, but it was Jane who was the most surprised. This was the first time she had admitted to herself, being talented let alone to someone else. William finally laughed and said. "There are no such things as witches, and there's no such thing as magic." Jane could feel her colour rising as he said.

"If you're a witch do something, do some magic for me." Jane knew that William was serious and he wanted proof, and she couldn't do anything. She felt totally helpless standing there powerless. She felt anger rising against herself and her locked-in power. She had to do something; anything just to prove it to him.

Jane was surprised to find herself gripping one of the iron rings inset in the top of the bollard with both her hands. Gripping the iron ring and finding she could feel the power as it surged through her and into her hands, and then with no restriction into the iron.

William jumped back and found himself stepping hastily away from the bollard as the wood started to smoke and the ring to glow. First it glowed a dark red, then orange and then yellow. Finally, as the iron started to spit sparks Jane simply pulled the ring apart.

William watched first in horror and then amazement as Jane stood holding the two glowing halves in her bare hands. Jane then held them out to him so that he could feel the heat on his face as she asked.

"Look can you do that?" Then quickly turning, she threw the glowing iron into the river before spinning away from William sobbing.

William stood looking at her only half-believing what he had just seen. Then seeing the woman he had come to love with her back to him crying, he reached out and gently took hold of Jane's shoulders, turning her to face him before pulling her into his arms and holding her head against his shoulder as he said.

"I think I'd better believe you hadn't I." He then kissed her on the forehead and said. "It doesn't make any difference, not to me." Then he held her close until her sobs faded to the odd sniff. Taking hold of her hands, he turned them over and looked at her palms. He was surprised to find there was not a mark on them; they weren't even dirty.

"I'm sorry," he said as he turned her hands back. "I shouldn't have done that." Jane taking his proffered kerchief wiped away her tears and then hesitated before asking.

"Do you still want to tell me what you started to tell me in the tea room? I will understand if you don't?" William looked at the woman in his arms and then kissed her full on the lips.

"Does that answer your question?" He then asked. "Why though if you have power like that do you need to keep it a secret?"

"For protection," she answered.

"For protection?" he repeated. "I would have thought you could protect yourself easily." Jane shook her head.

"No not for our protection but to protect ordinary people. Just think if it was known to people that...." Jane found she hadn't taken a breath, and she needed to breathe. "That witches are real. How many innocent people would be accused of being witches and persecuted? Not long ago witches were burned at the stake. Do you know how many died like this?" She waited for his answer. William shook his head, and Jane quietly answered.

"None, but hundreds of innocent women and children did, and we were too few to stop it. It took us years and even then there was still persecution. Like you said, a witch could protect herself but she cannot hurt another human under any circumstances. It's just not possible the oath taken when a wand chooses its companion prevents it." Jane turned away still not sure of William.

William pulled her around again to face him, and putting his hands first on her shoulders and then cupping her face in his hands he said.

"I think you are right, there is a lot I want to know about you, but first...." He fell silent as he took an envelope from his pocket.

Jane took it and slowly opened it; taking out a sheet of paper she began reading. It was a letter to his parents. In it, he was telling them about meeting her, and he was asking if they would mind if he invited her to stay for the weekend.

"Well" he asked. Jane thought to herself as she held the letter nervously. *'Celina would be away over the weekend. Claire and Marcus could manage the shop. Nobody needs me, so why not?'* Looking up at William, she said.

"You did say your parents lived by the sea didn't you?" William nodded not daring to speak.

"I've never seen the sea."

"Does that mean 'yes'?" he asked her.

"I think so, yes," she replied with a smile. William put his arms around her waist and to Jane, it felt so.... well, just so comfortable. Then pulling her closer he kissed her again. This time Jane found herself responding with more passion than she expected as something stirred within her.

For a time they walked in silence with both Jane and William's thoughts in a whirl. Suddenly, it seemed she could use her talent. Indeed she had used her talent and that must mean she actually was a Talent, a full Talent, but she had no wand. She hadn't taken the oath so could she do harm. That thought filled her with dread; she knew she needed to see Polly.

Then, there was the big question of William and just when to tell Celina. Jane thought about it and then decided to say nothing yet. After all she didn't want to upset Celina; she loved her too much for that and she remembered how her coming had upset Robert all those years ago.

While Jane was asking herself all these questions, William was struggling to come to terms with what Jane appeared to be, and asking himself if witches could be real. He had seen with his own eyes the impossible, and if witches were a part of the church, then what about all those tales of witches and the devil.

William found he wanted not just to know more about witches but also to know more about Jane.

Tuesday and Wednesday were taken up with various talks attended by the Carvel's at St Paul's school. Thursday brought some relief as the Carvel's had friends in London that were to be visited, and then finally there was the packing. Over the last few days Cook had prepared again and again meals that could only be compared to a banquet, prompting Celina to complain she was putting on weight, while Jane was saying it would be nice to have some peace and quiet again.

Thursday 14th Aug 1862.

Jane had been on tenterhooks wondering when Polly would arrive not wanting her to let slip about the broom. Relief finally came when Polly had informed them that she was going to call at Edinburgh University Hospital and would see them later.

Watching the preparations, Jane found she had difficulty in believing it about herself. The thought of flying still terrified her but now in a different and more exciting way.

Jane knew she would have liked to have flown back with Celina, but for some reason making the decision to fly with Celina terrified her more than the idea of flying with Polly. First, she wanted to try a short flight with Polly just to make sure, and apart from that, she wanted to be with William and see the sea.

Eleven of the clock saw the entire household in the stable yard ready to see everyone off. Jane was in tears as she gave Celina and her adoptive parents a hug and a good-bye kiss. Then she stood wiping tears from her eyes as she watched their brooms until they finally disappeared into the dark of the night sky.

Once she was back in the kitchen with the servants Jane found Cook offering cocoa to all. Seeing Jane Cook put her arm around her and gave her a squeeze as she handed her a mug saying.

"It hurt saying good-bye like that didn't it?" Jane wiped her eyes again and nodded as she replied.

"Someday I shall be able to fly with Celina; I just know it and I only wish it could be soon." Then giving her eyes one final wipe she picked up her cocoa and said. "For now I'm going to bed."

Friday 15th Aug 1862.

The clock had just struck one as Robert was advised, that a broom had landed in the stable yard. Robert made his way to the stable yard door, reaching it just as the night man opened it to a small man dressed in a heavy riding coat, and carrying a bag almost as large as himself.

Holding the lamp higher for a better look and still not recognising the man, Robert was just about to ask who he was when the man removed a hat to shake out curly brown hair and Robert saw a face he knew very well.

"Polly," he exclaimed, "is that really you?" Then looking her up and down he asked. "Where did you get the…." Polly quickly interrupted him by asking.

"Well am I welcome or not; I thought I was invited to your birthday?"

"Of course you are welcome but the clothes…. where did they come from?" Polly looked down at herself.

"These? I had them made for me special. After all no-one makes riding clothes for a broom." Then throwing Robert an impish smile she said. "I think Celina may be working around to some as well. Have the others arrived yet?"

"No you're the first; we're not expecting Father and Mother for another two hours at least." Then as he put Polly's bag down, he asked. "Polly, what have you got in this bag? It feels like it weighs more than you do." Polly grinned as she replied.

"They're my clothes of course; after all I can't wear these all the time." Robert leaving her bag by the stairs took her into his father's study where he had been waiting, and taking her coat he apologised saying.

"I sent the servants to get some rest and said I'd call them when everyone arrives. Would you like a drink, Sherry?"

Polly didn't really know much about alcoholic drinks, so she accepted a small sherry and settled back into a chair. Sitting there she felt content to relax and listen to Robert telling her about the orphanage. He told her of how he had visited it with his mother and then there was more news about Nancy.

However, fatigue and the sherry soon began to overwhelm Polly, and within half an hour she couldn't keep her eyes open. It had been a long day and when Robert offered to show her to her room she gratefully accepted, while at the same time refusing Robert's offer to wake a maid to assist her. Vaguely, she remembered climbing into bed and being asleep almost before her head reached the pillow.

Celina and her parents arrived just after three. This time Lady Mary had insisted that she be permitted to set the pace, and surprised both herself and her husband at the speed she set and maintained. With a little more time set aside for a rest, she arrived home in a much better state than when she had arrived in London.

"It just takes practice," her husband told her. Celina thinking it over had to agree. She remembered how her abilities had strengthened after first over stretching herself with the demon.

Jane

Friday morning dawned bright and sunny, and as it looked like it would be a nice warm weekend Jane informed Cook that she had decided to finally do something she had wanted to do all her life. She would go and see the sea.

"I'm going to be very brave and take the railway to Brighton," she told Cook. "There's someone I know whose parents live on the coast there, and I've been invited to come down for a visit, and as Celina is enjoying herself up north I think I will take them up on their offer."

That was almost the truth and Jane thought she had gotten away with it. That was until Cook gave her a knowing wink and touched the side of her nose with a finger, then Cook with another wink and a smile said.

"The less said the better." Then winking again she turned back to her baking before asking. "What's the young gentleman's name then?" Jane with a sudden blush and her nose in the air left to pack.

Waiting outside the imposing building of the London Brighton and South Coast Railway, Jane nervously looked around for William; she was hoping that nothing had gone wrong and secretly smiling to herself at cook's insinuation. It was twenty past the hour of four when a breathless William arrived with two tickets.

The engine painted a dark green with L.B. & S.C.R. painted on the tender was smaller than the one that had taken her from Ripon to York, and Jane found the coaches were not as luxurious, with at least half being only partly glazed.

William's tickets however, were for one of the better fully glazed coaches, and she even found to her surprise that they had reserved notices fastened on their seats.

William assisted Jane in climbing into the coach and then after taking their seats William said.

"It usually takes about an hour and a half, and my mother says she has arranged for us to be collected from the station, otherwise it's a five-mile walk along the coast." A shrill whistle and the noisy release of steam from the engine interrupted him, followed by a loud bang and a jerk as the train lurched into motion. Once they were on their way William turned to Jane saying.

"As we're the only two in here, why don't you tell me a bit more about yourself? After all," he said with a smile. "I'm sure it will be far more interesting than me telling you about myself.

Jane told him a great deal more about herself. She talked of how she had helped her father until the age of thirteen when she had been taken to the home of Lady Celina. This took a great deal of explaining before William even approached an understanding of the relationship between Jane, Celina and their respective parents.

By the time the journey's end neared, William still felt he knew very little about Jane. Principally because he knew only what she wanted him to know, and that left him very curious and wanting to know a lot more about her.

An elderly black man was waiting outside the station with a carriage and greeted William cheerfully. As William passed him the bags, William introduced him to Jane as.

"Moses, who is the man who does everything that is important for the 'old man', namely my father. He was on the boats with Father from the earliest days." William lowered his voice so Moses wouldn't hear him as he said.

"He's a fantastic fellow, and we all think the world of him." Leaving the station they turned down a nearby lane following it for about a mile until the lane turned sharply, and William pointing across a field said. "Look." Looking out over the fields all Jane could see was blue sky and small clouds for as far as the eye could see.

"Come on," he said calling for Moses to stop. As the Phaeton came to a rest, William jumped down and helped Jane descend the steps. Then with William holding her hand they ran over the grass to the top of a low cliff. Jane looked down onto a shingle beach where white-topped waves were breaking, and out over a sun sprinkled sea to where a boat with two brown sails was tacking against the wind.

"Is this the sea?" she asked. William nodded, and Jane said. "It's beautiful," gazing at it wide-eyed and enthralled. William putting his arm around her waist said.

"If you like after supper we can go for a walk on the beach." Jane just stood and looked drinking in the sounds, the sights and the smells. Finally she turned, reluctant to look away.

"Can we?" she asked. "That would be marvellous." They both stood in silence, with William holding Jane while she stood feeling the sun and wind on her face and enjoying every sensation. It was Moses calling them back that eventually broke the spell.

The Bowden's house stood on high ground overlooking the sea, and Jane found it was larger than she had expected with a number of out buildings to one side, while at the back of the house, Jane could see a paddock with six horses grazing. It was as they drew nearer that Jane found that some strange poles sticking up beyond the house were the masts of four boats, moored in a creek that ran into the sea just beyond the house.

As the Phaeton drew to a halt, Jane found a grey-haired woman wearing her hair pulled back in a bun standing waiting for them at the door. William taking Jane's hand then introduced her to his mother.

William's mothers greeting was genuinely warm, and his mother's smile Jane found made her feel truly welcome. Then taking Jane's bag and despite Jane's objections, she insisted on carrying it into the house. Inside the house, Jane found a man who she took to be William's father was making his way along the hall with the aid of a walking stick.

"Father," William's mother said. "Would you take them through and ask Jean to bring us some refreshments while I take Jane's bag to her room?" Then turning to Jane and William, she said. "I expect you will both need a little something after that long journey."

"I'll take the bag up later if you want Mrs Bowden," Jane volunteered.

"No my dear," Mrs Bowden replied as she started up the stairs. "You go and sit down: it won't take but a minute."

Jane looked around the sitting room admiringly, as she found it particularly unusual in the sparseness of the furnishings. In fact Jane found it had a spacious and open feeling utterly unlike the drawing rooms she had visited. It was as Mr Bowden approached and only then that she realised not only had he a bad leg, but also he was blind or very nearly so. Looking around the room again Jane now found she could see the reason for the lack of clutter and its spaciousness.

Jean, a small and dumpy woman with as Jane found later an infectious smile, soon returned with a tea trolley and a plate of sandwiches that she carefully placed on a low table just so, with Jane guessing that this was for Mr Bowden's benefit. William's mother returned and took charge of the serving as she explained.

"We normally have an evening meal about seven so this is just to tide you over." Then turning to Jane with a smile and getting straight to the point she said. "Now Jane, tell us all about yourself as we're all ears. William has been very reluctant to say anything about his life in London, he never even mentioned you until his last letter."

Jane made a start, and between herself and William, they told of how they met and how Jane worked as a buyer for a shop. The fact that Jane travelled around London looking at goods in warehouses and dealing with wholesalers brought the same comment from both William's mother and father as it had from William, with them asking.

"Isn't that unusual work for a woman?" Jane found herself once more explaining that though the work may be unusual for a woman, she enjoyed the work as it involved meeting new people and seeing new things.

Over the evening meal that consisted of a fish dish so good that she had a second helping, Jane heard all about William's life. It was largely a life spent on the fishing boats helping his father until he won a scholarship to Oxford. An iced dessert followed and over dessert, it was Jane's turn to tell about her life in the north.

Jane described how she helped her blacksmith father until at the age of thirteen she was taken to live at Brimham Hall. William's father and mother listened intently as she described a life totally different from theirs. Again, William found himself captivated even though he had heard most of it before.

The iced dessert had left Jane ready for a relaxed evening, but William reminded her of the beach, and so arm in arm they set off along the nearby creek following it toward the sea. Jane was surprised to find that the creek that had only a trickle of water in it upon her arrival was now almost full.

"The tide has come in," William explained as they reached what was left of the beach.

Down on the beach Jane found that the sound of the waves pushing the pebbles around was something she loved. She stood there in silence taking in the sound of the wind and waves as William skimmed stones over the sea and told her more about himself, including personal things from his childhood.

Fishing out on the boats, mending nets, and swimming almost before he could walk, William explained that he had fallen off the jetty so many times before he was three that Simon had taught him to swim for his own safety.

Early stars were starting to show as they made their way back to the house where William's mother told Jane that the 'necessary' was outside saying. "We are not quite as civilised as in London."

Jane was then taken up to her room where William's mother informed her that there was a chamber pot residing under the bed should she require it. In all Jane found the room was pleasant and the bed very comfortable, particularly as she was feeling extremely tired and eager for sleep.

Sunday 17th Aug 1862.

The railway deposited Jane and William back in London right on time. It was five of the clock on a warm afternoon after what had been for Jane a most agreeable weekend. Standing with William outside the station and waiting while he called a cab Jane felt on top of the world.

A copy of some of his mother's fish recipes was in her bag, and an invitation to join them again the next time William was able to return home. Last of all she had been given a very sweet kiss and embrace by William's mother.

Once they were on the train William told her how this demonstration of affection was totally out of character for her, saying.. "She must have really taken to you."

That was only one of the things she needed to discuss with Polly. New things were starting to happen to her. First, it had been the iron, and now to her horror she had leaned on William's mother.

Just as they were leaving and without meaning to she had definitely leaned on her. Indeed, she actually had heard his mother's thoughts not as feelings or emotions but as near to words as made no difference. She knew his mother liked her, and that she had been telling his father so. Realising this a shocked Jane had pulled back instantly. This was something frighteningly new and disturbing to her.

A cab arrived, and William gave her a wonderful kiss of a kind that made the cabbie smile. William then helped her up into the cab before passing her bag up to the cabbie and with his last words.

"I'll try to be a bit earlier on Tuesday, as I have no real lessons for now," still ringing in her ears the cab pulled away.

Jane arrived back at Belgrave House to find all the staff outside the house. Cook and Thomas hurried over to the cab and helped Jane down with Cook saying.

"Oh Jane I'm so glad that you're back." Jane could see Cook was in a state even before she said. "We can't go inside; it's the drains or something, and the smell, well it is terrible." Jane knew that smell and it was terrible, but she also knew that it wasn't the drains.

"What happened?" she asked Cook.

"We came back from church this afternoon, and this was how we found it."

"Has anyone gone in to the house?" Cook shook her head.

"No the smell just turns your stomach." Jane had to agree that it did and was thankful that it had kept the staff out. Celina was away so it was up to her. Suddenly, the word 'iron' came into her mind; she needed iron and all her instincts drove her to find it, and she knew just where to find it. There was iron in the stables.

"Stay here, I'm going to have a look around the back." Then leaving her bag with Thomas Jane made her way to the stable yard gates. They were locked, so trying the small side gate she found it unlatched and by pushing it open just an inch or two, she could see into the yard. It appeared deserted.

She let herself in and then ran toward the forge; pulling the doors open an inch and putting her nose to the gap, she sniffed the air inside. The air smelled of old fires and coal. Opening the door wider Jane let herself in.

Picking up a file, she held it in one hand. For some reason it felt wrong. Next a large iron punch nearly a foot long caught her eye. Picking it up she held it, finding it fitted comfortably in her hand as she felt her body accepting it. Yes she thought, though she didn't know why, she could feel this was just what she needed.

With her heart-pounding Jane then headed up the stairs to the kitchen door, fumbling in her bag to find her key and unlocking it. By cracking it open just an inch she could see into the kitchen, the smell was horrendous but the kitchen was empty.

Taking a towel off the range, she ran it under the tap before fastening it around her face covering her nose. Jane then hesitantly made her way towards the front of the house checking each of the many rooms in turn and finding nothing. Now, it was time to go up the stairs.

Reaching the first floor she found Celina's rooms had been disturbed, with the smell even worse in them. Holding the punch at the ready though not quite sure what she would do with it, Jane first checked their parent's rooms before looking in the rest of the unused guest rooms on that floor.

Then it was up the next flight of stairs to the floor above. On this floor neither Polly's rooms nor the guest rooms seemed to have been touched. Jane even checked in the attic but there was still nothing amiss, now that only left the servant's lower rooms.

Making her way down to the lower floor beneath the small kitchen Jane looked in the servant's rooms, and found that they were also undisturbed and clear. That only left the main kitchen and back rooms to check including the cellar. It was in the cellar that she found it.

A wraith was laid on the floor or rather most of one. The top of the wraith's head was missing, sliced completely off.

Looking at it and considering the height of the ceiling and the possible size of a portal, Jane thought. *'I suppose it forgot to duck'.* Turning back towards the servant's quarters she decided. *'First open the windows and then call for a clean-up team from Dickie.'* It was as she opened the kitchen window that it finally hit her; her legs felt like jelly and she had to sit down.

'What a fool' she thought. *'Walking in alone untrained and not even sure I could defend myself.'* She looked at the punch in her hand. Yes, it was hot to the touch but whether she could have used it other than as a red-hot piece of iron, she had no idea. *'Oh my,'* she thought, *'all these years I have refused training because I couldn't use it, and now I need it and there's nobody here to help me'.*

Jane, was shaking like a leaf and almost fainted as Thomas looked around the door asking.

"Are you all right Miss Jane?" Jane managed a nod while struggling to say.

"Open the front doors will you and let some clean-air blow through the house?" Jane watched feeling sick as Thomas still looking slightly apprehensive made his way through to the hall. Remembering the wraith, Jane called after him. "Don't go into the cellar."

Cook and Kate now arrived at the kitchen door with Kate asking. "Is it the drains?"

"No it's not the drains; just don't go down into the cellar." Cook hearing this turned white, and pulling out a chair and sitting next to Jane she asked.

"You don't mean?"

"Yes there's a dead one in the cellar so it's not very nice down there. Make me a drink will you please Kate?" Jane asked as getting to her feet and putting her hand on the cook's shoulder she said. "I'd better get it removed, open some more windows will you please?"

Dickie was horrified when Jane told him what was in the cellar and insisted that he came himself with the clean-up squad. It was as they watched the cleanup squad depart that Dickie asked Jane.

"Why, why are they after Celina? She's not the only Knight or even the strongest." Even as he said this he felt less sure about that. Celina had changed after the attack by the demon, she was now more confident in her abilities, and Dickie felt certainly more able to defend herself, as the episodes with the wraiths and bugs had proven. "When is she due back?" he asked Jane.

"In the early hours of tomorrow I believe."

"Do you mind if I stop?" a worried-looking Dickie asked. "I think I need to see her." A very relieved Jane replied.

"I'd be most grateful if you could, I don't know what would happen if they returned."

"That is a point; I wonder if Elizabeth felt anything, do you mind?" Dickie asked pointing toward the Telson; returning he said. "Elizabeth isn't back yet, her mother says she's been out of London all day, but she will get her to call as soon as she arrives home."

It was just after eight of the clock when Elizabeth called, and after hearing about the invasion of 'Belgrave House', she insisted on coming around saying. "If it happens again two wands are better than one." Dickie who still looked worried now asked.

"Do you mind if I make a call again?" Jane could hear him telling the Abbot about the afternoon and asking if Marjory could come over as he said. "The more wands there are the better." Returning to the day room and looking relieved, he told Jane. "Marjory is coming and she says she will be here in about an hour, after all three wands are better than two."

Dickie sat down and looked at Jane asking. "Why Celina, and what is it that they want from her, and why do they want her so badly?"

Monday 19th August 1862.

I arrived back from mothers in the early hours of the morning to find Jane, with Dickie, Marjory and Elizabeth in the house. There had been an attack by demons. Luckily everyone was at Church and no one was hurt. Later, Jane gave me the biggest shock or fright I have ever known. I'm afraid I lost my temper with her.

~~~

It was just after two in the morning when two brooms spiralled down into the yard of Belgrave House only to be greeted by a lingering odour of demon. Two dark shapes with wands in hand ran up the steps to the kitchen door to find the door unlocked, and the kitchen illuminated only by the red glow from the range.

Polly created a small glow and then followed Celina through into the entrance hall where a line of light was showing under the day room door. Celina couldn't help herself; she threw the door open startling the occupants.

Dickie jumped to his feet, but Marjory already had her wand in her hand and pointed at the door almost before it was fully open.

"Thank God it's you," she said heaving a sigh of relief.

"What's happened, and that smell, is everyone all right?" Celina asked stepping into the room with Polly pushing right at her heels and in time to hear Dickie say.

"Yes everyone's fine they were all at church when it happened, and by the time they returned the house was empty, that is apart from one dead wraith." Celina sat down white-faced and breathing heavily. Then as she unbuttoned her coat and pulled it open, she asked Jane.

363

"One dead wraith?"

"Yes it looked like it forgot to duck as it was going back through the portal. The ceiling isn't very high in the cellar and half the wraith's head was missing." Dickie with a grimace added.

"We found the other half of its head at the back of the cellar door." Dickie turning to Jane said. "It was Jane who called me, and I came around with the clean-up squad. After they had left I called for Elizabeth and Marjory; we thought three wands would deter any more intrusions until you came home."

Colour was slowly returning to Celina's face as she asked Jane. "Did you say the portal was in the cellar?"

"Yes in the large store room at the back of the servants' hall."

It was past four in the morning and starting to get light, when an almost-satisfied Celina stood with Jane and Polly as they watched Marjory and Elizabeth, with Dickie on the front seat of Marjory's broom disappear over the rooftops and into the night. Jane then took Polly and her bag up to her usual room. As soon as the door closed behind them Jane sat on the bed saying.

"Polly I'm frightened."

"What, about today?" Polly asked.

"No," Jane said shaking her head. "Not just today, things are happening to me, things I don't understand. Polly it's changing; it's starting to take control and I need to talk to you without Celina."

Polly sat down next to her and took her hand. She could feel a difference. Putting her arm around Jane, she said.

"Celina should go to the shop later today and I'm here until Wednesday night, so we'll most certainly have time to talk before I go." Jane wiped her eyes as she said.

I must go; it's Celina she can't do her own hair." In Celina's room Jane picked up the hairbrush and started taking the pins out of Celina's hair as Celina asked.

"Well how did the shop fare while I was away?" Jane could already feel her colour rising as she replied.

"I don't know; I wasn't there."

"You didn't spend all your time here did you?"

"No I did something I've wanted to do for a long time." Jane paused wondering if she should tell Celina everything. Eventually she decided to say, "I went to the seaside; I've never seen the sea."

"The seaside," Celina asked and half turned only to be pushed back by Jane as she said.

"Yes and I saw the sea; I went to Brighton for the two days." This time Celina did turn around as she asked.

"Was it with William; that was his name wasn't it?" Jane was blushing now as she replied almost in a whisper.

"Yes it was; he asked me and I thought it would be nice to see the sea so I said yes." Celina could see Jane's colour as she asked.

"Well did you?"

"Yes I did; I saw the sea," came the reply.

"Not that, you know the other thing men and women go away for." By now Jane was almost scarlet.

"No we didn't!" Jane gasped indignantly. "It's not like that at all; we stayed at his parent's home if you must know." Celina put her arms around Jane and said.

"I'm sorry I shouldn't have said that, but I'm glad you had a good time, after all we did. Robert was sorry you missed his birthday and so was I, I missed you."

"I missed you too." Jane said with tears threatening in her eyes as she hugged Celina.

"Enjoy yourself with William," Celina said encouragingly. "Its time you had someone else to think about besides me, and I know you have the same advantages as I do." Jane blushed again and said.

"Turn around; I need to finish your hair; after all some of us have to be up early this morning."

Celina lay in bed and was almost asleep as a stray thought wandered through her mind. *'Where did Jane call Dickie from on the Telson?'* As far as Celina knew theirs was the only one in the square. *'I shall ask her tomorrow,'* she thought as she drifted off to sleep.

Jane had more difficulty getting to sleep. She knew questions would be asked, and it frightened her; she knew Celina all too well.

Celina was sitting partially dressed as Jane was brushing her hair when she remembered about the Telson call, prompting her to ask.

"Where did you call Dickie from yesterday?" Jane taken by surprise answered.

"From the hall," Jane felt Celina freeze under her hands and instantly knew she had given the worst possible answer she could.

"Who came into the house with you?" was Celina's next question. Jane's heart skipped a beat as she answered.

"No-one, there was just me."

"You came into the house by yourself?" Celina asked incredulously.

"Yes," Jane whispered.

"You by yourself, knowing that demon spawn had been or were in the house." Celina said with her voice slowly rising and becoming shriller.

"Yes," Jane's head nodded of its own accord.

"You idiot you imbecile," Celina began, with idiot and imbecile being two of the mildest words that were repeated several times at ever increasing volume and shrillness.

"What were you thinking of? If there had been a live wraith in the house you, you wouldn't have stood a chance. I suppose you just walked in the front door and, and."

Celina who was now on her feet was holding Jane by the shoulders and shaking her as she said,

"You, you, I thought you had more sense." Jane could see Celina was now crying with tears running down her face. Suddenly, she had Jane in a bear hug holding her tight.

"I could have lost you do you realise that? I could have lost you." Now both were crying as Celina's emotions overwhelmed Jane too.

It was some time later when Celina walked into the breakfast room. Polly was waiting there having heard Celina along with the rest of the household, and Polly thought possibly some of the square.

"Are you going to the shop today?" Polly asked. Celina shook her head.

"I think you should," Polly said.

Celina looking puzzled asked. "Why?"

"I want to talk to Jane; I want to have a girl-to-girl talk with her to try to get her to accept some form of training."

Celina who was pouring her coffee now found her cup overflowing into her saucer. She set the coffee pot down carefully and placed her cup on a clean saucer before saying.

"Polly, if you can do that I'd spend a week at the shop."

"That shouldn't be necessary," Polly said. "After all I'm only here until Wednesday."

Much to her surprise Jane found Celina ready and waiting for a cab within forty-five minutes. Then with a cheery good-bye called to herself and Polly, she was away.

Polly and Jane were sitting in the window seat of Polly's room as Polly said.

"Right Jane, tell me what has happened." Jane sat looking at her hands resting nervously on her lap unsure where to begin; finally, she said.

"Two weeks ago William was walking me back to Rarities." Polly sat still and quietly listened, not asking who William was, or any other questions as she waited for Jane to finish.

"A dray horse had broken loose and was running away. Something or someone had frightened it. William tried to pull me out of the way but there were so many people in the road. Someone would be hurt or killed so I had to do something." She looked at Polly for understanding. Polly nodded her head still not saying a word.

"Polly, I pulled the horse down and stopped it. All right a big strong heavy man who knew horses could possibly manage it...." Jane fell silent looking at Polly willing her to understand.

"But not a slim woman like you, correct?" Polly finished the sentence for her.

"Polly I was leaning on the horse as I pulled it down." Polly sat back looking at Jane and thinking eventually saying.

"All right, but was that talent leaning, or just skill? You've worked with large and powerful horses for how many years?"

"Polly I definitely leaned; I've never leant like that before, and it's not just that; William wanted to tell me something. I knew he wanted to be more than a friend. Polly I had to tell him, I told him I was what he would call a witch, and then I told him about Celina." Again, Jane paused looking at Polly for understanding.

"I take it that you've finally admitted to yourself that you have real talent then?" Polly asked; Jane nodded.

"Go on then," Polly said encouragingly.

"He didn't believe me," Jane again looked at Polly still needing her to understand. "He asked me to do something, something magical. We were down by the river and I was so mad that I took hold of one of those iron ring things that they tie the boats too. I felt my barrier break down when I touched the iron ring, and then I heated it. Polly I made it glow red hot, so hot that I just, well; I just pulled it apart and threw it in the river."

"What happened then?"

"He said it made no difference to him, and he kissed me, and then he showed me a letter he was sending to his parents. He was telling them about me, and he was asking if he could bring me with him to meet them over the weekend." Jane paused as her feelings created by the memory threatened to overwhelm her.

"Then what?" Polly asked.

"I said I would go."

"No." Polly stamped her foot. "I mean what happened with you talent-wise?"

"It was as we were leaving his parents, William's mother was telling his father how nice she found me, and that she had suggested to William that I came with him the next time he was able.

"Well I know it's not nice to listen to private conversations...." Polly began, but Jane was still speaking.

"It frightened me," Jane was saying. "Because they were in the house, and I was outside in the lane. Polly we were already in the carriage on our way back to the station." Jane was now desperately searching Polly's face as she said. "I could hear William's mother inside my head."

Polly was shocked at Jane's revelation. Only a few of the most powerful Talents ever had that ability. She doubted whether Celina without a wand would be able to do it at the distance Jane was talking about.

"Go on," she said.

"When I arrived here I found the staff outside the house, and I could smell a demon. Cook had told them it was a problem with the drains, but I knew what it was and I think Cook did too. Then something sort of took hold of me; I knew I had to go inside and I also knew I needed iron, so I went around the back and took an iron punch from the forge." Jane shivered again at the thought.

"I went inside through the kitchen door and looked around the house. I don't know why I did it or what I could have done if there had been anything in the house. Polly I'm scared." Polly took Jane's hand only to find Jane was trembling as she said. "Polly it's getting away from me; I can feel it."

"Come on." Polly said getting to her feet. "Let's go down to the stables as I want you to try something for me."

In the stables, Jane showed Polly the punch, picking it up Polly swung it around just to feel the weight.

"It's quite heavy isn't it." she said giving it to Jane. As Jane took the punch from her hand Polly felt the iron change, it felt as if it became almost alive and was objecting to Polly having hold of it. Polly felt it was acting just like a wand, a wand that was in the wrong person's hand. Polly found a shudder running through her as she let the punch go, and then turning to Jane she said.

"Point it at the coal in the forge." Jane pointed it at the old coke and ash that hadn't been cleared from its last use as Polly said.

"Think of heat in the iron and try to push it into the coal." Jane willed heat into the iron only to find the end of the punch glowing bright orange and then yellow before dropping off showering sparks across the stone floor.

Polly stepping smartly back and lifting her skirts away from the sparks dancing across the flagstones said.

"Well at least it looks like you could give things a nasty burn, and you do have some control."

Jane tried again with a throwing motion, only to find a larger and hotter piece of iron dropping off the end of the punch. This time the sparks showered clear across the floor. Polly hurriedly moved further away saying.

"That's not going to work, try thinking of heat in the coal." Jane concentrated on heating the coke, and without even pointing the punch the small lump of coke she was concentrating on glowed bright yellow orange before it exploded with a loud crack making them both jump.

During the afternoon's experiments, it was found that all Jane needed was to hold something made of iron in order to produce about the same level of control as most Knights gain through the use of a wand. Experiments proved that wrapping some soft iron wire around her finger gave as much control as holding a horseshoe in her hand. Neither quantity nor quality seemed to make any difference.

As the forge was now hot with repeated casts as they called them for want of a better word, Jane spent the last ten minutes before returning to the house making a plain iron ring for her finger. This also gave the watching Polly an idea of how skilled Jane was as a blacksmith. After finishing and polishing the ring, she then had to persuade Polly not to tell Celina too much, at least not yet.

When Celina returned home, the first thing she did was to pull Polly into the day room to ask.

"Well did you get anywhere?"

"Yes," Polly replied as Celina settled into a chair. "She's going to let me try to help her, though first I think I'll have to have a word with Marjory as Jane's talent is something different and totally strange."

The fact that Jane was admitting she needed help was enough to satisfy Celina, but Polly warned her.

"Don't tell Jane that I've said anything to you though, as it may put her off or even stop her," so that evening as Jane saw to her hair, Celina had to be content with just asking about William.

As they talked, Jane was forced to admit that she had told William about herself. Explaining that she was different and also about Celina.

"What was his reaction?" was all Celina said. Jane decided to tell her the truth or at least part of it as she said.

"He wanted proof; he said he didn't believe me."

"So what did you do?"

"Well I made rather a mess of one of those iron ring things set into a bollard." Jane's face had coloured at the memory as she quietly said. "I think I can say they won't be tying any more boats to it."

To Jane's surprise, Celina who had seen Jane working with iron burst out laughing, and then with no further mention of the iron ring she said. "Come on then and tell me what happened next?"

"He said it didn't make any difference," and then quietly and going even redder she said. "He kissed me and asked me to meet his parents." Anxious to change the subject Jane quickly said.

"I brought back some recipes of his mothers; we're having one tomorrow as the cook's keen to try them."

"Is she?" Celina said as she looked up at Jane and asked.

"Would William like to come for dinner? I think it's about time I met this young man of yours." Jane looked doubtful.

"Oh it's all right Jane, I don't mind, and I know I can't hold on to you forever." Taking Jane's hand she said. "I'm not going to do a 'Robert'. I am really pleased for you; you know I am; after all if I wasn't pleased I know you would be able to feel it."

Jane didn't need to lean; Celina was clearly pleased and not in the least distressed. Yes, Jane could feel she was genuinely happy for her, though she did pick up a whisper of. '*When will it be my turn to find Mr Right?*'

"We can invite Elizabeth and Marcus if you would like," Celina said trying to console Jane. In the end, it was Jane who was feeling low and sorry for Celina as she made her way to her room. '*If only,*' she thought. '*If only.*'

Tuesday 20th Aug 1862.

Jane was waiting with tea and a plate of cakes on the table for William when he arrived. At first it seemed strange after the two days at the coast to be meeting in the tearoom again. Sitting there talking over the weekend Jane found she was rather shy about bringing up the subject of Celina's invite for the evening.

They were down to the last two cakes before Jane gathered enough courage to bring the subject up. Hearing Celina's invitation William was a little doubtful but Jane assured him that he wouldn't be on his own as she said.

"Marcus will be there to keep you company, and you will be perfectly safe as we don't have a cauldron large enough to cook you in," which made them both laugh. William thought it over as they demolished the last two cakes and finally decided. He had only his one small room at the school to look forward to; so he might as well accept the invitation and meet Jane's companion.

Celina greeted him and then introduced him to Polly, Elizabeth and Marcus. Marcus she introduced as a friend of Elizabeth, and the manager of Rarities. Jane then explained that Polly was a Knight of the Church, and that Elizabeth was not only a Knight of the Church but also a church doctor. Finding a moment when no-one was looking William whispered to Jane.

"Are they all really witches and Elizabeth a doctor, and Polly, well surely she's only a young slip of a girl?"

"Yes they are all Talents or talented just as Celina said. Polly and Elizabeth are Knights of the Church, and Elizabeth is also a church trained doctor specialising in infectious diseases." Then giving William a dig with her elbow she said.

"You'll notice none of us have warts, whiskers or long hooked chins or noses. Oh and Marcus is a perfectly normal man no talent at all." William had to laugh at this and then admitted he was puzzled.

"I still don't understand what makes a Talent different from a Knight?" Jane found herself explaining.

"All Talents have an ability of some form or another; however, very few Talents can use for want of a better name power. The rest do other things instead like nursing, divining, finding lost items or people. Things not requiring the use of...." Jane shrugged and then said. "I can only describe it as directed power.

"Now a Knight is a Talent who not only has the ability to use power but can also direct their power through a wand. Normally without a wand the power would go everywhere and most of it is wasted. Directed through a wand though it all goes just where it's needed."

William thought for a moment before he said.

"I think I understand," and then he asked. "Do you have a wand?" Jane shook her head feeling slightly embarrassed as she said.

"No my talents lie in other things, I'll explain later."

After the meal where they all voted that the fish dish that Cook had served was absolutely marvellous, with William being complimented on his mother's behalf. It was then that the conversation turned to as Jane quietly put it, "shop talk."

William was at first dubious and then horrified to learn that things like demons actually existed, and that the murders in the papers had been more than common murders. Marcus was cajoled into telling of his and Celina's near demise at the hands of a demon, causing Celina some slight embarrassment.

Celina and Elizabeth then told of the two bug episodes, complete with a description of Celina's encounter with the pipe-sucking gardener, and her new flowerbed in the park.

It was this and having read of it in the papers that really brought it home to William that what he had been hearing was real.

Finally William was treated to a graphic description by Celina of Jane's folly on Sunday, and what could have happened to her if the house had not been deserted. It was as he was leaving with the cab waiting that he remembered the brooms.

"I never did get to see a broom did I?" he asked.

"Next time," Jane said as they kissed goodnight.

Returning to Polly and Celina Jane stood in the doorway looking at Celina and asking.

"Well?"

"Yes we give him our seal of approval; he took the shoptalk better than I expected, don't you think so Polly?"

Polly, taking Jane's hand said. "He seems very nice so stick with him; I think he's good for you." Then turning back to Celina, she said; "but right now we need to get back to the shoptalk. What we need to know is why the demons are so interested in you Celina. Is it fair to say it must be something they know or think they know about you that we don't?"

"Yes obviously, but what?" Celina asked. Silence followed, as there was no apparent answer. Celina breaking the silence said.

"I suppose that I shall have to find and talk to a real-live demon and then maybe I can ask."

Wednesday 21st Aug 1862.

Polly and Jane continued experimenting with Polly eventually deciding that Jane's abilities were unique, and like nothing she had ever heard of before. The biggest difference however, was in Jane's shield, as far as Polly could tell Jane certainly had one, but not an external one like hers and Celina's.

More difficult to understand was that the power Jane used was very different. Yes, it came from within her, but if it was gathered, it seemed to be gathered and used in an entirely different way. It was as they rested that Jane broached a subject that had been worrying her.

"Polly, the oath you take as Knights of the Church, you know the one you take at sixteen when you're chosen by a wand?"

Polly, who had propped herself up against an empty barrel and was looking out of the door, heard something in Jane's voice that told her she was worried. She looked at Jane as Jane hesitantly said.

"When you take the oath it makes it impossible for you to harm a person, that's right isn't it?" Polly was shaking her head as she said.

"It's not impossible; it's just that it can't be done deliberately, after all it's always possible by accident. Why do you ask?"

"Well I was wondering if I could hurt someone or even kill someone, after all I haven't taken the oath."

"Would you want to?" Polly asked.

"Take the oath? Of course I would."

"No kill someone."

"God forbids no, but I don't want to be in a position where I did in, well in a fit of temper or something like that." Jane had just remembered two boys that she had half drowned in a horse trough, and how easy it would have been to do worse.

"Well as you haven't got a wand you can't take the oath; so just remember what you said and let that be your oath for now."

Polly was worried though; she trusted Jane, and the fact that Jane was worried helped Polly feel justified in her trust, but she also knew that Jane had more than sufficient power to kill with ease. Polly thinking about it decided to have a word with the Abbot as soon as she could.

"Well back to work." Polly had decided Jane should try for a glow globe, and so she started to explain to her the steps to try to produce one. After about half an hour Jane succeeded, but the glow was totally different to any that Polly had been able to produce. For a start, though no more than a pinhead in size, it was incredibly bright. Also it was actually cold; they found it radiated no warmth at all.

It also came as a surprise to both of them to find that Jane could control and move it at incredible speeds over several hundred yards. Further experiments proved that Jane's glow though cold could easily punch through the best steel sheets, leaving only a tiny hole just large enough to pass a bodkin needle through.

That evening Celina drew Polly aside asking. "Well what conclusions have you come to?"

Polly who had already decided that she ought to tell Celina at least part of what she had discovered when she eventually asked said. "She's different; I don't know if anyone has ever come across anything like her. Her power is totally different to ours and where it comes from and how she uses it is well…." Polly stopped unable to give an answer only saying.

"I don't know; it just seems to be a different power than ours. I'm going to have words with the Abbot tonight even if I have to wake him up. I'm worried, and Jane, well she is really frightened."

"Jane really frightened?"

"Well she is," Polly said. "She doesn't understand what's happening to her. It's not like with you; you had help. You had Dickie as a teacher and your mother and father to guide and support you, Jane is different, and she knows it. We have to feel our way from one thing to another, and we are never quite sure what is going to happen or how. She asked me today something that frightened both her and me."

Polly then looked up at Celina as she said. "She knows she hasn't a wand, and so she hasn't taken the oath, and now she's worried could she kill?"

Celina was horrified at the thought of Jane's killing someone and found herself listening in silence to Polly as she said.

"I asked her about it, and the thought terrifies her; I'm sure she doesn't want to be in the position where she has to make that decision herself. You know yourself how easy it would be to do harm under certain circumstances." Celina agreed as she said.

"Without a wand she can't take the oath as it just wouldn't work."

"Well that's why I want a word with the Abbot; she needs a wand of some kind but of what sort I don't know. I'm lost, and I need help with this," a worried Polly had to admit.

It was dark as Celina and Jane waved good-bye to Polly, watching her lift her broom toward the clouds Celina caught a faint sense of, *'Please Polly,'* from Jane, as she took her hand. Giving it a squeeze Celina said.

"It's going to be all right Jane; I've been told to keep out of it unless you want to talk so whenever you do I'm here, but I'm not going to ask." Jane continued to hold tightly to Celina's hand as she said.

"Thank you. It's not that I'm not ready to talk yet; it's just that I don't know what to say or possibly how to say it, but thank you for being so understanding."

Monday 8th September 1862.

After being gone for over two weeks Polly finally made it back for a few days. She landed just before eleven of the clock and was greeted by Jane with.

"How long are you here for?" Polly threw her a smile as she said.

"For a few days, no-one has told the Abbot that I no longer need time off every month so now I get a holiday almost anytime I want." They both laughed as Jane said.

"Well so long as he hasn't got a calendar."

"Oh he's officially a monk, and as he came up as a child through the Abbey I don't think he even knows why I needed a few days off every month; he just accepted it from Marjory. Has Celina said anything to you?"

"No, only that you told her not to ask."

"Have you said anything to her?"

"No," Jane said as she picked up Polly's bag, "but I know she's bursting to know."

"Where is she right now?"

"She's out with Elizabeth; I actually thought you were them coming back. A portal opened about an hour ago and as Elizabeth was here they decided to have a look." Jane having carried Polly's large bag into the kitchen and finding it was heavier than ever asked.

"What have you got in here rocks?"

"No just books, I'm delivering them to St Paul's." A clatter outside in the yard announced the arrival of Celina and Elizabeth.

"Warm the kettle please Polly and I'll get the mugs as they'll be cold after skulking around for an hour or so." Celina and Elizabeth were indeed cold. Celina was cold, complaining as she came through the kitchen door.

"It's surprising how the temperature drops at about three hundred feet." Then seeing Polly, she said. "Hello Polly It's nice to see you; I take it that you are stopping?" Polly giving first Celina and then Elizabeth a hug replied.

"If I can, that is at least until Wednesday." Celina having extracted herself from Polly's embrace held her hands to the kitchen fire warming them as she said.

"Polly you know you're always welcome, and your rooms are kept ready for whenever you need them. Is that drink ready yet Jane?"

"Did you find the portal?" Polly asked Elizabeth.

"No it had closed by the time we arrived, so we assume Celina's friend's having or has had a visitor again." Jane turned from making the drinks to say to Celina.

"I wonder if they're planning another attack on you as there seems to be one after a portal opens."

"Well if it's this week he's in for a surprise with both Polly and myself here."

"As long as it's not after Wednesday." was Polly's comment.

The following morning Celina volunteered to take the books to Dickie while Jane and Polly retired to Polly's spacious sitting room.

"Well I've looked right through the library." Polly said as she pulled out a book from her bag. "This is the only one I can find that might apply to you." She handed the book to Jane.

"It's a book on King Arthur," Jane said opening it.

"Yes and it's a very old one. It's unusual as it's written in a form of old English instead of Latin, and I found it a bit hard to read. It was written some years after he was buried, but it is very interesting. After reading it I think Arthur was talented but not in the same way as we are. Rather I would say he was more like you." Jane who was looking from page to page asked.

"Like me?"

"Well Merlin spent all of Arthur's youth trying to understand his talent. Apparently, it was different from any form of talent Merlin knew. It was only after a number of failed attempts that Merlin created a wand for Arthur."

"A wand," Jane said interrupting Polly and with excitement clearly showing on her face.

"Yes it's referred to as the lost wand of Arthur, everyone's heard of Excalibur, but few have heard of the wand. In the book it says the wand and Excalibur were part of each other, and apparently Arthur needed the sword first before Merlin was able to make the wand. It's not a thick book, and I don't read very fast but I read it all in one morning, so you read it first and then we will see."

Polly getting out of her chair stood looking out of the window as she said. "I think I need a walk and some fresh air; I'll be in the park if you want me."

Jane found Polly sitting on a bench watching the ducks swim on the pond. Sitting next to her Jane watched the ducks in silence for a time until finally Polly broke the silence by asking. "Well what have you decided?"

"Why did they call him the white King?" Jane asked taking Polly by surprise.

"I don't know, why do you ask?"

"It just struck me as I was sitting here watching the ducks, its right at the end of the book where it tells about the death of the white king." Jane hesitated and then said. "Thinking about it, it just says the white, it says nothing about a King."

"Have you seen the round table?" Polly asked. Jane shook her head.

"No why?"

"Well I have, and its built in twenty five sections all of different colours. There's a white section with a red one on its left, while on its right there is a black one, and I have been told that it was King Arthur who sat at the white section."

"Who were the black and the red?" Jane asked.

"I don't know, all I know is there are five grey sections with the Abbots sitting at four of them, and then every other place is a different colour." Polly turned back to looking at the ducks for a moment before she asked.

"Well what do you think about Arthur's talent, is it like yours?" Jane who was still looking at the ducks thought about it trying to put her feelings into words.

"It seems similar," she finally said. "I suppose it could be, and I think it is just as troublesome so what do you think?"

"I think that if it's not the same it's very similar, but there's no mention of King Arthur having a shield like you appear to have. We know he could be cut or burned, and certainly he could be killed." Jane looked down at her hands, both without a mark or blemish on them after years of work in the smithy.

"Come on," Polly said getting up and looking at the gathering clouds. "I think there's starting to be a chill in the air; let's go back."

Returning home, they found Celina stood in the entrance hall taking off her coat, and seeing both Jane and Polly together, she said.

"Good afternoon, and how have things gone today?" It was Jane who answered her.

"Polly brought me a book to read about King Arthur, and I think you should read it too; it's very interesting." Celina having a feeling that there was some purpose in Jane's request replied.

"All right; if you think I should I will." Over dinner Celina decided to ask what to her, she felt was an important question.

"Is it permissible while you're both together to ask how things are going?"

Polly and Jane looked at each other, and then Jane said. "It's all right you can tell her."

"Are you sure?" Polly asked. Jane looked at Celina and said.

"Tell her about what we did in the forge." Polly thought for a moment, Jane had said about what happened at the forge, or in other words, nothing to do with brooms. To Polly it appeared as if Jane was saying that it would be all right to tell Celina about this and this only.

So Polly explained how they had found out about Jane's affinity with iron. She told Celina about the trials with the punch, and Jane explained about the reason for her new ring.

Polly told her about Jane's glow globe, and explained how it differed from theirs. This brought about a demonstration, and it was a demonstration that proved to Celina just how bright something as small as a pinhead could be.

Tuesday 9th September 1862.

The day had been one of those hot sultry September days that hinted of rain with the odd rumble of thunder in the distance. In the teashop, Jane was relieved to be sitting as her feet hurt from the days' walking. Now she felt hot and sticky as she sat waiting for William. Stefano the waiter came to the table, by now Jane had mastered his Italian accent and had managed to pick up a smattering of Italian.

Today he was asking if she would like to try something new. Proudly, he told her they were selling ice cream. Though late in this summer season he said that they hoped to have it on sale as a regular item next summer. Jane who had not had ice cream since she had arrived in London immediately ordered two to be brought as soon as William arrived.

She didn't have long to wait; William arrived carrying a brown paper package, and by the time he was comfortably seated two glass dishes had arrived and had been duly presented. Each contained ice cream with a topping of chopped fruit. Stefano informed them with a great deal of Italian and very little English that it was a specialty of the house, and something new.

William was in a hurry, and he wanted to talk saying as he held up the package.

"We need somewhere quiet where we won't be overheard so I can show you this." Finishing their ice cream and drinks they quickly made their way to the embankment. Finding a quiet spot on the steps where they sat holding hands, watching the boats on the river and the people as they walked by. William began by saying.

"With the school being almost closed I've had time to look in the school archives and cellars for anything I could find about Demonology." Then he opened the package he had brought and held out a thick sheaf of papers.

"I've found a lot of old manuscripts, but this one is especially interesting. I was told it's over a thousand years old, so I've had it copied for Celina. It's a book written by a monk on what the language master says is Mam Cymru. I think that means the Mother of Wales, or as we now call it the Isle of Anglesey.

I had him translate it from Latin for me. It's taken him and three of his top pupils all week, and he says it's been incredibly difficult as some of the words seem to be an old language, a form of medieval Welsh and Latin mixed."

He then showed Jane someone hundred and forty pages consisting of neat lines of original writing, and then a second bundle of considerably more pages with the original lines written again, only this time with the school master's translation written under them.

Jane had a quick look through picking out odd bits of interest. One section came as a real surprise to her as it dealt with summoning of demons, not evil ones, but ones that were apparently friendly and helpful.

"Will it be of any use to Celina?" William asked.

"It will certainly be of interest, especially this bit on how they've summoned demons as summoning demons has always been a mystery. Celina will find this description here very interesting even if it's not complete." William who had taken out his watch and was looking at it said.

"I'm sorry I have to go; I have a class to teach at half after the hour of six. Professor Green is sick, and I have to tend his last remedial class this week, so can I see you on Sunday?" Jane nodded asking.

"Where?"

"I'll call for you after morning church about one." William stood taking hold of Jane's hands as he prepared to go. It was only then that Jane remembered about William's father's eyes.

"William, what happened to your father's eyes, that is if you don't mind me asking?"

"No it's all right; it was the same accident that broke his legs. When the cargo they were unloading fell on him one of the barrels burst and splashed a caustic substance on him. I don't know what it was but some of it went into his eyes and damaged them. Why do you ask?"

"I want to have a word with Elizabeth about him, to see if anything can be done."

"He saw a doctor, in fact he saw more than one doctor. They all said that the front of the eye is too badly burned to heal properly."

"Yes but they weren't church doctors were they? Celina's mother and father, and Elizabeth have certain advantages."

"Advantages?" William asked uncertainly.

"Yes, they're church-trained." Then without elaborating, Jane said. "I'll ask them and see what I can find out."

William looked quickly around and seeing no-one nearby he gave her a kiss, and then a second one before crossing the road and heading back to school.

Reading the copies Jane had brought in, Celina was disturbed and even a little frightened. The writings indicated that once a demon was known and summoned, it appeared to be relatively easily summoned back.

Even worse, though how was not described were the apparently simple requirements for opening a portal, and the apparent ease of doing so at the time of writing. More shocking still was the finding of a statement that the demons at that time were actually friendly and amenable.

"This," Celina said holding out the manuscript. "Has to go to the Abbot with Polly as soon as possible, but first I intend to have a copy myself." She thought for a moment and then said. "I must do one for father as well; I know he will want one."

Celina continued reading and the more she read the more puzzled she became. Finally, she decided it wasn't a monk writing it. Rather it was someone who was familiar with Latin, but who was writing in a mixture of languages from both the west of England and what is now Wales.

Celina's grandmother on her mother's side had been from an un-named collection of three small cottages about two miles from the hamlet of Bethesda and had always spoken entirely in Welsh. 'Nain' as Celina had called her had been Celina's favourite grandmother, and Celina had from an early age spent a large part of her summers with her. In doing so she had become fluent in the Welsh language and even mastered most of the odd dialects from the surrounding area, so she was able to see where and how the words where mixed.

Reading carefully, Celina gained various small insights about the writer as well. For example, there was the mention of a sister, Celina deciding that it was not a sister of a religious order but an actual sibling. Further more the Roman Aquae Sulis was mention as he made a journey there, and the taking of his children. Other passages referred to various happenings after the Romans had left with one at least two hundred years later.

Reading further she found mention of demons not only being summoned, but of humans also being called by demons. There was even a mention at one point of the writer himself going back with a demon. Then on the last page, there was a disturbing note of a visitation by three demons bringing word of some important happening.

It was here that the translation had become so garbled due to the original being a strange mix of languages. It left Celina feeling that the writer wanted to convey the fact that something significant had happened. Or that something had arrived among the demons, something that had changed where they came from. It was something that the demons had found wrong and feared.

Celina couldn't decipher the word. It wasn't Welsh or Latin or any language she recognised; she murmured to herself.

"Could it be Demon?"

Wednesday 10th September 1862.

Morning found Celina had taken up her pen and was making three copies of the papers supplied by William. Jane, to give Celina peace and quiet took Polly with her on one of her buying excursions to give her a look at the other side of London. Saying it would give her a change and might even be a little enlightening.

A quick call at the shop where they found a very excited Claire who couldn't wait to show them a letter she had received from her mother saying that they hoped to be home for Christmas. Reading the letter raised doubts in Jane's mind about Claire being allowed by her parents to continue working for them, prompting her to ask Claire.

"Do you think your parents will approve of you being employed here after they return?" It was a Claire showing a very independent streak who replied.

"They will have to accept that fact, as I have every intention of continuing to work for you. I think too much of the work we have put into this shop to throw it all away now."

Jane and Polly leaving the shop set off over the river. Once past the warehouses and docks lining the river, Polly found another London, a London she would never have believed existed.

It was a London of narrow winding streets filled with crowds of people ranging from the well dressed to those in rags. There were street markets and little shops with to Polly strange looking people who stood at their doorways looking for customers. Some were dark-skinned, others yellow-skinned, and others she couldn't begin to describe.

Jane made her way through the streets without hesitation, while Polly found herself fascinated by the many men who smiled and touched their hats or even removed them, and the number of women who smiling passed the time of day with them.

By the end of the afternoon, Polly knew what Jane meant when she arrived home saying her feet hurt as they had walked many miles over paving and cobbles.

Arriving home, they found a red-eyed Celina, who had spent all day copying the manuscript William had found. Celina had made two copies of the original ones, and a further two with her notes and comments attached. Seeing Jane and Polly Celina said.

"I'm going to keep the original ones of William's. Polly I need you to take one copy of the original and my notes back with you to the Abbot tonight." Celina gave Polly a package while keeping another.

"This one," she held up the other package. "I'm going to post to my father as I'm sure he will be interested." Then she asked Jane. "When are you seeing William again?"

"On Sunday, he says he'll call for me after church."

"Don't let him run away as I think I need a word with this interesting young man of yours. He seems to have found in his school library more than I found in the Abbey archives."

Sunday 14th September 1862.

I have found out how William's school managed to have records in its cellars that the church does not possess. The possibility of the church looking into and recording what is down there was discussed.

~~~

Attending church was normally a pleasant outing for Celina and Jane, but today it seemed a long and drawn-out service. It was probably no different from any other, but as both were anxious to return home the service seemed to last for hours.

Celina's mind kept wandering from the service to demons, old manuscripts and back to friendly demons, something she still couldn't believe. Eventually having said good-bye to the vicar and exchanged pleasantries with others of the congregation, it was home for a light lunch.

Jane and Celina sat anxiously casting looks out of the window with both willing William to arrive. One primarily for the pleasure of his company and the other one who hoped to extract every bit of information she could.

Their patience was rewarded, as a figure came around the railings of the park and across the road until it finally came to the steps leading up to their front door.

William never reached the door; Jane had the door open and without ceremony she hauled him up the steps and into the house, where his coat was almost ripped from his shoulders by Celina before he found himself being pulled into the study. Once seated there Celina called for tea and then started what was almost an interrogation.

First, she wanted to know how a school library had information that the archives at the Abbeys didn't have. A somewhat surprised William replied.

"The manuscript wasn't in the school library; it was in the cellars along with a lot of other things."

"In the cellars?" Celina asked in surprise.

"Yes as I understand it during the great fire, and with the school being close to the river and on a bend, it was largely out of the fire's path, and with the river and its water being so close it escaped almost all of the fire's effects.

The school suffered mostly from smoke damage whereas buildings in the direct path of the fire were burned to the ground." He waited as Kate served the tea and then continued his explanation.

"Other buildings, even the few stone buildings that survived were badly damaged, and so various churches and other organisations and people of high standing came to the school. They needed somewhere to store important manuscripts, books paintings and other valuables.

The school's roof had remained intact and was completely watertight so the governors charged for the school and its spacious cellars to be used for storage." He paused and looked from Jane to Celina.

"It's really as simple as that, and quite a lot of them never came back to collect what they had left so it's still in the cellars."

"You mean," a curious Celina asked. "There are many old books and manuscripts that no-one knows about down there?"

"Well they were never catalogued if that's what you mean."

"There could be anything down there," Celina said and then after giving it a moment's thought she asked. "I wonder if the church could get permission to catalogue them?"

"They could always ask," William replied. Jane seeing the interest in Celina's face decided it would probably be best if she invited William to stay for dinner. After William had accepted the invitation Celina brought out her copy of the manuscript and then startled William by creating a glow globe over the table.

"You get used to things like that in this house." Jane said nodding towards the globe. The three of them then gathered over the table and jointly went through Celina's interpretation of the Latin-Welsh translation.

"Well this manuscript has started something in the school. The master who did the translation has now developed an interest in what's down in the cellars. He says he needs something to spice up Latin classes as most of what he has been using is rather dry and of no real interest to his students."

"It will spice his class up if he summons a demon." Jane laughed.

"I think he's after ordinary Latin not a mixture like this, he says this took too much work to decipher, and he needs something simpler and easier to translate. You say you don't think it's a monk who wrote this," he asked Celina.

No look here." Celina turned a few pages. "Here he mentions his sister. Now I know a monk can have a sister, but I also get the feeling although he doesn't say so, that he's married." Celina flicked back through the pages.

"Here he mentions a visit to a Roman garrison and says he brought cloth back to make clothes for his children." Celina flicked through more pages.

"Then look at these bits, they are in an ancient west of England dialect a sort of mix between Welsh and Latin and that doesn't fit with the rest of the manuscript." Shaking her head, Celina pointed between two places on the page.

"This type of speech was in use what; two hundred years after the Romans left England so to me the timescale of the book is all wrong; it covers a length of time far too long to be the lifetime of one person."

It was approaching ten of the clock when Jane called a cab for William. Celina now discreetly left the two alone and retired to her room; she was not wholly satisfied with the evening, but William was leaving, and she didn't want to be a chaperone. Jane found Celina in her bedroom sitting with the manuscript open on her knee, but she seemed to be gazing far past its pages as though deep in thought. Looking up Celina said.

"Jane it just doesn't make sense; it goes against everything we know about demons, do you think William could get the original manuscript?"

"I don't know but I can ask." Jane replied and then asked. "Why?" Celina pointing to the pages in front of her said.

"I want to check the handwriting as I want to know if it was all written by the same man." Jane who had started to lay out Celina's nightwear asked.

"Do you think it was more than one man?"

"It must be, as I'm sure the time covered by this manuscript extends over hundreds of years." Turning the first few pages she said. "It says here that Suetonius Paulinus came to see him, yet near the end he mentions Maewyn Succat." Jane shook her head as she said.

"I'm not as knowledgeable about church history as you are, who are they?"

"Well Suetonius Paulinus was a Roman garrison commander when the town of Chester was no more than a crossing on the river Dee, and that is sometime before one hundred A.D." Celina waited as Jane brought her nightdress across before she said.

"Maewyn Succat is better known as St Patrick, and he lived about three hundred and eighty A.D. so that would make the writer of this scroll about four hundred or more years old. That is if it is the same man.

"Then there are other strange things; he says he went to Aquae Sulis with his children, so either several people wrote it or the writer was someone very old, and certainly not a monk. Then again, the manuscript William found could be a copy of several writers' works." Celina stopped again and shook her head, looked at Jane and said.

"No the manuscript reads as one not several put together."

"I'll see if I can meet him tomorrow just to see what he says," Jane offered as she picked up a hairbrush.

Monday 15th September 1862.

Jane had no difficulty getting to see William as she boldly went for direct access. Walking into the school's office she handed the doorman a letter addressed to Mr William Bowden. Then at half past the hour of four Jane was sitting waiting at their usual table. As William came through the door, Jane quickly looked around and catching Stefano's eye, she promptly waved four fingers.

William looked worried as he sat down asking.

"Is anything wrong?"

"No, it's just Celina and that translation; it raises more questions than it answers."

"How do you mean?"

"Well, Celina wants to know if it's possible to see the original manuscript, she wants to check the writing to see if it was all done by one person." William smiled and immediately replied.

"Yes it was as I checked that myself, and not only that I asked Professor Green what he thought. Professor Green considers himself to be our expert on old books and handwriting, and he said it was all in the same hand and that it had been written around three hundred and fifty A.D.

He also told me about the type of Vellum used, he says that it was goat skin and probably from Wales." Jane was impressed that someone could discern things like that in something so old.

"Is there a problem with it or the translation or anything like that?" William asked.

"No it's just that Celina found a few things that seem odd."

"Odd," William asked, "odd in what way?" So as she poured the tea, Jane began to explain.

"First the time frame it covers, well it extends over three or four hundred years. Then there's the fact that he seems to have children and that rules out the writer being a monk. Just little things like that. Then there is the mention of you-know-what's, which goes against everything we were taught about them, not to mention everything that has been happening lately."

"I see what you mean; I'll try to get the original. I'm not saying I can, but I will try." Then Jane asked.

"Do you think it would be possible for the Church to have a look at your archives?"

"I don't know but I suppose I can enquire about that as well. It seems nobody knows what there is down there, and really it all ought to be investigated and possibly catalogued."

Finishing their drinks, William walked a little way with Jane before they parted, William explaining.

"I have an extra evening lesson to teach tonight; it's annoying as there are only twenty eight boys left, and as I drew the short straw I have to get back to the school." They walked a short way further and then William, having heard a church clock striking turned to Jane and giving her a kiss said.

"I'm sorry; I have to turn back. I shall have more time to see you tomorrow as I have no lessons in the afternoon."

Jane arrived home before Celina, and by the time Celina arrived home Jane was sitting with her feet up reading one of the books from Celina's father's library.

"You're right about St Patrick," she said as Celina entered the room. "Did you know he was born in Wales?" Celina dropped into the seat opposite her. Holding her nose she slipped off her shoes, and then holding them with two fingers she tossed them across the room.

"No I didn't, but I do know that he was a slave in Ireland and that later he became a Bishop." Celina's stockings followed her shoes.

"Well that was before he went back to Ireland," Jane said holding up the book she was reading.

"Did you find out anything from William," Celina asked eagerly. Jane sat up taking her feet off the footstool and pushing it across to Celina as she said.

"I most certainly did; William has already had the scrolls checked by the school's expert on old books, a Professor Green, at least I think that's what he said his name was. The professor said that the parchment was goat vellum from about three hundred A.D." and then finishing with a flourish she said. "He says it was all written by the same man on that same Goat Vellum."

"I suppose what he really meant was that the Vellum was made about three hundred A.D. and not necessarily written then, but yes Jane it all fits." Kate chose that moment to enter and picking up Celina's shoes and stockings announce that dinner was about to be served.

After dinner, Celina settled down to start the book that Polly had left for her to read. Just as she put her feet up Kate announced a call from Elizabeth on the Telson. Taking the call, Elizabeth asked Celina if she could come over.

"It's nothing important; it's just that things have been fairly quiet apart from that one short opening, and I wondered if anything had happened at your end."

"Well you'd better come over and have a look at what's turned up here," was Celina's reply.

It only took Elizabeth about twenty minutes to arrive, and once she had settled in Celina produced the newly acquired documents, dropping them onto Elizabeth's lap as she said.

"These are copies of an original manuscript that William found in the school cellars, and he's had one of the masters at the school translate it for us."

Looking through it, it turned out that Elizabeth's Latin was as good if not better than Celina's Welsh, and so between the two of them several additional points of interest were found.

"Look here." Elizabeth said as she put her finger on the part she had been reading. "According to this it's much easier to open a portal in winter than summer. I wonder if that's why we only get short irregular openings now." Moments later Elizabeth almost jumped out of her chair again saying. "Oh look here, this can't be right, there's over a hundred years between these two events."

"Keep reading," was Celina's only comment. Elizabeth started flicking back and forth from page to page before turning the manuscript towards Celina and saying.

"It just can't be; if this is right this book, well it covers a time period of over four hundred years and yet it's all written in a first-person eyewitness manner. That would mean this man is over five hundred years old."

"Well they say Merlin was somewhere in the region of eight hundred years old when he died."

"That's only legend," Elizabeth retorted. "No-one lives that long, the oldest Talent on record lived to be about one hundred and seventy five and there's even doubt about that."

"Setting that aside for the moment," Celina turned a few pages. "Here the writing also indicates that demons at one time were friendly." Elizabeth felt that didn't ring true as she said.

"It could be just a ploy of some kind to get us to trust them."

"If that's the case," Celina asked. "Why warn us of terrible trouble and danger among the demons later on? Look it's these words here." Celina turned to the last page and pointed to the nonsensical lines. "What does that mean? The word Ixcte or whatever it is, it's certainly got the demons worried."

"Yes," Jane said, "so worried that it's been repeated three times."

"Three times?" Celina asked.

"Yes here in the footnote," Jane who had been looking at the schools original translation turned the last page over and pointed to the back.

"Here it is repeated three times." Celina blushed as she said.

"I never thought to turn the last page over. What else is there?"

"Notes about the various spellings, and he says here that some of the Latin and Welsh translations are only approximate, that's due to the changes in the English language."

It was striking eleven as Elizabeth made her way to the stable yard where she was just about to lift her broom, when Jane remembered to inquire about William's father and his blindness.

"I think you may find that Celina's father is the one to see about this as it's a job for a surgeon with talent to remove the damaged parts of the eye. It's usually done a small amount at a time, and Lady Celina's mother would then become involved to encourage the growth of new tissue. Between Lord and Lady Carvel, the restoration of his sight could be possible."

393

Wednesday 17th September 1862.

I was awakened in the early hours this morning to find there were intruders in the house. Strange things have happened to both Jane and myself. I have been shown things that were terrible beyond belief, and I would never have thought human beings could be so evil. My life has been changed forever, and now I feel I am no longer the same person that I was.

~~~

Celina found herself suddenly awake; it was not the slow awakening as normally occurs but a startled awakening to instant full awareness. Though her room was dark and quiet a trigger had snapped in her mind. She remained still and unmoving while letting her mind wander through the house searching. Then it happened again; a sharp awareness of the protective ward on the kitchen door, someone or something not belonging to the house had opened it.

Creating a small glow and looking across at the clock Celina found that it was just after midnight. Lying there she let her awareness drift back to the kitchen. Someone, in fact, two someone's not belonging in the house were now in the kitchen. Celina had barely swung her legs out of bed when Jane appeared at the bathrooms connecting door.

"You felt it too?" Celina asked.

Jane nodded as Celina in surprise asked. "You did, how did you?" Jane just shook her head as she said. "I don't know, I just did, possibly I felt it through you."

Celina picked up her wand and taking it from its sheath; she allowed it to attach itself to her wand safe before she closed the small glow globe saying.

"They're humans not demons that much I can tell." Then confidently she said. "It's probably burglars."

In the darkness, the two started to creep down the first flight of stairs only to stop halfway to listen as a voice came up from the kitchen saying.

"We ought to take some of these things; it seems a shame to burn them all, just look at this silver."

"Shut up," another voice came drifting up to them. "We're being paid to make sure no-one is alive in this house after tonight not to rob it."

Celina and Jane looked at each other as Celina lowered her shield and pulled at the power around her. It was as she lowered her shield that she felt a feeling of a strange cold anger come over her, one that somehow didn't seem to belong to her.

Startled she found her fingers of their own accord tightening on the wand that was once more in her hand. Together they started down the stairs again only to stop as two men came through the door from the kitchen.

One was small portly and carried a dark lantern with its shutter almost closed. The other man who was heavily built, tall and carrying two two-gallon metal jugs; gave a low whistle, and then they heard.

"This is some house." Then they heard the smaller man saying.

"I think we should see to the man and the cook first, a quick knife, and they'll be no more trouble." Then looking up at the larger man he said. "The maid's not bad-looking, you can have her." Only to have the larger man reply, "I want the red-haired one; I've never had a redhead."

Celina found the voices drifting up to her ears had sent a shiver down her spine. An anger was burning somewhere inside her, but it was a strange anger; it seemed remote and distant like it was the anger of someone else.

"Well we've got time to have plenty of fun with them all," the larger man's voice drifted up to them. Celina and Jane watched as the men went into the day room where they heard the smaller man say.

"Dump the oil here for now and let's see to the two we don't need." Celina and Jane made a quick but quiet run for the door to the kitchen. Taking a position on either side of the doorframe they stood with arms crossed and blocking the entrance to the kitchen and servant's quarters.

The men came out of the day room but crossed the hall into the study where the light from the lantern grew brighter as the shutter was opened slightly.

"Look at this," a muffled voice said. "They must be right rich toffs." The men could now be heard walking around the room making comments as they went.

"I'm having this," one said.

"Well put it down for now it'll only get in the way," they heard the other man say.

"That was my writing set." Celina whispered and then seeing the light growing brighter, she said. "Here they come."

In the hall, the lantern made splashes of light swinging from side to side across the floor until it stopped at a pair of bare feet belonging to Jane. Slowly, the light lifted to show first a pair of ankles and a small amount of a pair of legs, followed by the lace hem of a nightdress. From there the light rose rapidly to a pair of arms folded across a chest and then up to a blond-haired head. The shutter was quickly opened wider, to reveal a similar redheaded figure propped against the opposite doorframe.

"Bleeding Hell, would you look at this?" the tall man said. "The letter said they were a pair of beauties, and would you believe it here they are and all ready for bedding."

He reached into his coat and pulled out a wicked-looking knife. The smaller man with the lantern opened the shutter fully before placing the lantern on a table. It was the small man, who pulling a knife from his belt said.

"Better come over here me dears, that is if you don't want to get hurt. My friend here can be a little rough at times," then saying out of the side of his mouth as if not to be overheard. "You go and see to the others." Celina and Jane hadn't moved. Out of the corner of her eye, Jane could see Celina whose face was white, just as she knew her own must be. A curious detachment seemed to have taken hold of her. It was as if she was watching someone else.

Jane felt cold and calculating but not fearful, anger yes. Next Jane became aware of a strange silence in the hall; she could see the pendulum of the clock swinging but she couldn't hear the tick. All the small noises were absent, and apart from the four of them there was nothing that seemed real. Everything now seemed to be seen as if from far away and distant.

Jane glanced at Celina, who was still standing but now with her wand discreetly facing backwards clipped to the wand safe;

Jane looked closer. Somehow, it looked as if there were two hands; she could clearly see Celina's hand. Over the top of it was another hand, one wearing a ring with a black stone. Slowly, Jane became aware of a dark shape smaller than Celina that seemed to move with her, as if a slightly smaller woman was trying to occupy the same space.

Jane found herself standing shoulder to shoulder with Celina as the taller man said.

"Look let's have no trouble, just do as you're told."

Jane and Celina looked for an instant at each other and then without their conscious control both found their heads nodding in unison. Jane had caught sight of Celina's eyes before she turned back to the men, and it seemed like they were no longer Celina's eyes. If Jane had been able to, she would have shuddered.

Jane could feel there was something there that was no longer just Celina; she felt there was something with Celina that was angry and determined.

"Right you two, get in here," the small one said pointing to the day room. "Come on move." Celina and Jane moving shoulder to shoulder walked into the day room. To Jane, it was starting to feel as if she was in a dream.

"Take yourself off and see to the others, and don't be long." the fat one said to the taller one.

Jane felt she should feel something, fear for the servants fear for herself and Celina, or at least embarrassment at being stood before a strange man in just her nightdress, but inside she was cold and dead. Other than his voice nothing seemed real; she wanted to turn and look at Celina, but only her eyes would obey.

Jane found her body was obeying his commands without consulting her, while out of the corner of her eye, she could just see Celina where there was still a darkness surrounding her. That darkness did raise a feeling but only a slight one of curiosity.

The man looked them up and down and then said. "Sit over there and don't move or scream, I don't want to have to hurt you," and then with a smile he added. "Yet." Jane moved over to the sofa and somehow she knew that the same was happening with Celina. As Jane sat looking straight ahead, she felt Celina silently move to sit beside her.

The small man taking a sack from under his coat now started to fill it with small items from around the room, while all the time whistling to himself as he did so. Then faintly she heard a voice coming from the hall.

"I can't get in the bloody kitchen." followed by the tall one bursting in, only to stop just inside the doorway as he saw what his friend was doing.

"What the Hell do you think you're doing," the taller man said angrily. "We have to see to the others first and I can't get in the kitchen." The small man who had dropped the sack guiltily asked.

"What do you mean you can't get into the bloody kitchen?"

The tall man with a hint of panic in his voice came further into the room saying.

"There's bloody well something in that bloody kitchen door that won't let me pass." Jane found a slight feeling of amusement creeping over her as she watched his agitated pointing back towards the kitchen.

"Stay here, I'll do it," the smaller man said. "Don't let them move, and don't start with them until I get back." The smaller man then snatched the candle from the tall man's hand and turned towards the door.

He took four steps to the door and then bounced back as if he had walked into a wall. Dropping the candle he doubled forward with both hands going to his face. Jane watched as the candle fell turning once before it stopped in mid-air. The flame flickered, almost went out and then burned steady.

"What the Hell." The small man said, standing there with one hand covering his nose and looking at the candle.

Jane could see blood starting to run between his fingers and then down his face until it dripped off his chin.

Without taking his eyes off the candle he reached forward with one hand toward the doorway.

Jane found her eyes turning to the tall man who was standing with his eyes open wide, staring unblinking at the candle. Then with an effort she turned her eyes back to look at the smaller man.

He pressed one bloody hand against something blocking the doorway. As Jane watched he pulled his hand away as if he had touched something hot, leaving the red smear of a hand-mark hanging in the air. To Jane it seemed as if the doorway was blocked by glass, as the hall was just visible in the candlelight that shone through.

The small man turned back to the two women, and Jane found her eyes turn to look at, and then fix on the blood dripping through the fingers covering his nose. She found herself counting the drops as he demanded. "What the hell's going on?"

He looked first at Celina and then at Jane. Jane remained silent; her eyes still locked on his bloody fingers as she reached twenty-one. He aimed a slap at her face that should have knocked her across the room, but he might as well have hit a marble statue for all the effect it had on her. Swearing and nursing his hand he backed away from Jane and then still cursing; he turned to Celina.

"You," he hissed at Celina. "You tell me what's happening?" Pulling her to her feet and towards him, he started to shake her like a rag doll. With his hand now away from his nose, Jane unable to look away watched as the blood splattered across the front of Celina's nightdress while his hands left bloody handprints on the sleeves.

Celina remained silent and unresisting; until he released his hold leaving her to fall back onto a chair. He turned back to face Jane. Jane found herself watching still unable to pull her eyes away from the blood that was dripping from his nose and down on to the front of his coat. Pulling Jane towards himself, he took hold of her left hand, and started to push the point of his knife into her palm.

Now not only did Jane look away from the dripping blood to look at her hand; she also found she could feel something; relief as she found her shield was working to protect her just as it had done with the slap.

There wasn't a sound as Jane looked up to watch his face, watching fascinated as his eyes bulged. He pressed harder and then harder, until his bloody hand slipped on the knife handle, forcing him to use the palm of his hand to try to force the knife into Jane's immobile palm.

Somewhere in Jane's mind a feeling intruded its self. This time it was a slight feeling of amusement with her thinking that if he succeeded in pushing the knife through her palm, he would probably put the knife through his own palm as well.

As he pushed harder the knifepoint at first started to glow red, and then orange. The man watched fascinated, all the time pushing down on the knife. It was as the knife blade buckled, and in a shower of sparks ran to form a small sparkling puddle in Jane's palm, that he dropped what remained of the knife, which like the candle turned once in falling and then remained slowly cooling in mid-air.

"What the bloody hell's going on?" he asked again looking first at his knife then at the now cooling steel in Jane's palm.

The tall man was still looking at the candle hanging in mid-air, and now he pointed a trembling finger towards it as he said. "Look Mick, look." The small man now appeared to realise the things that his eyes had earlier seen and his brain had failed to register.

"What's happening?" he asked again, and then looking at Jane, he asked in a voice that now trembled slightly. "Who are you?" Then taking hold of Jane and shaking her, with fear starting to show not just in his voice but also on his face, he demanded. "What's happened to the door, and what the Hell are you??" It was then that Celina who had silently risen to her feet finally spoke.

"The door," she said with a shrug of her shoulders. "It is blocked, and at this moment nothing is happening." To Jane's ears Celina's voice sounded cold, distant and devoid of emotion.

The small man spun to face Celina shouting. "I bloody well know it's blocked, but how?" Now with more than just a trace of fear showing in his voice he again asked. "Who the Hell are you," and then with a tremor noticeable in his voice. "What the Hell are you?" The man fell silent as whatever had become Celina put a finger in front of her lips to silence him before she whispered.

"Who am I…. I am your nemesis, and what am I…. I am your worst nightmare; that is what I am." Celina looked from one man to the other and then with her finger removed from her lips said. "Now the question is just who are you?" Celina paused waiting, and then she repeated her question.

Both men were now stood unmoving, and to Jane they appeared to be frozen as if in a bind and unable to move, standing, staring at Celina. Jane could see the fear struggling to show in their eyes and on their frozen faces.

Getting no answer and in a voice so hard Jane felt it could shatter stone, Celina now demanded.

"I will have your names." The feeling of detachment was starting to fade from Jane. She was in her night attire in front of two strange men, thankful for the dim light she tried to pull up the front of her nightdress, only to find herself still unable to move.

The man with blood still running down his chin and dripping freely down his coat was struggling to work his mouth as if his face was frozen; finally he said, "Mick." Celina then turned to the other man who managed to utter. "Dave."

"Why are you here?" Celina asked.

"To kill everyone in this house," Dave replied.

"Why?"

"We get paid for it," he replied. By now their faces were beginning to look more normal, and their speech became faster as Celina asked.

"By whom and how much were you paid?" It was Dave who answered saying. "We don't know who; our instructions came in a letter with five hundred pounds for each of us." Celina now asked him.

"Do you do this often?"

"It's our line of work,"

"Tell me more about it," Dave now turned fully toward Celina. To Jane it looked as if both men became more relaxed as with a broad smile at the memory Dave began.

"A month ago there were two spinsters, and someone owed them a lot of money, well he found it cheaper to pay us than them." Then there came a nasty chuckle as he asked Mick.

"Ugly-looking pair though weren't they?" Jane felt sick as the men started taking it in turns to recount what they did before burning the house and what was left of the two sisters.

Jane found she could move her head just enough to look at Celina, only it wasn't Celina's face; it was only half Celina with another face all mixed into hers. The two men continued reminiscing as Mick now took up the tale.

"Dave, do you remember that farmer in Surrey, you know the one? After we killed him and his wife, we found the children. The boy was no good, so I knifed him. Do you remember how he squealed for about ten minutes," he chuckled. "Just like the stuck pig he was?"

"The two girls," Dave interrupted. "You made a mess of the little one though didn't you; she nearly got away."

"Well she didn't," Mick chuckled again at the memory. Jane looked at Celina; she had never seen such hatred in a face before. Yet it seemed as if Celina was fighting within herself or with someone only she could hear, while at the same time she was speaking both sides of an argument.

"No I can't." Jane heard her croak. Then Jane heard what she could only think of as another voice saying. "Yes I want you to; they deserve it. I've shown you all their evil."

Celina was now shaking violently as she croaked "No." Then the other voice coming from Celina's mouth said. "You've seen all that they've done and the horrors they enjoyed inflicting."

Although Jane was hearing both sides of a conversation, she did not understand either.

"No I can't, the oath, no! No!" It came as almost a shout from Celina as she stood immobile. Looking at her Jane could now see the indecision clearly showing on her face.

The two men continued reminiscing, turning Jane's stomach. She would have covered her ears if she had been able to move that much. Suddenly released, Celina turned to them and her wand flicked forward from the wand safe. Grasping it, she made a small movement with the wand not even pointing it at the men and Jane breathed a sigh of relief as they fell silent. A thankful Jane could now see that Celina was herself again.

Celina's wand flicked back reattaching itself to the wand safe, then drawing herself up to her full height she placed the palms of her hands on the tops of their foreheads. The two men stiffened, and their eyes went blank as Celina held them like this for possibly half of a minute before removing her hands. Jane could now move enough to see the tears running down Celina's face.

Jane's eyes were drawn back to the two men, where she could see a rapidly fading red mark about the size of a half crown in the centre of their foreheads. Jane felt a wash of relief when she heard Celina speaking in her normal voice give orders to the two men.

"Now you will go where you are told, leave by way of the stable's gate and turn right into the alley. When you reach the end of the alley turn right again and then take the next turning left. There is a police station there, go inside and tell them about every killing that you have done before tonight. Of tonight's happenings you will remember nothing. Now go."

Jane now found the wand was back in Celina's hand as with a flick of it; she dismissed the two men who fought their way through the door and rushed out turning towards the kitchen.

For a moment, Celina stood as if in a daze. Then as Jane heard the kitchen door slam, she saw Celina slump into a chair and bury her face in her hands as she cried, sobbing as if her heart was breaking.

"I could have done it," she sobbed, "and I wanted to do it." Jane put her arm around Celina. For the first time feeling the cold and finding they were both shivering.

Celina pulled away, seeing for the first time Jane in her nightdress covered in blood.

"What's happened?" she gasped. "Why are we…?" She stopped still looking at Jane.

"Something happened didn't it? I remember a woman. She told me things she wanted me to do, things that were horrible, things that she wanted me to do to those two men, but I couldn't do it to them because of the oath." There was a haunted look in Celina's eyes as she looked up at Jane. Then Celina put her arms around Jane pulling her close as she said.

"Jane she told me how to circumvent the oath and…. oh dear god Jane, it's so simple; I could have done what she wanted."

"Was it so bad what she wanted?" Jane asked remembering with a shudder and a sick feeling what she had heard. "They deserved all I can think of."

Celina shook her head as taking a breath she said.

"She was going to impale them and then turn them over a fire as their flesh was burned off." Celina was now looking at Jane but Jane was certain it was not her that she saw. "She was going to start at their feet and then work up." Celina looked up at Jane now seeing her again as she said.

"She was going to keep them alive and do it over and over again, at least once for every murder they had committed." Jane could see the horror in Celina's face. Celina shivered, and Jane didn't think it was just with the cold.

"She was going to keep them alive, and she could do it. She showed me how because it was me who was going to have to do it for her. Jane I know how to do it. Oh Jane it was horrible." Celina was now violently shivering, and her teeth were chattering.

Jane put her shoulder under Celina's arm and lifted her to her feet saying. "Come on into the kitchen, there should still be a bit of a fire left in there."

Once in the kitchen Jane settled Celina in the cook's chair by the fire where a few embers were still glowing in the grate. Jane in her haste and not bothering with the fire irons cleared the dead ashes from the grate with her bare hands, and then pushed the few embers into a pile.

Pulling a handful of sticks out of the stick box, she laid them over the ashes. Finally, she heated them with a thought until they burst into flames.

Jane waited for them to burn steadily before she added some coal. Only then did she take two glasses down from the dresser and at the same time retrieve one of Cook's bottles of brandy from the top shelf in the pantry, brandy that Cook always claimed was for cooking. Jane poured two good measures before passing one to Celina and asking.

"Do you know what happened, do you remember?" Celina still shaking drank half of her brandy in one go. Then coughing and gasping she shook her head.

"It was like a dream; I remember getting to the kitchen passage but then everything changed. It was as if I was a passenger in my own body," she shuddered. "It was horrible; there was a woman with me doing things I could never do." Celina stopped and thought, and then said.

"No she was showing me how to do them; she said that I must be the one to do it not her." Celina took another sip of brandy.

"Then she sort of took over; she made me make them tell her or me everything they had done. Everything, not just what they said out loud. I had to see into their memories and feel their feelings." Celina started sobbing again as she asked.

"How could people be so evil? They deserved to burn." Jane topped up Celina's nearly empty glass.

"At one point there was also a man in my mind." Celina hesitated as her head came up. "No he was with me; he spoke to the woman in me.... what was it he said?" Celina's brow now creased in concentration as she tried to remember the exact words.

"No sister of mine, no; if you make our daughter do this thing you will corrupt her as them. Times change let her punish them as she will. Show her what she must do and then let us depart. Our daughter must remain strong and pure." Celina paused taking a drink before she said.

"Then she showed me, and I knew how to make them confess to the police; not just confess but relish doing it for a whole day. I made them want to tell the police everything."

By now Celina had stopped shivering with the cold, and Jane was wondering if she could go for their coats, as worry about Thomas hearing voices and getting up had started to intrude its self.

She was just about to ask Celina if she would be all right when there was a clatter outside the kitchen door, and then it flew open. Both leapt to their feet as a figure appeared in the doorway. It was

405

Polly who stood there shivering with just a coat thrown over her nightdress.

"Are you all right?" Polly asked, grabbing hold of Jane in a hug while tears were running down her face.

"I had a nightmare and I had to come." She paused looking around. Her eyes widened as she saw for the first time that things were definitely wrong.

Seeing Celina sitting there red-eyed and tearful, and with Jane standing by her side with the bloody streak of a hand across her face and blood smeared over her nightdress. Polly's pale face went even whiter as she asked. "It happened didn't it?"

"What happened?" Jane asked, and then not waiting for Polly to answer she said. "Look after Celina, we need something to wear." Jane almost ran out of the room, returning with hers and Celina's coats. Once with their coats on Jane started topping up their glasses again. By now, Polly was sitting at the table and having seen the blood on Celina and Jane's nightdresses had started visibly to shake.

"Is that Jane's blood or yours?" she asked Celina, pointing a trembling finger at the smears on Celina's nightdress. Jane with a shake of her head answered "neither," as she filled her glass and passed it to Polly. She was just reaching for another glass when Polly started choking.

"Careful its brandy not sherry," Jane told her as Polly wiped tears from her eyes. Jane put some more coal on the fire and then after washing her face, she sat down opposite Polly saying. "Now tell us about this nightmare."

Polly took a sip from her glass and as the colour slowly came back into her face she said. "It was strange; I was here with you and Celina, but in my dream it wasn't always Celina. Some of the time it was another smaller woman with dark-red hair. I really remember the dark-red hair as it was just like Celina's." Polly blinked owlishly and then pulling herself together said.

"You Jane, you seemed to be surrounded by a white haze." Polly looked at them blinking.

"You were stood in the kitchen doorway watching two men. It was so strange. They said they were going to kill Cook and

406

Thomas, and you went into the day room with one of the men. Then lots of things happened. It's all so confusing and then the man, no the men started to say some things and." Polly's colour came back all at once as she took another drink.

"I can't tell you what they said it was horrible, and then." Polly found she needed another sip, "and then the woman became totally Celina. She wanted Celina to do something, and it seemed as if there was someone else with me. I felt as if there was this man, and he knew this woman shouldn't have Celina do what she was asking her to do, so he said no." Polly hesitated.

"Yes, it was the man who said to the woman…." Polly took another sip of brandy and murmured. "Its all confused and I must get this right." She closed her eyes and concentrated before saying. "No sister of mine no, if you make our daughter do this thing you will corrupt her as them. Times change, let her punish them as she will. Show her what she must do and then let us depart. Our daughter must remain strong and pure.' I think I got that right, and then I woke up and found I was flying over London."

Polly took another sip and Jane topped up all three glasses again as Polly said. "In my dream I felt that there was this man, and that the woman was his sister. Yet I also felt that he considered Celina to be the daughter of his sister just as I felt he was her father." Polly shook her head and then drained the glass.

"It's so confusing," she said. Then looking into her empty glass, she held it out for Jane to splash another inch into the bottom of all three glasses. Jane looked at the bottle finding by now it was almost empty.

"It doesn't make sense." Polly said. "How can a man be the father of his sister's daughter?" Jane and Celina looked at each other as Polly asked.

"It wasn't a nightmare was it? It really happened didn't it?"

Jane put her hand on Polly's as she replied. "Almost exactly as you said." Then between the two of them, they told Polly all about their ordeal, with Jane saying. "At first I thought the men had some sort of talent because I couldn't do anything to stop them…."

Then Celina interrupted her saying. "It was as if it was a dream happening to someone else, at least most of the time. It was this strange woman who took complete control of me." She shuddered and said. "It was horrible; she made me do what that man said." She paused to finish her brandy.

"Then this woman spoke to me…. No it wasn't actual words; I just knew what I had to do or rather what she wanted me to do and how to do it. Then I had to make them tell me all they had done, everything, it was." Celina had to stop unable to go on or put into words what she had experienced from the men's memories.

Jane could feel her distress as she sat there elbows on the table with her hands covering her face, being reduced to tears whenever she allowed herself to think about what she'd experienced through the minds of the men.

After hearing from Jane of what the woman had wanted Celina to do Polly turned to Celina and said.

"If you could have done it you should have done it; they deserved it all of it."

For a moment Celina seemed about to agree, and then she remembered the words of the man who was apparently the woman's brother, and what he had said. With a shake of her head she said.

"No if I had I would be as bad as them." She stopped her hands covering her ears in a vain attempt to stop the memories.

It was hearing the clock strike half past the hour of three that decided them that the time had come to get some sleep; that was if any of them could. Polly was the first to attempt to leave the table saying.

"I must get back to the Abbey before it gets light." Getting to her feet she stood swaying, and then by holding on to the edge of the table she made her way almost to its end before her legs gave way. Celina, swaying only slightly stood blinking owlishly and looking down at Polly crumpled on the floor. Eventually, she said.

"She's drunk." Jane picked up the empty bottle and looking at it said.

"After a third of a bottle of brandy I'm not surprised." Polly was indeed out cold. Celina looking at Jane said.

"I think we should get her to bed don't you?" Jane made an attempt at lifting Polly only to collapse over her giggling. Celina studying the situation decided it was up to her to get Polly into her bed. Celina's wand however proved to have a mind of its own lifting anything in its way but Polly. Between them, they managed to carry Polly up to her rooms.

Then as she was already in her night attire, they put her straight into bed. Jane having seen Celina to her room and into bed made her way back to her own room. Standing in front of the mirror, and seeing the blood smeared down the front and side of her nightdress, she found she felt dirty.

Stripping off her nightdress, Jane kicked it across the room standing naked in front of her mirror and looking at herself, she still felt.... She didn't know what.... Maybe dirty may be violated; she shuddered. Leaving her nightdress on the floor she slid into bed. It was about a quarter of an hour later when her bedroom door opened and she found Celina looking in.

Celina finding Jane still awake asked. "Can I join you; I can't sleep?" Jane moved over as Celina slid in beside her showing no surprise at Jane's naked body. There was a brief struggle before Celina's nightdress joined Jane's on the floor, and then after about half an hour and feeling more relaxed; they finally fell asleep in each other's arms.

It was early for Jane to be awake. Unable to sleep, she quietly slid out of bed and made her way to the bathroom. First she attended to her morning needs before turning on the hot tap, only to find slightly warm water flowing into the bath. Jane sat on the edge of the bath twirling one finger in the rapidly cooling water and decided that Thomas must have let the boiler go down.

Disappointed at the warm water and really wanting a bath, Jane watched the water swirl as she reviewed the previous night's happenings in her mind. Watching as the water slowly rose up the side of the bath, seeing six seven and then eight inches of tepid water, she finally turned it off.

Jane looked down at her hand looking at the iron ring on her finger, and then looked back at the water to find steam rising and the water was now hot, almost too hot. Jane lowered herself into the bath relaxing in the hot water. She needed to be clean; not just in the few places where the man and his blood had touched her but also in other places where she was relieved that he hadn't touched her.

Selecting various bottles from the side of the bath Jane poured some into the water, and then with others she lathered herself. Finally pulling the pins from her hair she sank backwards under the water. Her hair had grown longer in London, and now wet and let down it reached almost to her hips. Sitting she reached across for the jug on the stand and then absently filling it from the tap, she poured it over her head finding herself gasping at the rush of cool water. She'd forgotten that the boiler must be down, but the water certainly awakened her.

Shivering Jane reached for a towel, and then she froze. The water, she had used her talent entirely without thinking. Jane sat in the cooling water for long minutes wondering how such a change could have taken place.

Holding up her hand, she looked at the ring on her finger. Had she changed so much and if so was it because of last night? She pulled a bathrobe towards her.

Jane wandered back into the bedroom to dry her hair while Celina was still sleeping. Now standing in front of the mirror and watching herself towelling her hair, Jane felt clean again. As she dressed she ran through the night's happenings in her mind. Something or someone had taken over her body and made her do things against her will.

Reliving the memory of it again made her shudder. Something or someone had also taken over Celina.

Jane remembered how she had seen a woman's shape mixed in with Celina's as if two people were occupying the same space. The woman Jane felt certain had been the same one who had shown Celina how to do things, horrible things, and had almost forced Celina to do them against her will.

Jane considered the possibility that she had been shown things as well. Polly had said she saw her in her dream. In the dream, something white had surrounded her just as something black had surrounded Celina. Could it be? She shook her head; she didn't know. Celina stirred threw out an arm and then sat up and looked around. Jane throwing her hair over her shoulder said.

"Good morning, are you ready for a bath?" Celina gave a shudder as she replied.

"That sounds wonderful; I feel dirty, dirty and used." Then Celina held out her arms and said.

"Thank you Jane, I couldn't have slept last night without you." Jane came over, gave Celina a kiss and then went to run her a bath, this time not bothering about the boiler.

Thomas was full of questions about the two jugs of lamp oil in the study, and shocked to hear that he had slept through an attempted burglary. Jane assured him that Celina had dealt with it and there had been no need to worry, as they had all been perfectly safe.

It was almost midday before Polly made her way down to join them in the study, looking frail and very much under the weather as she gingerly lowered herself into a chair. Celina sat in silence as Jane went to see Cook about making Thomas's favourite hangover cure. Returning Jane gave Polly the glass.

"What's this?" Polly asked as she took the glass.

"It's Thomas's cure-all." Jane replied. "Drink it." Polly looked at the thick brown evil-looking mixture and then downed it all in one gulp.

Celina and Jane waited expectantly, but nothing happened. Polly just sat there and looked blankly into space. Finally, she hiccupped once and said.

"Actually, it's not that bad." Then as she gave Jane the glass back she asked. "Did I have much to drink?"

"Half a bottle of brandy." Jane replied.

"I don't remember, I remember telling you about my dream and then you and Celina telling me about some men, and then it all gets rather mixed up."

"Let's just put it this way," Celina replied. "Someone wants us dead and was willing to pay one thousand pounds to accomplish it." With that comment, Polly sat bolt upright in her chair asking.

"Mr White hair?" Celina nodded as she said.

"That would be my guess; we've been expecting something since the last portal opened. Maybe this time they tried normal

411

methods rather than demons, and it has to be someone with access to large sums of money."

"Well our Mr White hair seems to have plenty," Jane said as she picked up Polly's glass. Then as she made her way towards the kitchen, she called back. "Cook is making some strong black coffee for Polly." Polly shuddered as she said.

"I should have been back at the Abbey before now."

"Its all right, Jane called them on the Telson first thing this morning and said you weren't well."

"What are you going to do now?" Polly asked.

"Well," Celina said putting down the paper. "There's nothing in the morning paper, so I intend to wait for the evening one."

Polly frowned not understanding Celina's meaning as she asked. "The evening paper?"

"Yes, I want to see if they arrested our two friends." Then as Polly had only a vague drunken recollection of the early morning's conversation, Celina had to explain to Polly again about her instructions to the two men.

"What if they didn't believe them?" Polly asked.

Jane who had returned with the coffee said. "If they don't believe them, I shall go after them myself and I shall have no worries about taking them apart by brute force."

Polly had a gut feeling that Jane was more than capable of pulling arms and legs off that was if she was annoyed enough. As it was they didn't have long to wait before a voice could be heard from the street calling. "Special edition, mass murderers arrested," sending Jane hurrying out with coins in hand. Jane returned with a single fold of newsprint with the headline.

'Mass murderers give themselves up. Fourteen murders claimed.'

Despite the beneficial effects of Thomas's cure all Polly left that night adamantly vowing never to touch brandy again. Later as they retired for the night, Celina made sure all the wards she had previously set not only on the house but also the additional ones on the alley gates were all intact and working.

Celina had a nightmare that night, and again the following night. After that Jane shared her bed for several nights until Celina had recovered enough to sleep alone. After their ordeal, Jane found a change in Celina. The knowledge imparted by the strange woman was having a profound effect. Celina had been forced to face the seamier side of life, and now the little girl in her had gone.

Monday 6th October 1862.

Mother and father have let it be known that they are making the journey down to London on Wednesday, and will be staying for a few days. That will be most nice.

~~~

Word was received that Lord and Lady Carvel were to arrive early Wednesday morning and would be staying until Friday night. The cook and Kate went into a frenzy of preparation. The cook wanting to try one of William's mother's fish dishes sent Thomas to the market with strict instructions on just what to buy, while Kate and Jane had the task of making sure the master suite was ready.

Celina was overjoyed wanting her mother to see the shop now that all the alterations and improvements were finished, while Jane couldn't wait for Tuesday to see William and tell him of the impending arrival. Now she would be able to ask her adoptive parents about possible treatment for William's father's eyes.

The party arrived early just before midnight on the Tuesday, having made better time than expected. Celina's mother put it down to the extra flying time she had put in, in her new role as inspector of children's institutions, while quietly confiding to Celina, that it was her father, who had called for the rests on the way.

Later that morning Celina's father was meeting with the board of a company who wanted to run a Telson cable under the sea to Ireland, and then possibly on to America.

While her father was occupied Celina arranged to take her mother shopping followed by lunch in the restaurant they had used for her birthday, and finally calling at Rarities.

Lady Mary was most taken by the portraits created by Sally, and insisted on paying to have one of herself with Celina and Jane done there and then. Celina arranged for it to be framed and collected the following day. Dinner was over, and they had all retired into the study before Jane could bring up the subject of William's father's eyes, and finding to her surprise that it provoked a heated dispute between Celina's parents.

There was no contention over whether or not it could be done as both were in no doubt about that. Rather the dispute was regarding the best way to treat the eyes both during and after the operation. Jane had mentioned the fact that William's father had avoided earlier treatment because it meant cutting the eye, and that the doctors could not guarantee success. Now Jane was relieved to hear Lord James say.

"I wouldn't have the faintest idea how to use a scalpel," and that he considered them, "though useful in certain hands often barbaric.

Tuesday 14th October 1862.

William was waiting for Jane as she entered the teashop anxious to hear her news.

"Yes it can be done." Jane said taking William's hands. "Father that is Celina's father said that for him it is a relatively simple operation, although it is time-consuming for the patient as it has to be done a little at a time, as new skin has to grow back before any more of the damaged skin can be removed. It takes a surgeon to remove the damaged skin, and a church doctor to encourage the growth of new skin.

Celina's father says he is prepared to do it along with mother, but your father would have to go into the hospital at Ripon for treatment, and it would mean a stay in Ripon of about three to four weeks."

William thought it over and then asked. "Will you come down with me this weekend and explain, as father is terrified of operations?"

"Of course I'll come, and then I can assure your father that our father operates without using a knife, and that it is totally painless. Don't forget that both he and mother are church-trained."

"I keep forgetting you have two mothers and fathers," William said taking her hand. Jane laughed as she replied. "I'll see Celina and arrange to come with you; when and what time?"

"Friday," he replied giving her hand a squeeze. "The same train as last time and I'll get the tickets."

That evening when Jane broached the topic Celina said she had no objections at all. It was Jane who had a sudden disappointment as Celina told her that Polly was making her feigned 'monthly time' visit that same weekend. The only thing that cheered Jane up was that Polly would be staying until Thursday.

"Is she still using that excuse with the Abbot?" Jane asked. "I would have thought he would have gotten wise to it before now."

"Well he is technically a monk, and I don't know as he would know that much about women, and who's going to embarrass him by mentioning things like that?"

Jane was laughing as she replied. "Well I say good luck to her as I already think they put too much on our dear Polly.

Friday 17th October 1862.

Friday saw William at the railway waiting as Jane was helped out of a cab, and then as they hurried to the platform he told her that he had already spoken briefly to his father.

"I didn't know you had a Telson," Jane said.

"We don't; I sent father a telegraph, and he went to the postal office to call me at school last night, and he sounds very interested."

Moses was already waiting at the station as the train arrived ready to take them and their bags to the house.

"Hello Moses how is everything," William asked swinging the bags onto the rack. Moses looking back over his shoulder said.

"Your Mother and father have gone to your aunt Daisy's this afternoon; your mother says she's had a bad fall but they should be back tomorrow on the two o'clock train."

"Aunt Daisy is my mother's elder sister who lives just outside Little Hampton. She's quite a bit older than mother and getting rather frail, and we're all really fond of her." Before William could say more Moses said.

"Your mother says she's arranged for Lily to stay overnight." Then chuckling to himself he said. "To keep an eye on you." Jane could hear him still chuckling under his breath as they left the station yard.

"Lily used to be our maid until she retired about five years ago, but she still comes in occasionally to look after the house if Mother and Father are away." Then William leaned closer saying. "She's as deaf as a post and can't see a thing without her glasses." Then looking up, he asked Moses. "Where's Jean?"

Moses looking over his shoulder replied. "It's her weekend off." William nodded and explained to Jane.

"Jean has one weekend off every two months to see her mother."

Arriving at the house, William and Jane entered through the kitchen door startling an elderly woman sitting by the fire, who by leaning heavily on a stick struggled to her feet.

"Is the arthritis bad again Lily?" William asked almost shouting.

Lily nodded smiling at his inquiry while looking curiously at Jane. Not giving her time to answer William said. "This is Jane; she has come to see my father."

"They're not here; they've gone to your aunts. She's not very good as she's had a fall and hurt herself." Then looking at Jane and obviously not having heard William fully Daisy asked. "Who's this then?"

William raising his voice even further and leaning close to her ear said. "This is a friend of mine; she's come to see Father." Lily squinted at Jane and said.

"I can't manage your bags; you'll have to take them yourself." Jane picked up her large bag and Williams small one and took them both up to the first landing; there she paused smiling as she heard Lilly shouting at William in the kitchen.

"You're a right one letting the young lady carry her own bags." Jane arrived back at the kitchen just as Lily said.

"I'll see to something for you to eat." Jane pulled a chair round in front of the fire and said.

"You sit here Lily; I helped William's mother the last time I was here so I know where most things are. You stay here, and I'll see to a meal for us all." Lily protested very loudly but still lowered herself carefully into the offered chair, and within a few minutes was snoring quietly.

"Snoring is about the only thing she does quietly." William said with a broad grin.

Jane noticed that once Lily was seated, and the meal was on the table that she packed away an awful lot of food for one so old and infirm, and as Jane said to William later.

"She put all of it into such a small body."

By the time everything had been cleared away and the kitchen made tidy again Lily was definitely ready for her bed, and was soon heading for a little room off the kitchen that was her bedroom. William seeing Jane watching said.

"Once she couldn't manage the stairs mother had a bed put in the old pantry for her." After seeing Lily safely to her bedroom door, William returned and poured them both a drink as he said.

"I'll bet this is the latest Lily's been up for years," and then as he looked at the clock. "Ten past ten and she's only just to bed." He then settled down next to Jane, who cuddled up pushing under his arm and yawning.

"She's not the only one ready for bed is she?" William said laughing. "Let's finish our drinks as the fire's low, and it's getting cold."

In the hall, William looked for the bags. "Where did you put the bags?" he asked.

"Yours is in your room and mine is on the landing." William picked up a candle lighting it before blowing out the hall lamp, and then taking Jane's hand he started up the stairs.

On the landing, he stopped to put the candle on a table and turning to Jane, he put his arms around her before planting a kiss first on her neck and then with kisses working around to her lips. Jane felt something in her stir as she returned his embrace and felt his kisses.

One longer kiss and what had only stirred was now fully awake as his lips met hers again. They were alone in the house for all practical purposes. "Should she?" It would be so easy. She didn't need to lean to know that he wanted her as much as she wanted him. He broke away looking at her.

"It's going to be cold tonight, your room in the attic…. well, it gets very cold," he finished lamely.

"Does it?" Jane murmured.

"I know a warmer place."

"Do you?" she whispered. Sudden doubts started entering her head as William took her hand and gently guided her down the hall to his bedroom door. At the door, he put his arms first around and then under her; before lifting her off her feet, he carried her through into the bedroom.

Jane watched as fear, anticipation and want vied with her emotions as the bed drew closer and the bedroom door swung slowly closed, leaving the two of them in total darkness.

Jane woke as usual at six of the clock only to find that the stub of a candle was still alight in her room. This was followed by. *'Why is Celina in bed with me?'* That thought was quickly followed by the realisation that it was not Celina but William laying at her side. Suddenly, memory came flooding back. *'Yes, they'd done it.'*

Looking to her right, she saw William lying beside her still asleep with his tousled hair resting on his pillow. She reached over and ran her fingers down the side of his face feeling the stubble. It was as she did this that Jane remembered her bag was still on the landing, and not knowing Lily's habits Jane decided she had better move it promptly.

Getting out of bed and shivering in the chill morning air, she quietly opened the bedroom door and with a quick look over the banister to see that Lily wasn't about to see her, she ran across the landing to retrieve her bag.

Dropping the bag just inside the bedroom door Jane dived back into bed thankful for William's warmth as once more she snuggled up close to him. Jane felt him stir and then an arm slid around her shoulders pulling her closer.

"We really ought to be up and about," she murmured rather unconvincingly as she attempted half heartedly to push William away, while her. "Before Lily comes looking for us," was smothered by a kiss. It was some time later as William lay there comfortably in the warmth of the bed watching her that Jane was able to make her way to the washstand.

Missing her morning bath, Jane felt she was definitely smelly and in need of soap and water. Reaching the washstand, Jane found to her dismay that the pitcher was empty. William seeing Jane holding the pitcher slid out of bed saying. "I'll go and get you some water." Then putting on his housecoat, he gave her a kiss as he passed. Reaching the door he turned, returning for another much longer kiss before finally leaving the room altogether.

It was a busy morning for Jane, as Lily left shortly after a hearty breakfast and leaving Jane with a kitchen that needed to be cleaned, and arrangements made for a proper meal ready for William's parents' return. William had volunteered for the hard work of pumping water and filling the water tank of the kitchen range.

Even then Jane found that the kitchen fire had not been lit for long enough to provide hot water for the washing up and cleaning. Jane not wanting to wait had put the breakfast things into a sink of cold water, water that to William's amazement became hotter with every dirty item that Jane placed into it.

Cleaning and preparations over, William seeing Jane looking out toward the sea suggested a walk on the beach to which Jane readily agreed, and within ten minutes they were walking along the tide line.

Finding a sheltered spot on the cliff top where they could watch the ships passing by. Sitting there and holding hands William told her stories of his father's days fishing the English Channel. Sitting, cuddling and kissing they found the time had swept by without notice, and by the time they realised this it became a frenetic rush to get back to the house.

It was too late for William to harness the horse to the Brougham so Jane did it in record time. Then it was Jane taking the reins and driving the carriage into town ready to meet the train.

William and Jane met his parents at the station, where William's first words were.

"How is Aunt Daisy, and how seriously is she hurt?"

"Getting better," his mother replied. "There's nothing broken just bruising." William's father said.

"She says she fell all the way down the stairs, and the doctor thought she might have broken some ribs."

The Brougham having been loaded with the small amount of luggage William's parents had, set off along the coast road. Along the way, William's mother pointed out various points of interest until arriving home, and with the luggage unloaded William's mother asked.

"What did Lily feed you last night?"

"She didn't; Jane did." William replied not giving Jane time to answer.

"You didn't?" William's mother said as she turned to Jane. "I left strict instructions with her that all it wanted was heating up."

"Well I did." Jane replied; "and it's a good thing you made plenty. I've never seen someone so small pack away so much food at one sitting." William's father burst out laughing as he said.

"That's our Lily; she eats for four and by that I mean four crews."

William's mother was surprised to find that Jane, who had found some herbs and spices similar to those used by the Indian restaurant, had already started preparing a meal for their return. William searching in the cold room found his mother had some suitable game hung and ready for eating, and though not quite what the Indian restaurant used Jane had still decided that it would provide an unusual and exotic meal.

Now it was William's mother's turn to help Jane in the kitchen. and though the meal Jane was preparing was not truly Indian, it was still very like one provided by them. It was a meal that Jane served with a wine that William's mother had provided.

The meal was hot and spicy, and it came as such a delicious surprise that it left William and his parents all wanting more.

"It's a good thing Lily's gone home," William's father was heard to say to his wife as he started on a second helping.

Jane later explained to William's mother and father as much as she understood about the proposed operation on William's father's eyes.

For a time this created something of a problem. To them, it seemed as if she was talking about the use of magic, so Jane then had to explain first about church doctors and then about the Knights of the Church, and that meant explaining about herself and Celina. After that it naturally called for a demonstration of her power.

The following morning after breakfast, William's father announced.

"If there is a chance of me seeing my grandchildren, then I want to take it." It was then that William's mother asked.

"How much will it cost?" Without any hesitation Jane replied.

"Usually a voluntary contribution to the hospital of any amount that can be reasonably afforded is all that is asked, as it helps out with some of the cost of running the hospital." Having considered this William's father asked.

"Only part of the cost, how else is the hospital funded?"

"A part of the hospital's income comes from these voluntary contributions, and then there are some charities that help. Other than that my father pays most of the hospital's day-to-day costs." Jane had replied not realising that she had referred to her father as paying most of the hospitals costs, but William's mother had.

"Your father pays?" William's mother queried.

"Oh well I mean our father, or rather my adoptive or…. maybe William you can explain."

William did his best to explain about Jane and Celina's relationship. How from the age of thirteen Jane had lived with and come to know Celina's parents, Lord and Lady Carvel as her surrogate mother and father. Just as in a similar manner, Celina called Jane's parents mother and father. It was all rather confusing and Jane wondered if anyone other than herself really understood.

Jane found the remainder of the weekend was wonderful and over far too soon. Arriving back home, Jane found Celina, Polly and Elizabeth gathered in the study where they were discussing bringing Nancy down to London for Christmas. Jane came through the door just in time to hear Celina suggest to Polly that Nancy be brought down no later than the twenty-third so that she could join in putting up the Christmas decorations.

Christmas was immediately forgotten when Jane was seen walking through the door. With Celina wanting to know everything about Jane's trip to Brighton and William's father's reaction to the news that it could be possible for him to see again, before telling Jane.

"We heard last night that Mother's coming down again on Thursday as there's a seminar she wants to attend on Friday, so you can ask her about William's father then." Jane almost bouncing on her chair at the idea said.

"That's good and then I shall be able to tell William straight away."

"Is it that urgent?" Elizabeth asked.

"I think it is now that he's found there may be hope for him; he feels he wants the operation sooner than later. After all he's not seen his wife or William for fifteen years, and as he's in his late fifties now he may not have that much longer to see them."

Elizabeth quickly understood; being a Knight or even anyone of reasonable talent did confer certain advantages. Celina's mother was now in her early seventies and could expect another fifty or even sixty years of active life. Even a minor Talent could expect to see eighty or ninety years.

By contrast, William's father now in his late fifties might only live another ten years or quite possibly less. To Elizabeth, it was a sobering thought reminding her of her talented mother and her father with no talent.

It also reminded Jane of something else that had been said.... 'Grandchildren.' His father had also said that he wanted to see his grandchildren. Jane felt certain that children wouldn't be in her future for many years, and she had to admit to herself probably not with William. Something inside told her that she and for that matter Celina, had a long way to go before thinking about children.

Later that night as Celina sat in front of the mirror getting ready for bed; Jane was brushing her hair and wondering how to start.

"You haven't asked." she finally said.

"Asked what?"

"About Brighton." Celina swung round on the stool. "You didn't?"

Jane nodded and then turned Celina back to face the mirror.

"Did it hurt and did you bleed?" Celina asked. Jane watching Celina in the mirror shook her head as she said.

"Yes a little, but it was so quick…. it was over almost before I really felt it, and as for bleeding I never noticed so it couldn't have been much."

"What was it like?" Celina asked.

"I can't describe it." and then thinking about it she said. "Do you remember the village girls and what they used to say? Well, it was nothing like that. It was just well far beyond that."

"Would you do it again?" Celina asked watching Jane's face as she replied.

"Yes I would." Celina put her arms around Jane and said. "I'm so happy for you finding William; do you feel different now you've done it?"

Jane shook her head as she said, "no, not really any different at all." Celina sat in silence thinking until Jane said.

"There, we're all finished." Getting into bed Celina said.

"Someday Jane, someday, I don't meet enough men; that's my trouble." Then with a smile and looking up at Jane she said. "At this rate I may have to walk the streets and give it away."

Jane surprised that Celina even knew of such things bent over the bed and gave Celina a kiss as she said.

"You'll find someone; you've plenty of time yet but wait for the right man and the right time; it makes a real difference."

Friday, 24th October 1862.

After her meeting Lady Mary returned to her two daughters in high spirits and bursting to speak to her husband on the Telson, so it wasn't until after dinner that Jane asked about William's father. Her mother decided on the spot that another Telson call to her husband was in order, telling Jane that a surgery date should be scheduled promptly and then leaving Jane waiting in the dining room while she made the call. Then upon her return she said.

"It's all settled your father says if Mr Bowden can get to Ripon for the third of November. We can have someone pick him up from the Railway station and take him straight to the hospital, and that way he will be able to see by Christmas."

Jane was so excited that she couldn't wait for the morning as she wanted to take a cab immediately to the school.

"Jane dear," Lady Mary said. "I don't think going to the school at this time of a night will be appreciated." Lady Mary pointed at the clock that was showing that it was well after ten of the clock.

"William may already be in bed, and not only that he won't be able to speak to his father tonight anyway. Why don't you call him first thing in the morning?"

"Mother's right Jane," Celina said. "If you call about eight of the clock tomorrow, that will be best." It was a very reluctant Jane, who had to agree.

The next morning as eight of the clock was striking, Jane called the school, and then she had to wait about twenty minutes for William to call back. Jane sat and fidgeted until Celina finally told her to sit still. When the call came Jane ran to the Telson easily beating Kate in getting there, and not waiting for William to speak she excitedly said.

"William, I've spoken with Mother last night, and she called our Father, and he says if your father can get to Ripon on the third of November he will see him and your father will be able to see before Christmas. What do you think of that?"

William was spluttering unable to get out what he wanted to say; finally, he managed. "It will be a miracle; I know father will jump at the chance. I'll get a letter off and posted this morning, so he should get it on Monday."

Jane took a deep breath hoped for the best and said. "Why not go down there this morning, and then we can tell him ourselves?"

"Why not," William said with a growing eagerness of his own. "I think there is a train at ten of the clock this morning, can you be there?"

Jane looked at Celina, who was standing in the doorway and asked. Celina nodded her consent and then with a knowing smile said. "Stay longer if you want and come back Sunday."

Jane turning back to the Telson quickly asked. "Do you think your parents will mind if we stay and come home on the usual train Sunday?"

"With news like that we could stay a month," was William's excited reply. Replacing the Telson, Jane hugged Celina as she said.

"Thank you, you know I don't like leaving you too often."

"I know and my hair suffers terribly," Celina replied feigning a pout and patting her hair. "Now you go and pack and I'll have Kate call a cab."

With no one to meet them it was a long walk from the station to William's house carrying their bags so both were glad to see the smoke from its chimneys as they rounded the last bend in the lane. William's mother was outside and saw them as they turned the bend.

"William; Jane," she called. "Is everything all right?" Running to his mother, William threw his arms around her as he said.

"Yes Mother everything's absolutely perfect, where's Father?" Seeing the excitement on William's face, she said.

"He's in the house why?"

"Come on," William said taking his mother's hand. "Let's go in and then we can tell you both together."

William's father had heard them coming and was standing waiting in the hall; hearing William, he asked. "William is that you, and have you brought Jane?"

"Yes Father and we have brought you some good news as well, tell him Jane."

Jane waited until they were all seated, and the tea had been sent for before she said.

"Celina's mother came down late on Thursday, so I didn't get chance to speak to her until after dinner on Friday. It was only then that I had the opportunity to ask her about your eyes." William's father now leaned forward waiting tensely.

"Mother called our father on the Telson, and he says that if you can get to Ripon on the third of November he will see you, and you should be able to see by Christmas."

William's father sat with his head resting on the chair back as tears started to fill his eyes, while his wife reached out and put her arms around him crying too. Reaching out she pulled Jane toward her and whispered.

"Thank you and thank your mother and father too, that will be our best Christmas present ever."

It was later when Jane and William's mother were alone that his mother closed the door saying. "Jane I need to have a word with you." Jane who had been looking at William's book of pictures he had painted of boats turned to William's mother waiting.

"I want you to know," William's mother began and then paused looking embarrassed as she said. "I am not saying I approve of what you and William did last time you were here, but I do like and approve of you."

Jane felt her face turn scarlet as she struggled to gather her wits to ask. "How did you know?"

"Don't be silly," William's mother said, starting to smile at Jane's obvious embarrassment. "Remember I'm the one who sees to the sheets."

Jane who had to sit down before her legs gave way felt she had never been so embarrassed in all her life. Then Celina came to mind hanging in a tree with her skirts caught up, and now for the first time she began to understand just how Celina had felt.

Jane's head went into her hands covering her face as William's mother put an arm around her shoulder and said.

"It's not that bad my dear. I remember William's father and myself. You're not the first, and you won't be the last.

426

Oh yes I know things are different among you young things now, and I have to accept that times have changed." William's mother's voice changed sounding to Jane regretful as she said. "You have choices we never had." William's mother pulled a chair across and sat next to Jane as she said.

"What you do on your own is your own business, and we can't stop that, but please don't expect to do things like that when we are here. It's too late to change things now so I just expect you to be careful. After all, we don't want any accidents do we? I know there are things you can use now that William's father and I never had." Jane finally composed herself enough to say.

"Yes it's all right about that, I will decide when to start a family, and I have no intention of having children out of wedlock."

William's mother closed her eyes, and Jane caught a look of pain as it crossed her face. Then William's mother taking Jane's hand said.

"I wish I could have done that. After William, I had six miscarriages. In my day we had no...." William's mother stopped again looking embarrassed, and Jane could see the sorrow now showing on her face.

Jane tentatively reached out and put her other hand on top of William's mothers, and then she found herself leaning and giving comfort as she said.

"I'm so sorry." Wiping away her tears, William's mother getting to her feet said.

"Well I'll let you tell William," and then with a smile she said. "Oh and I'd better tell you that father knows as well, I felt it was only right that I told him." That started another blush for Jane.

"Father, he'll be all right with you," William's mother said reassuringly. "He liked you even before he knew about the operation, and he says you are good for our William."

The remainder of the evening was so busy and full that Jane never had an opportunity to speak privately to William, so it came as quite a shock to him when as they reached the landing Jane told him quietly. "Your parents know about us and last week."

William who had been about to take Jane in his arms with the intention of a rather passionate kiss, now found himself holding her at arm's length shocked and anxiously asking, "how?"

"It was the sheets," Jane replied. "I never gave them a thought, but they gave us away." Then pulling a startled William towards her, she gave him a kiss before quickly running up the stairs to her attic bedroom. William standing in shock watched her as she turned on the landing and disappeared into her room.

Saturday 1st November 1862.

We had visitors over both Saturday and Sunday, as William's parents stayed with us before their journey to Ripon. I must say I found them to be most delightful company.

~~~

Celina arranged in advance for William's parents to stay with them over Saturday and Sunday. This way they could take the express to York early on Monday, and be rested and refreshed before the surgery the following day. Although William's parents had known Celina's family had money, Belgrave House still came as a shock.

Celina created an equally surprising impression by not being anything like they imagined a Lady from a high family to be. Later and talking to William's father and describing Celina, William's mother said.

"Celina is so like Jane in manner and looks, that it's hard to believe they're not sisters."

It was after dinner Sunday evening that William asked Celina to demonstrate something of her talent for his mother, and so the ever-amazing glow globe was called out to perform. It shone so brightly that even William's father could experience it in spite of his limited vision.

Monday 3rd November 1862.

On the Monday morning of their departure for Ripon, William was allowed two hours off school to see his mother and father off. William and Jane stayed with them as they waited to board the London-Edinburgh express where their first stop would be York, where they would arrive shortly after eleven. From there they would then have a little under an hour to wait before catching the local train to Ripon, to arrive there at around two of the clock.

Jane, who considered herself a seasoned long-distance railway traveller as she had made that same journey once before. Now she felt she was able to assure William's parents that it would be a pleasant journey. Seats had been reserved on both railways and as Jane had said.

"Refreshments are available for you at York just outside the Station at the Railway Hotel." Celina's mother had also arranged for them to be met at Ripon by one of the house carriages, which was to take them directly to the hospital.

Jane had thoughtfully given William's mother the address of a small hostelry and as Jane had told her. "It is just a short walk from the hospital, and I know that the beds are clean and the food is very good."

As the train pulled out of the station Jane putting her arm around a worried William said.

"Don't worry, I'm sure that your mother and father will have a most comfortable and pleasant journey, and I know Beth will look after them."

"Beth? Who may I ask is Beth?" William asked.

"My sister." Jane laughingly replied. "She and Billy run the 'Coachman's rest,' just a short walk down the road from the hospital."

It was just after eight of the clock, and dinner was being cleared when a call came for Jane on the Telson. It was William's mother calling from the Coachman's rest, with the news that the initial examination had been good, as she told Jane.

"We saw Lord and Lady Carvel, and they examined William's eyes." Jane hadn't known William's fathers name was William not that it came as much of a surprise, but she made a mental note to ask William after his mother's name.

"Lord Carvel said the damage was more severe than he had expected, but that it was entirely repairable. Lord Carvel says, as both William's eyes are affected he will do both eyes together. He also explained how it would only require an initial two-day stay in hospital and then William could go out for three days.

He would then have to return to the hospital again for another two days. All together the treatment would take about four or five weeks as the entire front of both eyes has to be removed and then re-grow." Jane was delighted as she said.

"I'll get hold of William for you first thing in the morning; I can't contact him tonight as the school office will be closed until eight of the clock tomorrow." William's mother then said.

"I've taken a room in the hostelry you recommended, and they say it's all right for William to stay there with me for the three days he's out of the hospital, and you were right about the people running it; they are very nice."

"I knew they would be," Jane said with a laugh. "I've known Beth all my life, after all she is my sister."

That took William's mother by surprise, as Beth was very much like her mother in looks.

"Your sister, she looks nothing like you," William's mother exclaimed, and then said. "Still I must say she is a very good cook, and I will give credit there where credit's due. I've got to go now, but I would like to ask one more thing of you. Moses is looking in on the house daily during the week, but if William could call one or two weekends. You too Jane if you wish, just to keep an eye on the house as it would reassure us both." Jane felt that strange feeling in her stomach and her heart give a thump as she said.

"I'll have a word with William in the morning."

****

Morgana rested on her shovel and wiped the sweat out of her eyes; it had been hard work digging the grave, but it had given her satisfaction doing it this way, and now Manora could rest, indeed they both could.

Morgana wiped her brow again and looked down at the grave remembering how Manora had spent many of her last days sitting looking over the narrow strip of water at the mainland. Morgana felt a prickle of tears as she remembered how she had liked to sit and watch the change of the seasons on the mountains, and now looking at them Morgana felt that the view would be hers to keep.

Turning she looked at the small stone and turf shelter that had been their home for the last ten years, Morgana knew it would be lonely and empty now.

Reaching into a fold of her wrap Morgana took out the fifteen gold coins that Manora had kept all these years along with a square of deerskin. With tears filling her eyes, Morgana read the letters burned into the skin so many years before, her gift of freedom to Manora.

Wiping the tears away, Morgana pushed the square of deer hide away and then digging deeper into her wrap she pulled out a small square of stitched leather.

Encased in it was a lock of Merlin's hair. Morgana stood looking at it thinking it had been a long time. Finally deciding she closed her eyes.

The instant her eyes closed she knew Merlin's shield was open to her. 'Merlin.' she thought as she extended her mind.

'At last!' she felt him reply. 'I've waited for you for over a year. Where are you?'

'On the west coast over on the big island, why?'

'I need a close link as there is something I want to show you.'
Morgana was shocked. It had been many years, indeed they were children the last time either of them had requested even a hand link; eventually she asked. 'Is it that bad, can't you come here?'

'No I can't, and yes it is that bad. You need to see what I have seen and as soon as possible.'

Morgana suddenly found herself sitting down, finding her legs had unexpectedly become very shaky. A hand link or a close link meant Merlin could see all her memories and thoughts, everything about her if he chose. Her thought was uncertain as she replied. 'I don't know Merlin; it's been a long time.'

'I'm sorry sister but I have to show you something very strange. I promise I won't peek into your mind; I'll just show you this one thing.' and then there was silence in her mind.

Morgana listened to the wind and the birds calming herself, and remembering that a close link worked both ways, so as Merlin trusted her, she would trust him. She replied. 'All right Merlin; I do trust you, show me.'

Morgana opened a path through her shield feeling Merlin press against her as he entered her mind. A flood of memories followed. Merlin's memories of a certain village, and then he was gone. Replacing her shield Morgana said. 'I'm sorry Merlin; I shouldn't have distrusted you but it's been so long.'

'Look at the memory Morgana', he urged. 'Do you remember?'

Morgana did indeed remember. As she allowed his memories to be unveiled in her mind, the old childhood fears of monsters in the dark returned. Morgana sat frozen feeling ice flowing through her veins. The images were of monsters.

'What are they?'

'I don't know,' Merlin replied. 'I had hoped you might know, or know as to what could have caused that sort of condition in the dead.' Merlin could almost feel Morgana shaking her head as he waited for her reply.

'I just don't know; have you found any more?'

'No just them, and I've wandered around this area for over a year now.' Sending her thoughts back again a frightened Morgana said.

'Merlin, I think that we should keep ourselves open all the time, at least for now. That way if you find any more like this you can link with me immediately, and please Merlin, do take care, I still love you.'

'And I love you too sister,' his thought came back. 'Be well,' and with that Merlin was gone leaving a large empty space deep inside her.

,

****

Tuesday 4th November 1862.

It was midday when William returned Jane's call eager for information. After telling him about his father's meeting in the hospital with her father and mother, Jane then told him about his mother asking him to keep an eye on the house, though not saying anything about herself. His reply made Jane's heart leap as he said. "I think we ought to go down, if not this weekend then the next."

"Whichever you think best," Jane replied trying to sound as calm as possible.

"Meet me after school this evening as usual, and then we can see about a meal."

As Jane neared the teashop, she could see William waiting outside for her. He opened the door as she approached to find their usual table unoccupied. Over a pot of tea, they discussed where to go for a meal. William was unsure not having eaten out much in London.

Jane immediately thought of the Indian establishment. The one where she had obtained the special spices and herbs for the meal she had cooked in Brighton. All his family had enjoyed the food that she had cooked, and the restaurant wasn't far away, so Jane put the idea forward explaining to William that during the day the restaurant served meals on the ground floor for the dockside workers. Then at seven of the clock they changed to an upper class establishment with meals served on the elegant first floor.

William readily agreed and they took their leave of the teashop. Being early and as it was a pleasant evening, they took a walk along the embankment. It wasn't long before William stopped and putting his arm around Jane's waist they stood looking out over the water watching the boats on the river. Standing looking at the boats William turned Jane towards him and hesitantly asked her.

"Will you be coming home with me this weekend?" Then he stopped starting to look somewhat embarrassed.

"Of course I will, that is if you want me to."

"Well will you…. again…. you know,"

"If you want me to," Jane whispered.

433

William looked even more embarrassed as he said. "We ought to use you know, precautions." Jane looked up at him with a smile and said.

"I already spoke of this with your mother; I don't need to take precautions. I'm a Talent and Talents only start a family when they want to."

Puzzled William asked. "How do you mean?" Jane found her embarrassment rapidly disappearing, as she had to suppress a laugh at the bewildered look on his face as she replied.

"I have full control over that function of my body, and I shall decide when I start a family, and that won't be until I am married." William breathed a sigh of relief, and then his expression changed somewhat as he asked.

"You mean we can whenever we want, and as often?" Jane looking at him nodded not saying a word.

William still looking embarrassed said. "You don't know how worried I was after that first weekend, and then over the last few weeks I've been thinking I might have you...." He stopped not wanting to say the word.

"It's not that I don't love you, and I know my mother and father would be pleased to have you as a daughter. However my salary isn't yet that great, and when I marry I want to be able to support my wife in a home of our own." Jane with a smile and a kiss to William's cheek replied.

"You don't have to worry because I'm not, and I have no intentions of permitting that just yet."

Then arm in arm they turned and resumed their walk crossing over the river. As they walked the streets, Jane told William of the three ruffians who had attacked and tried to rob her and Marcus only a short distance from where they were.

Then Jane found herself having to reassure William that no-one would dare attack them, as with her being a woman and the reputation she now had as a street fighter guaranteed their safety.

It was only a short distance further before they turned into what looked to William to be a warehouse. Once inside he found that not only was it a very exclusive restaurant, but that Jane was well known and liked by all the staff.

434

***

With Celina's acceptance of William and her blessing, wonderful weekends in Brighton followed one after another. Even their final weekend accompanied by Celina wasn't spoiled. William found Celina's company delightful, and her presence made it a perfect last weekend.

Celina now not only saw the sea for the first time but she saw a stormy sea, with the waves breaking over the beach and beating against the low cliffs.

Eventually Celina made her way back to William's house cold and wet to the skin with rain and salt spray, her state earning her a reprimand from Jane, who complained.

"Just look at you, wet through. Why didn't you use your shield?" To which Celina happily replied.

"I thought it was high time I found out how I would feel being cold and wet."

William's response to this was a laughing. "Well, how does it feel to be cold and wet like a normal person?"

"Horrible," Celina replied with a wry smile. "I need a hot bath as I'm chilled to the bone." William was still laughing as he told her.

"Well a bath here in this house is taken in the scullery, in that tin bath hung up on the scullery wall and with water that comes from the pump in the kitchen," so for the first time in her adult life, Celina had a bath in a tin bath. However, as a concession to Celina being a guest it was placed before the fire in the kitchen. Her only other deviation from the normal was, that she heated the water herself and kept it that way until she was finished.

****

435

Spring ~ 210 AD

The hair prickled on the back of Merlin's neck. Something was making its way along the side of the river toward his little camp, and whatever it was it was not attempting to hide its advance.

Merlin moved away from the fire and into the darkness, giving his eyes time to adjust to the evening gloom. Whatever it was that was approaching; it wasn't a human of that Merlin was certain.

Slowly, a form was starting to materialise out of the shadows and beginning to take shape. Whatever it was it was slightly smaller than Merlin, and it was making an ever-increasing amount of noise as it approached.

It stopped for a moment at the edge of the trees and then slowly came closer, until Merlin could see one of the creatures he had last come across thirty years ago.

Merlin lifted his staff and as he did so the creature stopped. Merlin watched in surprise as it squatted down and then looking at Merlin it slowly raised its hands upward palms open before turning them down flat to show the back of its hands.

Merlin lowered his staff warily watching and waiting, and as he did so he searched the surrounding woods with his mind to determine if it was alone or if there were others. Relieved Merlin found nothing.

Merlin didn't like killing other than for food, and he certainly felt that eating one of these creatures was out of the question, so as it appeared to pose no immediate danger he stood and waited for it to make some meaningful move.

Still squatting it now lowered its hands to the sand between its feet, and smoothing the sand in front of itself, it began to draw lines in the sand. Once it had finished it slowly rose and moved back, retreating almost to the water's edge where once again it squatted down and waited.

Cautiously, Merlin made his way over to where the creature had stood. Merlin creating a spark of light looked at the lines in the sand studying them intently.

A drawing showed a man and the creature together doing something with the sand. The man, who was clearly holding a staff *and wearing a fox skin hat with a bushy tail visible was obviously Merlin.*

Pushing the iron-shod end of his staff into the sand Merlin squatted beside the picture. He looked toward the river to where the creature still squatted in the gloom. Making up his mind Merlin beckoned for the creature to approach using a gesture unmistakable in any language.

Wary of each other at first, their confidence gradually increased until setting all fear aside, they earnestly began trying to communicate. The night didn't last long enough as they began first with drawings in the sand, and then gradually added words in their efforts to make themselves understood.

The creature drew images in the sand that depicted two separate types of creatures. One looked to be enormous while the second was much smaller, to Merlin obviously like the one squatting and creating the sand pictures.

Merlin understood that he had already encountered the larger creature in the past, and now he was meeting the smaller form. Knowing this his trust along with his knowledge progressed rapidly.

The creature when it spoke, spoke in a language of sounds Merlin found mostly impossible to reproduce, but as near as Merlin could say them the sound, "Sishky," represented itself while the sound. "Cesdrik," referred to the larger creatures.

The Sishky's drawings showed that the Cesdrik had enormous strength, and that they were almost impervious to powers such as those practiced by Merlin. The Sishky then using what Merlin understood to be a wand demonstrated that it possessed abilities that were very similar to Merlin's.

With additional drawings and words, it became apparent the Sishky and Cesdrik were enemies. As best Merlin could understand it, the Cesdrik wanted to capture the Sishky alive possibly to use as slaves. However, because of the difficulty Merlin experienced in explaining this concept, he wasn't entirely sure.

The sky was growing light in the east as the Sishky made it clear that it would have to leave. Using gestures and additional drawings, the creature indicated that it would return at nightfall.

As evening fell the Sishky returned, and they resumed their efforts at communication. During the night, it became clear the Sishky wasn't being taken as slaves, but were being used for something far worse, something that often resulted in their deaths. Merlin began to understand that it was something that had to do with a being that was called Ixcte.

Toward daybreak the Sishky made it clear, it wished to show Merlin something down by the river. They had only gone a short distance along the river before Merlin found himself stood in a small grassy clearing where the Sishky spread a line of dirt along the ground. Taking its wand, the Sishky started to call, and as it did so a ring of light appeared to hang in the air.

As Merlin watched the ring of light grew larger until looking through or into it, Merlin found he could see an expanse of what looked like a meadow, covered with blue grass and sprinkled with blue leafed plants. Some of the plants had flowers of many vibrant colours, and in the distance; he could see what could only be blue trees. Behind all of this was an orange-yellow sky.

The Sishky indicated that it would return at nightfall, and then it stepped through the circle to join two other Sishky waiting. Having joined them the three Sishky stood and watched Merlin as the circle collapsed down to nothing leaving a strangely pleasant smell in the air unlike anything Merlin had ever known.

****

Thursday 18th December 1862.

William's parents stayed with us again on their way back to Brighton. Both sang high praises of my mother and father. William's father says his eyes are now perfect.

William's mother and father stayed overnight with Celina and Jane before travelling back to Brighton. William's father was delighted that his eyes were working again after fifteen long years.

438

As he hugged both Celina and Jane, the tears ran down his cheeks and into his beard. It was a sad farewell for all of them as Jane and Celina saw them off at the station. William was holding a tearful Jane close as he said to her.

"It's not for long, and I shall see you right after Christmas."

Saturday 20th December 1862.

Polly arrived for Christmas in the early hours of the morning, and after a late breakfast, she set off with Jane on a shopping expedition. They arrived back in the afternoon with what was called a Christmas tree, which had to be set into a container of soil to hold it upright. With the container that Thomas finally produced turning out to be a brass coalscuttle.

After that, they produced their other purchases comprising of two boxes of fancy glass decorations that had to be unpacked and checked for breakages. In the end, it was decided to wait for Nancy's arrival before decorating the tree and some of the rooms. Polly experimented with casting a number of small glows scattered about the branches of the tree, saying that it was much safer than candles.

"That's very nice," Jane said. "But can you make them flicker like a candle?" Although Polly tried she could only get one or two odd ones to flicker, or all of them together. Celina herself was feeling a little despondent; it had been three years since she had been home for Christmas. Celina found herself thinking. *'If only Jane would fly.'* What with the shop to run and other obligations, Celina could see flying would be the only way they could make it in time.

Secretly, Celina had hoped that Jane, much as she would miss her might have accepted William's offer to go to Brighton for Christmas, not that much that she would have suggested it though, as Jane was too much a part of her.

Now Celina wandered around the house uncertain of what to do. She had already wrapped all of her presents, and between her and Jane, they had decided that all but Polly's would go under the tree on Christmas Eve.

Her wandering took her into the kitchen where she found the cook sitting to one side of the fire with a glass of something in her hand, while Kate was sitting on the other side of the fire knitting. Celina looking at Kate's knitting decided that it looked like something for a baby or a young child. Kate seeing the look said. "It's for my sister Miss; she's expecting her first."

At Cook's invitation, Celina pulled a stool across and accepted the glass that Cook had poured for her, of what turned out to be sherry. The cook then put the bottle on the table so Celina changed her stool for a chair and pulled it a bit nearer the fire. From the front of the house faint sounds of laughter drifted in from Jane and Polly, but sitting and listening to the click of needles, the cook scribbling in a book, and the pop of the fire; Celina felt strangely comfortable.

As she sat there with glass in hand, her thoughts drifted back over the past year. Who would have thought she would have been the target of so many attempts on her life? She took a sip from her glass.

Then there was Polly, so much power in so small a girl. Celina's thoughts turned to how Polly had shown her so many things she would never have dreamed of.

Next her mind drifted to Jane and how she was finally beginning to show some real talent. Then there was William, a man who seemed truly to care about her. The thought of Jane and William brought her round to thinking of the recent attempted murder of the whole household, and she suddenly went cold all over in spite of the fire.

The foundation of her life as a Knight of the Church disappeared that night. Until that time she had always been comfortable in the knowledge that the oath prevented her from killing in a fit of temper or passion, or even hurting someone deliberately, but now it was gone.

Someone or something had taken her over that night and implanted in her the knowledge of how to circumvent the oath, so in effect Celina knew she was living without the oath now.

It was as she was thinking of this that she became aware of the fact she was sitting in silence. The click of needles, the pop of the fire and the cook's pen scratching on paper had all ceased.

Around her now was a sense of sorrow. She could feel it deeply. It was a sorrow for doing something. It was a sorrow for someone her; me losing her; my temper and wanting to force Celina to do something she naturally did not want to do. It was as these thoughts drifted through her mind that Celina found she had been relaxed to that dream-like point of letting her shields fade almost to nothing.

A thought intruded into the silence that seemed to say. *'I'm sorry; I should have listened to my brother before telling you. You are.'* The thought was fading as another came to her. *'Never needed the oath.'* It faded further and then she heard or felt…. *'Untrained and so powerful, I'm so proud of you.'*

A pop from the fire made Celina jump; startled into raising her shields again she almost spilled her drink. Had she lowered her shield or had she just been asleep and dreaming? She looked at Kate and the cook who seemed to be carrying on as before. No she didn't think she had been sleeping; yet somehow she felt better just as she had when her mother had praised her as a little girl.

Sunday 21st December 1862.

Church lasted longer than usual and was followed by the singing of Christmas carols outside the church gate. A local band having first complemented the service was now doing the same for the carol singing. To the entire congregation, it was a joyous experience for the season.

Back home sitting in the study the conversation eventually came around to King Arthur.

"Have you had a look at that book I left?" Polly asked.

"No, I don't believe I have yet; where is it?" Celina said as she started pulling the desk drawers out. "Oh here it is," she said as she pulled it from a drawer. "I might as well have a look now."

441

With a glow over her shoulder to give her plenty of light, Polly and Jane left her in peace saying they were going to play a board game in the day room.

Celina found the book to be old, different and interesting, with outstanding illustrations that had been brilliantly done. The intriguing nature of the work made the reading go quickly and so by half past the hour of six of the clock Celina was almost at the end of the book.

Reaching the death of King Arthur, she found the illustration of his tomb to be beautiful and detailed; with the inscription on one end shown exactly as it had been hundreds of years ago, although Celina knew it had been almost weathered away by now.

She had just turned the page when something made her turn back and look again at the illustration of his tomb. Looking closer she found that what she could see in the illustration didn't quite match what was written in the book. She read the text again; it said.

'These walls protect within all that is left of the days of my life.' Then she looked at the illustrated engraving again. Unable to see it clearly she pulled out a drawer and extracted a glass. Magnified through the glass it looked like Welsh, and yet not Welsh. She looked again and, yes it was Welsh. The text was Welsh but not thirteen-hundred-year-old Welsh.

"That's strange," she said aloud. "A fairly modern Welsh passage written in a book that's nearly twelve hundred years old." Carefully, she copied out the inscription from the illustration and then began to translate it and compare it to the text in the book.... it didn't fit. She tried again.

"'Mae'r waliau cerrig, *These stone walls...*" Yes, she was sure that was right. Then the next bit. "Diogelu o fewn *Protect within....*" Yes, that was it. Then some words were missing. Quickly, she inserted the rest of the words from the illustrated inscription.

Translating them and holding the paper up, she now read the inscription aloud. "These stone walls protect within...." Celina put in the spaces for the missing letters before fitting in the last of the letters. All the days of my life. There weren't enough spaces, but there was space for y llyfr o'r holl 'The book.'

These stone walls Protect within The book of all the days of my life. Celina almost dropped the book. She couldn't believe it; a slight mistranslation and 'The book of all the days of my life' would become 'The Book of Days.'

"Jane, Polly, come quickly," Celina called. The door flew open and Polly wand in hand burst through the door with Jane just behind her. They found Celina holding the book out and actually shaking. "Lo…. Loo…. Look," she stuttered.

"What?" Polly and Jane asked in unison.

"This," Celina said as she thrust the book out showing the picture of King Arthur's tomb. Polly took the book and with Jane peering over her shoulder, they both looked at the picture, neither of them seeing the reason for Celina's excitement. Finally, Jane said "so?" Celina pulled the book around and then ran her finger over the print as she said.

"In the book it states that the inscription on the end stone says. 'These stone walls protect within all that is left of the days of my life.'

"Yes so?" Jane asked again finding the strangest of sensations starting to come over her.

"Well it's the right number of words, but it doesn't fit the illustration. Look here." Celina took the book and laid it on the desk. "Here with the glass you can see the spaces left by the missing letters, look; it doesn't make sense." Polly and Jane looked baffled so Celina continued.

"If you count the spaces left by the missing letters and fit letters in, this fits." She picked up the paper she had dropped on the floor, putting it next to the book to show them.

"These stone walls protect, right that's clear enough. Now put in here and here these two letters that are missing." She pointed to where she had pencilled them in. "Now that one is correct, do the same again here, it then continues without any missing letters or spaces to say. 'The book of all the days of my life'. Now, however, you must retranslate. 'The 'book of all the days of my life.' A simple translation from Welsh could be 'The Book of Days.' The real book of days is in King Arthur's tomb." Polly and Jane both stood eyes fixed on the book.

"You know that could be right," Celina heard Jane whisper under her breath. Then Polly asked.

"Do you think we ought to go there and look?" Jane suddenly looked up as she found herself overcome by an overwhelming need to say.

"Yes it is right; I know it is, and you must look tonight; I don't know why but I just know it, and it must be tonight." She pulled Celina away from the desk and holding her shoulders said.

"Please, you must go tonight. I just know it." Polly put her hand on Celina's arm and said.

"Look Celina, look at Jane, can't you see it?" Celina found herself staring at Jane as for an instant a faint white outline seemed to be surrounding her before it flickered and disappeared as Jane collapsed sobbing into a chair.

"Please go," she said weakly. "Hurry there isn't much time. I don't know why but I know you must go now."

Celina immediately made up her mind pushing Polly out of the study and saying. "Come on take a coat."

Grabbing a coat hat and gloves for herself, and even though it was too large for her Celina pushed one of Jane's coats at Polly, along with a hat scarf and gloves.

As they ran through the kitchen startling Cook, Celina called. "Get Kate to take a brandy to Jane and stay with her until I get back." Then they ran for the stables with both of them now feeling that there was something far more demanding than just curiosity driving them.

Flying alongside Polly and with Polly pushing her broom to its limits it was the fastest Celina had ever made the journey to Glastonbury.

Arriving in haste, they both slid their brooms to a stop just a few inches from the stones of King Arthur's tomb.

Walking around the tomb, they both created glow globes for light. Polly stood closest to the tomb with her glow over her shoulder as she studied what was left of the inscription.

444

"How do we get inside?" Celina asked brushing the mass of hanging dust and stone covered cobwebs away. "There doesn't seem to be an entrance."

Polly walked around the tomb carefully running her hands along the stone.

"The way in must be where the inscription is," Polly said as she stood at the end of the tomb, and then looking up at the slab of stone that formed that end of the tomb she said. "It has to be here, nowhere else would make sense."

Stepping back she moved her glow closer to the stone causing it to grow brighter as she did so. Then Polly stepped forward, and placing her hands on the end stone, a stone slab some seven feet high and five feet wide. Polly spoke one word. "Open."

With a grinding sound the slab moved, hesitated and then pivoted slowly upwards and out, displacing the soil along its bottom edge. The light of Polly's glow which she had hanging in the air in front of her now illuminated a flight of stone steps leading down.

"How did you know to do that?" Celina asked.

"It just seemed the right thing to say, you know to open things," and then looking down the steps. "I never really expected it to work."

With her glow illuminating the steps and seeing what was hanging in front of her, Polly no longer sounding at all sure said.

"Look at those cobwebs, there must be spiders the size of tea plates down there; I suppose we have to go down?"

"I think so," Celina replied with a shudder, and then said. "I hate it when spiders-webs slide across my face, ugh." Then wafting a monstrous one out of the way she started down wafting her hands to keep the cobwebs away from her face. Polly hesitated and with a shiver, she hurried to catch up. Grasping Celina's proffered hand she said.

"Use your shield; it will keep the cobwebs away." With their two glows now hanging just above their shoulders so as to clear the low ceiling they descended. Polly counted twenty shallow steps before coming to a landing where they changed direction turning to the left.

Another twenty steps brought them to another left turn. Two more flights of identical steps and left turns finally brought them to a door. Looking back at the steps Polly said.

"We've been going down in a spiral, so we must still be under the tomb."

"A long way under it," Celina replied. "Look it's all solid rock and bone dry."

"Don't say that." Polly exclaimed as a shiver ran through her.

"Say what?" Celina asked.

"Bone," Polly replied. "We're inside a grave; that is if you remember." Celina ran her hand over the door in front of them, only to find once again that it was a solid slab of stone.

As she pushed on one side, Celina felt it start to give under her hand's pressure. With another harder push and more grinding of stone upon stone it started to pivot and open inward. Celina wafted away the dust and cobwebs, rubbing her nose and trying not to sneeze as she peered into the gloomy darkness ahead.

With Celina sending her glow into the darkness, they found themselves standing in the doorway to the burial chamber, and looking at the body of a man lying on a stone plinth.

His mail, mostly corroded to a red dust, and decaying leather clothing had rotted away to almost nothing. The skin where it remained looked like dried parchment. Celina decided he was just bones lying on stone. The skull itself rested on a stone pillow directing its eyeless sockets toward the door.

Both women hesitated to enter; apart from the body, the room was empty. Celina and Polly both jumped grabbing a hold of one another, as something scuttled across the floor.

"It's all right Polly," Celina said peering around the door trying to see where whatever it was had gone, "no doubt just a large spider." She then looked up again looking over the stone plinth and the body to find she could see in the glows' light that there was yet another door.

"Come on," Celina said as she took Polly's hand again. Easing themselves around the stone plinth they made their way to the door.

The door once again was a solid slab of stone. Celina pushed at it, and as before with a grinding of stone upon stone and a cascade of dust, it opened to reveal what looked to be a small empty room. Celina raised her glow higher to see an ornate wooden lectern placed at the far end of the room; on it was a book.

"That's it," Celina whispered excitedly, and leaving Polly standing in the doorway she moved reverently closer, until she could run her fingers over a perfectly preserved leather cover. Opening it, she found written on the first page:

y llyfr holl ddyddiau fy mywyd

Turning to the next page she was greeted by a beautifully illuminated and artfully drawn gilt-edged decorative rubric. It was followed by closely written words. For some reason, the fact that they were inscribed in modern Welsh didn't register. With Celina, it was as if the book had hypnotised her. Lifting her glow higher she continued to read.

Her surroundings faded from her awareness as she became totally engrossed in the words that flooded into her mind. How long she stood there reading she had no idea. It could have been minutes or hours, but she did not stop until the book finally released her.

The book was a journal of Merlin's life written in exquisite detail and set forth over thirteen hundred years earlier. In it, he shared with the reader, his knowledge and his life. Having read the book Celina now knew all she needed to know of the stones of destiny, the ring of blood, everything and that tonight being the dark of the moon made it the pivotal night. The book had imprinted Merlin's knowledge about many things, in how long.

Celina turned to ask Polly, only to find her slumped sitting on the floor shivering and as white as a sheet. Horrified Celina dropped to her knees as Polly's eyes fluttered open. Looking up with terror in her eyes, Polly flung her arms around Celina's neck clinging and sobbing.

447

"Polly what's wrong?" Celina asked trying to free herself from Polly's embrace. Polly clung to her all the tighter as she sobbed out. "The book, the book."

"Yes I read the book," Celina replied uncertainly. Polly violently shook her head as she said.

"No you didn't look." Celina looked up to find that the room had gone, and with it the lectern and the book. They were back in the tomb. In utter confusion, Celina looked back to Polly again as Polly grabbed Celina's face and pulled it toward her sobbing.

"You didn't read a book." Still holding firmly to Celina's face she sobbed. "You read me." Celina was now totally confused.

"No I read a book," she said looking around for the room. "The Book of Days I read it with my own eyes." Between the sobs Polly said.

"No it was me you were reading, and as you read it, I lived it all, every waking moment of Merlin's life; it's all in here." She let go of Celina with one hand to point to her head. "Every thought, every deed, and every spell it's all in here. I don't know how but it is. He wants to take over my mind, but I won't let him. He keeps on trying; trying to move into my mind but something stops him."

Celina rocked back in shock, but Polly grabbed her shoulders and pulled her back asking. "You know today's date don't you?"

"Yes I know it's the winter solstice and tonight is also the dark of the moon. I read about it in the book." Then with anxiety creeping into her voice Celina asked. "Can you stand? We have to find out just where it will be and stop it, and we don't have much time."

Polly holding on to Celina began struggling to her feet, and then with Celina's help she managed to walk to the stairs. Shaking herself, Polly said. "I think I can manage now; it's easier if I have something to concentrate on."

Her glow appeared over her shoulder where it flickered like a candle in the wind until Polly got it under control. Then with Celina following she started up the stairs. They were about half way to the first turn when they heard the door below them close.

By the time they reached the surface Celina knew she had completely lost track of time and was desperate to find a clock.

"Are you able to help?" Celina asked holding Polly's hands and feeling her trembling. "Do you think you can find Marjory? I think we may need her help."

"Of course I'm able to help," Polly replied trying to sound more confident than she felt, "and I will find Marjory."

"Bring her to London," Celina said. "I'll meet you there but first I need to find a religious site. A site with five sacred artefacts forming a circle around a central object, and I think I will need Claire for that, she's turning into quite the expert on Britain."

Ixcte ~ 5.

Something stirred deep within Ixcte. At first, it was just a flash of red, and then the red was fully there and blazing in all its power. Finally, as if deliberately taunting Ixcte the red's presence slowly faded from Ixcte's awareness.

Ixcte felt fear stirring. First, the black had returned and now the red. The red was always the hard one to find, hiding and striking without warning. First it had been the black, and now the red....

How long would it be before the white returned? It was too late now Ixcte was helpless. The time of the opening of the gate was far too close. Surely, it was too late for the black to interfere now. Nevertheless, fear surged through Ixcte. The gate must be opened, and it must be opened now.

***

Celina mounted her broom as she heard a church clock strike the quarter hour.

"Not much help," she murmured as her broom lifted toward the clouds. Celina knew that Claire had a book in the shop, and she was sure it had something written in it about sisters. Something about five sisters rang a bell in her mind.

As Celina dropped into the back of the shop darkness blanketed the yard. With the darkness and her haste, she almost overshot the yard only just stopping in time. To Celina's horror, the front of the broom was actually touching the back wall of the shop as she stopped.

Not bothering with a key, she simply used a thought to unlock and open the door. Then running through the shop and into the office, she began to search the desk. Using a glow for light she frantically pulled drawers open, pulling out books and papers and yet there was no book.

A new thought sent her running up the stairs to the top floor where she looked along the shelves lined with books, and still there was no book.

In desperation, Celina looked around her until her eyes finally rested on the Telson. It seemed an age before the controller answered and then after he answered, she felt as if she stood for hours drumming her fingers and waiting to be connected. At last, Claire's uncle answered.

"Hello Mr Ellis its Celina, is Claire there?" and then there was that interminable wait again until she heard Claire's voice saying. "Hello Celina, is something wrong?"

"Claire, this is very important; I need that book you had last week, the one on Britain, is it in the shop?"

"No Marcus has it; he wanted to read it before it was sold." Celina took a deep and grateful breath. The words she had dreaded hadn't been spoken.

"I'm sorry I'm in a terrible hurry. Oh and are your parent's home?"

"Yes," Claire said with obvious excitement. "They arrived yesterday and they're staying at a hotel in London, so I will be spending Christmas with them."

"Tell them I look forward to meeting them after Christmas. I'm sorry Claire I have to go; it's another of those you-know-what things, so just in case I don't see you before, have a nice Christmas."

There was a shocked silence for a moment and then Claire said. "Celina, please be careful."

The words echoed in Celina's ears as she replaced the ear speaker. Standing for a moment resting her forehead against the wall and breathing heavily, gathering her breath she turned away from the Telson saying to herself. "Marcus."

Almost falling in her haste she ran down the stairs and out into the back yard, locking the door in passing as she had opened it, with a thought. Then lifting the broom vertically she turned for the home of Marcus. Once above the rooftops and pushing hard it took only a few minutes to reach Marcus's house where a light was burning in the kitchen.

Celina dropped the broom down heavily in the back garden, and was off it and running for the door before the broom had finished sliding across the grass. Running up the steps to the back door she hammered on it calling out.

"Marcus, Marcus," the bolt slid back, and she found Marcus stood before her. "Celina," he began but Celina pushing past him said.

"Marcus I need that book; the one Claire was reading and she says you have it." Marcus pulled his eyes away from the dust and cobwebs covering Celina and pointed to the kitchen table where a book laid open under the lamp. Celina breathed a sigh of relief as she asked.

"Have you come across something, anything with or about five sisters in it, or anything with five in it and to do with the church?"

Marcus shook his head as he said. "No why?" Celina's heart fell as she explained.

"I need a religious object or rather five objects together arranged around a sixth." Marcus glanced at the book and then asked.

"Does it have to be a Christian object or can it be Pagan?" Celina stared at him as she thought for an instant about what she had learned from reading in the tomb before answering. "No, yes, and why?"

Marcus picked up the book and turned a few pages, and then he said. "Well these are the five sisters; they are five Iron Age stones that are arranged in a circle, and in the centre there is an altar stone. They are thought to be a Druid place of worship, would they do?" Celina read furiously for a moment and then said.

"It's in Cumbria near Keswick." Marcus suddenly put two and two together and definitely didn't like the answer.

"This has something to do with demons doesn't it" he asked. Celina looked up from the book and rattled off.

"Yes it has; it has to be the winter solstice and the dark of the moon and tonight's it. Everything will be right at midnight tonight, and all they need to open a permanent portal is the five objects upon which to place the jewels, and a centre object to hold the star." Celina pointed to the book, "and the five sisters will be perfect."

"What about the ring of blood?" Marcus asked.

"A ring of blood that is it, it's just what it says it is, a ring of blood put around the outer edge of the five stones to make a circle, and it has to be given by one living willing human." Celina stopped for breath before saying. "I've got to stop it."

As Celina turned to go Marcus caught her arm and holding her back he said.

"Wait, I'm coming with you." Celina stood held by Marcus halfway to the doorway; hesitated half-turned and replied. "No, it's far too dangerous." Marcus who was still holding her arm pulled her fully round to face him saying.

"Look what happened last time. You may need help and possibly ordinary normal help, and I'm coming." He grabbed a coat off the back of the door, and then he reached into a cupboard taking out a pistol. If not it, the twin to the one Celina had named 'the cannon'. Taking a box of cartridges and shaking some of its contents into his hand, he then pushed the loose cartridges into his coat pocket. "I'm ready," he said blowing out the lamp.

Back in the garden Marcus fastened the lap strap tightly as Celina fastened the new shoulder straps for him saying.

"I'm flying fast so keep these fastened tight, first though I have to see Jane."

Jane was watching from the kitchen and ran down into the yard as Celina landed. Celina gave her no time to ask questions as she had started calling her instructions to Jane even before the broom had reached the ground.

"Call Elizabeth and get her here, just tell her that we will need her. Let her know that Polly has already gone for Marjory and that they are both coming here. When Polly arrives tell her it's the five sisters in this book, on page one hundred and five." Celina thrust the book into Jane's hands.

"It's in Cumbria near Keswick, and I'm going there right now, so tell them I'll see them there." Then she was off again before Jane could even open her mouth to object. As Celina turned her broom to the north, she shouted down. "It's going to be tonight at midnight; it's the winter solstice."

Jane stood frozen and frightened; the fear was not for herself but for Celina. Celina and Marcus against what? She turned and ran into the house for the Telson. Waiting for the call to go through seemed to take forever until at last Elizabeth's mother answered the call.

"Hello Mrs Gibbard, its Jane Celina's maid, is Elizabeth there?" Having asked she then stood waiting for an answer that seemed to take forever to arrive though it was only a moment.

"No," her mother's reply came back. "She's working until midnight. Can I give her a message?"

"No thank you it's urgent; I'll call the hospital myself." The night porter took the call and when Jane asked for Elizabeth, he told her she was somewhere in the hospital and implied that it would be difficult to find her. In desperation, Jane said.

"It's urgent, very urgent would you please find her and tell her that it's Lady Celina calling for her."

There was an immediate change in the voice and manner from the porter as he said.

"Oh if that's the case I have instructions to find her immediately. Do you want to wait, or I can have her call you back if you wish?"

"Please have her call me; I'll stay by the Telson until I hear from her, and it is very," and then with great emphasis; Jane again stressed the words. "Very urgent." It was only a matter of minutes before the call came back.

"Celina," Elizabeth asked.

"No it's me Jane. Celina told me to call and tell you that it's tonight at midnight. Tonight is the winter solstice and Celina knows where it is going to be, and she has gone there with Marcus. Can you come over here now? I don't know what I can do."

"She's taken Marcus!" Elizabeth almost screamed into the Telson.

453

"I don't know why she has, but she has."

"Probably his idiotic idea," Elizabeth's reply came back, and then she asked. "What about Polly can you find her?"

"Celina says she's already on her way here with Marjory."

"All right, I'm on my way now and keep them there until I arrive." Then the Telson went dead leaving Jane standing holding the Telson and shaking all over.

It was less than ten minutes later when three brooms landed one after the other in the stable yard. Jane feeling sick and helpless watched them from the large double doors as Elizabeth, who was the first into the hall had just time to ask.

"Where's Celina gone?" before Marjory entered followed closely by Polly. Jane hurrying them into the study spun the book around on the desk and pointed to the open page as she said.

"Here, the Five Sisters. Celina says that's where it's going to occur and it's going to be at midnight tonight."

"Midnight, how far away is it?" Elizabeth asked looking at her watch.

"Roughly two hundred and fifty miles," Marjory answered. "I know because Fredrick and I, well we used to go there for picnics during the summer, but that was before he passed away."

"We'll never make it," Elizabeth said sitting down. "It's past nine of the clock now." Jane could hear the distress in her voice and knew she was worrying about Marcus.

"We've got to try," Marjory said, and then looking at Polly she said. "Polly might."

Polly looked up from the book and replied. "Yes I can, you two set off now and go on ahead, oh and keep a glow above you so that I can find you above the clouds." Then pulling at

Jane's oversized coat and her flimsy skirts she said. "I need to get changed, I can't fly that far, or that fast in these." Then she turned to Marjory and said.

"You had better tell Elizabeth about her shield and everything else she needs to know for the flight."

Polly and Jane watched as the two brooms disappeared into the night. Polly pulling the oversize coat off as she started towards the stairs, hesitated as she reached the foot and turned to see Jane still standing at the open door staring into the empty sky.

As Jane turned Polly felt her heart wrench at the look she gave her. With a lump in her throat, Polly said. "I'll get changed and catch up with them." Then to reassure Jane, she said.

"Don't worry I know Celina will be all right," and with that Polly ran for the stairs. Jane returned to the study and was about to sit down, but having seen Polly run for the stairs; she found it was all too much for her.

Hearing the thunder of Polly's feet on the stairs, Jane made her decision and shouted. "Polly wait for me; I'm coming with you."

Polly had just reached the landing and hearing Jane; she missed the top step and fell full length. Rolling over she heard Jane running up the stairs.

"Are you all right?" a worried Jane asked as she reached her.

"You're what?" Polly asked.

"I'm coming with you." The look on Jane's face told Polly that frightened or not Jane was determined to go. Jane turned and ran for the next flight of stairs to collect Polly's bag from her room and take it to Celina's room.

Polly watched Jane from where she lay on the landing only half-believing what she had heard. With a last look at Jane, Polly rolled over and pulling her skirts from under her; she half ran and half fell into Celina's room.

Jane threw Polly's bag of flying clothes on to the bed before she started searching through Celina's wardrobe. Polly pulling her flying clothes out of the bag turned to Jane.

"What?" Polly began and then paused. It was as Jane stepped out of her dress and draped it over the bed that Polly became aware of a strange sensation at the sight of Jane undressing.

"Merlin," she muttered, as with a shock she realised what she was experiencing was Merlin's feelings within herself. He was there, and now she understood that Merlin was looking at Jane through her eyes. Polly immediately closed her eyes and thought. *'No if you are going to see any woman undressing you will have to wait and see me.'* The thought shocking both herself and Merlin, the shock to Merlin was enough to allow her to push Merlin back out of her mind.

Hurriedly, she turned away from looking at Jane, who had chosen a plain grey woollen dress.

"Do you think this will do? It's light but warm." She asked as she held it up for Polly to see.

"You'll also need a coat, gloves and a good scarf or hat to cover your head." Polly replied pulling her own dress off, while at the same time taking care just where to look.

After what seemed an age to an impatient Jane, they were both ready and standing by the broom. Jane had approached the broom with a certain amount of dread, and now as she stood nervously looking at it she felt sure that two hundred and fifty miles in two hours would be called serious flying by any Knight's standards.

She reminded herself that she had sat on this one before, and that Polly had even lifted it a few feet into the air. Once Jane was seated Polly adjusted her lap strap and pulled hard as she said.

"Keep it tight as it's only a loan broom so it doesn't have a fancy harness like the one Celina has fitted to hers."

It was as Polly lifted the broom that the sound of the kitchen door opening caused Jane to look down. Cook, Thomas and Kate were now standing looking at them and watching as Polly lifted the broom and rose quickly above the wall. Once above the wall Polly pointed the broom up at about forty-five degrees and said. "Hold tight."

Jane held tightly to the hand bars and pushed her feet firmly against the footboards. Polly pushed, and Jane felt the enormous power behind the broom's acceleration, as Polly launched the broom like a rocket from a tube.

Jane found it was like a large hand forcing her back and trying to tear her hands from the bars. Someone was screaming, and Jane had a feeling it was her. For a moment Jane felt the terror of plunging into what in the dark looked like a solid wall but turned out to be clouds, and then minutes later they were through them.

Once through the clouds Jane found the most wonderful sky she had ever seen. The stars overhead shone like diamonds covering a sky as black as soot. It was a sky no longer dimmed by the smoky air of London. Here the Milky Way was a brilliant band of misty coloured light crossing the sky. Speed ceased to have any meaning under that wonderful expanse of heaven. Jane felt the broom vibrate under her as Polly increased their speed. Gathering her breath, Jane asked.

"How high are we?" Polly thought for a moment before answering and then said.

"The clouds were very thick, so I should say about fifteen thousand feet. I'm using my shield to help us to breathe so are you all right? You're not short of breath or your ears hurting or anything like that?"

"All right, it's marvellous!" Jane exclaimed. "Dear God just look at that sky and the broom, the broom. It's accepted me. It's not pushing me away any more so now I can fly with you and Celina."

"Well I'm glad to hear it so as you're all right I'll go higher where we can travel faster." The vibration from the broom rapidly became worse as Polly pushed even harder and Jane felt the broom rise upward under her.

Jane had lost all sense of time when Polly called out. "Look there they are those two lights down there!" Jane looked where Polly was pointing. Far in front and a long way below she could see a small white light shining against the cloud tops.

"How far away are they?" she asked. Polly looking down guessed.

"About thirty miles, as we're very high compared to them."

"Will we make it there by midnight?" a worried Jane asked. Polly looked at the stars before answering.
"It's going to be close, and I think Marjory must have been coaching Elizabeth; I have to admit they've made better time than I expected."

It was about half an hour later when Polly and Jane slid in alongside Marjory asking. "How much further?" Marjory pointed to where they could see the cloud far in front had a reddish tinge to it.

"I think that's it, about fifteen minutes or maybe twenty no more," she said, and then gasped as the sky in front lit up.

***

"We should be near by now." Celina called to Marcus. "Over there." Marcus said as he pointed slightly left. "There's a glow in the clouds."

"That's it hold on tight," and with that Celina dropped the broom sharply down into the clouds. Only to find below them a night as black as a coalmine, and to make it worse she found it was raining, a fine misty rain. Peering forward through the mist and rain the one thing Marcus could see that was still visible was the red glow in the mist.

"Its there," he called over his shoulder to Celina. "I would say about a mile away." Pushing her shield as far forward as she could and trusting it to guide the broom clear of any obstructions Celina flew on flying blind through the fog and darkness. *We must be in a valley.* Celina thought finding as they drew nearer that the glow was actually reflecting back at them from the clouds above.

Suddenly she felt something brush her shield; it was the ground and it was coming up fast. Celina found herself thanking Polly for her lessons that night as she felt the broom lift to follow the land.

As they neared the top of the hill, the rain turned from a fine misty drizzle to rain, and the glow gradually became a visible shape. Drawing closer still the glow could now be seen as a dome of light bright enough for Celina to see the stones standing inside it.

Marcus on the front seat could see that the dome was just outside a ring of five stones creating a circle of about forty or fifty yards in diameter. He could also see between three of the stones that there was a gap where a complete dark segment was missing from the dome. "Look over there, is that a man?" he called back to Celina as he pointed to one side of the stones. As they neared the stones, Celina swung her broom closer to that side of the stone circle, watching as a man staggered to a stone, almost collapsed and then held on to it as if exhausted.

As he did so another segment of the dome shimmered into visibility. It took one look for Marcus to see that only one segment remained between the stones to complete the circle and the dome.

458

Marcus

Marcus could feel they were descending rapidly. Twenty feet then ten feet and at last Celina dropped the broom less than ten yards away from the man. Marcus suddenly found his safety straps undone. *'Celina must have done it.'* He thought as he came off the broom, staggering and then almost falling as the bracken pulled at his feet.

"Stop him; don't let him complete the circle." Celina shouted to Marcus as she started to run for the large stone in the centre. "Whatever you do, don't let him complete the circle." Marcus heard, as from the corner of his eye, he saw her push through the glow and into the dome.

Marcus was now running towards the man who he could see was almost halfway to the last stone. As Marcus watched, the man for some reason seemed to lose his direction as he half turned staggered and fell to the ground.

Running towards him, Marcus watched, as he seemed to have trouble getting back to his feet. Swaying, he stood only to lurch away from the last stone before turning in a wide circle to stagger back towards it.

Gun forgotten Marcus reached him bringing him down with a shoulder charge and knocking him out and away from the circle, with the force of the blow rolling them both down the slope and away from the stones.

Landing on top of the man, Marcus found him struggling with a strength that amazed him. He was somehow slippery and Marcus found it hard to get a firm hold on him. With a show of strength that Marcus wouldn't have thought he had left the man shook him off sending him rolling down the hill. Marcus on his hands and knees watched as the man staggered back to his feet.

In desperation Marcus threw himself forward, managing to get both arms around the man's ankles pulling him down again. Holding fast to his legs Marcus risked a quick look for Celina and found her about halfway to the circle's centre stone.

In that quick glance, Marcus gained the impression that she was running as if against a strong wind. It was a sight that Marcus remembered for the rest of his life; the vision of Celina running with her hair loose and streaming out behind her.

Marcus was brought back to the here and now as the man rolled pulled one foot free and landed a kick to Marcus's shoulder and then a second one to his chest winding him. Gasping Marcus held on desperately.

Celina

Celina punched through the red glow with her wand held in front of her like a weapon. She could see the altar stone standing about five feet high in the centre of the circle, and that there was something deep in a hollow at its top that was emitting a red glow.

She ran twenty yards and then ten, but the closer she drew the harder it became as something seemed to be holding her and pushing her back. Celina felt as if she was running through molasses and finding every step was an effort. She risked a quick look toward Marcus, relieved to find that he had the man down.

Despite all her efforts, she hadn't covered half of the last ten yards, and she could feel her strength rapidly ebbing. Now her legs felt like jelly; her corset was too tight, and she felt she couldn't breathe. Colours were flashing before her eyes. Three yards to go…. her legs were threatening to give way…. three feet remaining…. At last, she reached out with her left hand and almost falling as she reached up and over the top of the stone and into the hollow.

Unable to see she felt her fingers touch and close on something just as her legs gave way. Then she fell, and continued to fall.

She found herself falling for what felt like miles and miles. Celina vaguely wondered if she was falling into Hell itself. As she made up her mind that she must be dead and going to Hell, she felt the presence of someone falling with her. It was a comforting presence that took hold of her hand….

Marcus

Marcus was lifted off the ground, and then rolling down the slope until a bush of some sort stopped him. Opening his eyes, he looked up the slope only to find he had been blinded by the brilliance of the flash as the dome collapsed. All he could see was a large purple afterglow floating in front of his eyes.

Sitting up and rubbing his eyes repeatedly with hands that felt somehow sticky he tried to look around but all he could see were slowly fading red and purple rings. *'Up the hill,'* he thought. *'I need to be up the hill'.* He felt his way following the rise of the ground as the afterglow faded from his eyes.

He almost walked into one of the stones before he was able to see it, finding that it was now leaning at an angle from the collapse of the dome. Peering into the darkness, he called out Celina's name. Getting no answer, he made his way toward where he thought the centre stone should be.

Eventually, he found its remains now only three feet of jagged and broken stone left drunkenly standing. Turning Marcus almost fell over something. Reaching down in the dark his hand found Celina lying at its base. Marcus still barely able to see felt around to find her face.

Touching it he found it was icy cold. Panicking he felt at her throat and almost cried with relief as he felt her pulse. Pulling his coat off Marcus put it over her, and in doing so finding both his hands and coat sticky with something.

"She needs warmth," he said to himself. "She needs a fire." Marcus looked around but all he could see was wet bracken heather and gorse. Searching in his coat pockets and then Celina's, Marcus eventually found several scraps of paper, and feeling at the bottom of the centre stone he found some nearly dry bracken and dead grass. By now, he could see a little better and making his way from stone to stone, he managed to gather a small amount of fairly dry burnable material.

With a prayer, Marcus put a Lucifer to the paper and then fed the growing flame carefully with small pieces of bracken. Once he had managed to get a few fronds to burn he gradually added more until he had a small fire.

It was by the light of the fire that he found that his hands and the coat covering Celina were covered in blood. Horrified he stood looking at himself, only to realise that it must have come from the other man.

Relieved Marcus gently eased Celina into a more comfortable position, after which he went to attack some gorse bushes, and this time returning cut and bleeding from the gorse. Now with a reasonable fire giving some warmth he settled down with his back to the stone, and holding Celina's head on his lap he prayed for someone to arrive.

It was about fifteen minutes later when the broom carrying Polly and Jane ploughed into the bracken almost throwing them off. Jane flung herself forward with a scream of, "Celina." before she threw herself across the prone body of her friend and companion.

"She's alive," Marcus assured her. Jane running her hand across Celina's face looked up at him and said.

"She's not here." Turning and looking up at Polly, she repeated. "She's not here," before she broke down crying.

Two more brooms slithered to a stop. The first one carried Elizabeth who was undecided whether to throw herself at Marcus or Celina. It was Marcus who decided for her as he said.

"Elizabeth, look at Celina will you? She's unconscious." Elizabeth's medical training took over as she dropped onto her knees by Celina, only then noticing the blood covering the two of them.

"It's all right it's not ours," Marcus said seeing the look on Elizabeth's face. "It's Dr McDonald's; he's somewhere out there, dead I think." As Elizabeth turned back to Celina Jane looked up again saying.

"She's not there; it's just a body her mind's not there." Elizabeth put her hand on Celina's forehead and turning to Polly she said.

"Go to Celina's mother and tell her that Celina's hurt and unconscious. Tell her we need to get her home as soon as possible."

Polly never said a word but dragged her broom out of the bracken, threw herself astride and was away immediately disappearing into the night.

The fire was starting to burn low, so Marjory produced a glow to give heat and light as Marcus eased himself out from under Celina.

"What's this?" Elizabeth asked. Elizabeth could see that Celina's wand was still held tight in her right hand, but she also had something clasped in her left hand, something black and burnt. Elizabeth tried to open her hands only to find that both her hands were locked and immovable.

Marcus was bringing his second load of bracken and heather back when he found the body.

"Elizabeth," he called out. "Have a look over here will you?" Elizabeth produced a small glow as she left Celina in Jane and Marjory's care and made her way across to Marcus.

There lying on the ground was a man with white hair and with more blood on him than Marcus would have thought possible. Elizabeth turned him over to reveal a deep cut right down to the bone across his left wrist.

"I think the cause of death was this." She said pointing at his wrist, "and by the look of it lack of blood. I suppose this is how you come to be in the state you're in, and just what were you doing??"

Marcus who now having seen by the glows light the bloody state that both he and the body were in, found he was starting to feel sick as he replied. "Holding him and trying to stop him completing the circle."

"What was he doing here, and what do you mean? Complete what circle?" Marcus pulling his eyes away from the body asked.

"Do you remember the ring of blood?" Elizabeth nodded. "The one we thought the demons always had?" Marcus swallowing hard as his stomach threatened to empty itself said.

"Well, the ring of blood is just that; a ring of blood around the perimeter of the circle given by one willing human." Elizabeth looked down at the man by her feet and then back at Marcus before saying.

"I don't think they will get many to volunteer twice." Elizabeth had just checked the time on her pocket watch as being half after the hour of one when a broom circled down to land. It was Polly with Lady Mary.

Lady Mary ran over to Celina, and having dropped to her knees she pulled from her bag a crystal, a small bowl and a box of glass vials. Taking the crystal, she held it in her hands over Celina's forehead and closed her eyes.

She remained kneeling like that for two or three minutes as Jane watched desperately hoping that her mother would be able to bring Celina back. Finally, and with relief in her voice Celina's mother said.

"It's not physical, there is no injury to her body but her mind is somewhere else." She reached down lifting first Celina's left and then her right hand.

"I think we'll leave these where they are for now," she said looking at Celina's wand and the blackened object still clenched in her left hand. "I don't feel it would be a good idea to forcibly remove them."

Taking out a small dish, she poured a small quantity of a dark liquid into it. Dipping a second crystal into the liquid, she placed the crystal on Celina's forehead, and then putting her hand over the crystal she waited.

With a shake of her head, she removed the crystal, cleaning it before wiping Celina's forehead, only then did she repack everything in her bag as she said.

"She is totally exhausted, far worse than when she fought the demon, so first we need to get her home and then we must wait. Her body's hold on her mind is still strong so I believe it's just a matter of time." Then turning to Jane, she said.

"Will you stay with her? She needs you." Then looking at Jane in surprise as she realised for the first time the significance of Jane's presence she asked. "How did you get here?"

It was another hour before Lord James arrived with the large broom. Then Lady Mary insisted that Jane should ride back with Celina which she did holding her close all the way.

"The body of Dr McDonald," Lord James said after having had a look at it. "Can be collected in the morning, as I don't think he will be going anywhere tonight."

Autumn ~ 232 A.D.

Merlin stood and looked at the mountains rising in the distance. It had been many years since he last looked on the mountains of his birth. Resting on his staff, he tried to remember just where his long-gone village used to be.

He shook his head as the memories eluded him; it was too long ago. Shifting the pack to a more comfortable position on his shoulder, he made his way into the foothills knowing he needed to reach the coast before the arrival of winter.

Merlin found that the stretch of water between the island and the mainland had surged with the tide, and now surrounded by the surging water, he found he understood the reason why the fisherman had told him that it was not a pleasant place to cross.

Merlin found himself gripping the sides of the frail skin boat as the tide pulled it first one-way and then another. The fisherman paddled furiously, first on one side and then the other as they slowly made headway toward the far shore.

At last it was a relieved cold and wet Merlin who stood on the shore and watched as the fisherman pulled his boat through the shallows.

"By all the gods," Merlin muttered to himself. "I've got to go back eventually; I hope Morgana knows a better way."

Picking his way between the rocks and piles of driftwood Merlin finally reached dry ground and stopped. Turning to the fisherman he fumbled in his belt for the promised coppers and then paid for his passage in full, before adding an extra copper having now experienced the crossing himself.

Casting around with his mind Merlin picked out the general direction of Morgana, and turning in that direction, he studied the climb from the beach and the steep wooded rise beyond towards the centre of the island. Only then with a groan and grumbling to himself did he finally make a start.

It took Merlin four days picking his way through steeply wooded hills and valleys before finally he reached the area overlooking the straits and the mountains of the mainland. Evening was fast approaching as he came in sight of a fair-sized stone and turf dwelling.

Despite the distance and the gathering darkness, the figure standing and watching for his approach was even after all the ensuing years still familiar. He drew closer and then before he realised it; he was running, running toward a woman who was running towards him.

It was the chill of evening that finally set them walking back to the house. Looking at his sister, he was pleased to find she looked just as he remembered her, and that this memory was one memory that hadn't faded over the years. He found himself wiping tears from his eyes as for some reason he wanted to cry.

Morgana also was overjoyed to have her brother back with her again after how many years of separation, she could no longer remember just how long, but it had been she knew, far too long.

Morgana looked at him again, finding his hair was longer, and he had a beard, but it was still Merlin. She found herself smiling, seeing that Merlin was wearing what seemed to be a ridiculous and battered fox skin hat. Looking at it, Morgana couldn't resist it; she had to tweak its tail as she followed Merlin into her home.

Morgana had a meal waiting and she sent Merlin to wash while it was laid out. That evening Merlin felt that he had never tasted meat as delicious as in the meal that Morgana served. He had no idea what kind of meat or what the vegetables were that she had served with it, but he completely cleaned the bowl, and even wiped it out with some of the best bread he had ever eaten.

Finally, Morgana cleared the low table and put things away. When she eventually returned to Merlin, she found him fast asleep.

The following morning, clean-shaven and with his hair trimmed, Merlin looked just as he had when they had parted long ago on the banks of a long-lost river. Sitting in the morning sun, Morgana decided that now was as good a time as any to talk.

"Well," she asked expectantly.

"Well what?" Merlin replied.

"You must have had a reason to come all this way, and I'm sure it's not just my cooking."

Merlin sat for a moment leaning back with his eyes closed before he asked. "Do you remember that village I showed you?"

"I remember," she replied with a shudder. "Did you find any more like it?"

"One or two," he replied slowly. "Seven I think it was." Morgana sat waiting but Merlin just sat with his eyes closed still leaning against the house wall.

"What's this got to do with me?" she finally had to ask.

"Oh about twenty years ago, I was camped somewhere." Merlin opened his eyes and sat forward. "I can't remember where but something came looking for me."

"Something,"

"Yes something, it wasn't a man; it was a Sishky."

"A what?.

"A Sishky," he replied.

"What's a Sishky?" Morgana found herself asking.

"It's a long story and not a very nice one." Merlin replied somewhat evasively.

"Go on then tell me, we've got all winter." Morgana assured him. Merlin began slowly and hesitantly saying.

"It came upriver to find me not trying to hide and making enough noise so that I would know it was coming. I was just about to try and destroy it when it sat down and raised its hands with its palms away from me."

"It did what?" Morgana asked.

"You heard me," Merlin retorted. "Anyway it then drew a picture in the sand. The picture was of it and me together looking at the sand. I assumed from this that it wanted to talk, and we've been talking on and off ever since."

"Do you mean to say you talk by drawing pictures in the sand?"

"No, by now it understands what I say, and I can understand what it says. Now when I find words that I can't say, I can just speak as I would normally, and it understands me, and it is the same for words it can't say it says them in its language and that way we understand each other quite well.

The Sishky are surprisingly intelligent and friendly. They can also do much of what we do; more and better in some things and not as good in others."

Morgana sat thinking and then asked. "If that's the case why kill the villagers?" Merlin leaning back against the wall explained.

"It wasn't the Sishky who killed them. There are three intelligent types of beings where they come from. First, there are the Sishky, which are small and about my height. Then there are the Cesdrik, which are twice my height and very strong. The Cesdrik are resistant to most of our powers, although they are not able to do much power-wise themselves.

Then there is Ixcte. Ixcte is something different, and it doesn't belong in their world. It came from another world to theirs probably by accident. At first, it was small about the size of a slug but over the years it grew to be powerful and huge.

It feeds by taking over its victim's mind and making them come to it. Only small things came at first, insect like things, and other small living things. Then as it grew it could command larger and larger things. Finally, it found the Cesdrik.

At first, they were small and it just fed off them. Then it started to breed them to make them larger to be able to use them as slaves as well as food.

Now here's the nasty part; it feeds like a spider. It has arms with a mouth on the end that it bites its victim with, and then it injects venom like a spider does. It doesn't kill immediately, but as the internal organs slowly dissolve Ixcte feeds on the liquefied contents, and also; it feeds off the pain of its food. It keeps them alive and in pain for about an hour before it sucks them dry leaving just an empty shell."

Morgana sat there not knowing whether to believe him or not. Finally, she asked. "What has this to do with us?"

"Two things, first Ixcte is going to need more food and very soon, and by that it means us. Secondly I like the Sishky and they're fighting a losing battle against it. Normally, they live a very long time and like us; they exist in families.

I don't know how it works, it did try to explain but it was too complicated for me to understand. A Sishky family unit consists not of a man and a woman but of three individuals and in their life they normally have only five or six young, rarely more."

Morgana sat quietly looking out over the straits at the mainland absorbing and pondering over what she had been told as Merlin sat watching her.

"Well go on then," she finally said. "I still want to know what all this has got to do with me."

Merlin sat in silence as she watched waiting until he said. "Well, they want our help."

Once more, silence followed as she waited for Merlin to continue; until eventually, her curiosity made her ask. "How can we help them if we are here, and they are there?" Merlin sat in silence and then finally he said.

"They say they can teach us a lot about our ability."

"Such as?" Morgana asked.

"Well for instance, I managed to kill that first one but I don't really know how, and I haven't been able to do anything like it since. They say they will teach me and show me how I did that and other things."

Morgana sat looking at her brother and then asked again. "Yes but I still want to know; what's it got to do with me?"

"Like I say, they want our help." There was silence as she waited before asking.

"Against Ixcte, it's there and we are here, so how can we help just the two of us?"

"We have powers they don't, and the powers we do have are more destructive while theirs are more.... well, for a better word creative." Morgana hearing this still wasn't satisfied. She felt there was still more to come.

"You're not telling me everything. There's a catch so tell me now."

"They want us to go to their world to learn from them, and then they want us to stay and fight Ixcte with them. They also hope we can teach them some of our abilities so as they can better defend themselves."

Morgana was already on her feet and backing away, saying.

469

"No! No way am I going into some other world filled with strange creatures. I may be old, but my minds not that rotten yet. No, not me, there is no way am I going."

Merlin sat quietly and watched as she stormed back into her home.

Monday 22nd December 1862.

A sombre household met for breakfast that morning, with Celina lying in bed as if dead, and Jane sitting with her refusing to leave her side. Polly also sat glumly blaming her late arrival for Celina's condition.

Finally, Lady Mary decided enough was enough, and that it was time at least for Polly to look like a woman again. Taking her into one of Celina's sister's rooms she started to pull out clothes, and finding some to fit, she pestered Polly into getting changed.

It was as Polly removed the trousers that Lady Mary's eyes widened, and she burst out laughing. Having a struggle to compose herself she finally asked. "Where did you get those?"

For a moment, Polly was confused looking up at her blankly. Lady Mary then pointed to Polly's undergarments and said.

"Those undergarments, just where did you get them?" Polly looked down saying.

"They were Robert's; Jane let me use them as trousers aren't that pleasant otherwise."

Lady Mary still laughing replied. "Yes I can imagine they aren't."

Lady Mary and Polly eventually returned to the day room with Polly looking a little less upset, less like a boy, and a lot more like a lady.

It was dark, and the candle had burned down to a stub when Jane awoke. She had fallen asleep across Celina's bed still holding Celina's hand.

"Jane," Jane heard Celina's whisper. "Are you awake?" Jane jerked upright.

"Celina," a pinprick of light appeared at Jane's fingertip, not much brighter than the candle but illuminating Celina's face.

"I've seen things Jane," Celina said as she lay with her eyes closed. "Horrible things," then she asked. "Is Polly here?" As Celina spoke she moved and her hands relaxed allowing the object she had held clenched in her left hand to fall to the floor. It lay there blackened and twisted; it was what remained of the star of destiny.

Seeing that Celina's hands had finally relaxed Jane reached over and held out the sheath for Celina's wand, sliding it over the wand before Celina let it go.

"Jane, I need to speak to you and Polly."

"In the morning." Jane said. "Your mother will want to see you first."

"My mother, what is she doing here in London?" Celina asked in surprise.

"You're at home in Ripon not in London," Jane told her. Celina tried to remember, but her brain felt like it was stuffed with wool.

"Yes now I remember; we went to the circle.... did we stop it?" she asked anxiously.

"Yes you did you and Marcus." Jane reassured her as she reached across and pulled the bell.

Almost immediately, Celina's mother was there to be closely followed by her father. Jane moved aside standing waiting nervously as her mother examined Celina. Finally, her mother relaxed and said.

"She's all right, still very weak but all right, so I've put her to sleep for now as what she needs is proper sleep and rest." Then turning to Jane she said. "You young lady, you must go directly to bed." Looking at her again, she said. "Or get something to eat and then go to bed, you look worse than Celina."

Celina woke the following morning and within minutes was feeling as bright as a button. She was obviously in fine spirits and claimed she had no residual problems apart from her left hand that was still slightly burnt; on hearing this, her mother was soon attending to it with a minor pain block.

Celina's only remaining complaint was that she was not allowed out of bed, so it was the middle of the morning before Celina Jane and Polly finally managed to get some privacy.

"Exactly what happened?" Polly asked Celina.

"Well I'm not really sure; I remember getting my hand on the star and then…. Then it was as if I was falling. I seemed to fall an awful long way; it seemed like miles but all the time I was falling, I felt as if I was not alone.

There was a presence there, as if a woman was falling with me; it was almost as if she was holding my hand. As we fell, she told me things somehow putting them in my head, so I knew that I had to see something important and that she would show it to me.

"Then when I finally stopped falling I found myself under an orange sky with red sand below me. It was as if I was flying, but I had no body. I flew for miles; I think it must have been over a desert,

Then I followed some demons across the desert; it was like following a trail of ants. I don't know how far we travelled but I had to follow them a long way until I saw it.

It was enormous. It must have been at least half a mile across and it snaked across the sand like, well like a snake or a massive river. The thing itself was hundreds of feet high and five or more miles long."

Celina stopped to think for a moment before saying. "I know what it looked like…. It was as if the sea had dried up around an island, that's what it looked like.

As we got closer I could see what looked like millions of the demons. At first I didn't know what they were doing. I flew along for possibly two or three miles before I realised." Celina now had her eyes closed and her face had lost what little colour it previously had, and she had started to shake with the memory.

"I finally realised that it wasn't a building or an island; it was actually alive. It was a great red-brown slug-like thing with millions of thin legs, or at least that's what it looked like.

There were two head's, each with horn-like eyes rearing up out of it. They seemed to rise up hundreds of feet above its body. Each head had four eyes just like a slug's eyes standing out on stalks and twisting and turning." Celina shuddered.

"Around the base of where the heads came out of the body there was a fringe of thicker and longer tentacles that reached down over the sides and across the sand. Then as I came closer I could see that all along its body the legs were really long thin tentacles some of them hundreds of feet long, and each one was attached to a demon.

The woman with me told me that it was feeding off the demons by sucking their insides out. I watched as each one was sucked dry and then a demon would remove its empty shell, and then another demon just walked up and took its place." Celina was now shaking as if cold and sitting with her eyes open, but Jane felt not seeing, and the look. Jane couldn't describe the look on her face other than a kind of sick revulsion.

"As we got closer I could feel it; it was like I was almost inside its mind. It was then that I felt its hunger, it doesn't just feed on them physically." Her hand reached for Jane's taking hold for comfort, and Jane could feel the sickness in Celina's heart as she remembered it.

"I knew that it also feeds on their pain. It injects something into them just like a spider does and it dissolves them from the inside out. Only this venom doesn't kill, they stay alive right until the end. I could feel their pain, and I could feel its enjoyment of their pain and the way it fed off it before they died, and then." Celina's shaking stopped for a moment or two, and then it started again as she continued to say.

"I could taste what it tasted like." Celina had to stop unable to go on as Jane held her close. Celina's shaking stopped, and she started speaking again.

"The woman told me that it's hungry, and it's grown so large that soon it's going to be eating faster than the demons breed. That's why it wants us, and that's why it wanted a permanent large portal. It wanted to extend itself into our world and take over our minds and feed off of us just as it does the demons. That's how it hunts; it takes over its prey's mind and then draws it to it."

Both Jane and Polly were now holding Celina's hands while Jane pulled the covers up around Celina, who was shivering again and staring into the distance.

"It wants to make us a source of food. It's frightened of something from our world. After that something pulled me away and I was back here."

She looked at them with eyes focused on something only she could see and said. "The creature like an island, it has a name. Its name is Ixcte." She blinked and looked at them, looking at them as if she had just awakened.

"Now I want to get up," she said. Pushing the covers back she swung her legs over the edge of the bed, and getting to her feet she said. "Jane where are my clothes?"

When Celina arrived in the dining room Lady Mary was annoyed, and more than a little mystified. Celina should have been in bed totally exhausted, and yet here she was as bright as a button and full of energy. It should have taken at least three or four days for her to recover.

Lady Mary knew that when Celina had been put to bed her talent had been completely depleted. It was at least as bad if not worse than when she had destroyed the demon. Now Lady Mary watched Celina talking to Jane and Polly and couldn't believe or understand her rapid recovery.

After talking to Jane and Polly Celina turned and looked in her mother's direction.

"Mother," she said crossing over to her. "I was just wondering; would it be all right seeing as we're all here now if everyone stayed for Christmas?"

"I assumed you were, or at least you Jane and Polly."

Celina kissed her mother and said. "Good now we only have three things to sort out."

"Three?" her mother asked curiously.

"Yes, first Polly had arranged for Nancy to spend Christmas with us in London, and now we won't be there. Second, all the presents are still down in London and need to be brought up here, and third; I'm worried about our staff down in London. All though I rather think they will have made arrangements with friends in London by now, I know Jane says Thomas has."

"Well I suppose that Polly can go and collect Nancy first thing tomorrow morning. I take it Nancy knows Polly's a Knight?"

"Yes mother I believe she does, or at least she knows she's a witch."

"Well that's settled then, and we can either put a bed in Polly's room, or better still if we give Polly your sister Anna's rooms Nancy can have the adjoining bedroom. As for the presents, your father can take Mr Ross tonight and collect them; he can also see the servants at the same time."

"Thank you mother; I knew you couldn't resist inviting us all." Then after giving her mother a hug, Celina bounced her way back to Polly to give her the good news.

After hearing Lady Mary's plans, it was an overly excited Polly who ran across the room and threw her arms around Celina's mother saying.

"Oh Lady Mary, thank you so much!" Lady Mary extracted herself from Polly's embrace and then held her at arm's length as she said.

"Now Lady Polly, there's just one thing we have to make clear. If you continue to call me Lady Mary, then I shall have to call you Lady Polly."

Polly looked totally lost as she asked. "If I don't call you Lady Mary, what can I call you?"

"Well as you haven't a mother you can either call me mother as Jane does, or just plain Mary, after all that's what I was before I claimed my wand, and then I would be permitted to call you Polly."

"But you're married to Lord Carvel a proper Lord with a proper title, so surely I should address you correctly?"

"Listen Polly, James sets far more store in his church title than his parliamentary one. When we were in college, we were eight Ladies and two Lords and none of us used our titles. I didn't know James was the eldest son of Lord Carvel until after he had asked me to marry him." Polly stood back and looked at Lady Mary a moment before replying.

"I don't remember my mother, so will it be all right if I call you Aunty Mary?" Lady Mary reached out, and took Polly into her arms and hugged her. There were tears in her eyes, and she was sure there were tears in Polly's eyes too.

Wednesday 24th December 1862.

Before first light Polly was away on Celina's broom wearing a dress and actually looking like a Lady as she headed for the orphanage. Tucking the broom among the branches of the little wood that had been used before, Polly made her way along the lane to the main door of the orphanage.

A pull of the bell brought a smartly uniformed girl of about ten to ask her business. Polly was then shown into the same room as on her previous visit where she was again asked to wait.

Now standing there she found herself a bundle of nerves as she waited for Nancy. It was only a few minutes before Mrs Philips and Nancy arrived, with Nancy carrying a small bag packed with her few clothes.

"Good morning Lady Cavendish," Mrs Philips said. "Would you like a warming drink, as I believe it is rather a cold morning and we have hot chocolate ready?"

Polly who was very tempted by the thought of hot chocolate decided against it saying.

"I'm afraid we have quite a long journey in front of us, and I would like to get us both home before Christmas is over."

Mrs Philips herself saw them to the door and wished them both all the best for the Christmas season.

It was several minutes later that Mrs Philips suddenly found herself wondering. *'Strange, where did she leave her carriage?'*

Once away from the orphanage Nancy asked. "Are we really going to London?" Polly who was holding her hand looked down and said.

"Not this time, this time we are going to stay at Lord and Lady Carvel's for Christmas."

"Who are Lord and Lady Carvel?" Nancy asked curiously.

"Lord James and Lady Mary Carvel are the parents of two friends of mine, Celina and Jane, and I know you'll like them."

"How are we going to get there?" and then with some trepidation she asked. "Are we going on a broomstick?" Polly had a feeling Nancy didn't really expect a yes as she said.

"Yes we are, as Celina has very kindly let me use hers especially to collect you."

"Go on, there's no such thing as a flying broomstick. It's all made-up everyone says so."

It was at this point that Polly stopped and looked around before turning to Nancy asking. "What about this then?" As she spoke she lifted a branch and pointed underneath. Nancy stared for a moment and then asked. "What is it?"

"That Nancy," Polly said. "Is a real broomstick that flies." Then with a smile she held out her hand, and the broom lifted off its rack and moved towards them.

Nancy squealed with either delight or fear, Polly wasn't sure which as the broom floated backwards out from under the trees. Looking around, Polly found Nancy with fists pressed against her mouth and her bag dropped in the lane as she backed away from the advancing broom.

The broom settled into place with its footboards about six inches above the ground waiting. Polly picked up Nancy's bag and fastened it behind the rear seat before holding out her hand.

Nancy slowly came toward her with eyes wide with wonder and asked. "Does it really fly?" Polly put one arm around her as she answered.

"It had better, or we're in for a very long cold and…." looking up, "wet walk back." She then held out her hand as a snowflake settled on her palm.

Nancy was now shivering whether from cold fright or just plain excitement; Polly wasn't sure which as she fastened Celina's additional safety straps over Nancy's shoulders. Polly then mounted the broom and lifted it off the ground. There was a squeal from Nancy as Polly with unusual care lifted toward the clouds. While in the clouds, snow fell heavily across Polly's shield, but once they rose above them the sun shone pleasantly warm.

Above the clouds, Polly found that she could push without alarming Nancy, so they were about halfway back to Brimham hall when Nancy, who had been watching the slow-moving clouds, looked over her shoulder asking. "We're not going very fast are we?"

"Aren't we," Polly asked as she partially slipped her shield aside and for an instant an icy wind slammed into them taking Nancy entirely by surprise, and leaving her breathless and shivering as Polly said.

"We're going at least a hundred miles an hour."

Celina's mother eventually dragged Celina back to her bedroom insisting she wanted to check Celina and make sure she was recovering properly, while Celina was adamant that she had fully recovered.

"Look Mother, I feel fine."

"So you say," her mother replied. "But I still want to make sure that there are no lasting after effects." Her mother opened her bag and took out the same crystal she had used earlier. Placing some oil in a dish, she immersed the crystal and placed it on Celina's forehead, resting her hand over it. Celina lay quiet for a time and then pulled a face at her mother.

"Stop that," her mother said. "I'm concentrating." Celina then crossed her arms over her chest and played dead. It only took a few moments, and the examination was complete, but Lady Mary remained bewildered.

Celina seemed to be fully recovered from total exhaustion in only one day. No one recovered his or her talent that fast. She cleaned the crystal and put it away, after which she wiped the oil from Celina's forehead. Now sitting back and looking down at her daughter she asked.

"All right, I want to know how you do it."

"Do what?" Celina said as she opened one eye to look at her mother.

"Recover so fast, it's not normal; you have a way of regaining your strength far faster than a normal talent, so how is it done?"

Celina sat up to face her mother, thought for a moment and then said.

"All right Mother. I do have a way and so do Polly and Marjory, but were not allowed to tell other people," Then with just a hint of a smile Celina asked, "so are you other people?"

"No, I'm a mother," Lady Mary replied with an equal smile in return. Celina, now with a sly grin said.

"Good then I can tell you. When Polly was at the orphanage she did things to help the other girls, mostly to protect them and herself."

"Yes I know that," Lady Mary said wondering where Celina was leading. Celina continued ignoring her mother's interruption.

"Yes Mother you may know that, but what Polly didn't know was the correct way to use her talent, so." Celina shrugged. "She did what she had to do her own way. When you or I use our talent all the energy we use comes from within us." Her mother nodded and said.

"Yes it comes from inside and when we use an excessive amount, we have to regenerate it within ourselves, and it leaves us tired until we do."

Celina shook her head and said.

"No mother as it turns out that's wrong. Polly never did it that way."

"She must do, there' is no other way."

"No mother there is another way, Marjory and Polly have worked it out and in doing so they discovered why we are different from ordinary people. Marjory says that everyone has a type of inner shield that keeps us well, 'us'. The difference between us and other people is our inner shield is faulty."

Seeing the doubtful expression on her mothers face Celina asked. "Are you following this Mother?" Whether her mother was following Celina or not she nodded saying. "Go on."

"Well it turns out that a power actually exists all around us, the same power we need when we use our talent. Normally the inner shield keeps it out but like I said our shield is faulty, and it let's some leak in and when enough gets in we can use it."

Celina's mother sat silently thinking and then said.

"You mean when we use our talent we use up what we have inside us, and then we have to wait for some more to leak in?"

"That's it exactly Mother, only Polly never used her store of this inside energy, she always used it directly from the outside, and because of that she has always had unlimited power, and so she never feels tired after using it."

479

Celina's mother nodded and said. "Yes if what you say is true I can understand that, but you were exhausted yesterday."

"That was yesterday, when I woke up today all I had to do was lower my shield and let the power rush in, and then I was fine."

Lady Mary sat on the bed with her hand resting on Celina's. She was a doctor and a healer, and she knew she was one of the best. It was her awareness of people's internal malfunctions and health that made her a good doctor. Resting her hand lightly on Celina's was all she needed to understand what she had been told.

Through her hand, she could feel something in her daughter; it was something she had never felt before in the resistance to intrusion that everyone has. She could feel the shield that kept a person an individual. The resistance that as a Doctor Lady Mary was so good at slipping past in looking for illnesses and problems in her patients. In Celina, it was different, in Celina it was fluctuating. First it was there and then not, and then it was back again.

Lady Mary then probed even deeper until she became aware of the flow of something into Celina. She noticed that it flowed most freely when the shield was weak. She next probed for the energy, but it shied away from her as she looked for it. It was almost as if it ran away from her yet if she ignored it, it was there. Puzzled she withdrew her awareness.

Celina looked at her mother and then raised one eyebrow and asked. "Well, what did you find?"

"So that's how you do it? Is that it, can it really be so easy?" she asked clearly astonished at her findings.

"Yes Mother it really is, but once you understand how to do this and start using power this way it is vital for you to remember one thing. Don't ever try to gather power and then use it with your shield up. Whatever you do don't, if your shield traps it, it will bounce back at you and release itself on you. Do you understand what I mean?"

Lady Mary opened her mouth to answer and then went pale as she thought through the devastating consequences of such an act. They both turned as Jane opened the bedroom door and with a smile asked. "Is she still with us?"

Lady Mary rose to her feet and cheerfully replied. "She most certainly is, and she's fit and well."

"Good because Polly has just arrived with Nancy." Jane then held the door open for their mother, who with a backward glance at Celina left them.

Nancy stood looking up at the house. Looking at her Polly could see the fear in her young eyes. To Nancy, the house was enormous. Even partially hidden by swirls of snow it was far larger and more imposing than the orphanage. Polly racked her broom in the stables and then taking Nancy's hand they started toward the house. After a few steps Nancy suddenly held back whispering.

"We can't go in there; it's a Lord's house." Polly put an arm around Nancy and pulling her close she said.

"Yes it is, and it belongs to Lord and Lady Carvel."

"Are you a servant here?"

"No, like I said I'm a close friend of the family, and we have been invited to share Christmas with them."

"No Polly, I can't go in there." Nancy said now with a tremor of fear showing in her voice. "It's too posh for the likes of me; I need to go in by way of the kitchen." Polly turned Nancy to face her and said.

"Nancy, it's all right you're with me, and I'll look after you now just as Celina looked after me when I first came here. Don't you worry about a thing, besides you already know Robert?"

"Is Robert here?"

"Robert is coming home today and he should be here very soon, so come on and let's be out of this snow."

Together Polly and Nancy climbed the steps to some magnificent doors where to Nancy's surprise she found that a smartly dressed man had opened them as they approached. A young woman took their coats and other outdoor clothing as they entered the hall, and then in a daze Nancy was shown into Lady Mary's reception room.

Finding a room filled with what to her were posh people caused Nancy to hang back and press into Polly's skirts trying to hide. Seeing a child so nervous and near to tears, Lady Mary immediately took charge. Dropping on her knees in front of

Nancy, she took her hands gently in her own while leaning just a little to ease Nancy's fears as she said.

"Come now Nancy, you know me and you know Polly, and Robert will be here soon." It was as Lady Mary knelt before her that the face that had seemed familiar took on a name; Dr Carvel. With a feeling of relief, Nancy managed a small nod as she heard Lady Mary say.

"Now do you see that Lady with the red hair?" Lady Mary pointed to Celina.

"That Lady is my daughter Celina, and the one with the blonde hair is my other daughter Jane. Now Polly here hasn't got a mother, so she calls me Aunty. I know you haven't got a mother, and Polly is like your big sister so will you call me Aunty as well, will you do that just for me?" Nancy nodded timidly.

"Now I'll let you in on a little secret. Jane the blonde lady there isn't really my daughter, but I love her just as much as I love Celina, so can I love you too?"

A very, very quiet, "yes" came from Nancy.

"Now as it's Christmas how would you like some nice new clothes?" There was another little nod from Nancy. Lady Mary turned to Jane and said.

"Jane I'm sure that after having seven girls in this house, we can find something to fit our new addition to the family, and I think your expertise with hair will also be needed."

Then with Jane holding her hand, Nancy was escorted out of the room with just one backward glance at Polly, who gave her the biggest smile and wink she knew how.

It was almost two hours later when a new Nancy returned. She was beautifully dressed in some of Celina and Jane's outgrown clothes. With her hair washed scented and re-arranged by Jane, she looked a very new Nancy, so new that Robert didn't recognise her when he finally arrived.

With the weather having been cloudy all the way both to London and back, and with low cloud and snow over London it was possible using the large broom to make the journey in the daylight, allowing Lord James to return home in the afternoon.

All the presents except one were placed in the hall under a tree, a tree that Polly had dragged Robert and Nancy out to cut. Then they spent the rest of the evening decorating it. As the newly purchased tree decorations had remained at Belgrave house,

Polly finished this tree off with hundreds of little glow lights spread across the branches. Seeing Celina's look of surprise she said quietly. "It's a Merlin thing; I'll tell you more about it later."

It was later that night that Jane quietly informed Polly that Nancy had never seen a bath for just one person before, and it hadn't taken much to persuade her to try it. What with the hot water, scented soap and other things to enjoy it took longer to get her out of the bath than to get her in.

Thursday 25th December 1862.

Breakfast was a rushed and excitable affair with everyone, including the house staff wanting to see the back of it. With having a tree the presents were arranged in two rings. The inner ring was for family and the outer ring for the household servants. It was a family tradition that presents between family and servants were the first to be opened. After that the family opened their personal presents.

After all the presents from under the tree had been opened, Lord James asked. "Now what about that big one, the one we had to leave in the old tack room?"

Celina and Jane looked at each other and then in perfect unison said. "The big one, that's for Polly." Then each taking hold of a hand they rushed Polly out to the stables where they stopped just outside the old tack room door. While Celina covered Polly's eyes with her hands, Jane pulled the doors open....

"Now you can look," Jane said. Polly stood still for long moments unable to believe her eyes. It was like nothing ever built before. Longer by about three feet than a normal two-seat broom, it was a conveyance the like she had never dreamed of.

In front of the first seat was a covered luggage area tapering from a blunt point at the front, and continuing back and up to the first handgrips making a large storage container.

While at the back another large covered luggage container ran from the back of the rear seat and down to the flair of the tail.

The footboards seats and handgrips were all positioned differently from a normal broom. With the seats being more substantial and padded for extra support on sharp turns, all of this giving a more relaxed and comfortable riding position over long journeys.

Finally, the whole thing was exquisitely painted and decorated in two shades of red, with a small brass fire-breathing dragon mounted on the front box. The whole broom with its smooth lines was so sleek and shiny it looked as if it was doing a hundred miles an hour while still sitting on its footrests.

Jane went to the front and released two clips to open the front storage area revealing a space large enough to hold Polly's bag with ease. Celina did the same at the rear showing another ample storage space. Then patting the shaft Celina said.

"It's fifty percent thicker and made to take at least one hundred percent more push without vibration."

Polly found her arms around Celina and tears running down her cheeks, and then noticing Jane within reach she pulled her into the embrace as well with Jane saying. "Celina really had to twist some arms at the Abbey to make a broom like this; Claire drew a picture of it, at least what she thought it should look like and then Marcus put his ideas to it, namely the dragon."

"Then we had it built," Celina said excitedly. Polly was by now sitting on a barrel crying as looking up at Celina, she asked. "Is it really for me?"

"I owe you my life Polly, at least twice, so Jane and I decided to buy you a broom worthy of the fastest witch in the sky." Lord James coming over handed Polly her coat and hat, saying.

"They say you're the fastest there is, so I'd like you to take me for a flight and prove it." Then pulling on his own coat he walked over to the broom. Polly looked at all the smiling faces and then pulling on her coat and hat, she turned to Lord James and said. "Your steed awaits you."

Lord James settled himself into the front seat with a nod of approval at the comfort given by the new style of seat. Finding the safety straps were similar but sturdier to the ones on Celina's broom, he again nodded his approval.

"Ready," Polly asked, and then with a lift she flew the broom out and into the yard. Once outside Polly lifted to about four feet above the ground and said to Lord Carvel.

"Are you sure you want a true speed test?"

"I'm certain of it," he replied with a smile. Polly then looked over to Celina and her mother, and with a wink said.

"You are my witnesses, so just remember that he asked for it." Then she pointed the front of the broom toward the clouds and pushed. With a howl from Lord James, and in the blink of an eye, the broom was just a small dot in the sky.

When Polly and Uncle James as he now insisted she call him returned, he was enthralled. He vouched that Polly had indeed pushed a broom the fastest and highest he'd ever flown, and he wanted to know all about the new broom's design. After some discussion, he said that both he and Mary "simply must have one."

Polly fairly radiated happiness and smiled back her joy. Just watching her, Celina and Jane both felt that it had capped off a wonderful Christmas morning.

Polly

It was some time after eleven of the clock, and Celina was in that state that was neither awake nor asleep when a light tapping at her door brought her fully awake. Then the door opened, and Polly's head peered around it and asked.

"Can I come in?"

Celina pulled herself up propping herself against the head of the bed and then beckoned. Polly came and sat on the bed saying.

"I've spoken to Jane and now I want to thank you too. I never expected anything like a broom. It must have cost an absolute fortune and how did you get the bond so perfect?"

"Cost doesn't come into it," Celina said. "If it wasn't for your training, I am quite sure I would be dead. Both Jane and I know that so I don't want to hear any more about it; and as for the bond I just told them about your wand. It's famous you know. Now;

485

seeing as you're here and we're alone I'd like to talk a bit more about what happened in the tomb? For a start, I actually saw and read that book of Merlin's." Polly shook her head as she said.

"There was no book." Celina protested.

"Polly it was on that lectern in the room, you know the room after the one with the body in it." Polly shook her head again insisting.

"Celina there was no second room, I was the book. When you thought you were reading the book you were actually reading memories, memories of Merlin's that were in my head. While you thought you were reading the book, I was living all of Merlin's life in my head. I lived through every bit of his five or six hundred years or more. I haven't sorted it out yet, but it's all in here." Polly tapped her head and then not giving Celina chance to object, she said.

"I don't know yet who the warlock was but Merlin had arranged it so that when this warlock came along with a woman Talent to open the tomb, he would be able to access the latent memories in the man's mind. He would then be able to live again by taking over the mind of the man." Celina looked in horror and stopped Polly by saying.

"Taking over your mind?" Polly shook her head as she replied.

"It all went wrong for him. When he and Morgana knew they wouldn't return they arranged for King Arthur to return and make the necessary arrangements. Merlin wanted Arthur to make all this possible for him. I don't know what Morgana arranged just Merlin.

Anyhow King Arthur was hurt in the return and didn't survive, and well; everything went wrong.

Merlin hadn't intended it to be thirteen hundred years until the right someone came along and entered the tomb, but by that time not only had it all gone wrong time wise, but that someone was a woman, me and not a man."

Celina sat there looking at Polly, who was shivering with the cold night air. "Get in," she said pulling the covers aside for Polly.

Polly slid into the bed and snuggled down under the sheets and eiderdown as she said.

"He had planned on a man but he ended up with a woman, and it didn't work. According to Merlin, our minds aren't the same. He says it's like two stars, a star with five points and a star-shaped hole with six points. No matter how you turn them the five-point star won't fit into a six-point hole." Aghast Celina asked.

"Do you mean to tell me that Merlin's inside your head and you can talk to him?"

"No it's not like that, it's hard to explain; it's like a memory of a conversation you had a long time ago. I can think of something, and then I remember an answer only its Merlin's answer. Or I'll remember something and its Merlin asking me something; I don't hear him as such."

"Just who is Morgana?" Celina asked. Polly blushed as she said.

"Don't get this wrong, I was shocked at first but now I think I understand." Polly took a deep breath and still blushing said.

"I'm an eighteen-year-old virgin…." then she blushed even a brighter red at what she was going to say. "A virgin, and yet I know just what it's like to make love and to love someone, to love someone and watch them grow old and die.

Celina I know what it's like to have children and grandchildren and to watch them die too. I also know what it's like to end up being hated because you don't grow old. I know all of this, and I understand what it's like to know that you cannot ever give yourself truly to another, but I know all this as a man not a woman."

Polly took Celina's hand as she said. "Morgana was Merlin's sister, Morgana of the Fay or Morgana-le-Fay. She was a very powerful healer and witch, possibly more powerful than Merlin, and even he admits that. They loved each other as brother and sister for hundreds of years. However, with no other human being to love." Celina could see Polly was embarrassed, but she carried on saying.

"They came to love each other not as brother and sister but as man and wife. They loved each other like that for hundreds of years." Polly stopped looking at Celina and seeing the shock in her eyes said.

"Yes I felt like that too until I realised that they had no-one else. They were alone and it just happened. No-one deserves to be totally alone for hundreds of years."

Celina started to say something, but Polly was saying. "Don't say they could have other lovers; you can't. You can only have acquaintances, and it's not the same as loving. Just imagine having someone you loved for fifty years pleading for you to let him or her die. Yes die of old age; I know I couldn't stand it and neither could they. They tried, and it broke their hearts." Polly sat there looking at Celina; tears were running down her cheeks with the memory.

"Merlin gave his life for our world. If he hadn't he would still be alive today." Polly's grip tightened on Celina's hand as she said.

"Celina, I'm the same now; I'm part-Merlin, and I'm going to go on and on just like he did, and I'm frightened. I wanted to love Robert. He's asked me to marry him." Celina took hold of Polly's hand with hope in her eyes, hoping for Polly as a sister.

"You're going to aren't you?" she asked. Polly looked down and shook her head.

"No I can't, I couldn't put Robert through what Gwyneth went through with Merlin or Julius with Morgana."

Celina was shocked but then she started to understand as she asked. "Have you told Robert?"

"I said I'd think about it and let him know tomorrow." Polly looked up at Celina as she said. "I think it's tomorrow now. I've just heard the clock strike twelve so with your permission…." Polly slid out of bed.

"I'm going to his room, and then I'm going to make love for the first time as a woman."

"Then what?" Celina asked surprised at finding that she didn't feel shocked.

"Well I'm going to make him happy for the next few years and then…." Polly paused still with tears in her eyes, "and then I know it's going to break my heart but…." Polly took a shuddering breath before saying. "I'm going to find him a nice wife who can give him children, so they can both grow old together and play with their grandchildren."

Celina squeezed her hand and finding tears in her own eyes she said.

"Go, go and make him happy I do understand; I think." Polly half-turned towards the door and then as if coming to a decision she turned back asking.

"What will your Mother and Father think will they?" Polly fell silent not quite knowing how to put her fear into words. Celina took her hand again saying.

"I'll have a word with mother and father; I know they will understand as it's quite common for young powerful talents to have short term." Celina shrugged. "After all it's not every Talent, especially if you're a woman who can find a talented."

Again, she struggled trying to find the word she wanted finally saying. "Companion who will live as long as you will; my mother and father are very lucky to have found each other. They will understand, now go."

Polly started towards the door and then stopped again and turning back she said. "I take it that you know about the oath?" Celina felt shocked and then realised that Polly had Merlin's memory.

"You mean about hurting people?" she asked. Polly nodded. Acceptance was finally coming to Celina now that she could put a name to the woman.

"I think it was Morgana who explained it to me that night." They looked at each other, and then Polly turned and walked away.

It was shortly after Polly had left that the connecting door opened, and Jane stood there.

"She thanked you then?" Jane asked. Celina beckoned and said.

"She thanked me and more." Then pulling the covers aside she said. "You had better get in."

Jane slid between the sheets listening without saying a word as Celina repeated what Polly had told her. By the time Jane had finished asking the few questions she had the clock was striking two.

"No more questions?" Celina asked. Jane snuggled down, wrapped her arms protectively around Celina, and said.

"No, no more questions." Then with a giggle, "I suppose by now Polly's a woman."

"She had better be" Celina replied. "If not Robert's reputation with women will be in tatters." Both of them laughed as the glow went out, and it wasn't long before two nightdresses fell to the floor.

As Celina finally drifted off to sleep somewhere from a long way away a voice said.

"Sleep well my daughter; sleep well."

****

Lady Celina ~ Knight of the Round Table.

Book 2 of The Knights of the Church.

A. E. Staniforth.

It was late with the first stars already bright in the sky as they left the forge a scene of many happy hours for them and continued out of the village. Jane fanned herself saying.

"I wonder with this weather if we're due for a storm?" Celina looked around the rapidly darkening cloudless sky saying.

"If there is it will be later; I don't think we'll see it before we get home." Crossing the beck they turned with the road as it passed through a small copse of trees.

It was as they reached the trees that Celina's overenthusiastic charger started to pull and then refused to go any further. Finally, and despite Celina's best efforts rearing back into Jane's horse pushing it off the road and onto the grass.

Snorting and rearing both horses backed up fighting their riders. Celina's horse twisted bucked and then tried to turn back towards the village with Jane's horse attempting to follow.

Despite Celina leaning heavily to try to calm it, her horse bolted leaving the trees at a gallop with Celina fighting for control. Something large caught the corner of Celina's eye distracting her.

Whatever it was, the horse had seen it too, pulling sharply to one side it stumbled and almost fell. Righting itself, it stumbled again and threw Celina, with Celina falling heavily and rolling in the grass.

Jane seeing Celina's fall tried to pull her horse over towards her, but it refused, rearing and backing away. Fighting Jane her horse reached the beck but in the dusk missed the bank edge and fell, almost rolling on her.

Struggling to her feet she made a grab at the reins and missed. Jane found herself sliding in the mud on the bank and falling again. Struggling back to her feet she looked for Celina.

Things, lots of them, thin dark and spindly like two-legged ants were converging forming a circle around Celina. Celina had her wand out, strikes lighting the conflict throwing them into the mass of bodies as fast as she could, but Jane could see there were just too many attackers.

As Jane watched, several reached Celina's shield and now unable to open it to use her wand she was trapped. Jane knew that as they pressed closer and closer, it would be only a matter of time before Celina grew tired, and her shield started to fail.

Jane desperately lifted her hand and threw a series of microscopic glows at the wraiths; nothing happened. Her ring had fallen from her finger and was now lost in the mud.

"Celina," Jane screamed. Celina looked in her direction.

"Run Jane run!" Jane heard over the chittering and whistles from the mass of wraiths.

"Go to the village and get help." Jane looked, hesitated then decided that Celina needed help, and fast. Lifting her skirts she turned and ran.

Jane had always been athletic for a girl, often running races with her brothers and more often than not beating them even though they were older than she was, and now she ran as never before. Jane knew she was running for Celina's life.

The quarter of a mile to the village took forever until at last with her head swimming and breaths coming in great gasps she saw her father's forge and then the house. As she entered the village, something pulled her, not physically but still irresistibly towards the smithy.

The doors were locked; Jane stood panting barely able to stand with her forehead pressed against the doors. Taking hold of the iron lock and without conscious thought, Jane found she had turned the lock feeling it drop open in her hand.

Pulling the door open and looking inside she found the glowing embers from the fire still giving a little light. Her eyes were drawn to the back wall where the sword hung.

Panting her hand pressed against her side and bent almost double with the pain, she wove her way through the clutter until she was able to reach up, and tentatively she touched the sword.

Then for the first time and with trembling hands she lifted it down surprised at how little it weighed. Holding the scabbard, she put her hand around the hilt, the leather binding feeling warm to her touch. The grip fitted her hand perfectly. She pulled, and....

* *

<u>The world of Lady Celina.</u>

Please don't look to your History books for my England or London of 1860. Remember that the England I live in has had more than six hundred years to divert from your history. Some street and roads mentioned in London may have the same names but not necessarily be in quite the same place, and also the parks and squares may have been moved.

After the reformation of the Abbeys and the acceptance of witchcraft by some sections of the church, the church became the instigator of change and progress rather than the suppressor, and due to this technologically and medically in many ways my England is far in advance of your England.

Take for instance, the railways; having had an extra hundred years of development, the railway engines would be more like your Mallard than the Rocket. Mainline steam engines would be sleek, powerful, and able to maintain high speeds over long distances.

The steam carts and coaches would be powered by small, light and powerful steam engines fired by paraffin or lamp oil. The steam engine being so highly developed also hindered the development of the internal-combustion engine. Though a simple stationary engine had been developed and was being used as a gas engine, fuelled by coal gas following the spread of the gas main.

Electricity, though well ahead in the area of communications, basic electricity was very much in its infancy, (Mostly due to a lack of an efficient means of generation.)

Medically, look to your years 1920 before penicillin, but up to 1950 in other areas.

Socially and morally.

In manufacturing and employment, our equivalent would be spread in your time over the years 1920-1950.

Working conditions in domestic service and industry would be spread over the years 1920 to 1935.

Lady Celina Carvel

A brief history of Lady Celina's England

132 BC: Birth of Merlin

135 BC: Birth of Morgana

480 AD: Birth of Urther Pendragon

511 AD: Birth of Prince Arthur, son of Urther Pendragon

530 AD: Death of Urther Pendragon: King Arthur takes the Throne at Camelot

535 AD: King Arthur and Merlin set about a grand tour of his Kingdom

547 AD: King Arthur creates The Knights of the Church

548 AD: King Arthur creates the round table. Fifteen Knights of the Church sit at the Round Table and King Arthur appoints the first High Abbot

559 AD: Death of King Arthur at Glastonbury

1536-1540 AD: Dissolution of the Monasteries by King Henry the VIII

The next threat to the Knights of the Round Table occurred in 1537 when King Henry VIII tried to destroy the power of the monasteries. The High Abbot of Glastonbury refused King Henry's demands and was summoned to London, where after a meeting with King Henry he was incarcerated in the tower under a charge of treason.

Later that night King Henry woke from a troubled sleep to find the High Abbot sitting in his bedchamber. More disturbing still, King Henry found he was unable to summon help, move or speak. The High Abbot then dictated his terms to King Henry about certain Abbeys. The High Abbot then, releasing his hold over King Henry, put him back to sleep before taking his leave. The following morning King Henry found that not only was he not only unable to speak of the night's events, but also he was unable to eat. Having fasted for several days, he again summoned the Abbot, who once more dictated his terms to King Henry.

The eventual acceptance by King Henry of the High Abbots terms saved five Abbey's immediately, with King Henry the VIII being forced to give the five a Royal Charter of rights, while accepting from six others an oath of allegiance making King Henry the head of the church in England.

1555 AD: Of the five posts of High Abbot, only two are filled; a shortage of suitable candidates at the Abbeys creates a crisis. Separating the post of High Abbot from the Abbey, and opening the post to all male talents solved this crisis. Also at this time it was reluctantly agreed to allow women holders of a wand, the right to hold the title Lady, and to be admitted to the Order of the Knights of the Church.

1585 AD: With female talents outnumbering males by seven to one, and usually being more powerful, the church finally admitted defeat, and opened the post of High Abbot to all talents holding a wand. At the same time, the Order of Knights of the Church was separated from the Knights of the Round Table.

1591 AD: The Abbey of Watersmeet, along with three villages and associated farms, disappears.

1705 AD: Birth of David Anderson

1725 AD: Birth of Richard Telson

1730 AD: First practical locomotive demonstrated by David Anderson, pulling fifty tons of coal at twenty miles an hour for twenty miles on an iron track. For this feat, Mr Anderson claimed a prize of 100 guineas

1739 AD: David Anderson and Lord Edward Carvel started the first public railway system between Durham and York, with the intention of extending it to London in the south, and Edinburgh in the north. On the inaugural run, the engine managed the amazing average speed of thirty-five miles an hour.

1742 AD: Demonstration by Richard Telson of a practical form of communication by wires over ten miles. At first, it was looked on as just a novelty, until Lord Edward Carvel bought the rights in 1745 for two hundred guineas. Lord Edward Carvel had seen it as a means of long-distance communication on the railway, but it was eventually opened up for public use and became what is now known as the Telegraph.

1762 AD: The Great Fire of London.

   August the 21st. The hottest and driest summer in living memory ended with high winds blowing from the southeast. Disaster struck just before midnight, with the shock of a violent earthquake striking London.

   On the south bank, a naval warehouse had over eight hundred barrels of pitch stored on two upper floors, while in the cellars, half a hundred barrels of gunpowder were stored awaiting dispatch to the fleet.

   An oil lamp in a watchman's hut was knocked over in the first tremor, starting a fire, and within twenty minutes the warehouse was a raging inferno. The resulting explosion blew burning pitch over an area of half a mile on both banks of the river Thames.

   On the south side, the wind blew the flames to the river, while on the North bank, the flames spread rapidly. The buildings being mostly wood with thatch or shingle roofs were tinder-dry. With the high winds and tinder-dry buildings, the flames were spreading faster than a horse could run. Whole families were burnt to death in their beds, while others died trying to run before the flames. By dawn, most of the North of London was a smoking wasteland. Very few of the poor survived, and the few that did, did so by taking refuge in the few stone buildings and churches. The dead were uncountable, many being cremated with no remains found. It was estimated in that one night over one hundred thousand souls were lost.

For the next three months Parliament debated what was needed to restore London without success. Winter was close and a large number of what could only be called hovels had sprung up into towns, with these areas now themselves becoming a fire hazard.

The King on returning to London informed Parliament something must be done before London had another fire. Parliament with relief passed the problem back to the king, 'saying that they would bow to his judgement.' The king passed the problem to his new wife Charlotte, who, knowing nothing of London, immediately called for advice from politicians, high families, the church and merchants.

Within weeks the Queen realised they were all only interested in forwarding their own interests and not that of what she now considered the people of her city, London.

The Queen decided without informing her husband or her advisers to send four of her guards out into the remains of London, to bring back six people from the streets. The guards returned with a Vicar, a doctor, a shopkeeper, an architect, a thief and last of all, as they politely put it, a woman of the streets. To which the Queen is reputedly said to have replied.

"I am perfectly aware of her profession; after all I do believe there is some argument as to whose is the oldest, mine or hers."

From then on, as people opposed to her decisions put it, an unholy alliance was formed. An unholy alliance that resulted in one of the first planned cities, a city planned from start to finish producing a clean city with wide avenues, parks and open spaces, all intended to make north London the most beautiful and fire-resistant city in the land.

1769 AD: Demonstration of voice communication over a wire given by Richard Telson, who then sold fifty percent of the rights to Lord Edward Carvel for one thousand pounds. Now having coverage over most of England and Wales it is being installed in Scotland, and as become generally known as the Telson.

Lightning Source UK Ltd.
Milton Keynes UK
UKOW01f0449131016

285173UK00001B/17/P